# PRAISE FOR ELLA CAREY

"With snappy dialogue, impressive historical details, a sense of adventure and courage on every page, and even a love story, Ella Carey has hit all the markers that make fine historical fiction."
—Ann Howard Creel, bestselling author of *The Whiskey Sea*

"Ella Carey skillfully interweaves two women's lives and two eras in this passionate story about art, music, and the high cost of keeping secrets."
—Janis Thomas, bestselling author of *What Remains True*

"A fascinating world, beautifully described. I love how Ella Carey writes. She took me there completely."
—Carol Mason, Amazon Charts bestselling author of *After You Left*

"A captivating novel of romance, art, and deception. Ella Carey writes with such compassion, evoking two women and the landscape of two different eras so that one can see them."
—Elise McCune, bestselling author of *Castle of Dreams*

"Ella Carey explores the geometry of love in the Bloomsbury set. Hers is an intriguing story where triangles of obsession, desire, and devotion are entwined with a mystery that reaches across generations. Highly recommended."
—Elisabeth Storrs, author of the Tales of Ancient Rome saga

"Historical fiction at its finest! This is one of those books that makes you say 'Wow!' when you've finished it. From breathless descriptions of Australia to love and sacrifice, this story had big moments that still felt intimate. I was very engaged with the characters and genuinely cared about what happened to them. I look forward to reading more from this author."
—Camille Di Maio, bestselling author of *The Memory of Us* and *Before the Rain Falls*

"An absorbing tale that kept me turning the pages! Set in two time periods, I found the 1940s section fascinating, learning about the modernist art movement in Australia post–World War II with its interesting characters. The novel alternates between this bohemian way of life and the corporate pressured world of publishing in 1980s New York. It portrays well the experience of a woman in such a world. The story kept my interest by switching back and forth between the two romantic storylines and—with a satisfying twist towards the end—it was an enjoyable pacey read. Stunning cover too!"

—Janet MacLeod Trotter, author of *The Tea Planter's Daughter*

"Ella Carey's *Secret Shores* flies off the page as the intricate plot points dance together to perfection. I couldn't put it down. A must-read!"

—James D. Shipman, bestselling author of *It Is Well*

"Ella Carey's *Secret Shores* is an irresistible setup—the singular passion of true love, the complicated pressures of inheritance, and the value of struggle. Insightful, full of historical drama, and with a stunning twist that will keep you turning the pages, *Secret Shores* earns a spot on the shelf of Ms. Carey's bestsellers."

—Consuelo Saah Baehr, author of *Three Daughters* and *Fortune's Daughters*

"Ella Carey's *Secret Shores* is a poignant, star-crossed love story that spans decades and distance and offers a fascinating glimpse into the challenges and cultural clashes of post–World War II Australia. It is a compelling dual-narrative story with immersive historical detail and a plot that will keep you guessing until the very end. Devout readers of Carey's stories will be thrilled, and she is sure to create new fans with this latest novel!"

—Jane Healey, author of *The Saturday Evening Girls Club*

# BEYOND

## *the*

# HORIZON

A NOVEL

# ELLA CAREY

LAKE UNION
PUBLISHING

Published by Lake Union Publishing, Seattle

www.apub.com

Amazon, the Amazon logo, and Lake Union Publishing are trademarks of Amazon.com, Inc., or its affiliates.

ISBN-13: 9781542091398
ISBN-10: 154209139X

Cover design by Shasti O'Leary Soudant

Cover photography by Richard Jenkins Photography

Printed in the United States of America

*In memory of the thirty-eight Women Airforce Service
Pilots who died flying for the United States during
World War II, and also in memory of Tom Lawson,
pilot, who so generously helped me with the flight scenes.*

# AUTHOR'S NOTE

While this novel is inspired by the true events surrounding the Women Airforce Service Pilots during the Second World War, the characters and story are products of my own imagination.

In the novel, letters are written between characters during the war. Some parts of their correspondence would have been censored in such a way that Eva and the other characters would not have been able to see the censored text, but for the sake of the story, I made the authorial decision to let the reader see the censored information.

# CHAPTER ONE

*Los Angeles, 1977*

Eva nearly sent her bag of mandarin oranges tumbling all over the farmers' market floor. Alex was racing toward her, elbowing his way through the Saturday-morning crowd. He rushed along ahead of his father, who was panting and puffing close behind.

"Mom." Alex pushed back his shock of dark hair to reveal brown eyes that held traces of a determination rare for her laid-back adolescent boy. "You have to see this."

"Alex. Enough. I've told you, son. No." Eva's husband, Jack, lunged toward a piece of paper that their son was clutching, but Alex raised it high, holding it way above his father's head.

"You guys!" Eva pushed her sunglasses on top of her dark curls. "Please!"

Jack wiped a hand across his sweaty brow. The fine lines around his own brown eyes seemed to be etched deeper than usual, and his thick gray hair was sticking up in tufts.

"You need this, Mom." Alex thrust the piece of paper toward Eva.

"No." Jack snatched it from him.

"Mom has the right to know. Whatever your stupid ideas are, Dad. Give it to me."

"She may have the *right* to know, but it won't do her any good." Jack glared at their son.

"Honestly, what is the problem?" Eva said.

"Mom." Alex's words rushed and tumbled out. "I met a woman today who flew planes in the war, just like you did." The look on Alex's face sent Eva's thoughts back to her own youth faster than a backdraft rekindling an old fire.

Eva reached out for a plastic chair next to one of the tables in the middle of the market. She sank down. The sound of Alex and Jack scraping back the other two chairs seemed to come from a distance.

"You didn't mention my name?" Her voice sounded disembodied, and she fought to control her thoughts that wanted to fly to a myriad of faraway places, anywhere but here and now.

"We were waiting to see *Star Wars*." Alex dropped his voice a couple of notches. "Me and Denny and a few of the guys. I did mention that you flew planes too."

Eva brought her hand up to clutch at the red silk scarf that hung loosely around her neck.

Alex took a swipe at the paper and snatched it from his father's lap. The gleam in his eyes was triumphant.

"Alex." Jack's tone was a warning growl.

"Cut it, Dad." Alex handed the paper to Eva. "There you go, Mom." Jack rested his head in his hands.

Eva scanned the paper. Slowly, her hand floated up to her mouth.

"There was a woman handing these out, working the line while we waited for the movie. She told me she flew in the war just like you did." Alex's voice ran a counterpoint while Eva read on. "She was trying to get signatures to support the Women Airforce Service Pilots. They've got a whole group of them—ex–women pilots like you, Mom—in Washington. Lobbying Congress. Apparently, they're about to go to a committee hearing. They're fighting to be recognized as part of the military because they never were during the war. What do you think of that?"

Eva kept reading. Her eyes flew over the words.

"Isn't that what you were, Mom? A WASP? This woman was very cool, and she said that the WASP wanted to be a part of the force, like in *Star Wars.*" He chuckled, his eyes lighting up. "She got us all on board. Cool strategy, don't you think?"

"It's part of your mom's old life that she doesn't like to talk about, Alex. You know that. Leave it alone." Jack cut in while Eva read.

"*Anyways,* I told her you flew too," Alex went on. "It was pretty neat, actually, because Denny and Ralph and the others, well, they didn't know you'd flown in the war. They all think you're cool anyways, of course. But the fact that you flew airplanes in the war kinda blew their minds."

The sounds of the market, people doing their everyday shopping, started to swirl. Eva fought to focus, to listen to Alex's voice.

"They've got the support of the son of the dude who was the chief of the air force during the war, and also Barry Goldwater, who flew with your outfit, apparently—and they are going to congressional hearings now. But they're struggling."

"Henry Arnold's son," Eva said. "That would be Bruce Arnold. I recall his name was Bruce. Hap's son is supporting this, you say?"

"Eva!" Jack's eyebrows shot to the roof.

"Yeah, I think the guy's name was Arnold. But the woman said most of the congressmen also fought in the war. They don't believe the WASP should get military recognition."

"There was a battle over this during the war. But we didn't win. Obviously."

"Eva!" Jack placed his hand over hers. "Not now."

"Anyways, thing is, the woman said that if you were a WASP, they would love to have you join them. You could go to Washington to help.

And testify too. You'd be awesome. I got the woman's phone number. Do you want it?"

"I can't. I just couldn't—"

"But, Mom, why not? You deserve that."

"But I can't remember—"

"It will help you remember."

"Alex!" Jack thumped his fist on the table. "Do you not listen to a thing I say? Your mother does not discuss the war. It's best left alone."

Eva jumped at the sound of Jack's fist.

"Have a mandarin orange, Eva. You look faint." Jack crinkled Eva's brown paper bag open. He pulled out a fat mandarin and started peeling it.

The fruit's sweet scent flooded the air. Suddenly, it became hard to breathe, and the sound of an old prop engine throbbed in Eva's head.

# CHAPTER TWO

*Camp Davis, North Carolina, January 1944*

*Eva flicked open the door to the women's private alert room. She stood for a moment, framed underneath the warning sign that read,* **WASP Nest! Drones Keep Out or Suffer the Wrath of the Queen!**

*The North Carolina wind howled, sending the sand drifts surrounding Camp Davis into gritty swirls that tried to burst through the cracks in the makeshift building. Eva shivered. She pulled her standard-issue, men's size forty-four flight suit closer around her slight frame.*

*A small group of women pilots sat waiting in the anteroom. Her close friend Helena held a bowl of mandarin oranges. "These are liquid gold, girls! Just when you thought bathtub gin was the epitome of sophistication, I give you this: a mandarin orange!"*

*She threw one across the room toward Eva. Eva caught it, her whip-fast reflexes kicking in after months of military training.*

*"Thought it might help while we wait for assignments," Helena said. "The weather's wild out there. Even by Camp Davis standards, flying's going to be tough. And given it's our first time with the boys throwing spotlights all around our planes, we need all the food we can get tonight."*

*Two WASP stood up from another table, ready to go out on searchlight missions.*

*"Those oranges were for the men," Helena said. "But I stuck my chin out in the mess hall and convinced them that we deserved some fresh fruit too. We've already put in a full day of target towing up and down that beach while the boys shot at our planes. Nina and I came back with bullet holes in the fuselage because some fool missed his mark, and then we had a blown tire on landing, so I thought we deserved a treat."*

*Eva peeled the ripe fruit open, its tangy scent freshening the room's stale air.*

*When the mandarin eating was done, the other girls headed toward the runway, sending a swoop of icy air into the small room. Eva pulled on her leather flight jacket, grabbed her helmet and goggles, and followed them out.*

*Eva braced herself against the bitter-cold January wind. She crossed the runway to the waiting A-24. Across the field, searchlights from the antiaircraft guns circled and swooped in the dark.*

*Eva helped the ground crew do the preflight inspections, then pulled herself up onto the A-24's wing, swaying against the buffeting wind. She climbed into the rear cockpit.*

*Helena was already in front. Once Eva was settled, Helena yelled into the wind and the sideways rain, telling the ground crew to remove the chocks and clear the runway. Helena fired the engine and requested permission to taxi.*

*Eva focused on the glimmering instrument panel in front of her. She watched the speed indicator. Helena lowered the flaps on the wings and took off. She made a gentle fifteen-degree turn. The plane bumped in the wind, rising above the swampy undergrowth and vine-covered trees that surrounded Camp Davis.*

*"My bed is gonna be awful welcome after this day," Helena said.*

*Eva grinned. "Couldn't agree more. My day was longer than a triple shift nailing rivets."*

*"Eva?" Something sharp pierced Helena's voice.*

*"Roger."*

*"I'm seeing some spatters of oil on the windshield. Keep an eye on the oil-pressure gauge."*

*"Sure."* Eva frowned and scanned the instrument panel. The indicators on the planes the WASP were given were sometimes faulty, so Eva knew she could not always rely on the readings. The oil gauge was bobbing up and down. *"It's shifting up and down a little. Are you sure you're seeing oil, Helena?"*

*"Hard to be certain in the dark."*

Eva kept her eyes trained on the gauge. Once they'd reached the correct altitude, planes flew above them in a circuit. They were in a holding pattern. Searchlights beamed around them in the dark. The male trainees were learning to operate radar-controlled searchlights to track bombers and indicate targets for antiaircraft guns at night. The lights dazzled the cockpit, searing into Eva's eyes, just as they would for any enemy crew.

There was a cough in the engine. It started to lose its rhythm, that rhythm any pilot was comfortable hearing. Eva had become attuned to listening for everything that might go wrong with an engine.

*"I'm not liking this, Evie."* Helena's voice crackled through the radio.

The plane bumped hard.

*"This isn't just roughness. The oil gauge is falling now."* Eva ran through options in her head. And only one seemed viable. A forced landing.

*"It's too close. It's almost redlining,"* Helena said. *"It's happening so fast."*

Outside, the light continued to swoop in eerie circles around them, illuminating the instrument panel and only highlighting the plummeting oil gauge. Out of the corner of her eye, Eva saw a jagged strip of lightning streaking down toward the ocean.

*"The cylinder head temperature is rising dramatically."* Eva fought to hide the nerves that pierced her insides like a collection of spikes. *"We need to look for a place to land."*

*"Going to execute a forced landing."*

If the engine locked up, the propellers would stall.

"Keep your speedometer steady, Helena. The faster we go—"

"The more likely the airplane could catch fire. Oil is spreading over the canopy."

Helena's voice sounded small.

The plane skated over a belt of trees, lapping at the tops of them, shearing leaves and branches, metal chafing foliage, sickening, grating, chilling.

"Trying to accelerate and lift, to get beyond the trees to land. How long do you think we have until the engine fails, Evie?"

"No idea. Just keep it steady."

Helena's shoulders were rigid in the front seat.

Suddenly, Eva was fighting to breathe. Smoke filtered through the cockpit. A thick, rank odor spread through the air like an unwelcome ghost.

"Oh, Evie." Helena's voice was shaky. "Fighting to maintain airspeed. Emergency procedure."

"Activating emergency ventilation procedures." Eva reached up. She pushed her rear canopy open. Freezing air blasted and swirled around her. The wind roared. Rain pummeled her face, soaking her lap and the cockpit, saturating the spreading smoke. Eva's arms shook and her heart thumped in time with the beat of the rain. She had to concentrate. Told herself how she'd flown open cockpit in the rain a thousand times during training out in Texas. Told herself how Helena was a good pilot. Told herself they were not going to die.

Eva forced herself to focus on the procedure that had been drilled into them over and over again.

"Keep the airspeed up to extinguish the fire, Helena."

"Executing a forced landing as soon as we get beyond these trees."

The plane heaved and shook like a bag of ball bearings over the forest. Helena fought to lift the ricocheting nose upward.

"We have to assume we could be glider pilots any second now, Helena."

"Are we gonna make it, Evie?" Helena shouted the useless words.

"You need to come around by three degrees now, Helena." They had to turn a little to move toward the base and not stay stuck above the trees. Eva *forced herself to stare at the artificial horizon, a glimmering, tiny flicker of a beacon in the pouring rain.*

*"Roger."*

*"Maintain altitude now. If you need me to, I'll take over." The plane bounced; it might as well have been a balloon filled with air. Eva cursed herself for all the jokes they'd made about planes falling into Dismal Swamp and never being seen again.*

*The props stopped.*

*Suddenly, the engine froze. Eva reached for the throttle and felt it flapping back and forth.*

*"Please," Eva whispered into the screaming wind. "Please, save us now." In the distance, thunder growled.*

*"I'll handle the radios," Eva said. "You handle the aircraft. Switching to the tower frequency."*

*"I'm slowing down a little. Turning off the ignition switch."*

*Something dark spread through Eva's stomach and hung there. "I'm switching frequency to the control tower right now, Helena. Give me one minute."*

*Eva's fingers were slick on the little knob. Rain pelted her hands. Her entire body felt like it was being melted by the rain. "This is Baker Forty-Seven. We're at one thousand feet. Mayday, Mayday, Mayday. We've lost oil pressure."*

*"We'll scramble the fire trucks and meet you there."*

*"Roger."*

*Eva fumbled with the controls, switching back to Helena. "Push the nose forward to keep the airspeed up now, Helena."*

*The plane bounced upward. Suddenly, the air base spread below them. Eva clutched the sides of the plane.*

*"Put the landing gear down now, Helena. Unlatch your door prior to landing." Eva reached out and unlatched hers. She saw Helena still fighting the steering controls. "Unlatch your door!" Eva shouted. "Brace for impact and run on landing!"*

*Helena yelled, "I have to turn the airplane on an angle!"*

*Eva saw Helena scramble for her door handle. Eva closed her eyes for one second, nausea surging up through her throat.*

*Helena pulled the nose up again, turning the plane sideways with the rudder. The plane skipped.*

*Eva grasped hard on her handle, ready to exit on impact, ready to run.*

*"Remember to run!" she managed to shout.*

*The plane crashed and skidded. A second, sickening crack ripped into Eva's ears. Pain ricocheted through Eva's body, up her side, searing into her head, tunneling deep into her legs.*

*She heard the wail of sirens.*

*She smelled the stench of smoke.*

*But one thought pushed her to yank on the door handle and get out of the plane. One thought kept her pulling herself across the tarmac, dragging her body along.*

*She had to save her friend.*

*Los Angeles, 1977*

"Alex. I told you not to bring this up. Look at her. She's spaced out again." Jack's voice sliced into the air.

"Sure, Dad." Alex's voice was small.

Jack shook Eva's shoulders. Eva lost her balance and tipped off her chair.

Gradually, the sounds of the market grew louder and louder. A stall owner shouted about potatoes. The roar of the burning plane receded away into the distance. Eva put her hands out on the asphalt floor of the market. She started to push herself forward, to crawl along the ground. The noises around her came into focus. People talking. Laughing.

*It's not the tarmac.*

*It's the market.*

"Mom, Mom, where are you going? Let me help you up. I can't believe you pushed her, Dad. You knocked her out of her chair."

"She tipped, Alex."

"I'll go get the car." Alex again. "Mom, you don't need to walk home."

She felt Alex place his hands under her arms, hauling her up to a chair. In front of her, a glass of water sat perfectly still. Alex held it up. Gently, he guided the glass to her lips.

"She can walk, Alex." Jack glowered in the background.

"Alex, please stay with me." Eva's hand shook as she rested it on the table.

"I'm out of here." Jack turned and disappeared into the busy street. He sounded as mean as he had when Alex had stayed out too late and broken curfew when he was sixteen.

Alex pulled out a chair and sat down opposite her. "I'm so sorry, Mom."

"It wasn't your fault, sweetheart. I just . . ." She could still hear the prop engine, but it was only faint. "There was an accident back then. I was involved. It came back just now. It was like it was haunting me."

"You never talk about the war. Are you sure you're okay?" Alex leaned forward, his eyes running back and forth over her face, filled with love.

"One of my close friends was killed in the accident. I was her copilot." Her words would come only in bursts.

"Oh, Mom. I didn't know."

"I have trouble recalling the details. I tried so hard to remember the accident after it happened, and over the years, I guess I just gave up."

"That's so sad." Alex looked down, darkness haunting his face.

Shadows of her own past seemed to linger between them. Eva's heart still beat fast with the memory of so long ago.

"Just now, I finally saw something new. I was crawling to the plane, trying to save Helena. I was so worried that I hadn't done enough to help, that my copilot's death was my fault."

"That's horrible." He drew a hand up to his face.

Eva looked down at her hands. They sat folded neatly in her lap on her dark-blue skirt. It was the same color as the official WASP uniform, the Santiago-blue fitted jacket and skirt she'd been so proud to receive for her graduation, such a gorgeous outfit to wear after months in flight suits, broken only by beige pants and white shirts for ground school.

Alex leaned forward. "All you've ever told me is that you don't keep in touch with your old friends from the war. That you lost touch."

"I tried. I wrote letters, and they never wrote back." Her voice sounded distant, lost now. It was as if she were trying to recall some stray note.

"They must have moved away."

"We'd all been so close." Eva felt for the familiar comfort of her scarf and ran her fingers down its soft length. "Eventually, I blocked out the war like it never happened. We were told to pick up our lives and never talk about it. I never knew what really happened that night."

"Jeez. Mom." His voice shook, and her heart lurched out to her son. "This ex-WASP. She told you they were getting together again? Now?"

"She was so great, I wanted to tell you," Alex said.

"When we joined, they told us we'd be made military. Our leader, Jacqueline Cochran, fought Congress back in '44. We were disbanded at the end of that year. They wanted the returning men to have jobs. We were all sent home." Her voice filtered off again.

"Mom, you've got to go. The reason they're fighting again now is because the government just announced that the air force is going to train women as pilots for the first time."

"Well, it's not the first time. We already flew air force planes and lived on air force bases back in World War II."

"Don't you think that the WASP deserve to be recognized? And don't you think you deserve some answers about your accident?"

Eva's heart contracted at the dearness of him, but she heaved out a sigh. "I've promised your father. I'm done with the past."

"Don't listen to Dad. He doesn't get it." Alex's expression tightened. And Eva saw all the complexities of his relationship with his father in that one look. All the times she'd tried to stand up for Alex, all the times she'd tried to step in and put a stop to the conflict that Jack caused with their son. All the times Jack had turned on her and told her to keep out of it.

"Women died."

"What, Mom?"

"Women died while flying for the United States. All of them had undertaken military training, and they died doing their duty for their country."

"The woman today said they've got the bill approved by the Senate." Alex's voice was soft, filled with the sympathy she knew was imbued in him.

"So it's gone to the House."

"The reps are proving a much harder battle, she said."

"How long did you talk to her?" In spite of everything, Eva felt warmth flicker through her insides.

"The line for tickets was *very* long. It's a very big movie, *Star Wars*."

"Oh, Alex!" Eva caught his dancing brown eyes with her own.

"Go for it, Mom. For you and Granddad."

*"Granddad?"* Eva's voice came out solid and strong now.

"Granddad." Alex was firm. "He used to tell me how you loved nothing more than to fly when you were young. That Grandma tried to convince you not to fly for the air force, but you were headstrong and you wouldn't listen to her. He would want you to fight. I know it."

"Oh, I was a bit determined back then." Eva chuckled.

Alex dropped his voice. "Sounds kind of familiar."

For a brief moment, Eva shared a smile with her eighteen-year-old boy.

"Dad will be here in two minutes. I have to ask, wouldn't they tell you about your accident?"

"The WASP records have been hidden for over thirty years."

"You've got to go to Washington. Promise me you'll go." His eyes searched her face, his expression so vulnerable that Eva's heart wanted to break in two.

"I'm *saying*, supporting some movement to militarize women pilots is not a good idea." Jack stood framed in the doorway of their bedroom in the house in Hancock Park. They'd lived there all their married life, and they'd raised Alex there. Alex would most likely move out when he went to college next year, but for now it was still their familiar nest, even though it had become riddled with arguments during the last three months over Eva's decision to go to Washington and help fight for her sisters in the WASP when the bill went to Congress. Eva folded the last sweater from the pile of clothes on their bed, its everyday pale-green quilted cover smooth as always. She zipped up her small red leather suitcase.

"I doubt I'll be gone long."

"Look how crazy the past makes you. You space out, have these episodes where you just sit and stare. You don't need that. Stay home."

Eva sighed. "Jack, for over thirty years, I've done what you said. For the first time, I'm doing what's right."

Jack took a step toward her. He placed his hands on her shoulders, standing over her.

Eva took a step to the side. Mimicking her, he took a step too, blocking her way.

"Really? You're going to stop me?"

"You gave up flying. I gave up acting. That was the deal. I've kept my side of the bargain."

14

Eva looked up at him. She focused on the expression on Alex's face when he had urged her to go, remembered the unfathomable determination that she'd so admired in those fellow WASP of hers, remembered that girl who'd marched out the door with her suitcase in her hand and a whole pile of confidence back in 1943.

Eva felt her lips forming a strong-willed smile. "I'm not going flying. Yet."

# CHAPTER THREE

*Washington, DC, 1977, Congressional Hearings*

THE COMMITTEE: Mrs. Forrest, can you give us a summary of the Women Airforce Service Pilots during World War II?

EVA FORREST: During the Second World War, 25,000 women applied to be members of the Women Airforce Service Pilots; 1,830 were accepted, and 1,074 passed flight training. We filled the need for more pilots to do noncombat duties at home, freeing up the men to fight overseas. We flew over sixty million miles for our country, bombers and fighters and every other type of plane. We started in 1942, and for the next two years, we ferried planes across the country from factories to airfields. We towed targets so that young men could learn to shoot at enemies. We test-flew new airplanes and planes just back from repairs. We served as flight instructors for the military, and we test-flew radio-controlled planes. Thirty-eight of us were killed in the line of duty. Men weren't the only pilots in World War II. There was a group of women, us flygirls, who were ready and willing to do our part too.

*Los Angeles, July 1943*

Eva stretched her legs across the sofa in the little house in Burbank, resting her feet in Harry's lap. Nina sat on a cushion on the floor. Benny Goodman played on the gramophone, and every now and then, the crash of Eva's mother's pots and pans rang from the kitchen in back.

"You could teach me to fly." Eva nudged Harry with her foot. "After all, you're a certified instructor. I know we're friends and all, but you'd be a grand teacher."

Harry took a sip of his beer, tipping his blond head backward in that slow, sexy way that Eva loved, not that she would ever confess as much to him.

"Every time I take you up, Evie, you're the pilot. You take control of the plane. So why bother with your certificate? You've already done hours and hours of flying with me. I know you haven't taken off or landed a plane on your own yet, but you're on your way to being a very good pilot already. You've logged up good hours so far, just by being up there with me." He tapped her leg with his tanned hand.

"I've heard talk of a callout for women to take over ferrying airplanes so the men can go off to war," Eva said.

Harry stayed stock still, his free hand still resting on Eva's leg.

"If I don't teach you, then you'll get your certificate yourself."

"That's right."

Nina leaned on her elbow, her long dark ponytail swinging behind her head. "If you get your certificate, I get mine too."

Harry stood up, his six-foot frame dwarfing the small room. "How about we start right away. I'll give you lessons."

He moved toward Eva's dad's desk. "Mind if I borrow a couple pieces of your dad's paper, Evie?"

Eva nodded, her gaze flicking to Nina. "My mom's not going to like this."

Nina shrugged. "How can we stay here doing nothing when we both know we could be doing something? When we both love to fly and women are being recruited."

Harry sat back down on the sofa. "Let's see what you two know already. Then we can build on it all from there."

Nina moved up to sit between him and Eva, and Harry started sketching out a neat diagram.

"Remind me what you need to check for landing?" He pointed the tip of his pencil at his drawing of an instrument panel.

"Fuel pump on. Mixture rich, check doors and harnesses," Nina said.

"At five hundred feet, you set the flaps, and slowly decrease the speed. You need to be at a landing speed of eighty miles per hour." Eva had flown enough with Harry that she could recite most of this by heart.

"Impressive. Nina, what next?"

"Pull back the throttle, left hand on the stick, right hand on the throttle, carefully juggling both so you are controlling them just as they need to be. You're a born teacher, Harry. You could go teach grade school." Nina winked at Eva.

Harry raised one eyebrow in an imperceptible move. "Don't push it, Nina. I'll find a second instructor for you at the airport. I'll teach Evie. You're gonna be way too much hassle."

"Oh, we all know how you love Evie best." Nina leaned her head back against the sofa, but she giggled. "I've long become used to being third fiddle."

Eva felt a flush spread up her chest and through her cheeks. She pressed her hands into the sofa and sat on them.

Next to her, Harry drew a picture of a fluffy cloud.

"You'll both love being alone in the sky. The excitement of going up solo for the first time is something else. And, Nina, there are some great instructors. I'll find one for you."

"I'll probably sing to myself," Nina said.

"And as you go over the hills," Harry whispered, drawing his arm up into the air in a smooth arc, "the updraft will pull you up, and the downdraft on either side will pull your little plane down. You'll learn to trust your instincts up there, just like you do on the ground."

Eva's instincts were telling her only one thing, and that was that her crush on Harry just got a thousand times stronger at the sound of the lilt in his voice.

"How about you and I go up for a fly tomorrow after our shifts end, Evie?" Harry straightened out his piece of paper. "I have to take a plane up for testing, and I need a copilot. Someone who can take over the controls. After that, I'll sort out formal lessons for you in a real training plane."

"I'd love that. I just . . . you know, I wish Dylan could be doing this with us. I wish he could fly too. I want to fly for him, and for all the others like him," Eva said.

Eva had tried so hard not to be furious about their friend, the boy who used to hit home runs and fix broken-down cars and throw popcorn at the back of her head at the movies. Now, all that was left of Dylan was a vacant shadow of the boy who'd grown up alongside them, after being hit by a shell in Tunisia, with no doctor to come quickly enough to save his leg.

"I like your reasons for learning to fly," Harry said. "I admire them."

The following afternoon, Eva looked up from the endless rows of P-38 Lightning fighter hard-noses lined up for riveting in the Burbank factory where she, Nina, Dylan, and Harry worked. Although since Dylan came back, he'd had to drop out of the aircraft-designing program because of his physical limitations and what the company saw as a loss of motivation, and he only did mundane clerical work now.

Dylan backed his wheelchair away from Eva a little. "Break's over," he said. He caught her gaze, and his eyes locked on hers. "Harry told me you and Nina are thinking of enlisting as ferrying pilots. Don't do it. It's not worth it."

"Dylan—"

"Eva, don't." His expression hardened. He rolled away up the aisle, back to the little glass office where he had to work these days, to the job he swore that he hated, over and over, every day since his return.

Harry strode down the long assembly line from the walled section that was off limits to everyone except those who were assisting with an airframe designed around the British Goblin—the most powerful jet engine they had. Harry had been chosen for the project. He'd always worked harder than anyone Eva knew.

Eva watched while he stopped and chatted with Dylan. The expression on Dylan's face turned from hardened to listless when Harry talked to him. Harry caught Eva's eye, patting Dylan on the shoulder and making his way over to her.

"How are you enjoying working under a tarpaulin?" Harry came to a halt right next to her and leaned against an upturned P-38 nose.

Eva was still getting used to the entire factory being camouflaged by a huge burlap tarpaulin painted with scenes from the countryside.

"Reminds me of those forts we used to make in our backyards."

Harry cracked Eva's favorite crooked smile. "Nina was way too bossy, even back then."

"Oh, I don't know. You've ended far higher up the ladder than we can ever hope to go. Working on the secret development of a new jet fighter while we two are stuck out here playing Rosie the Riveter? I'd say someone got the better deal."

He shifted a little, frowned back at the direction in which Dylan had gone, and crouched down next to her. "I'm taking a Ventura up for a test flight, if you're still keen."

"You haven't changed your mind after last night?"

"I know better than to stand in your way when you're determined to do something, Evie."

"Oh, I see."

"And anyway, today I'm on the lookout for a copilot who's willing to take out a plane that's been damaged but should be just fine if handled well."

"Then I'm your girl."

"I'm sure you are." He tweaked the end of her nose. "Did I tell you how gorgeous you look in that boiler suit? I hope none of the men here are giving you any trouble, kiddo. Because if they are, you can send them all to me. If anyone tries anything with my little friend, they'll know about it, believe me."

*Little friend* . . . "Surely you know I'm only here for the planes, Harry. Bomber, fighter, Ventura, you name it, I'll fly it," she said. *And I'm stuck on you, so even if some other man did try something, they wouldn't stand a chance . . .*

"Promise me you'll never lose your passion for flying, Evie." His eyes crinkled.

"Promise I'll never lose my passion for anything." Eva sighed at her surroundings, front ends of airplanes pointing upward like a group of giant silver eggs.

"Good." His voice was quiet.

"Not seeing Lucille tonight?" She wiped a hand over her perspiring forehead.

Harry's girlfriend, Lucille, had a dad who had been a star in the pictures during the twenties and was famous for having turned into Hollywood royalty.

"No. We're taking this Ventura up, you and me. That was the deal, that's what I'm doing."

The sound of machinery starting up somewhere in the factory pierced the quiet.

"Meet you out at the airfield in half an hour?"

"I'll be ready." Eva turned back to finish her shift. The sound of Harry's footsteps clicked through the hangar.

She couldn't wipe the grin from her face.

Eva walked out to the operational airfield at exactly five past five, moving out to the runway at Lockheed that was protected by strings of alfalfa growing overhead. Harry checked the quantity of fuel in the cabin tank on the wing. He came over to stand next to her once he was done.

"Preflight checks all carried out, Evie. This little beauty's good to go."

Eva admired the twin-engine bomber that would be loaded onto an escort carrier or a cargo ship by crane tomorrow. From there, it would move to the Pacific.

Harry stood aside to let Eva climb up onto the wing. She swung herself into the flight compartment. Harry settled into the dual cockpit next to her, and Eva felt a thrill at the sight of the sky through the big glass nose. She pushed aside thoughts that in the frame of war, bombs would soon be stationed down there in front of where they sat right now.

"Evie, you can check the escape hatch is securely fastened."

Eva reached up to check it.

"Now I'm removing the elevator and aileron locking bars, releasing the rudder locking bars. You adjust your seat, Evie."

"Aye, aye, Captain."

Harry let out a snort, and Eva grinned.

"Okay, smart girl, now I want you to adjust your rudder pedals. Are you sure you can reach them, honey?"

"Oh, they're made especially for women like me." Eva lifted the pawls, moving the pedals so that all five foot five of her could reach—just.

"Now turn on the instrument switch."

Eva moved it to "On."

"Double-check our fuel and oil."

Eva checked the right side of the instrument panel. "Roger, sir."

"Evie . . ."

"Roger, Harry."

"Checking the low-level indicator lights are working." Harry pressed the lights down. "Carrying out a few more checks pertinent to the Ventura. The bomb bay door control is closed, the eight-gun nose needs to be retracted, and the gun safety switches are set to 'Safe.' The rocket switch is off too, so you know."

"Oh, I'm so pleased to hear that. Don't want to drop a rocket on my own neighborhood today. Although, Mom's making wartime fish pie for dinner. It's tempting to blow that up."

Harry's eyes crinkled from the side.

"Seriously, if I'm going to try for a ferrying job, I'd better get used to a whole bunch of different planes." Eva concentrated on the knobs and dials in front of her.

"That is true." Harry continued checking the aircraft. "So, we have no fire extinguishers on this airplane. You've got to keep the engine mixture under control, and then you'll be fine."

Eva shuddered at the thought of fire. This plane seemed safe as a rock.

Harry called out takeoff instructions to the ground crew. "Evie, you can start up the plane."

She turned on the engine, and it started to beat beneath her.

"Warm up your engine and adjust the throttles to one thousand rpm. I'm going to carry out your engine and accessory checks, and I'll take over to taxi."

Eva watched Harry's hands move deftly over the controls, taking in what he was doing.

"We want the wing flaps up. See that the cabin doors are closed and the turn gyros are uncaged. Move the tail wheel lock control to unlocked, Evie, and release the park brakes with your toes."

"Doing that."

"I'm advancing the throttles to taxi. You steer the plane, Evie. Don't overuse the brakes."

Eva took hold of the control stick.

"Never gun your engines."

"Using a steady flow of power."

"Right. You can watch me take off this time, but soon enough, you'll be doing this yourself." Harry's fingers were steady on the instrument panel, and then he turned the parking brakes off. "Seat belt tightened?"

"Seat belt is good."

Harry taxied down the runway and took off, the plane moving in a smooth arc over Burbank. Eva felt a thrill that she was in the place she adored, with one of the people, or were she to be truly honest, the one person, whom she loved most in the world.

"Right, Evie. You can fly her now."

Eva took the plane into a gentle turn, her heart soaring as the valley spread below them, the dusty streets where they'd grown up and gone to school set out in straight square grids alongside the camouflaged Lockheed factory.

The urge to spread her wings farther than Burbank, to get beyond the confines of her upbringing, felt stronger than ever when she was up here, in the air.

"Now there's no acrobatics allowed in this aircraft."

"Oh? What a shame."

Harry's soft chuckle sounded through the communication device. "Tell me about this plan of yours. Tell me about ferrying airplanes."

"I can tell you what my ma says. 'No one will want to marry a pilot.'" Eva mimicked the words her mom had told her over and over again.

Harry laughed, sending the radio crackling this time.

"If I must leave, why don't I go be a dancing girl? Why don't I entertain the troops? Can you imagine, Harry? Me? Mom's worried I'll be a danger up in the sky, but I tell you, I'll be much more of a liability to the world on a stage."

"Oh, come on. You'd be entertaining. Gorgeous."

Eva felt her eyes narrow into a pair of calculating slits. "No, I would not!"

"Ferrying aircraft or bust?"

"You know why I adore you? You understand."

He was quiet for a moment. Eva was only more aware than ever of his close proximity, of the way he always stared straight ahead when he was thinking something through.

"Eva?"

"Huh?"

"I have news of my own."

The thrum of the prop engine seemed to deepen. Eva turned toward the desert mountains that formed a ring around the valley. Up here, the heat over the San Fernando Valley glistened and shimmered while in the distance, the soft-blue California coast sparkled.

"I'm going to join the US Navy. Dive-bombing."

*No.*

"I'll be training at Cecil Field. In—"

"Florida."

"Just like you, I can't stay home while men like Dylan have come back injured. I want you to understand, just like I have understood for you."

Eva forced herself to stare out the front of the plane.

Gently, Harry placed his hand on hers. Carefully, he took over the controls. "I know that it's still raw," he said through the radio. "I know how much you miss her. And I know how you worry about anything happening to any of us, Evie."

Sometimes, Eva thought Harry was the only person who understood. Her parents never talked about Meg's death. Her mother could not bear raising the topic of the sister Eva had lost, the daughter her mother had adored. Eva knew that, but sometimes, she just wanted to remember how having a sister had felt.

Perhaps she'd tried to replicate what she'd lost when Meg died by keeping Nina, Harry, and Dylan extra close. But her mother's own protectiveness always seemed to tighten around her like a vise. She'd taken to flying to alleviate it. Up here, her mother's restrictive attitude seemed so far away it didn't matter. It was the only place she could be herself these days, the only place in her life where she felt free.

And if Harry was going, she'd definitely have to go too, or she'd go insane. That cemented it.

*You have no idea how much I care about you, Harry,* she wanted to shout. And she couldn't say anything because of Lucille. Because Harry would think the little girl who lived around the block had gone crazy if she told him how she felt. He'd tease her or, worse, be kind. She hated the thought. It was deplorable. She was not sophisticated enough for the likes of him.

"The navy wants to train pilots with experience in fleet-type air-craft, men who've finished flight training."

Eva bit on her lip until it hurt.

"I'm going with a group of ten boys."

*Nine of them will die.* Bombing was the most dangerous mission he could have chosen. Everyone on the factory floor had been following the news—on top of the usual risks, planes the navy had been flying were falling apart in midair. Crashing into the sea, wings falling off. Scores of US planes had been lost in bombing missions in the last few months. Yes, Harry was experienced, but faulty planes were too much of a match for anyone.

"They say they've chosen men who they think will quickly become proficient in Helldivers."

"Helldivers?" Eva's voice sounded disembodied in the speaking tube.

*Dead targets.*

26

"Harry—"

"I have to go."

"We both know what the losses have been in the Pacific the last few months, and flying at such low altitude, you'll be a dead-easy target." Fear laced her voice. She watched Harry's hand, steady on the controls.

"They need pilots who can keep a level head."

*I'll go insane back here waiting, knowing you are risking your life while I'm fixing rivets . . .* "I can't stay here while you're doing that."

"We'll work toward it together. You, me. Nina."

A frown tightened Eva's features. She would rather lose one of her own limbs than have anything happen to Harry.

# CHAPTER FOUR

THE COMMITTEE: What was it that led you to join the WASP, Mrs. Forrest?

EVA FORREST: It was the love of flying. I was taught to fly by a very dear friend when I was working as a riveter at the Lockheed factory in California. And the chance to do something for my country in its time of need, when women were being called to help, seemed a marvelous thing. If I could fly and help, well then. There was nothing better than that.

Eva went back through the factory floor. The news that Harry was leaving seemed even more real and desolating down here in the eerie, silent hangar. Pieces of Venturas, Hudson bombers, and Lightnings stuck up at angles all throughout the room. Eva drew her jacket closer around her and marched toward the empty locker rooms.

"Evie?"

She turned. It hurt that it was Lucille who had the right to yearn for him, while she would do so privately, on her own. But he was doing exactly what she expected him to do. He was being the man he'd grown into, no longer the child she'd grown up with. The boy whom she'd known nearly her whole life.

"Where are you going now?"

Eva stopped at the door that led to the locker area. "Meg's grave."

He reached out, placing his hand over hers where it rested against the door. "Want me to come with you?"

Eva stared at the cement floor. Her feet encased in heavy boots looked solid enough. She wished she were standing on firmer ground. "You don't have to."

"I'd like to," he said. "I'd be honored to come with you, if you'd like me to."

"Thank you."

"I don't want you to have to deal with that on your own." His words hung in the vast space.

"Thank you," she said, her heart full of the things she could not say to him.

Half an hour later, Eva walked alongside Harry through the narrow streets of Burbank, past the rows of little factory-issued houses. The colors that people had painted their homes used to captivate her when she was young, but now, the pinks and greens and blues seemed faded.

As they came to the large cemetery, Eva stopped.

"You okay?" Harry rested a hand on her shoulder.

She resisted the urge to lean into him. Instead, Eva stared at the impersonal cemetery where her sister lay. "I'm okay."

She made her way, head bowed, toward her sister's grave.

Eva's heart quivered at the sight of the man standing by her sister's headstone. Her father looked so very much older than his forty-seven years. His hair had turned almost white since Meg's death. Eva stood still for a moment, Harry beside her. Her father bent down to place a single rose on Meg's grave, his movements stiff, like those of a man twenty years older than he was.

Her father turned and shook Harry's hand.

"It's been a long five years without her." Gerald Scott's eyes held that singular pain that losing a child can bring. "And yet, it seems like yesterday that she was a little girl riding her bike around these streets."

Eva leaned her head against her father's shoulder. Five years this week since they'd lost her.

Her dad stood there, quiet alongside her for a moment. "Nina's mom has been talking to your mother. You can understand that your mom is worried sick about this flying idea that you both have. To lose one daughter has been impossible, but the thought of you taking such a risk is making your mom ill."

Eva clutched at her cardigan. Beside her, Harry reached out and took her hand. Meg's grave seemed so small and helpless. The fact that her remains were buried down there was too much to bear. And every time Eva came here, Meg's last few desperate hours of trying to cling to life came belting back into Eva's mind.

Influenza had raged through her sister's body, tearing at her breath, coating her lungs, causing her heart to beat so hard and fast that she gasped and stared helplessly at Eva and her parents until, finally, it gave out.

Death had claimed Eva's sister before the war had taken hold.

Eva stared at the birthdate on the little gravestone. Her birthday. She and Meg had not just been sisters. They'd been identical twins. There was not a second Eva did not miss her, not a minute of her life she did not care, not a day that she would let pass without reaching up and entwining her fingers through the twin pair of silver necklaces that they'd been given when they both turned sixteen. Meg's last birthday. Since then, Eva had forced herself not to think the unthinkable, that from then on she'd been living only a half life.

She stood and looked at the grave in silence. She was sure that Meg would have flown right alongside Eva and Nina for their country if she could. They'd shared a passion for airplanes, she, Meg, and Nina. Eva and Nina had clung on to it, almost out of loyalty to the third strong member of their little trio of friends. No one would replace Meg. Never. But somewhere, in her heart, Eva thought that maybe they might enjoy training to fly with other women. And she was certain that Meg would give them her blessing for doing that.

"Remember those air shows you used to take us to, Dad?" Eva ran a hand over her father's stooped shoulders.

He stood, stock still, his hands in the pockets of his favorite old trousers. "Oh yes, dear. You and Meg used to love telling me the names of all the airplanes."

"We did. And I still pride myself on the fact that I can tell a Douglas from a Curtiss."

"Bet you're taking them all apart in your head, Evie, whenever you look at them," Harry said.

Eva looked up at him.

He tilted his head, smiled at her.

Warmth flooded her heart.

He reached out, stroking her head. "You're going to have a fine life, Evie. She'd want you to live it to the fullest, you know that."

"I know." Eva leaned down and touched her sister's headstone.

"Thank goodness we still have you, my darling." Her father's voice was quiet in the gathering darkness. He was silent for a moment. "Could you break it to her gently? You know I'd never stop you from going."

Eva started. She turned, catching Harry's eye.

Her father stayed motionless, looking at the grave. The expression on Harry's face was one of regret and hope and love and fear and everything that this awful war held.

"Yes, Dad. I'll break it to Mom gently."

31

"I heard you kids last night too, talking about ferrying airplanes, when I walked past the sitting room to go to bed. I understand, but please, take care of yourself for all our sakes."

Eva rested her head on her father's shoulder. He reached out, encircling her with his arm. Next to her, Harry stood straight and tall and dignified. The two men she loved most in the world.

The sound of the screen door slamming rang through the house. Eva rushed down the narrow hallway from her bedroom. Nina's voice, greeting her parents, sang out like the sound of a young bird in an otherwise silent nest. Eva grabbed her best friend by the arm and led her to her bedroom, bursting to talk.

Nina threw herself down on Eva's bed and reached for the canvas carryall she'd brought in with her.

"Look what I've got to show you, Evie!" She coiled her long ponytail up on top of her head and turned her wide blue eyes to Eva. She shuffled down on Eva's pillows, arranging them and patting them so that Eva could lie down right beside her.

Nina pulled out a magazine—the latest issue of *Life*.

Eva reached out and ran her fingers over it. "Oh . . ." On the cover was a photo of a girl pilot in braids, sitting on the wing of an air force plane.

"She's real." Nina turned the cover toward Eva.

"Shirley Slade." Eva's eyes drank in the picture.

"Uh-huh." Nina turned the pages.

Eva leaned her head on her best friend's shoulder. "Women Airforce Service Pilots. Seems their leader, Jacqueline Cochran, the famous aviator, wants to show what we girls can do, Nina!"

"I've already spoken to Ma. She's all for it. Heck, she'd fly a darned plane herself if she could get out of here. What's more, she's agreed to fund my flying lessons," Nina said.

Eva sighed. She sat up, crossed her legs, and frowned at the familiar patterns on her neatly pressed quilt. She reached across Nina and grabbed a notebook and pen from her bedside table and took off the lid from the pen. "First, I'll speak to Mom, which I'm not even going to dwell on right now. Then once we have our pilot's licenses, according to this article, we need to pass a physical examination and a regular entrance exam to even be considered for WASP."

Nina flipped through the magazine's shiny pages. "It will be tough if we do get into the training program. It's in the middle of Texas. A place called Sweetwater. Holy heck. Look at this, Evie. Says here that the girls deal with scorpions, rattlesnakes, and locust plagues."

Eva scribbled down notes. *Scorpions? Can I handle them? Locusts? You bet!*

"Constant nose-to-the-grindstone work. Long days, ground school, flight training, calisthenics."

"You're being too practical," Eva said.

"Can't help it. That's me."

"Go on."

"Open-cockpit flying in one-hundred-degree heat."

"No problem."

"Blizzards in winter."

"Fine."

Nina let out a loud sigh. "The washout rate can be up to fifty percent, although, so far the girls are doing better than their male counterparts. Okay, hold on, Evie. Imagine getting in and then failing and being forced to come back home! The *indignity* of it . . ."

Eva lay back with a puff on her pillows. "The other girls will be darned well determined. Determined like we are. We'd make some grand new friends." Eva turned to Nina. "Meg would be happy for us."

"She would." Nina whispered the words.

"And the flying . . ."

"There's nothing like flying to make a girl feel she's able to sing." Nina lay back too, staring at the ceiling.

"You don't really know what the world is until you've seen it from above." Eva felt a new determination.

"Beats the view from the factory floor under a P-38 any day."

"In, then?" Eva gripped Nina's hand.

"Oh, in."

# CHAPTER FIVE

THE COMMITTEE: What did you know about the leader of the WASP, Jacqueline Cochran?

EVA FORREST: We knew that she was the most famous woman aviator in the US. She grew up in poverty, worked as a beautician, and started her own company, then became involved in aviation and competed in air races, winning them and running her own multimillion-dollar cosmetics business. She set aviation records, both for men and women. We were in awe of her.

THE COMMITTEE: Did you truly think that Mrs. Cochran's achievements were in any way indicative of what the average woman could achieve?

EVA FORREST: Here was a woman who had done what men had always done. Her rags-to-riches story inspired us. Well, she definitely inspired me and my friend Nina Rogers. We were two girls who'd grown up in humble circumstances.

Eva sat opposite her parents at their red Formica kitchen table. Her mother's powdered vegetable soup simmered on the stovetop. A plate of homemade biscuits sat untouched in the middle of the table, and three cups of coffee were arranged like three goalposts. The coffee had turned cold.

"Flying airplanes won't get you a husband." Ruth Scott picked at the brown hairpins that held her hair into a wispy bun.

Eva's father sat with his hands folded in his lap.

"My whole life isn't about getting married, Mom."

Her mom sat back. "But your work at Lockheed is important. To our community. And our family. Your father lived with threats of layoffs during the thirties, but we still kept on, to support you through your school years. We need young people like you to stay here. To support those who have been here for you all your life, dear."

"Dear. There's no need for that." Eva's dad's tone was soft, cajoling, but Eva could hear the smear of pain in his voice.

"Before the war, Lockheed was struggling."

"War helped the factory . . . I know the story, Mom."

"We are not rich, Eva."

"Ruth." Eva's father had switched gears to warning now. "We are fine. We have stability. The factory is slammed trying to keep up with the war orders."

Eva leaned forward, clasping her hands, her gaze passing in earnest from one parent to the other. "I'm trying to do something more for our country. I hate that Dylan has come back maimed."

She felt the memory of Meg hanging between them in this room too. Eva took a glimpse at her empty spot at the kitchen table.

"Charity begins at home, dear, and families need their girls. Eventually, you'll meet some nice boy at the factory, and we'll all be together. A family, Eva. Goodness knows, families are more important than ever in war." Her mom smiled, her mouth spreading in an

I've-won-this-argument kind of way. She sat back, settling her hands on her apron. Willing Eva to defy her.

*A family.* "But I'm hardly ready to begin to think about settling down, Mom." Her mother had been stripped bare by her grief at losing Meg. And so had Eva. But lately, something new had kicked in. Eva felt an urge to live her life for the both of them, for herself and her lost sister. It seemed more urgent than ever that she make the most of the opportunities that came her way.

"Ferrying planes around might seem glamorous and exciting, but believe me, the excitement will wear thin once the reality of military training hits." Her mom was firm.

Eva's father wouldn't meet her eye.

Eva dropped her voice. When she spoke, it was as if some new force had entered between them. The atmosphere had become loaded with something that was not there before. "Mom, Dad, have you ever experienced a true taste of freedom? Have you ever known what it feels like to soar, high over the land? It's as if nothing matters when you are up there. It's as damned close to infinity as you can get."

"Eva!"

"Sorry for my language, Mom." Eva reached out a hand. "You know how much I love to fly."

Her mom stiffened in her chair.

"It's nothing against you, Mom. I need to spread my wings—"

"You could train as a nurse if you feel you *must* get away from us."

Eva leaned her head in her hand.

"You are bored here in Burbank! You are bored with your dad and me."

"No."

"It's not seemly, this idea of going off to fly airplanes." Her mom's voice moved from irritated to hysterical. "Please, I wanted to sort this out sensibly with you . . ."

Her father stood up. He went to stand behind her mom, encircling his wife in his arms.

"I can*not* let her go." Her mom reached up to clutch Eva's father's hand. Her face crumpled like a small child's.

There was one string Eva could pull, and she hated to pull it, but right now, she saw no other option. She took a deep breath and said it. "Mom, I'm an adult. I have the right to do as I please. I'm sorry, but it's not a matter of you letting me go."

Ruth Scott pulled out her handkerchief and let out a loud sob. Eva tried to reach out to hug her mother, but she stood up, turned, and swept out the kitchen door. Her father raised a placating hand Eva's way. He trudged after his wife up the hall.

Eva stood up with a clatter, her heart hammering and her chair falling backward onto the floor. Pushing open the back door, she ran around to the front garden before coming to a crashing halt in the street. She stood there, chest rising and falling. Now she was starting to feel lost in her own home.

The streetlights flickered on, and she turned to stare at the yellow-painted house where she'd lived all her life. She stood poleaxed while her mom came to the window. For one brief moment, their eyes met, before her mom pulled the drapes shut with a flourish. This was her parents' house, her parents' life.

She should be allowed to choose her life too.

Eva placed her hands in the pockets of her skirt. She marched up the road, head down, brow creased, stopping outside the house that she knew as well as her own. Harry's father's green hedge was soft in the gathering twilight.

Eva walked up Harry's driveway, past his window, his bedroom, the place where he dreamed at night.

The sounds of laughter rang through to the garden.

Eva's shoulders hung heavy as she pushed the back screen door open. Harry sat with both his parents at the kitchen table. And next to him, her manicured hand resting in his own, was his girlfriend, Lucille.

Eva stopped dead in the doorway. For a flash of a second, she considered backing up and going home. But home was a hornet's nest. Should she go sit in a park somewhere?

"Evie." Harry was up out of his seat instantly. "Is everything okay?"

Was she so transparent? Eva stood up to her full height.

"Hello, Harry, Mrs. Butler, Mr. Butler, Lucille . . ." Eva's voice surprised her. It sounded normal. But her eyes locked with Harry's, and she knew that she hid nothing from him.

"You look like you've seen the factory ghost, my dear." Mr. Butler stood up too. He was a perfect older version of Harry, same fair hair, green eyes, tall, handsome.

Eva heard Lucille's intake of breath. Out of the corner of her eye, she saw the way the girl patted her blond hair. Eva was an interruption, and an unwelcome one.

"I didn't realize you had company. I'm sorry." Eva's voice cracked on the last syllable. She started to back away.

But Harry was right alongside her. "Mom, Dad, Lucille, can you excuse us a moment?"

Eva turned toward the door. "No, it's fine. Bad timing."

Harry went to open the screen door. "Come and talk to me outside."

"It's a hot night out there. Harry, you'll boil." Lucille's voice tinkled, and the screen door squeaked.

Eva shot Lucille an apologetic look.

Lucille pouted. Even in annoyance, her red lips formed a pretty shape.

"Sorry, I'm not much company for your folks right now," Eva apologized.

Harry took her arm. He led her over to the wide wooden swing that his dad had built. Eva had spent hours there as a little girl, singing while she sailed over his backyard.

Harry sat down on the wide seat. He reached out a hand and pulled Eva down next to him.

"Tell me how it went at home."

"Mom is crying. I wish I could have her blessing. But I can't stay here. Do you understand?"

"Of course I do." His voice was tender in the dark night.

Once the words started coming, Eva couldn't stop. "Ever since Meg died, I feel like I've been just existing. Pushing one foot after the other. Nothing feels alive anymore. But when I'm up in the sky, with you . . ." She turned to him, eyes huge.

"I know." He rested his arm around her shoulder.

"But I can't possibly leave my mom like this."

Harry stroked her hair, smoothing out her curls. "Evie, deep down, the last thing your mom would want is for you to live a half-dead life. She's just scared of losing you, is all. But you're going to apply to ferry planes around the US, not—"

"Fly Helldivers on bombing raids as a dead target." She gripped the base of the swing and placed her feet squarely on the ground. The swing came to an abrupt stop.

"You know me." His voice dropped. "I can't sit here, just like you can't. We both know that."

"When I think about what's going on in France . . ."

Harry pulled her closer. "Unlikely to happen here, Evie."

"But look what happened to Dylan! You might not come back, you might not come home. And we could lose the war."

"Okay. Here's what we do—"

"You should get back to Lucille," Eva interrupted him, staring at Lucille talking to Harry's mother in the kitchen, their figures silhouetted in the window, close together. Lucille's glance out to Eva and Harry was sharp.

"Evie, listen to me. First, we need to get your mom feeling a bit better about the situation."

"Maybe I shouldn't go. Maybe she's right. Maybe I should focus on finding a beau."

In the kitchen window, Lucille flicked a hand through her blond hair and turned away. Eva bit hard on her lip.

"Nina's mom has agreed to fund her flight lessons. I'll teach you for free."

"You don't have to do that."

"Evie." Harry dropped his voice. Even in the darkness, she could sense him processing something difficult that he wanted to say to her. "Would it make things easier for your mom if she knew I was involved in this? If she knew it was me who was teaching you to fly?"

"She worships the ground you fly over."

"Sometimes, you gotta make the most of a little worshipping."

A weak laugh escaped Eva's lips. "Oh, you are too funny."

"Here's what I've been thinking. Tomorrow morning, and every morning after that before work, I'll give you your flying lessons, until you are a fully licensed pilot. I'm convinced that once your mom's seen how hard you're working, she'll be proud of you."

Eva looked up at him. He smiled at her with his eyes. Moonlight shone on his handsome face.

"I'll meet you in front of my house at four thirty sharp in the morning." He ruffled the back of her head. "You'd best go get some sleep. Because tomorrow is lesson one. I'll be ticking off all your accomplishments as we go. And first thing tomorrow, we're going to work on taking off."

"You help me take off." Eva turned away from him, her face burning.

Lucille stood framed in the screen door, staring out at them, her feet clearly visible in their red pumps.

Eva tore her eyes away from Harry's girlfriend.

"You okay?" he asked.

"Thank you." The moment they'd shared was suddenly ripped apart.

"See you in the morning, kiddo."

"Good night, Harry." She drew her cardigan around her and went out into the silent street.

# CHAPTER SIX

THE COMMITTEE: What did you think Jacqueline Cochran's intentions for women pilots were? To turn a group of women into military pilots?

EVA FORREST: My understanding was that Jacqueline Cochran wrote to Eleanor Roosevelt back in 1940 to raise the idea of starting a women's flying division in the Air Corps. Mrs. Cochran's intention was to place qualified women pilots in noncombative aviation jobs in order to release more male pilots for combat roles. She put together plans for a separate women's unit of the Air Corps, to be headed by herself, with the same standing as the Women's Army Auxiliary Corps, which was given full military status in July 1943. In 1941, General Henry H. Arnold suggested that she take a group of female pilots to England to see how women were being employed successfully in the Air Transport Auxiliary in that country. Jacqueline Cochran agreed, but she also worked toward her goal of starting a women's flying corps in the American military back home. She and her husband were friends with President Franklin D. Roosevelt and Eleanor Roosevelt. Jacqueline convinced the president to support her idea of using women pilots to help with the war effort, and he asked Jacqueline Cochran to research a plan to train these pilots.

Eva grabbed her little alarm clock and turned it off at four fifteen, before her mother could hear it and appear in her slippers and robe. Eva rushed through dressing herself, her fingers fumbling with the practical fitted dress that she'd left out the night before. She fixed herself a quick breakfast of toast and a little butter in the silent, immaculate kitchen and let herself out into the warm early-morning air.

Her pace quickening, she hurried down the dark street, the streetlamps casting pale pools of light on the road. Eva's heart accelerated too, at the sight of Harry standing outside his house already, and she grinned when Nina came trotting toward them from the opposite direction.

"Good morning." Harry stepped out and pulled Eva into a hug. "How are you?" His words were muffled into her hastily brushed curls.

"I didn't see Mom last night when I went back inside. I only hope she'll come around."

"We'll make sure of it." He let go of her, turning to Nina.

"Good morning." Nina reached forward and gave Eva a quick hug. "How did it go with your mom last night?"

"Less said, the better."

Nina linked her arm through Eva's, and they kept pace alongside Harry walking down the street. "I'm sure once she sees you flying solo, she'll be proud of you, girl."

"I'm not so sure."

"I've been thinking." Harry strode on Nina's other side.

"Oh yes?" Nina let go of Eva's arm, running a little ahead and turning around to face them.

"If we do this every morning for three weeks to a month, you'll get your licenses quickly enough. In the meantime, I think you should both go ahead and apply for WASP. You can send in your certificates once you have them."

"Sounds like a gas," Nina said. She swung her carryall around over her head.

"Nina, I've found a teacher for you. Paul is an excellent instructor. He's been teaching people to fly for years. I telephoned him last night, and he's briefed and ready to teach you."

Nina tilted her head to one side and skipped around ahead of them. "I'm jealous that Evie gets you as a teacher."

Harry's chuckle was rich velvet in the dark. "Evie and I are a good team in the sky."

Nina's eyebrows shot upward, and a mischievous grin lit up her features.

Eva shook her head, and Nina came back to walk alongside them again.

They rounded the corner to the local airfield, and Harry moved straight toward the glass entrance door. Out on the runway were a couple of jaunty primary trainers. Eva felt the stir of excitement in her veins.

A man who looked to be in his late forties with a sharp, clean haircut came and held the door open for them.

"Nina, this is Paul. He will instruct you," Harry said.

"Nice to meet you, Nina." Paul shook Nina's hand. "Let's start outside today. I want to look over the airplane and see what you know."

"Evie, come on in with me. I want to run through takeoff procedure. Then, if you feel ready, we'll get you to take off." Harry moved to the little coffee station. "Coffee for fortitude? Going up in an open cockpit as the sun comes up is exhilarating, but you're going to be tired all day at work."

"Coffee would be marvelous, thank you, Harry."

Harry handed her a steaming cup of coffee and led her to one of the round tables that were dotted around the small airport lounge.

"Now," Harry said, "the primary trainer is a tail dragger. The wheels are under the wings, with another wheel under the back. The tail stays on the ground while you take off."

Harry drew diagrams on a notepad, and Eva looked over his shoulder at the neat details he set out on the page.

An hour later, her head full of information, she did a final check over all Harry's notes.

"Let's go," Harry said. "That's enough ground instruction for today. No need for instrument flying now. The sun is coming up." Pink streaks started to spread fingers of light over the distant dry hills.

Eva took the flying goggles and helmet that Harry handed to her and followed him out to the runway. She tingled with anticipation and climbed up on the primary trainer, standing on the small wooden wing and sliding into the front cockpit. The ground crew moved around the little prop plane, and Eva leaned out the open cockpit. She called for the very first time. "Chocks away!"

Eva waited while they removed the triangular pieces of wood that were wedged under the wheels.

Next, following Harry's exact instructions from the copilot's seat behind, Eva checked that the hand brake was on and called everyone to get clear of the propeller. She pushed the mixture lever all the way down with her hand to make sure the engine mixture was fully rich.

"Later, you'll adjust this again in flight," Harry said to her through the radio. "It'll start running rough if it's too rich."

"Roger." She took an air-pressure reading to check the height above sea level on the ground and turned the engine on, the prop buzzing in her ears.

The control tower gave her permission to taxi, and she took the plane out to the holding point right before the runway, tested the ailerons, checked that the engine was running smoothly, and increased the throttle, just as Harry had instructed her to do back in the airport.

"Perfect, Eva."

She switched the radio to tower frequency.

"Foxtrot Thirty-Eight requesting clearance for takeoff."

"Clear for takeoff, Foxtrot Thirty-Eight."

Switching the radio back to Harry, she made a right turn to the runway, checking her wake turbulence and watching her speed on the instrument panel. She took in a breath and pulled back on the throttle, her heart hammering as the plane scooted down the runway.

The little training plane lifted in a perfect arc. Eva fought the compulsion to cheer.

"Well done," Harry said.

"Thank you." She felt the first tingles of success.

"Now, maintain your runway heading for another five hundred feet, then turn gently."

Eva kept her eye on the turn and balance indicator until it was time to make the fifteen-degree turn.

The sun streamed over the horizon beyond the hills, and the whole of Los Angeles was spread below her, the morning sun warm on her cheeks.

"You're a natural." Harry's voice came through the radio. "But, sweetheart, that was something I already knew."


Late that afternoon, Eva lay on the back lawn with Nina, drowsy from her early start and long day fixing rivets, although even riveting seemed to take on a new allure after her lesson with Harry, and to think there would be a string of mornings learning to fly. Well, that made up for the monotony of factory work.

"What if we were to get letters from Jacqueline Cochran herself?" Nina said. "Are we honestly going to make the grade?"

Eva leaned on her elbow and pulled her sunglasses up to rest on her curls. "Us, up in front of one of Mrs. Cochran's women? Being interviewed? I'm worried I'll forget my own name!"

"I still can't believe we're doing this for real, Evie. Even if I feel like it's something we were born to do. It feels right, and yet, at the same time, it's happening so quick. Paul says he'll accelerate my license. He's spoken with Harry. We're lucky to have them both helping us out."

"We're always lucky to have Harry. And Paul sounds just grand."

Nina was quiet for a moment. Eva felt her friend's eyes on her. "You okay with Harry joining up?"

"He won't stay here for anyone."

"I know how much you care about him."

Eva stared up at the sky. Above her, a bank of wispy clouds rolled across the Californian blue. "Well, I think he has the same problem we do. He just wants to go."

"But when it comes to Harry, I know how hard it's going to be for you to see him leaving." Nina shot a glance toward the kitchen window, but it was closed, and Eva's mom was nowhere in sight.

"All I can think is that he's a wonderful pilot. I can't bear to think of anything more than that."

She felt Nina's fingers lace with hers.

# CHAPTER SEVEN

THE COMMITTEE: But ultimately, Jacqueline Cochran trained you as civilians ferrying planes, not as military pilots. How can you argue that she seriously intended you to be anything else?

EVA FORREST: I am certain that Jacqueline Cochran's intention was that if women were fully trained in the military fashion, then they could contribute to the war effort. She wanted to prove that we were capable of making an important contribution. And she wanted to give us a place in aviation. What's more, Jacqueline Cochran was not the only woman keen to employ women pilots to contribute to the war. Nancy Harkness Love, who worked for Air Transport Command, employed twenty-five elite women pilots to ferry planes from factories to bases in the US in March 1942 while Jacqueline Cochran was in England with her group of twenty-five of our most qualified US female pilots being trained with British female pilots in the military. Jacqueline's women pilots were the first American women to fly military aircraft overseas. They delivered planes from factories to bases for Britain's Royal Air Force. Jacqueline came back home intending to apply what she'd learned about women flying for the military in England to our air force.

Eva tore around the block to Nina's house, a precious letter clutched in her hand. She rushed up Nina's driveway, fumbling with the side gate and heading straight to the open back door. Eva knocked out of politeness, but Nina's mom, Jean Rogers, was right at the kitchen window. She waved Eva inside.

"You come in here, girl." Nina's mom untied the pinafore she wore around her ample frame. In a flash, Mrs. Rogers eyed the envelope that Eva was clutching. "You got the same letter as Nina there in that hand of yours?"

Eva heaved a sigh of relief. "I'm sure glad to hear Nina's got one too."

"Haven't been able to make head or tail of my girl since she got home from the factory tonight and opened the envelope. She's so panicked that you might not have gotten one that she can't sit still."

"Well, turns out that's one problem we don't have to face. The WASP interview's next week, and Harry says we'll both have our pilot's licenses by then. But I expect there'll be girls with ten times our qualifications applying. I can't see why they'd choose the likes of us."

"Don't ever denigrate yourself, Eva," Jean said. "I've raised Nina to have no pretensions, but I don't believe for one moment in putting yourselves down. You girls have as much passion and skill for flying as anyone else. They'll be wanting to train you anyway, it's just a case of checking you have the gumption and the courage to fly for them, that's what it'll be about."

Eva wished she had as much confidence. "Not sure if they interview every applicant."

Jean placed her hand on Eva's shoulder. "Honey. Stop worrying about it. Just go and answer their questions, and you know what? You show them what you and Nina got."

"Evie?" Nina scuttled into the kitchen. "Tell me you're going to an interview like me."

"You bet I am." Eva raised her letter in the air. "I'd be happy to go to any interview on the basis that I'd never have to nail another rivet alone." Eva scanned the letter yet again. She still couldn't believe it.

Nina encircled Eva in a hug. "Oh, thank goodness." She read Eva's letter too. "We're on the same day."

"Harry says I'll have my license by the weekend," Eva said.

"Harry's a good boy," Mrs. Rogers said. "I've always said it." She eyed Eva.

"Yes, we're more than aware of that, Ma."

Eva felt her cheeks turning pink. How many people had recognized her crush?

Nina spread the interview notice out on the table. "It's from Captain Henry H. Arnold. The chief of the whole air force."

Jean placed a plate of cookies in front of them. "Look at you girls. Letters from the chief of the air force. You go for it. Mark my words, you won't regret it."

Eva took one of Jean's famous cookies. Nina had told her that Jean was working her ration papers so that the important things could still be baked.

"It's an opportunity that women of my generation would never have had. That's why I say it's doubly important." Nina's mom folded her arms and stood proud and strong by them both.


One week later, Eva held her brand-new pilot's license in her hands outside the house where the interview was being conducted. Her best pale-pink summer frock clung to her curves, its dark-red velvet belt sitting just so around her waist. Her feet were encased in unfamiliar patent-leather high heels. She'd done her curls up in a ponytail, and now, the heat of the afternoon swirled around her and Nina as they stood waiting to be let into the house where Jacqueline Cochran's friend would interview them.

Eva was utterly in awe of Jacqueline Cochran. The more she'd learned about her, the more she'd panicked. After growing up in poverty in Florida, she was recognized as America's foremost living female aviator, and she held records for her competition wins.

And now, Eva was here in her pink dress alongside Nina, all dressed up in blue, to be interviewed for Jacqueline Cochran's WASP.

Were they crazy?

Eva fought the urge to turn right around and go back home.

But Nina was walking along the path through the flowery front garden of the grand Los Feliz house, stepping with all the snip-snap and confidence that her sassy mom had put into her head.

Eva pushed away thoughts of her own mom's tear-stained face when she'd seen Eva filling out her application. Telling her mom that Harry was training her had helped a little, but the fact was, nothing was going to convince her mom that leaving home to fly airplanes was ever going to be a safe idea. She took in a shaking breath and followed Nina right to the front door.

Nina was called first into the interview. Eva was told by a delightful elderly man to wait in a lovely sitting room. Eva would lap up a room like this to sit in every night. Serene-blue easy chairs and sofas were set on a deep-blue carpet, and on the coffee table, books on planes were set out. The woman doing the Los Angeles interviews must be some elite flying compatriot of Jacqueline's.

Eva hovered in the room, only to be distracted by a set of French doors that looked out on the lush garden outside. On a stretch of wall beside the charming doors was the grandest set of airplane photographs Eva had ever seen in her life. She was staring at a gorgeous photo of three little Bell P-39s flying in a row, one above the other in formation, their noses up. Next to it was a photo of altogether different beasts: two grand Boeing B-29 Superfortresses, their noses menacingly short, flying above a cloudy sky.

"Enjoying those?" a voice boomed behind Eva.

She jumped, her face flushing.

"Terrific plane." The elderly gentleman who'd let them into the house smiled at her with his pair of bright eyes above his gray mustache.

"I'm sorry, I was taking a look. I was excited to see you have a photo here of such a new aircraft."

"You know something about the manufacturing of planes?"

"Well, I know this baby is ten times harder to build than any other bomber we've made in the United States so far. I know that it's only up for delivery this month and had its first flight in September last year."

"Do you now? I'm impressed."

Eva felt a little emboldened by the gentleman's appreciation of her interest in planes. "May I ask where you got this photograph, sir?"

"Can I ask you a question first?"

Eva's heart skipped a beat of delight at the chance to chat with someone who seemed genuinely interested in talking with her in turn.

"What do you know about these planes?" he said.

"Well, sir. I know that the B-29's a technical nightmare to build. Its engine power, weight, and wing loading and even the structure are something else, but it's more advanced and more capable than any bomber ever. It will be interesting to see how far this plane can go."

The old man's expression was sharp, and his eyes lit up. "I agree, my dear. That's why when a friend who was involved in the design of it told me all about it, I asked for a photograph to display on my little wall up here."

Eva's eyes widened. Here she was, already among folk who were right in the thick of things when it came to planes. "You know someone who was on the design team for the B-29?"

"Why, certainly, I do." He leaned a little closer to the photograph. "But I'll tell you this. My wife could have designed planes if she were given the opportunity. She's a fabulous pilot and a wonderful woman, and she knows what she's talking about when it comes to aircraft. I sense you know a thing or two as well, dear. And you have turned to flying?"

"I am keen as anything to fly for Jacqueline Cochran. At the moment, I work at Lockheed, but just tightening bolts."

"Well, tight bolts are important!" He turned back to the photos on his wall. "I'm also fond of the little Helldiver."

"It can go two hundred eighty-one miles per hour," Eva said, almost absently.

The man jolted upright next to her. "And it can fly at twenty-four thousand feet! We're seeing it in action in most of the Pacific battles."

"Yes." Eva drew her arms around her waist. It was the plane that Harry was most likely to fly.

"I'm impressed with your knowledge. You know, if you are successful with Jackie's outfit, you'll have to learn how to fly every type of plane there is. It won't be a case of just getting to know one plane. You'll have to get to know 'em all, inside and out. And you sure have an interest."

"Well," she said, "I only hope I can do them all justice, then, if I'm successful and if I get into WASP. I tell you, I take pride in the fact that I can memorize the specs of a plane. And in my spare time, sometimes, I read airplane books for fun!"

"Eva Scott." The woman conducting the interview appeared at the door. Nina was standing next to her. She had that concentrating, fixed expression she used to wear when they had math tests at school.

Nina put her head down and moved toward the front door.

"Good luck, young lady," the old man said. "Dear, you have a real plane enthusiast here. And she knows her stuff."

The woman standing at the door of the interview room stepped aside. "Do you have your pilot's license now, Eva?"

"I sure do, ma'am," Eva said, and held the license out that she'd worked so hard toward with Harry, placing it right in the woman's manicured hand.

"Well, I'm pleased to hear that. Why don't you step right inside?"

When the interview room door clicked closed, Eva felt the inevitability of what she was doing for the first time. If this was the beginning of a new life among a new sort of people, Eva was more than ready to take it on.

Even though Eva stumbled a little through her interview, she did well in her physical, and she hoped that the interviewer's husband might put in a few good words for her with his wife.

One hot August evening, Eva found a letter from Henry H. Arnold, chief of the air force, propped up on her pillow, waiting for her when she came home from work. A pink-and-yellow sunset simmered outside, and the house was silent and empty.

It was bingo night at the local community center. Her mother and father hadn't missed one of those evenings in years. Eva felt a momentary stab at the thought that her mom had seen the letter from Henry H. Arnold first, and now she would not be home when Eva opened it and read it. The envelope looked poignant waiting there alone on her pink coverlet.

Eva slid a letter opener into the thick, quality envelope, and Nina tore into her bedroom.

"I'm in! Evie, I'm not doing this without you. I swear, if you haven't gotten in, I'll wash myself out of WASP training right at this moment. Now."

Eva scanned the letter with Nina right behind her, her eyes running down the words and her heart beating a strange new tattoo in her chest.

"Oh, I'm in too. We've done it!"

Nina grabbed Eva into a hug and held her fast against her chest. "I swear this is going to be the best thing we've done. I know it's right. It just is. You realize what this means?"

"I know," Eva said. "A future away from the factory. A future that could mean anything. Look what Jacqueline Cochran has done with her life!"

"The freedom to fly and be paid for it. The chance to contribute in a real way to our country and to the war."

Eva held her best friend at arm's length. "Let's swear we'll make a success of this. Let's swear that we'll do everything we can to make good of this opportunity."

Nina wiped a stray tear from her eye. "You know how many girls want to be WASP?"

"Thousands."

"The acceptance rate is less than ten percent! That's what the interviewer told me. One in ten, and we got in."

"I have no idea why."

"Well, neither do I, honey, but I sure am not questioning the decision!"

Eva held Nina's gaze. "Have you told your mom?"

Nina stood up a little taller. "She said she had great faith in me, that I could do anything if I put my mind to it."

"And that you can."

The sounds of Eva's parents coming up the driveway loomed in the still summer night. Nina gave Eva a quick hug.

"Bye, Evie. I need to go back and make plans with Ma." Nina took a step back, catching Eva's eye and holding it. "And you come over anytime if you need to. Don't put the news off."

# CHAPTER EIGHT

THE COMMITTEE: On her return to the US from England, Jacqueline Cochran was tasked with training a new Women's Flying Training Detachment known as the WFTD. Cochran was to *train* women pilots to supply Nancy Love's Women's Auxiliary Ferrying Squadron, the WAFS, that was all, and these were all just civilian women pilots. You will understand that if these women are given military recognition, we will have every other civilian group in the country applying.

EVA FORREST: Nancy Love's WAFS and Jacqueline Cochran's WFTD, the predecessors for the WASP, were the first women pilots to fly US military aircraft in this country. We are not training women to fly military planes for the first time now, in 1977. Even the early WAFS recruits back in 1942 were all experienced female pilots. Jacqueline Cochran saw that very soon these pilots would be doing more than ferrying planes from factory to military base for the war, so Henry H. Arnold came up with the acronym WASP. The WAFS and WFTD were merged into Women Airforce Service Pilots in mid-1943. They were amalgamated and got full military training.

THE COMMITTEE: You say that the WAFS and the WASP were the first women military pilots in the US, but the point is that Cochran did not go to Congress and apply for militarization for her women pilots when the WASP was formed.

EVA FORREST: If Cochran had insisted that the WASP were militarized in 1943, we might have had that recognition. But the country was in desperate need of pilots. Jacqueline Cochran agreed to hold off militarizing the WASP, and instead, she put all her efforts into getting the scheme up and running, assuming that the women's excellent records and service to our country would guarantee Congress's approval. But this never happened. So she went on without congressional recognition.

Eva hovered by the kitchen door of her home, the letter from Henry Arnold offering her a place in WASP training clutched in her hand. Her father's lighthearted chitchat was accompanied by responses from her mom that could only be described in one way: short.

"Hello there." Her father smiled at her, his cheeks flushed with traces of red wine, visible even in the moonlight.

"Dad, Mom." Eva held the screen door open for them.

Her mom stepped over the threshold first, wiping a hand over her tired brow.

"Well, that was a mighty successful bingo evening." Her dad pulled out a handful of coins from his pocket. He spread them over the kitchen table with a clatter. "Our next outing to the movies is on me, Ruth."

Eva's mother struck a match to light the gas and put the kettle on for coffee. Eva felt a stab of guilt at the way her mom's hands shook like a pair of fluttering leaves.

"We did not take great risks, Gerald. I would never be one to gamble with anything I hold dear."

Eva caught her father's eye. She pulled out a chair and sat down, preparing for war.

"We'll be sure to use the small winnings to go to the pictures," her mom said. "Eva, perhaps you'd like to join us? We could see what is playing in the next couple weeks and pick something. A family outing. How about that?" Her mother's gaze was quick and surefire, and it landed like a dead weight on the telltale envelope in Eva's hand.

"Dad, Mom, I have some news to tell you."

Her mom moved over to the cupboard. Pulled out two coffee mugs. "Who would like a cup of coffee? Eva?"

"No. Thank you."

"I will, dear." Her dad's voice was measured, quiet. He pulled back his chair and sat down.

The linoleum squeaked under Eva's mom's practical shoes. Slowly, she collected a teaspoon, then went back to get some sugar from the cupboard, twisting the lid on the jar with a flourish. "I heard that Jackson Watson's turned to drinking and gambling since he lost that boy of his to the war. Folks are terribly worried Jackson Watson will make an attempt on his own life."

Eva placed the WASP offer down on the table in front of her like a deck of cards.

"Mom, Dad, I got accepted to WASP." Her announcement spun in the air, took on a life of its own, and lingered like some precious, fragile spirit.

Her mom pulled the kettle off the burner. She turned the gas off. Her back to Eva, she poured coffee into two cups. She thumped Eva's dad's coffee down on the table. A pool of brown liquid spilled over the rim of the cup and spread.

"I'll get that." In a flash, her dad was out of his chair and at the sink.

Eva dared risk a glance at her mother's face. Under her thinning hair and the dark circles that pooled under her puffed eyes, her cheeks were as white as one of her freshly washed towels. She yanked out her chair and sat down in it. The chair that had been hers ever since Eva and Meg were little girls, the chair where she'd read to them while they drew at the kitchen table, pigtails swinging and faces frowning in concentration, the chair her mom had sat in when they rushed home from high school to tell her all the gossip of the day. And the chair her mom had slumped down in, refusing to get out of all night after they came back from the hospital on the day that Meg had died.

"Congratulations, sweetie." Gerald busied himself wiping up the brown mess.

"Thank you, Dad. I am so honored to be accepted. They only take around ten percent of girls who try out."

Her mom stared at her cup of coffee as if not seeing a thing. "I suppose you won't even be able to come to see a picture with us now."

"Mom—"

"Why are you doing this?" Her mother's words struck like a hammer against hard rock.

Eva fought an urge to move across to her mother, to hold her, but she knew her mom better than that. Her mother's strength was not in emotional outpourings of love. It was in being there. And now, Eva was leaving home, perhaps for good.

"I've explained why I'm going. You know why I want to fly. I've told you how Harry has been teaching me. You are so very fond of him."

Her mother turned, her eyes catching her daughter's. Her mom might be reserved, but that didn't stop her seeing things. It didn't stop her knowing her own daughter's mind. "It's because Harry is going. You won't stay here without him. That's it, isn't it?"

"Please, give me more credit than that. There are so many reasons why I know I should do this. I admit, I can't just wait here while my friends contribute to the war, but also, this is something I feel is right. It's something I need to do."

"Best thing you could do is wait here for him. Be here for him when he gets home."

Eva softened her tone. "You know that Harry is dating Lucille. There is no point in me waiting at home for him, Mom. I may as well do something useful."

But her mother's tone was low and dangerous. "Your feelings for him will not stop because of other people. It's the same thing as love not stopping when someone dies. You have no idea what it's like to lose a daughter. If you did, you would not be risking your life going to fly those ridiculous planes."

Eva shot her head up toward her mother, a knife piercing and twisting deep inside. Did her mom not realize that Eva loved Meg too? That she had lost the sister who used to stroke her hair at night until she fell asleep? The girl who had shared every part of her young life?

"Why not tell him how you feel, dear? Surely that would be easier than all this rushing off and proving that you can do what he can do."

Eva folded her hands on the table. Stared at the patterns in the wood. The feel of her mother's metallic gaze bored into her.

And one thought hit, hard. Was she as stubborn as her mother?

"Ruth . . ." Her father coughed. "I think that's enough. Leave Evie alone."

Her mom pushed her coffee away and laced her hands.

"I love you both," Eva said. She stood up and kissed the tops of their heads. "I don't think we should go on anymore tonight. I hope, one day, you will give me your blessing, Mom. Thank you, Dad, for your understanding and support."

Her mother's silence followed her up the empty hallway to her room.

The community hall was decorated with stars and stripes and streamers the night before Harry went off to war. Eva walked into his farewell party alone, the red dress she'd decided to wear for courage and confidence feeling all wrong when she laid eyes on Lucille. She wanted to run back home and get changed when she saw the demure light-blue dress that Lucille had chosen to wear to bid farewell to the man they both loved.

A photographer snapped photos of Harry and Lucille in front of the band. Lucille tilted her head and smiled at the photographer, her porcelain skin shining and her blond hair done up in an elegant chignon. Her blue chiffon dress was gathered at the waist with a sparkling diamanté clasp, and the soft skirt swirled around her long legs.

"Beautiful." The photographer sent Lucille an exaggerated wink. "Can we have one of you alone, sweetheart?"

Harry stepped aside, a look of indulgence on his face, and Eva stood still, heart thumping, her mother's words ringing in her head.

The glamour of Hollywood shone like the lights on a film set all around Lucille tonight. It was as if she were from another world.

After a few seconds of not being able to tear her gaze away, Eva felt a tug at her elbow.

Nina was right by her side.

"You look gorgeous." Nina dragged her away from her vigil. "Stunning."

Eva sighed. She hugged her friend, whose five-foot-two frame was encased in a bold little black number. "You look just lovely yourself."

"Come with me." Nina marched her determinedly across the room, her long hair swinging to her waist. She'd pulled it half up in the front, and it looked mighty fashionable.

Dylan's wheelchair sat on the outskirts of a group of their old school friends. Eva felt her heart go out to him, and any thoughts of Lucille were obliterated at the sight of his stump of a leg sticking straight out in front.

Nina took hold of the handles of his chair. "Dylan, I swear you're gonna have a good time tonight."

"Hurting today?" Eva asked, crouching down next to him.

Dylan stared straight ahead. Eva wished she could help him with the battles he was facing in his mind.

"I heard you're going despite my best warnings, Evie." His tone was flat.

Eva searched his face. "I am. I have to. I hope you understand."

"I will pray every day that neither you, Nina, or Harry have to face your own failure for the rest of your life. And yes, I understand, all right."

She leaned in closer to him. "Dylan, you were the first of us to join. None of us can even begin to imagine what you saw out there in Tunisia, what you went through." She'd heard stories of tanks being blown to bits around him, bursting into flames while being attacked by German guns. "For my part, I send prayers of thanks each night that you came home alive."

Dylan's empty gaze did not falter. He adjusted himself, grimacing with the effort and easing his leg in the wheelchair. Out of the corner of her eye, Eva saw Lucille twirling and posing for the photographer, a gorgeous smile lighting up her features.

"At least someone's enjoying tonight," she said, hoping to cheer him a little.

But Dylan gripped her hand. The intensity of it caused Eva to startle a little. He leaned up to her ear. "I sure hope Harry sees the light, because I for one can't see myself becoming friends with Lucille. And I'd love it if Harry ended up with a friend. I can't see myself hanging around here in Los Angeles, but I have to tell you—"

"Dylan—"

"What are you two gossiping about?" Nina leaned forward from where she held Dylan's chair. "Evie looks like she's about to go into a dead faint."

A waiter came around with a tray of champagne, and the band played the last few notes of "As Time Goes By."

"Champagne?" Nina took two glasses and handed one down to Dylan. "Goodness knows where they got this stuff from. Although Lucille's been bragging about her daddy to no end, so I'm supposing he's responsible."

Eva took a glass, one hand still encased in Dylan's.

Harry sashayed across the room, Lucille clinging to his arm.

"That was so darling." Lucille tittered, her eyes glittering over them all. "The newspaper man told me they'd label the photo, 'Hollywood princess must wait for her soon-to-be Helldiver hero to come home.'"

Harry looked at Lucille with adoration.

Dylan tightened his grip on Eva's hand.

The band struck up "It's Always You."

"Oh, how perfectly sweet. This is our song, Harry." Lucille reached up and tweaked him on the nose.

Nina choked on her champagne.

"For me, it will always be you, my love." Lucille took Harry's arm and led him to the dance floor, wrapping her arms around his neck.

Eva tipped back her champagne and took a big gulp.

"Once our training starts, there will be no time to get blue over any boy, Evie." Nina placed her hand on her hip and glared at Lucille and Harry.

"Thank *goodness*," Eva murmured. "If there are no boys at Sweetwater, I'll be ten thousand times happier than any girl in the world."


Once the last dance was done and the lights were turned up, Harry moved to the door to say his farewells with Lucille right alongside him, hugging all their old friends. Eva clutched the folds of her red dress and waited in line with everyone else to wish him Godspeed.

Eva shook Lucille's manicured hand when she got to the front of the queue. She accepted Lucille's kiss politely and then found herself face to face with Harry. She wanted to either turn around and run or reach out and hold him and never let go.

Dylan's wheelchair glinted beside her. Nina still held on to it, steadfast, and they both chatted with Lucille for a moment. Eva was certain Nina was giving her time with Harry.

But all she could do was stare at him, the boy whom she might never lay eyes on again. It was a likelihood. She'd lain awake most of last night imagining him diving in a bomber plane somewhere out over the Pacific. She'd forced herself not to visualize everything that could go wrong, with the plane, with the Japanese, with sheer bad luck over the ocean. In the end, unable to sleep, she'd padded around the house like a grieving widow.

Harry's eyes caught hers. His mouth worked a bit, as if he were trying to think of something to say. In the end, he shook his head in one small, imperceptible movement. He reached out for her, pulling her into a rough hug.

Eva buried her face in his shirt.

"You're going to love the flying. You know that." His voice was rich and deep and so honest that Eva fought to still her heart. "For pity's sake, stay safe."

"You too," she said. "You too, Harry. And thank you. Thank you for teaching me to fly."

He held her at arm's length. "That was my pleasure. I enjoyed every minute of it. It was an honor to help you to fly."

Hardly knowing what she was doing, the streetlights a blur in the darkness, Eva somehow fled outside.

The neighborhood heaved with silence, and it was as if Harry had already left.

Heat licked the air at the train station several days after Harry's party, days that had been a whirl of packing and goodbyes and Eva's mom sulking with pursed lips around the house. The train loomed on the tracks, and Eva stood with Nina and their parents on the platform, crowded with other young folks going off to war.

Nina threw her kit bag on the ground and wrapped her arms around her mother.

"You take care, girl," Nina's mom said, her chest heaving with the effort of fighting tears. Jean Rogers would reserve her crying and her weeping for when she got home.

Eva reached for her dad first. "Take care of Mom," she said, hugging him hard.

Her mother stood clutching her handbag beside them.

She let herself slip into the warmth of her father's embrace. "I wish I didn't know so much about airplanes," he said into her ear. "Sometimes it's not a blessing to be an aircraft mechanic, especially when your daughter is going to be at the mercy of those darned metal birds we put up into the sky. I'll keep making the ones I work on as safe as can be."

Eva stepped back but still maintained a loving touch. "Dad, you know it was you who put that love of flying into my heart. Thank you."

"I know, my love."

Eva turned toward her mother, her hand lingering in her father's for a moment.

Her mother stood opposite her now, implacable, yet looking somehow small out here, dwarfed by the grand surroundings. It was as if her mother had taken on a less menacing demeanor away from home. Eva wanted to hold her and never let her go.

The crowds surged around them. Shouts were obliterated by announcements over the loudspeaker. Signal men whistled and people called goodbye to their loved ones.

"We'd best get on the train, Evie." Nina was next to her.

Eva stood there, eyes locked with her mom's.

"Goodbye, sweetie." Ruth Scott reached out and tucked a stray curl behind Eva's ear.

Eva stood, handbag in front of her, her khaki cotton suit feeling absurd and formal now. She wished she could fold back the last few heart-wrenching years and try to reconnect with the woman who had raised her.

Was it too late?

Her mom reached into her pocket and pulled out a small handkerchief wrapped in a little clear plastic slip. It was white, and on it were embroidered two letters, *M* and *E*. Meg and Eva.

"You'll meet new sisters out in Texas," her mom said. "But don't forget your old one."

"Never." She batted at the tears that fell down her cheeks.

Her mother pressed the small handkerchief into Eva's hands. Eva leaned into her mother's embrace, holding her close, before she had to turn, linking her arm through Nina's.

Eva tucked her mother's gift into her jacket pocket and went to the waiting train. She didn't look back.

# CHAPTER NINE

THE COMMITTEE: Mrs. Forrest, you have not made clear how it was in any way a disadvantage for those early members of the WAFS and WFTD and the WASP to proceed without Congress recognizing them as part of the military.

EVA FORREST: Right from the outset, there were clear disadvantages to not being military. Jacqueline Cochran's WFTDs were given worn-out planes and bad equipment. They had no fire trucks, no crash trucks, and only one ambulance, and that just on loan at the Houston airfield, where the WFTD was trained before the move to Avenger Field in Sweetwater, Texas. The women had to fly the dregs that the military did not want. There was also a lot of resentment from male instructors who did not want to have to teach women.

As for further disadvantages, the WFTD was told they would have no housing. They were told to find their own housing. They had to find their own food, there was no funding for meals or any food for them, and they had to find their own transportation to and from the airfield. They were there from 7:45 a.m. until 9:00 p.m. They all had to share the one public restroom on the base, which was usually dirty. They had no uniforms and no allowance to buy uniforms. One woman told me she would not put her dog in the room she had to live in and pay for in a nearby motel. She had to share with rats. When the girls were finally issued uniforms, they were men's uniforms. And far too big for the women. One, and only one, class graduated from Houston in April 1943, and they were given no wings because they were not military. So Jacqueline Cochran bought them silver wings and paid for them herself.

But still, the flight training program expanded. Women were still willing to come and fly. Jacqueline moved the program to Avenger Field in Sweetwater, Texas, to provide proper accommodation for the girls who wanted to fly and to help with the growing need for pilots. Avenger Field had been used to train male pilots to go to Britain, but they were vacating those facilities. So the program was moved there.

THE COMMITTEE: In spite of these disadvantages you've listed here, it did not stop the women or deter their enthusiasm, so why complain?

EVA FORREST: You have to understand, we women were getting to fly. My understanding is that the morale did get very low at Houston with the bad planes, lack of food, and everything else, so the girls did what they could do to cheer themselves up. It was just what we did so that we, too, could feel that we were a part of things, even without the benefits and regulated safety nets that being military would have brought.

Eva leaned her head on the train window, staring out at the flat plains, her eyes closing every now and then and her body aching from all the hours sitting up. Right now, the war seemed as endless and formidable as this journey across Texas, and yet so very far away that it seemed there was little chance anything was real out here in this moonscape of a place. But the war did matter, and it was real, as real as the fact that the dirt driveways that led to the ranches that spread wide and strong over the Texan plains might be empty of boys if everyone didn't play their part. The headlines on papers at every station shouted the same things, the P-38 aircraft that were being built back at home in Lockheed were seeing action in Europe, the Pacific, and North Africa; the Nazis were kidnapping Polish children with Aryan characteristics; and in the Pacific, photos of the "war without mercy" were accompanied by disturbing slogans saying "Kill Japs, Kill More Japs."

Eva knew nothing was going to stop her playing her part. And nothing was going to stop Nina either. For the first time in their young lives, something they did was really going to matter.

"Next stop, Sweetwater." Nina pulled their last two apples out of the bag on her lap, handing one to Eva, taking a bite out of the crisp fruit herself.

"Thank you." Eva held the apple for a moment. The last piece of food from home. Straight from the tree in Eva's backyard. Well, it must not go to waste. She took a bite and turned to Nina, taking in her red-rimmed eyes and the way her hair stuck out in tufts above her two long plaits.

"I sure hope that the arranged transport doesn't keep us waiting too long." Nina leaned her head on Eva's shoulder. "I never thought we'd get here. This journey is something I'm not keen to repeat too often."

"You're faring better than me, I think. Last time I went to the restroom, I nearly keeled over with tiredness."

The two older women who'd been sharing their compartment were both fast asleep. Eva envied them their ability to conk out. All the way, she'd had trouble sleeping. The chance to stare at the landscape had given her the opportunity to reflect on Meg, Harry, and also her mom. One of them gone, one on an ungodly mission, and her mom so sad that it hurt.

The train finally pulled up at the Sweetwater train station, heaving and spluttering to a stop. Eva said her goodbyes to their two traveling companions and followed Nina down the long corridor out to the platform.

A hot wind blew around the isolated station. Nina looked around instinctively for the way out.

"This way," Nina said, her kit bag next to her on the ground. "We've done it. We're here. The last few weeks have been such a whirlwind. I can hardly believe that we made it to Texas somehow."

Eva looked down at her little friend. "I'm so relieved to be doing this with you."

"Oh, me too." Nina picked up her bag, hauling the canvas tote over her shoulder. "Couldn't abide doing this myself." She marched off down the platform, whistling "Comin' in on a Wing and a Prayer," Eva keeping pace.

They came to the end of the platform and turned to the front entrance of the station, where they stopped for a moment under a wide veranda on the sidewalk. Heat simmered up from the road. A lone car pulled up, caked in dust and dirt. A man got out, said goodbye to his driver, put on his hat, and ran toward the still-waiting train. Other than that, the road was empty. Eva's head suddenly spun with tiredness, and she leaned on Nina's arm.

"Here we go." Nina breathed the words. She stood up to her full height, her senses clearly alert. "I'd say this is likely our lift."

Eva yawned, unable to fight the wave of fatigue that engulfed her whole body, dragging her down. She'd become used to the rhythm of the train, and the heat was something else out here. Flies bothered her constantly, zipping around her face.

She looked where Nina was pointing, as a great lumbering sound rattled up the road. "Oh my, is this the way they travel in Texas?"

They were faced with a cattle truck, its cage in back lined with benches.

"I'd say we'd better get used to it," Nina murmured.

The truck pulled up, coming to a shuddering halt. Eva coughed. Dust blew into her nostrils, her mouth. She'd likely swallowed ten flies. The dust-caked window was hauled down slowly, and a woman in her fifties peered out.

"How are all y'all?"

"Well, we are just fine, ma'am. Thank you for asking." Nina wiped a hand over her sweaty face and beamed.

"You going to Avenger Field?" the driver asked in her Texan drawl.

"Yes, ma'am." Nina was perky enough for the three of them.

The woman leaned over in her truck, her sweaty armpits leaving damp pools on her thin floral dress, but her hair was done up neatly in a fashionable style on top of her head, brought into a high roll at the front. "Right you are, girls. Let me see now. Miss Nina Rogers and a Miss Eva Scott?"

"That's right, ma'am. I'm the Nina Rogers you are looking for, and this beautiful girl here is my friend Eva Scott."

"Well you'd best git in here with me. My name's Rebecca. You're the last two trainees to arrive for your class. You come all the way from Alaska or sumpin'?"

"California, Miss Rebecca." Nina was clearly in a chatty mood.

Eva thanked goodness for her friend's perky disposition right now.

"You look dead beat." Rebecca frowned at Eva. "The heat is sumpin' awful around these parts. You'll be boilin' in them wooden sheds they've built for you to sleep in, boilin' outside too, though. That's Texas for you." Rebecca climbed out of the truck. "The girls in your class are all chatterin' up a dust storm already. Most of 'em arrived last night and were put up at the Blue Bonnet Hotel. I done fifteen round-trips to the station today alone, and this morning, that truck was full of girls from the hotel. Packed in like a tin of fish, they were, and the noise! I can tell you, young girls can talk. I'll be glad of a cool drink when I git home and a swim in the pool."

"You have a swimming pool?" Nina followed Rebecca to the back of the truck.

Eva trudged along behind.

"Well, of sorts. We got a nice local swimming pool and all here in Sweetwater, and a smart hotel. You'll git to know 'em both well enough. This is a close little community out here, and we're gittin' used to having a whole bunch o' lovely girls staying in our heart. When the WASP first came, mind you, we was quite suspicious. But that Jacqueline Cochran, she started up a thing where the girls would come to the townsfolk for Sunday lunches to git to know us. Once we got to know 'em and to share some of our hospitality, well, they were part of our community soon enough. Although, we won't see you that often. We'll hear you, is all, flying them planes overhead."

"Well, that sounds mighty nice," Nina said. "I'm sure the girls were grateful to you all, Miss Rebecca."

Eva stepped up into the back of the cattle truck, following Nina, who was already settled inside. Rebecca pushed the bars shut.

"Now you girls make yourselves comfy, and we'll be there in no time."

Eva wanted to lie down on the wooden bench and go to sleep.

"You okay?" Nina nudged her. "I'm of a mind you'll not be wantin' to look like a girl who is half-asleep when we arrive at Avenger Field."

"I promise I'll wake up once we get there," Eva said.

"Here. You lean against me, Evie. I'll prop you up."

They traveled for another half hour, the hot wind blowing hard against either side of the truck, the rattling engine too loud for them to talk. Eva watched the old cotton fields with one eye open, and she counted at least five oil wells on the way to Avenger Field. Finally, Rebecca turned off the main road to a slip road, passing a couple of hangars in the middle of nowhere. Once they got past them, an airfield spread out, and Eva sat up, shading her eyes with her hands. *Just look at that.*

Rebecca pulled up with a jolt and came around to open the truck. "That's my job done for the day. Welcome to Avenger Field."

"Thank you, ma'am." Eva, suddenly wide awake, was down on the ground before Nina had stood up. Dry red dust swirled up around her legs, forming a film that coated the air. A barbed-wire fence ran the length of the road. And Eva wondered, was that to keep people out or to keep the girls in?

On the airfield behind it sat over one hundred planes.

Eva took a long look at them. Behind her, the sounds of Nina saying her farewells to Rebecca were lost in the excitement of the sight in front of her. They were all there, little primary trainers, the PT-19As; basic training planes, the BT-13 Vultee Vibrators; and, finally, advanced training AT-6s. Eva made out groups of AT-17s with their Cessna twin engines. The planes twinkled in the harsh sunlight.

Twenty-two weeks surrounded by airplanes. Suddenly, she wished she could share this sight with Harry, because painful crush or no crush, her heart swelled with the excitement and the possibilities out here.

Nina was by her side, staring out at it. The sound of Rebecca thundering away in the cattle truck rang into the quiet air.

"Well, will you look at that." Nina whistled low.

A little farther up the road, there was an entrance, and two girls stood at the gate.

"Think we'd best haul ourselves up that way, given we're the last arrivals and all." Eva motioned to Nina. "Let's go."

"We'll get to see plenty of these babies over the next few months." Nina trudged along next to her.

Once they got to the gate, Eva stopped for a moment. A sassy-looking gremlin was painted over the entry. She wore a red top, yellow pants, and a pair of flying goggles, and on her back, she had a pair of little wings. She looked like she was airborne, and Eva couldn't help the giggle that rose in her throat.

"Well now, welcome, you two." A tall girl with neatly pulled-back auburn hair stepped forward and held out a hand. She looked immaculate and freshly washed and as if she dealt with one-hundred-degree heat every day of her life. "Welcome to your new home. I see you've spotted our mascot—Fifinella." The girl pointed up at the sign. "She's our protector, a nice flying gremlin. Fifi welcomes everyone who attends Avenger Field with a smile on her face."

The girl waited while Eva and Nina took in Fifinella.

"I'm Helena."

"I'm Eva Scott, and this is my friend Nina Rogers."

Nina stepped forward to shake the much taller girl's hand. "Charmed to meet you, Helena."

Helena scanned a list that she held. "They gave me the task of welcoming the girls to our class. It's something I can do. Organize folks." She pulled out a silver pen, a frown creasing her milky-smooth features, and placed a couple of neat ticks on her list.

Nina caught Eva's eye and raised a brow.

"We've been on that train for days on end," Nina said. "I hardly know up from down, and yet, I can tell you, the sight of those planes makes me feel like I've arrived home at last. But you look like you're as cool as the sea in summer."

"You've come from California?" Helena asked, looking up from their names on the paper. "No wonder you're exhausted."

"All the way from LA," Eva said.

The other girl standing next to Helena stepped forward.

"This is Nancy." Helena had a well-modulated voice that sounded like it came from the East Coast, from one of Boston's or New York's finest schools. They'd come prepared to meet all sorts of girls, and it seemed that the group would not disappoint.

"You desert girls are always swell. Welcome to Avenger Field!" Nancy was medium height with bright-red hair, and her face was covered with a spatter of freckles. "I hail from Cincinnati, and Helena here comes from—"

"New York or Boston?" Eva couldn't resist.

"Technically speaking, Los Angeles is no desert." Nina let out a laugh.

"Boston," Helena said, her eyes dancing from Eva to Nina. "But our friend Nancy here's much more interesting than me. She's a fully trained scientist. She loves to look at the stars. I'm afraid she's a lot smarter than me too. Her brains are going to put me to shame. But like I say, I can organize folks, so that is what I'm going to do, whether you like it or not!"

Nancy threw back her head and let out a loud laugh. "Oh, don't you be ridiculous, Helena. I'll tell you one of the reasons I *had* to apply for WASP. Because Texas here is one of the best places on this planet to look at stars. The night skies are huge and endless out here. Can't wait to get up in the air and fly in the dark. I tell you, it's going to be magical. Just you wait, girls."

"Well, I have to admire you," Eva said. "Instrument flying at night is something I'm not so experienced in. It's my least favorite thing. Anyone who has a handle on instrument flying is a clever girl in my books."

"You either love it or hate it," Helena said. "Let's hope Nancy inspires you to love it. It took me a while, but I'm at peace with instrument flying now."

"Helena here's a flight instructor back home in Boston." Nancy looked up at the tall girl with respect.

"Well, I can tell you two are going to be mighty helpful friends to have." Nina put down her kit bag and folded her arms. "A scientist and a flight instructor? Sounds like we came to the right place."

"Say," Helena said, eyeing Nina's bag on the ground. "We'd best get back inside now. And I suppose you girls don't have bay mates yet? Because Nancy and I are going to share with a girl named

Beatrice—Bea—she's a pal of Nancy's, from Cincinnati too. And we need another three girls to make up a bay. You two interested for a start?"

Nina turned to Eva. "Evie? What do you say?"

"Sounds just grand to me," Eva said. Sharing a bay for five months with five strangers was either going to be wonderful or a terrible nightmare!

"Let's get going." Helena glanced up toward the training base in the distance, the wooden buildings sitting stark in the wide, sunny landscape.

As they walked up the long driveway, Eva felt the full force of the Texan sun on her cheeks. Flying out here in open cockpits was going to be tough. As the other girls chatted alongside her, the plains seemed to stretch in endless silence, the reddish soil broken only by the blue horizon in the far distance.

"Here's the lowdown. Each line is a barrack, and each room in the barrack is a bay," Nancy said.

They came closer to the wooden buildings that would be home.

"There's only one bathroom per two bays. And twelve girls sharing them, with two showers between us all, I've been thinking about how long we'll have in there each morning." Helena added, "I've been inside. I like to scout around."

"Well, Evie and I'll be all right," Nina said. "We grew up in Burbank. No frills where we come from. But how will you do, Helena?" Nina looked up at the auburn-haired girl, her expression entirely innocent.

A flicker of annoyance passed across Helena's face, but after a while, she smiled down at Nina. "I'm not completely and utterly precious. I can manage perfectly fine, thank you, Nina."

Nina's cheeks reddened. "I'm sorry. I didn't mean to offend."

"I'm figuring sharing with you girls will be a sight better than sharing with four little boys. I have four brothers." Helena came to a stop at the edge of the long rows of buildings.

Outside the barracks, groups of girls milled about on the dry brown lawn. A fountain marked the entrance to the home of the WASP.

"That's where you get dunked after you do your first solo." Nancy stopped for a moment at the round fountain. The water spattered cool droplets in the searing heat.

"Oh, in that case, bring on my first solo flight," Nina said. "We're hardened Californian girls, but this Texan heat is something else. No ocean breezes, just dry winds, I imagine."

Another girl split away from the others who milled about on the dry, baked grass. She was tall and blond, and she raced toward them.

"I'm Rita," she said, coming to a screaming halt in front of them. "All the way from Oklahoma."

Rita shook Eva's and Nina's outstretched hands as they introduced themselves.

"Mighty glad to meet you, Rita," Nina said. "I'm Nina, and this is my oldest and dearest friend, Eva."

"Oh, how charming. Let me tell you, you are lucky to have a very good friend out here," Rita said.

"I sure know that, Rita."

"I'm Helena, and this is Nancy," Helena said.

Rita bit her lip for a moment. "I don't mean to be forward or anything. Or perhaps I do, but you girls know of a spare place in a bay at all? I'm here alone, and I promise, I'm no trouble!"

Eva felt an instant warmth toward the girl, and she saw Nina's eyes crinkling into a smile next to her.

Helena rested a foot on the edge of the fountain. "Well. It seems to me we've got a bay sorted. Nina, Eva, Rita, Nancy, me, and Nancy's friend Beatrice."

"Oh, thank you, girls. I promise you won't regret it. Hope the rest of the five months goes as swell as this afternoon has!" Rita's face broke into a huge smile.

A loud noise boomed over the lawn, and a microphone whistled.

"Come on, girls," Helena said. "Get yourselves over between the barracks now. Time to listen to our housemother speak."

Eva felt Nina's elbow in her side. "Think we're goin' to get used to Helena herding us all around like cattle? I'm not sure about this girl."

"Think we're goin' to have to get used to being herded like cattle in general," Eva said. "And if Helena wants to herd us faster, well, better her than me."

"Oh boy." Nina's face crumpled up into a pout. "This is going to be an interesting five months."

"It'll be grand," Eva said. It was the sight of the airplanes that had done it. The moment she'd spotted them, all her exhaustion from the long journey into this unfamiliar terrain had gone away. Because around airplanes, Eva always felt like she was at home.

A woman stood on a small podium between the two rows of barracks. She just reached the microphone, but the expression in her eyes was serious.

She introduced herself as Leoti Deaton, their housemother, responsible for their welfare and care while they were here. "Welcome to Avenger Field, girls. You will be Class Forty-Three-W-Eight. I'm known around here as Deedee."

Eva shaded her eyes. Deedee's blond hair was tied back into a tight bun, and she stood up perfect and straight in a navy dress jacket and fitted skirt, even out here in the heat.

"Before we begin, there are a few vital things that I need to say. I hate to start this way, girls, but first and foremost, you must be mindful of the opportunity that Jacqueline Cochran has given you out here. You need to be above scandal. Any wrong steps in moral conduct will be more damaging to us as a group than any mistakes you could make in your training." Deedee paused for a moment. "The fact is, we've had to close Avenger Field to outside traffic. We had daily forced landings from men making up mysterious malfunctions that seemed to disappear as soon as they landed. They all were here to check out our girls."

Rita let out a groan. "Oh, for pity's sake. What a lot of fools. As if we'd fall for that sort of malarkey."

Eva felt her mouth twitch. She was going to like Rita.

"We've had to ban social contact with our civilian instructors because they are all male, and also with army air force staff. Class Forty-Three-W-Eight, you *all* have to conduct yourselves in a manner that we'll all be proud of, and we expect you to do a good job of that. Mrs. Cochran is relying on you to do her justice. She works very hard for us all so we can train at Avenger Field. Please, don't let her down."

Eva sneaked a glance around the crowd of girls gathered on the grass. To a T, they all looked sweaty, hot, and excited. A shiver of anticipation passed through her. Nerves too. Based on statistics from previous classes, only just over half of them would graduate. She had to do everything to ensure she and Nina ended up in the right half.

"Please stick together and don't find yourself alone away from base. Especially at night."

Deedee turned a page on the notepad she held. "Now to the practicals. A typical day here starts with reveille at six hundred hours, and then we march to breakfast. After that, half of you will march to ground school. You'll get your khaki trousers and white shirts issued for ground school classes in the morning. The other half of you will dress in your flight suits, with your turbans to keep your hair out of the way, for going to the field for flight training. You've all provided your funds to buy the uniforms, so well done, class."

"Nearly wiped me out," Rita muttered next to Eva. Eva kept her eyes on Deedee, too scared to talk out of turn. "But I didn't realize I was payin' for a turban. I hate puttin' anythin' on top of my head."

"Shush, Rita." Helena nudged the blond girl. "You'll get us all in trouble."

Rita groaned.

"Then you'll swap classes, ground school or flight school in the afternoons, followed by calisthenics every day on the airfield for everyone," Deedee went on. "We march to dinner in, as they say in the military, the mess hall, and then we march to the field for night training. Finally, we march to barracks to go to sleep at twenty-two hundred."

Nancy was fidgeting a little alongside Nina and Eva. "Marching? I'm the most uncoordinated girl you've likely ever met."

"We don't allow talking while marching," Deedee proclaimed. "But you can sing."

A deep-red blush spread down to Nancy's throat.

"We are professional, and we want to make the WASP into something which you will always be honored to be a part of, class."

"Too much marching," Rita muttered. "I never heard of so much marching in my life."

Deedee folded her hands in front of her. "Don't think we are not as serious as the men. The washout rate is high, although at this point, we women are washing out less than our male counterparts in the military. And we are working toward becoming part of the military, as you know. We work by military rules out here. Don't get caught out on demerit points—watch that you keep your bedding neat. Your bays will be inspected every Saturday morning, and you'll need to line up while we do that. You need to adhere to the bedding standards that will be set out for you, and your towels must even be hung just so. Keep tidy, work hard, and always stay focused. That is the way to be the WASP that I know you all have the potential to become."

Deedee stepped down from the podium, and the girls milled around, organizing bay mates. Lugging her kit bag across the dusty brown lawn that ran between the barracks, Eva moved with her group toward one of the screen doors nearby and surveyed the row of six cots lined up against the wall inside. There was no mirror in the room, and there was one closet around six feet tall for each girl. Each trainee had a locker painted in a bilious yellow.

"Well, whoever put this together had a charming eye for color," Rita said. Standard white sheets and a rough gray blanket were folded neatly at the end of each bed.

"Bed makings have to be done with a slide rule and eight-inch tucks. Pillowcases to be folded around and under, and the second blanket has to be over the pillow to the exact half inch," Helena said.

Eva turned to her, wide eyed.

Helena raised a brow.

"You a schoolteacher or somethin', Helena?" Rita threw her kit bag down on her bed.

"Don't go messing your bed up, Rita." Helena laid her bag down carefully on the floor.

Nina sent Eva a wink.

Just then, a small dark-haired girl appeared on the threshold. She dumped her kit bag down with a loud thump on the bare floorboards, causing Eva to jump. She wiped a hand across her red face. Her pair of sharp brown eyes scanned the room.

Nancy moved over to her. "Bea! Come meet our bay mates."

Nancy made her introductions, and Bea shook all of their hands.

"I've been talking with Deedee." Bea spoke in a practical, forthright way. Eva looked at her and thought there would be no messing about with Bea. She'd see through everything and tell you exactly what was what. "Deedee told me that we're only allowed one picture on top of our lockers, so if you've got three beaux, you'll have to pick one. Lucky for me, I don't have any. I find most of 'em dull."

"Heck, that could be a problem for me," Rita said. "I guess the boys back home will have to be out of sight, out of mind. Not sure that I'd call any of them beaux, to be honest, more like a bucket of trouble."

Nina grabbed Eva by the arm. "I'll need a bed next to yours, just in case I have any dramas late at night. I need you within whispering distance, Evie. Imagine, we can talk all night if there's something pressing to gossip about."

"You'll be way too tired to be gossiping all night, Nina," Helena's voice sounded from behind them, and Eva turned in surprise. "We'll be flying so hard and so bent over our textbooks studying for ground school that we'll all fall asleep the moment we hit our cots."

"Don't you bet on it," Nina muttered, pulling a face behind Helena's back. "Is she for real?" she mouthed at Eva.

Eva giggled and shook her head.

"The two showers are a real sight." Nancy appeared in the doorway from the bathrooms. "We're going to be lining up in the mornings, and we'll have to be super quick if we're sharing with next door. I heard that when the very first class came here in April, there were no stalls around the showers, so I guess it could be worse. Some girls had an awful time of it and went crazy with embarrassment."

"We should get up early so we can use the showers first." Helena unzipped her suitcase with a flourish. Inside, her clothes were ironed to a crisp and folded so they sat perfectly flat. She pulled out a white blouse and hung it in her wardrobe.

Eva found herself staring at the organized, meticulous girl. She was going to have to watch her standards. If there were a lot of girls like Helena here, then the threat of washing out for those less organized could be real.

Eva sat down on her bed with a thump.

"Well, we'll have plenty of time to sort those practicalities out, Helena," Bea said. Her kit bag was already halfway unpacked. She looked up from where she was kneeling on the floor. "Deedee told me there's no leave into Sweetwater for the first two weeks. We have to stay at Avenger Field."

"Are you kidding me?" Nina said. "Rebecca, our driver in that great cattle truck of a thing, told me there's a swimming pool. How are we supposed to stand being without a swim in this heat for two whole weeks? And we can't dunk in the fountain until we've had our first solo flight. That's a tradition."

Helena stopped her unpacking and surveyed Nina. "Nina, it's fine to let loose in here, but mind you don't complain too much about Deedee's rules, or any of the other instructors, won't you?"

Nina threw her arms in the air when Helena turned back around. Rita caught the gesture and made a face behind Helena's back.

"Well, I'm awful panicked about the instructors. I've heard stories that they don't want girls learning to fly planes," Nancy said. "I'm braced for them not to be friendly. Mostly, I've heard they're men who don't believe we women are any good for the ferrying jobs."

"Someone asked me if becoming a pilot meant I was going to turn out fast." Bea stood up from where she'd been unpacking. She threw her short arms in the air. "I mean, me? Fast? You've gotta be kidding!" She did a little twirl on the spot. "If any folks knew me, they'd know the reason I like getting up in the sky is so I can be by myself. I'm just a hardworking girl. I was furious when folks back home told me not to hop on instructors' laps like a secretary would do."

"Oh my goodness me," Rita said. "You can't git away from gossip, even when there's a war on. You'd think folks would have bigger things on their minds."

Eva threw herself back on her bed and stared at the ceiling.

"Watch you don't mess your bed, Eva," Helena said. "They might come check us for tidiness."

Eva leaped up.

"Jumpin' Jehoshaphat, girls!" Rita shot across the room. "I've already got a scorpion in my wardrobe."

Everyone rushed over to stare at Rita's wardrobe. Bea appeared with a jar and deftly covered the little scorpion until it had crawled up the side. "Knew this place was famous for insects, so I brought this."

"Well, aren't you a treasure." Rita wiped her hand over her messed-up blond hair.

Bea bustled off with her jar and went outside, the screen door swinging closed behind her.

"Best get unpacked, girls," Helena said. "I think we have to be at dinner in half an hour."

Nina clutched Eva's arm. "Thank *heavens* I have you," she whispered, "because this is going to be one crazy time."

On her first morning at Sweetwater, the touch of Helena's hand on her shoulder woke Eva from the heaviest sleep she'd most likely ever had in her life. Slowly, she opened her eyes, watching Helena moving around the bay in her nightgown, gently waking everyone up. Nina was still curled fast asleep in her cot next to Eva's.

"Oh, patience love us!" Rita sat up, stretching her long arms wide in the air. "What on earth time is it, Helena?"

"It's five forty-five." Helena tapped Bea's shoulder. "I thought we'd get a head start on the showers before our friends in the next-door bay take over. I don't want any of us to be late on our first day."

Rita lay back and groaned. "Fifteen minutes more sleep, and I swear I would have been a different girl."

Eva felt the stirrings of a giggle. She pressed her lips together. The look on Helena's face was priceless.

"Well, I'm sorry to hear that, Rita, because I think we should be extra careful on our first morning. If we can get demerit points for not making our beds properly, the last thing I want to do is lose one of you girls over things that we can avoid . . . now that I've only just found you all." Helena's voice held a lilt of something wistful now.

Eva sat up and pushed her curls away from her face. She watched Helena continuing to wake girls up.

"Helena's right." Bea hopped out of bed, her blue cotton nightie plain and practical and her short hair sitting neat and tidy around her round face. "I for one am thankful for the extra fifteen minutes. And I'm looking forward to breakfast and my first day flying."

Helena was back at the sleeping Nina's side.

"Good luck." Eva pushed back her covers and stretched her arms above her head. "She's impossible to wake once she's out. I swear she stays up all night being quirky Nina. I used to think she was a fairy sprite when we were little."

Helena looked up, pushing a strand of her long auburn hair back from her beautiful face. "You girls have been friends for that long?"

"You bet. Since grade school."

That sad look passed across Helena's face again.

Eva leaned down and poked Nina on the arm.

The sound of Bea in the shower rang through the bay.

"Oh my, she's a singer," Rita said. She looked up from her wardrobe.

The sound of Bea belting out "Don't Sit under the Apple Tree" competed with the running water, and Rita started singing along.

"I'm next." Rita hurried to the shower room. "I can't fly without feeling human, girls."

Gently, Eva patted Nina on the shoulder. She looked all of twelve years old with her freckles and her hair spreading all over her pillow. She opened one eye finally.

"Time to get up," Eva said.

Right then, there was a knock at the door. "Girls, breakfast in half an hour!"

It was Deedee. And it was six o'clock.

"Yes, ma'am," Helena called back, and then looked at Eva with huge eyes. "Is that what we call her?"

"Sounds good to me," Eva said.

Helena nodded. "Remember, girls, three-minute showers each."

"Three minutes?" Nina threw off her bedclothes with a flourish.

"She's right, Nina. Mess hall in thirty minutes, and the next-door bay is going to wake up and be waiting in line for showers any second now."

Eva's hands flew through her wardrobe, grabbing a summer dress and laying it on her bed. Then she took it off the bed again, placing it on her locker in a flurry, and started making her bed in her nightie. She kept an eye on the line to the shower. She'd have to wash last this morning. She'd race to get her bed tidy first.

At 6:25, they were all breathless. Helena checked every bed with a ruler.

"Goodness, how are we going to do this every morning?" Nina's face creased into a mighty frown.

Eva wiped a hand over her brow. The sun wasn't even up yet, and already it was boiling.

"Nancy, you're an inch out on your measurements," Helena said. "You'd best fix it, and fast."

The sounds of screen doors in other bays slamming and Deedee giving instructions on how to get into formation to march to breakfast at the mess hall sent Nancy into a panic.

"Oh my," she said, scuttling off to her bed. "I'm sorry, girls. You leave me. Go get in line."

She ripped her bed apart, sheets flying in the air like sails on a boat.

"Not a chance, Nancy, we'll help." Rita rushed over to start pulling her bed into shape.

In a flash, everyone was tucking and tidying. Once they were done, Helena stepped in and measured Nancy's bed with her ruler.

Silently, Helena nodded.

Rita let out a whoop, and the girls rushed outside into the semi-darkness, nearly falling out the door.

"Well, good morning bay thirty-seven," Deedee said, her hair and makeup looking as immaculate as it had yesterday. Today she was wearing a pair of navy trousers with her dress jacket in the Santiago blue that the WASP would get once they did their first solo night flight.

Eva came to a shuddering stop behind Nina, almost falling into her shorter friend and knocking her flat. The sight of Deedee was again inspirational, and yet somehow intimidating. Would she and her bay mates ever reach such high standards in their dress, attitude, and demeanor once they were fully trained as WASP?

"You all might want to make sure you allow plenty of time in the mornings," Deedee said. "I'll make allowances since it's your first day today and all, but be careful."

Head down, Eva followed her bay to the formation.

"Right, split into two groups, girls," Deedee said.

The girls divided in a flurry.

They started to march across the lawn in silence.

But as they progressed toward the hangars, one of the girls started to sing in a clear alto voice, "Yankee Doodle Pilots." And after she'd sung a verse on her own, the rest of the group started taking up the tune. Soon they were marching and singing in time. Didn't seem to be that hard.

And out of the corner of her eye, Eva saw the glisten of planes on the airfield, and the sun rose up in the glorious wide Texan sky, bathing the lawn in fresh light.

Eva took a risk. She reached out and grabbed Nina's hand.

# CHAPTER TEN

THE COMMITTEE: It seems that the WASP not being military did not deter women from joining.

EVA FORREST: The fact that we were not militarized at the time did not stop us from joining. It simply did not occur to us that we wouldn't be militarized. However, as civilians, we WASP had no insurance, no burial and death benefits, no military rank, and no veterans' benefits. Men doing the exact same flying jobs alongside us were militarized and received all the benefits that brought. Men doing clerical jobs in the armed forces were militarized, sir.

THE COMMITTEE: Did you view the program as discriminatory against women at the time?

EVA FORREST: No, I viewed it as an opportunity. I was not aware that our pay would be lower than men's for exactly the same work. I did not know that women pilots who were applying for WASP were expected to have logged over twice as many hours as male pilots.

Eva marched back to the bay with her group, singing a grand rendition of "We Were Only Fooling," another WASP song that the girls had caught on to. While she picked up the tune and sang along with her classmates, Eva felt the stirrings of a chuckle over the fact that they'd been told they could have their scrambled eggs with brains. The mess hall staff were mighty cheerful, but Nina had turned green at the suggestion of eating sheep brains, and Helena had blanched at her plate of powdered eggs. But still, they'd all pulled together and made the most of the powdered eggs and tinned Spam, rather than brains. Bea had said she couldn't wait to write home and tell her folks how she thought she might come to like Spam.

"Twenty minutes to get changed, girls." Deedee turned on her heels and walked off.

"Jeepers, all this marching is doing me in already," Rita said. She pushed the door open. "But I love the singing. Now let's see how these babies fit. You know, I adore fashion. And the one thing I like about flying is having a good-looking flight suit. Lookin' forward to seeing some real flyboys once we're outta here." Rita held up the shapeless flight suit and let out a groan. "But these things look like somethin' a clown would wear in a circus! Goodness, I'm not puttin' this on!"

"Well, look!" Nancy had her flight suit out of its bag and held it up over her compact frame. "Size forty-four? How are we supposed to fly in these?"

Nina did the same thing. And was hidden like a little girl behind a huge oak tree.

"Nina!" Eva brought her hand up to her face and exploded into giggles. She bustled around with her package, pulling out a huge men's-issue suit and a long turban that was going to be foul in this weather over her curls.

"Zoot suits. That's what they call them." Bea stood helpless, the legs in her suit dragging halfway across the floor. "Air force can't be fussed issuing the right sizes for women. So we get the men's standard issues."

Nina had hers on. She waved her arms in the air, fabric flapping everywhere. "Evie, I'm in a swimming pool. Or more likely a giant swamp."

Eva bustled over to her friend. "Here, quick." She did what she could without a needle, rolling up the legs and the sleeves.

"If only we could wear a belt." Rita turned, frowning at her slender body encased in the voluminous thing.

Once Nina was done, looking like anything other than a pilot, Eva knelt down and fixed her own legs. Then Nina helped with her sleeves.

Helena was at the door. "Time to go, girls." She turned to them, her head wrapped in her turban, looking elegant even in this heat.

"My, you're a stylish girl," Rita said. She tried to wind her turban around her head and ended up in an awful mess.

"So glad we're moving to slimmer skirts to save fabric in wartime. Well, we can see where all the fabric's gone to," Bea said, her suit pooling around her small, sturdy frame. "Men's flight suits."

"Marching for your vaccinations, girls! Quick smart," Deedee called from outside.

Rita held up a pair of beautiful, shining black Texan boots. "I'm going to wear them with my zoot suit while I have my shots."

"Oh, so very elegant." Nina giggled.

"Those boots are somethin' terrific," Nancy said. "They'll help with the injections, I'm sure!"

Eva tripped on the way to the door, her shoes caught in the trousers.

They marched to the infirmary, and this time, someone started up a song that had them all roused up until the last verse, "Gee, Mom, I Want to Go Home." The last line gave Eva confidence for her vaccinations because they proudly sang to their mas that they were not going home. Once they were lined up at the infirmary for their shots for tetanus, yellow fever, smallpox, and typhoid, Rita started to turn a little green.

"Heck, the cowboy boots aren't doing the trick like I thought they would. Could someone stand in and have them twice for me?"

"You'll be fine. Think of something real nice, and don't look at the needle." Nancy rested a hand on Rita's shaking shoulder.

"Oh my!" Rita mocked a swoon. "I don't even have a decent beau back home to think about while I suffer this. What'm I gonna do?"

Eva's left sleeve was rolled up, ready for a needle that probably would feel extra sharp in the gathering heat. Rita pulled up the sleeve of her zoot suit, had her first shot, and fell flat to the ground in a dead faint.

Eva knelt down next to her along with Nancy and Nina.

"Rita?" Nina asked, but the tall blond girl's eyes remained closed, and traces of sweat bloomed above her white lips.

"Poor darling's gone and died with her boots on," Nancy said.

Rita lay quite still, her beautiful, shining boots sticking straight out in front of her and her toes pointing up to the sky.

Once they'd marched to the airfield, Rita pale and determined and insisting no one alert Deedee to her unseemly swoon, they moved into the two groups as they'd been directed, one for flight school, the other half for ground school. Eva filed with her bay mates into one of the tin hangars that overlooked the airfields.

Their flight instructor stood in front of the half class of girls. Eva eyed him. She, too, was nervous about the instructors. The stories that filtered around the mess hall were all about men who did not want to teach women.

Intense heat burned in the hangar. Eva's zoot suit was as useful as a fur coat on a bed of hot coals, and beads of sweat gathered at the edges of her turban. She was of a mind right now not to care that the instructors had insisted on turbans to wrap their hair under their helmets because the men were tired of the way the girls' hair flew out behind them, sometimes buffeting the instructors' faces when they were flying in open cockpits.

"Good morning, class. I'm Instructor Reg Tilley. I'm a civilian flight instructor."

Instructor Tilley swiped a gaze around the group. Reg's features were pointed and sharp. His movements as he marched across the room to his blackboard were quick and sure. Eva sensed that he would not suffer fools in the sky. She only hoped he was fair.

"Five flying periods a day. Five students assigned to an instructor, with each student flying an hour at a time. You'll march out in formation, and you must stay in the ready room or the flight line while you're waiting your turn to go up. Use the time for writing and studying. Once you start ground school this afternoon, there will always be work to do."

Eva looked out through the hangar's wide-open doors. The planes shimmered, hovering above the brown dust that hung in a light haze over the ground.

"You're going to start today with your pre-solo-training phase in our primary trainer, the PT-19A, in the tandem open cockpit with me behind you," he said. "Current WASP graduate pilots are delivering these planes all over the country, so it's important that you familiarize yourself with them here in Texas. Once I am confident that you are all ready, we'll move to a BT-13 Vultee Vibrator and then the AT-6."

Next to Eva, Nina let out a contented sigh.

"We want to get you flying in all conditions, and used to them as soon as possible. Over the next five months at Avenger Field, you'll experience flying in the intense heat of summer, and the blizzards and snowstorms that attack the plains in winter. The weather out here can change from morning to lunchtime and be completely different in the evenings. It is the best training place we can give you. A storm is predicted for today. There's no protection when flying in Texas."

"Fine by us," Rita said.

"Most of the time, you'll be flying with an instructor, only later on by yourself." He lowered his voice a little. "To be honest, I know that many of you have a lot of flying hours. I know that some of you could probably outfly your instructors. I want you to know that I believe women can fly as well as men."

Something shifted in the room—the girls stirred, and some of them put down their pens. An attitude like his was the last thing they had been led to expect. Bea sat up a little, eyes narrowing. Reg Tilley had just earned himself a new respect.

He moved to a large black fan and turned it on, sending a welcome flurry of air into the already stifling hangar. Eva thanked him silently. She felt her nerves relax a little. Instructor Tilley had already proven he'd be a good teacher.

Half an hour later, Eva looked down at her pages of notes about the specifics of the little PT-19A. Black clouds shifted across the ominous sky outside. The whole atmosphere out there had darkened. It seemed charged. Heat swirled, but the sky was octane.

The group made its way outside after the talk was done. Streaks of yellow sun broke through the gathering clouds, sending eerie patterns onto the airstrip.

Instructor Tilley divided the girls into flight groups. Eva was with Rita, Helena, Nancy, and Nina.

"Excuse me?" Rita put up her hand.

The flight instructor looked at her.

"What do we call you?"

"Sir," he said. "Or if you prefer, Mr. Tilley is fine."

Rita nodded. "Yes, sir."

The girls were quiet and attentive, boding well for their flight group.

A little primary trainer sat ready on the runway. Its blue fuselage and yellow propeller and wings looked uncanny, the colors almost electric in the strange light that hung over the Texan plains.

Reg moved toward Helena first. He handed her an inspection sheet, watching while she moved around the low-winged open Fairchild airplane to carry out her preflight inspection.

Eva frowned toward the horizon. The clouds seemed loaded, about to explode. But in spite of the weather, Reg climbed onto the plane's wing, settling himself in the rear seat while Helena climbed, in turn, up onto the wing and into the front cockpit. Helena called out to the ground crew to remove the chocks, then told them to clear the props.

Helena taxied the little Fairchild out to the holding point, increased her throttle, and executed a perfect takeoff down the runway. Eva stood with the rest of her flight group on the ground in the gathering wind and watched, craning her head upward while the plane went into a slow roll. But when they were inverted, everyone gasped, and Eva reached out to clutch Nina's arm.

Because the moment the primary trainer was flipped upside down, Helena was hanging out of the airplane.

Helena was holding on to the windshield, and her feet were sticking straight out behind her. Eva brought her hand up to cover her mouth. Reg clearly took control of the plane and let it keep rolling in the thunderous black clouds until Helena was back in her seat.

"My dears, did she forget to buckle her seat belt?" Nina gasped.

Nancy shielded her eyes with her freckled hand.

And Eva knew they were all thinking the same thing. Was he going to wash out Helena?

"Dear goodness," Rita muttered. "What was that girl doin' up there, and why?"

The little airplane came in for a neat landing. Reg was first out. Once Helena was on the ground, they talked for a moment. Eva's heart was full of feeling for Helena. She watched them walk back to the group, hardly wanting to hear the outcome, desperate to know at once.

Helena was a flight instructor. Helena had ten times Eva's experience in a plane.

Helena and Reg came to an abrupt stop in front of their flight line.

"Despite our detailed checks, the mechanics failed to secure the front seat belt exactly and properly to the seat." Reg turned to Helena with respect. "Due to Helena's ingenuity in quickly realizing she had to hang on to the front of the cockpit and keep her balance, rather than losing her head, she's standing alive with us today. We are bringing another airplane across for the rest of you." He frowned up at the ferocious black clouds. "I'm still looking forward to taking you all up."

Eva was next in line. Once a fresh Fairchild primary trainer was at the ready, once she'd carried out her preflight inspection with Reg right alongside her, just as Helena had done in the other plane, Eva stepped on the wing and climbed into the front cockpit.

If Reg hadn't been sitting behind her, she would have broken into song when the plane lifted off the ground, no matter the menacing weather, even with wind buffeting the aircraft and her forehead slick with perspiration. The base spread out below her, and the great menacing Texan sky started throwing welcome drops of rain into the cockpit. Eva felt her mouth widen into a grin.

She was flying. And flying made everything worthwhile.

# CHAPTER ELEVEN

THE COMMITTEE: Because Jacqueline Cochran did not insist on militarization for the WASP, was it then *her* actions that were detrimental to your chances of military recognition, rather than anything to do with Congress at the time?

EVA FORREST: In defense of Jacqueline Cochran, she was running the entire WASP training program. Even though she did allow the program to continue without militarization, she worried about trying to sort out the salary situation, acquiring insurance for us, death benefits, and adequate medical and dental care, and she had to sort these matters out herself. She was responsible for our moral image, for managing and disciplining us, and for discharge of WASP who broke the rules. She designed the Santiago-blue uniforms we wore officially and the wings that she paid for and gave us on graduation, and then she had to work out which bases we would be sent to after we graduated and how she could get all the bases to conform to air force regulations when it came to their dealings with us WASP. She was working on the issue of militarization, but she was also working on all these other things, and at the same time, her health deteriorated.

THE COMMITTEE: But while Mrs. Cochran was running your program, you were not trained in the full military way, like male pilots were.

EVA FORREST: The only aspect that our training did not cover was combat maneuvers, as the idea from the outset was that we would free up men for combat roles. Other than that, our training was exactly the same as that of male military pilots. In every sense, sir. We covered everything, from every aspect of ground school to all areas of flight. And out in Texas, we did so while freezing and roasting, in conditions that could only be described as tough.

A few weeks into training, Eva took one last look over the wide Texan plains that spread below the aircraft, the steady buzz of the prop engine a welcome companion to the great stillness below. The sky around her was azure, and only a couple of long slivers of wispy cloud were visible above the far horizon. Her first solo flight at Avenger Field had gone by like a dream, and before beginning landing procedures, Eva sent a little thought out into the sky for Meg. How she would have loved to be here with Eva and Nina and the other girls right now. Eva brought her hand up to the little silver necklace she wore for her lost sister, where it sat for as long as she could possibly wear it.

"Delta Forty-Two requesting permission to land," she radioed the control tower. *And this flight was for you, Meg,* she thought.

"Delta Forty-Two, permission granted."

Eva entered the circuit area.

"Calling downwind."

"Roger, Delta Forty-Two."

Eva continued downwind until she was at exactly a forty-five-degree angle, then turned crosswind and put her flaps down for landing. She reduced her speed and carried out her checks, Harry's voice in her head, reminding her to do everything thoroughly. She was more than keen to hear from Harry. Whenever the mail run came in, she would hope and pray that there'd be a letter. So far, nothing. She hated to think of the risks he was taking. If she could, she'd go dive-bombing herself if that would keep him safe.

At one thousand feet, Eva checked that her fuel pump was on, the mixture rich, checked her door, felt her harness to ensure it was secure. And once she was at five hundred feet, she started slowly decreasing her speed.

Eva frowned in concentration. Instructor Tilley would be checking her every move from the ground. It had been strange not having him in the back cockpit, but Eva had woken this morning early, knowing that she was ready to take the plane out solo and be assessed.

She had the PT-19A at landing speed at exactly the right spot. Eva pulled the throttle back with her right hand, her left hand on the control stick. Taking off and landing were instinctive to her after Harry's and then Reg's expert teaching, but she still made certain that she ran through procedures in her head to be sure.

She kept an eye on the airspeed indicator to maintain the right speed and not drop. The back wheel landed first, and Eva allowed herself a huge grin. She taxied back to the hangars and turned off the engine.

Once she was out and on the searing-hot pavement, she took off her helmet and unwound her turban, letting her curls fly loose. Reg stepped forward and shook her hand.

"Well done, Eva. I was extremely happy with that."

"I'm just thankful for the flying conditions."

"Credit where credit is due. I think you have a tradition to uphold . . ."

The moment he turned, it was as if he'd given permission to her flight-group mates to let loose. Rita was there first.

"Right, girls, let's get her up!"

Rita knelt down, and Eva climbed onto the tall girl's shoulders.

"Am I too heavy?" she squeaked.

"Nonsense, you're light as a leaf."

The others swirled around her. "Golly, you're going to enjoy the fountain." Nina laughed, grinning up at Eva and reaching to take her hand.

Nina's hair was still slick and damp from her dunking in the fountain after her solo right before Eva's. Rogers came before Scott, the way it had always been for them from the time they went through grade school. It was no different now that they were flying airplanes to help with the war.

Eva swayed on Rita's shoulders, and once they'd made the short journey to the little fountain at the edge of their training center, Rita knelt down.

Nancy, Helena, Nina, and Rita each took an arm or a leg. Between them, they swung her slowly into the fountain. Eva sank into the cool water, letting it wash over her for a moment before standing up, her zoot suit soaked, and throwing a fist in the air.

"Congratulations!" the girls yelled in unison, and in the sheer joy of that moment, Eva swore if there wasn't a war on, she'd be the happiest, most content girl in the world.


That night, the air was ever so still. No breeze came to soothe the oven-like Texan heat. Eva lay on her cot, sheets thrown off, arms folded behind her head. Rivulets of perspiration ran down her toned stomach.

Their calisthenics instructor had shown no mercy because it was searing hot. Instead, she'd pushed the girls harder as they jumped and followed every exercise out on the relentlessly hot tarmac. Eva's pulse had taken ages to slow down afterward, and even a cool shower had not given her relief.

She turned on her side. Nina faced her, eyes open, fanning her face with an exercise book.

"What's up, Nina?" Eva asked.

Nina stopped fanning herself. "I'm stifled and I can't sleep, Evie."

Eva sat up, pulling her knees toward her chest. "What say we drag our cots outside? If there's gonna be a breath of air, we're not going to see it in this bay. I heard that we have permission."

Nina sat up too. "Grand idea."

Rita sat up. "Wait. I'm coming too."

Eva scanned Bea's, Helena's, and Nancy's sleeping forms. Rita grabbed the top end of Nina's bed, and Eva and Nina backed out the screen door, holding the foot of the cot and placing it on the dry brown grass. Already, a number of cots from other bays were dotted around the lawn between the buildings. The soft sounds of snoring filtered into the quiet night.

Eva looked up. The stars glittered against the pitch-black sky. At least she'd have something beautiful to gaze up at if she still couldn't get to sleep out here. It sure beat the plain old ceiling above her bed.

She followed Rita and Nina back inside, padding in the quiet darkness, to bring the other two beds out before climbing into hers, lying, and staring at the night sky, allowing her mind to drift off, allowing it to float into thoughts of Harry and what he might have gotten up to today . . .

It seemed like only a flicker of time had gone by when the sky gradually lightened, the great blanket of darkness just beginning to reveal the pink sunrise that would bloom like a gorgeous bright flower over the Texan plains.

Eva sat up and stretched, swinging her legs over the side of her bed. She checked her watch, and it was only five thirty.

"Oh my!" Rita's shout hurled out into the air.

Eva jumped off her bed.

"Something's bit me."

In a flash, Nina was over to Rita too, pushing her braids behind her back. Eva scouted the ground.

"Help!" Rita shouted.

"Do you think it was a snake?" Eva couldn't see any critters.

"It's on my leg, in my pajamas." Rita's glance sprung around the field. "I've got to get them off."

"No men in sight, as if there would be at this hour," Nina said.

Rita heaved off one pajama bottom leg to reveal a great red swelling halfway down her thigh.

Eva glared at the sight of the critter crawling across Rita's bed. "I see the culprit." A three-inch scorpion scuttled through her sheets.

"Catch it in a jar! No, don't. Get some ice," Nina said.

Eva ran to the mess hall, rattled the door, almost slumped with relief when it bounced open, and hurtled straight to the refrigerator. Yanking the door open, she pulled out a handful of ice. She grabbed a clean linen tea towel, slammed the wooden drawer shut, and belted back out to the lawn, where a small crowd of girls had gathered around Rita.

Bea was in the middle of them, holding the offending scorpion in her jar.

Nina was bathing Rita's swelling wound with a wet, soapy towel.

"Brilliant, Eva. Pass the ice." Rita breathed. Her chest rose and fell too fast, and she was white with pain, her forehead running with perspiration.

"Lie down on your stomach," Eva said.

Rita wafted down onto her bed, her face contorting as she rolled onto her stomach. She clutched Nina's hand, her knuckles white, and Eva pressed the cold compress of ice against her swollen leg.

"Well, we've got your attacker, and as soon as the sick bay opens, we'll get you there," Nina said.

"You go get ready, girls. I can't move right now." Rita turned her head to one side, her face contorting into a grimace.

"She's right," Bea said. "I'll keep the attacker away until we've all showered and dressed. Then we'll get that cot of yours inside, make up your bed, and get you straight to treatment."

A group of girls had gathered to inspect the striped bark scorpion that flickered around inside Bea's jar.

"I've an idea," Helena said.

"Well, if it's good, I'll be glad to hear it." Rita spoke through gritted teeth.

Helena laid an arm on Rita's head. "I suggest we don't leave any bits of sheet hanging down from our cots when we sleep out here, nothing that could give a critter a hold."

"Brilliant, Helena." Rita winced. "My, this thing stings to high heaven."

"Ten past six," Helena said, her hand stroking Rita's head. "You girls go get in the shower."

Nina held the door open to their bay. "Rita was lucky. Those sorts of scorpions are the common ones. But that sure gave her an alarm bell she didn't need."

"The other day, I heard a tale of a girl waking up to find a two-inch-long roach eating a hole in her slippers," Eva said.

"Well, I heard that sometimes plagues of locusts come visit Avenger Field." Nina picked up her towel and slung it over her shoulder.

Eva shuddered. "Apparently, they line the runway so thick that the airplanes skid on them on landing."

"Ugh. Well, seems we have two choices. We either boil in our bays and don't sleep, or spend our nights crawling with critters."

Nina disappeared into the shower stall.

None of them mentioned that Sweetwater was the rattlesnake capital of the world.

Desert heat pierced the long days under the relentless sun. In the open-air cockpits, the sun seared through zoot suits, heads sweat in tight turbans, and faces burned until they were all red. Sweat trickled down the girls' cheeks while they flew, and their hair became wet pools, slick against their heads. Inside, during ground school, it felt like the barracks and hangars were on fire while they labored over algebra, navigation, and meteorology. Tin roofs absorbed heat. Their five o'clock calisthenics went ahead every day out on the tarmac in air like a furnace no matter what.

Talk in the mess hall over three good square meals a day was all about their next challenge—instrument flying in the Link Trainer, the dark, hot box that simulated night flying in a closed-cabin aircraft. The Link Trainers had no visual aids, only instruments and a radio connection to an instructor. It was the first step toward solo night flying, and anticipation about it buzzed.

Heat simmered up from the ground on the first day of instrument class, a slippery mirage that rose above the airfield. Eva took her seat in the sweltering Link Trainer room, her classmates pulling notebooks out and settling down.

A hush gathered over the room when the instructor strode to the front of the class, turning to face them and flashing a smile. Harry was handsome; Harry was the best man Eva had ever met, but the man standing in front of the class right at this moment was the most beautiful man Eva had laid eyes on in her life.

"Welcome to instrument classes. My name is Dan Parker." Instructor Dan leaned down to adjust his notes, his dark eyelashes fanning out over his cheeks.

Eva wasn't sure whether taking a seat in the front row was going to aid her concentration or hinder it, but she sure couldn't take her eyes off the instructor right now. Next to her, Rita sat back, crossed her legs, and let out a slow whistle under her breath.

"Instrument flying will be the most challenging flying you'll do. Overall, you'll get thirty-eight hours here at Sweetwater." Dan Parker turned to get some papers from a nearby table, and half the class took the opportunity to swivel around and gasp.

Rita nudged Eva. "It seems I'm about to break a cardinal rule," she whispered. "Let's see how long it takes me to get Mr. Parker here to ask me out. Conversations can be oh so private when you have an instructor whispering in your ear over a radio in a Link Trainer. Dates can be made, and no one will know . . ."

"And you'll be washed out for going on them, Rita," Bea murmured right back.

"Oh, but I excel at not getting caught," Rita murmured. "Other girls have dated instructors. I'll just have to slip in by midnight. But I'm getting ahead of myself."

Dan adjusted his notes. He leaned his tanned arms on the desk and addressed them all. It was so quiet that the sound of a pen scratching on paper would have stirred the air in the room. "I will be on the radio, talking to you and giving you instructions while you're in the trainer today."

"Swoon," Rita said.

"I'll give you a particular set of altitudes and distances to fly, along with simulated wind and weather conditions."

He strode over to the little metal Link Trainer box, which was only the size of a cockpit for one, and he opened the lid. "You climb under the hood, and you fly."

"Oh, yes you do, baby . . . ," Rita murmured.

Helena raised her eyes to the tin roof.

"Inside, the sensation is of actual flight. I'll be getting you to touch down under minimum visibility conditions."

Dan talked a few minutes longer, and Eva took down detailed notes. This was a vital part of their training, and while Harry had instructed her as well as he could in instrument flying, she was well aware that many of the other girls here had extensive experience flying at night—flight instructors Rita and Helena were two good examples. This was something on which Eva knew she had to work extra hard to pass.

Dan glanced at his folder. "Eva Scott, you're up first." He scanned the room.

Eva laid down her pen. This was not in her game plan. She had hoped—assumed—she would have the chance to talk to other girls about their experiences in the tiny trainer before she was assessed.

But Dan was waiting for her to climb into the blind trainer, and the class was watching her as well.

Dan held the lid open for her, and Eva took a deep breath and stepped inside. Once he'd closed the lid with a gentle thud, she forced herself to focus alone in the pitch dark, but instantly, the hot little box seemed to flare around her, the beads of sweat on her forehead feeling like they'd swelled to a million times their size. She jumped at the sound of Dan's sultry voice through the communication device.

"Prepare for takeoff, Miss Scott."

The instrument panel lit up, and Eva fumbled with the controls, somehow talking her way through takeoff with Dan, her hands shaking and wet. She struggled for air but still got the simulator moving, feeling the sweltering box moving with her.

Nausea swilled through her stomach. She shouldn't have had scrambled eggs this morning, or coffee, or juice, because right now she was feeling them all again.

"Close the throttle, apply full rudder, and look out for rough weather ahead," Dan said through the radio.

"Roger."

It was as if the whole world had been reduced to the confined, hot box. It was enclosing around her; she needed, desperately, to glimpse light. She had never been claustrophobic, but it was all she could do to stop herself from forcing the door open and bursting out of this inferno.

Eva fought to control her breaths, heaving them in and out with punches from her diaphragm, but the instrument panel was a blur of strange, misted shapes.

For what seemed like minutes, Eva followed Dan's instructions while heaving and gasping, licking her lips, feeling a wet trail of perspiration flowing down her face, from her armpits, down to her sweltering, shaking hands.

"The guiding beam will come on now. It will guide you to a safe landing when fog and darkness have obscured your vision. When you hear an interrupted note, that means you are coming into the path of the beam, and that's when you are taking up the true course."

The only word she heard was *landing*, and relief hit her like a freezing wind against hot bricks. She moved the control stick, knowing that she was not supposed to be able to see anything, and in the pitch darkness, broken only by the relentless bright lights of the panel, she realized in a fog of sweat and shaking that she'd forgotten to take the altimeter into consideration. She'd forgotten it even existed.

"You're losing height too fast." Dan sounded serious through the communication tube. "Get the plane level again. Try to gain some altitude for a moment, Eva."

But Eva's ears started to buzz. She struggled to keep her eyes open. Finally, she closed them for one second, giving in to the relative bliss of blackness, of the dark.

"You are way off course, Eva. Maintain some altitude and try again."

Eva's entire face was wet. "Sorry, sir," she muttered through the radio. She couldn't keep control of her hands, and her head swam.

"The pilot dies a horrible death." Dan's voice blurred.

Eva slumped forward into her hands. When Dan lifted the door open, the little box of darkness was flooded with bright, stunning light.

The taste of her own sweat exploded in her mouth. It was mixed, surely, with something else—blood. She'd been so distressed that she'd bitten her lip and drawn blood.

Eva stared straight ahead as, gradually, her eyes adjusted to the light and her heartbeat settled down to a slower rate.

She hated to think what she looked like, her face white as a sheet and her flight suit drenched with sweat. Slowly, she managed to ease herself out of the trainer, aware of Nina's hands coming to help her, easing off her turban, helping her across the crowded room.

Goodness knew she had to have washed out.

What would she tell her mother, her father? Harry? She'd failed in the Link Trainer while Harry was training to join bomber command.

"Eva." Dan Parker rested a hand on her shoulder.

Helena held out a glass of water for her. Eva felt the imprint of Dan's fingers through her sweat-soaked shirt. After a moment, she risked looking up at his face. There was no point in hesitating. He had no reason to do anything other than wash her out.

The expression on his face was kind.

"You are not the first to have that reaction. What happened to you in there is common, Eva. We'll get you to the point where you are confident in there and soon. The hot conditions today are something else. Your class is running at the most challenging time. It's like an oven in Sweetwater, so I don't think anyone's getting a good night's sleep. Being in that thing for the first time in this weather, in a hot tin shed? Well. You won't be the only one today. Let's put it that way."

Eva stared straight ahead. Even if he was being generous, the fact was she had failed an important exercise.

What if the same thing happened next time?

"Don't panic, and don't think about next time." His expression was serious. "Go back to the barracks," Dan went on. "Take a shower. Have a rest."

She stared at him.

"Helena Cartwright next," Dan called.

Helena moved away from Eva and started to climb into the box.

Eva walked silently out of class.

# CHAPTER TWELVE

THE COMMITTEE: Other WASP have told us that the moral expectations placed on you were different from those for male pilots. But how is that relevant to the government's decisions for WASP militarization?

EVA FORREST: I think it is relevant. The way we were expected to behave is indicative of the overall way in which women were treated differently than men. Our out-of-plane and classroom behaviors were scrutinized in a way men's never were. Even though we did not really realize that in those days, we were treated differently in every way. We were told we would be assessed on the way we walked, moved, and thought. We were expected to carry out all the training that men did, but we had to follow rules they did not have to follow, such as dressing modestly when off base, not being allowed to smoke in town, not being allowed to socialize too much. But we were still expected to look pretty and glamorous when the press came to take photographs of us.

A few hours after the Link Trainer fiasco, Eva sat on her bed with her legs crossed. Her ground school notes were spread around her—navigation, the theory of flight, weather, mapping, and math. She'd showered in cold water, washing the hot sweat from her body, but she hadn't been able to stomach dinner. The other girls were unusually quiet in the bay, some of them resting, some of them studying too.

"Mission accomplished." Rita burst through the door and threw herself down on her cot. She folded her arms behind her neck and stared up at the ceiling. "Plan A with Instructor Dan worked to a T."

Beatrice sat up on her bed. "Dating an instructor is a crazy idea. Dating is crazy, period. That's why I'm studying to be a librarian. I think I can avoid the likes of trouble if I avoid the likes of men. Don't do it, Rita. It's not worth it. You love flying too much. And we need you—the country needs you."

Rita lay on one side and propped herself up by one elbow. "Helena isn't the only one who was a flying instructor in our group, honey. Most of my students were men. I've met plenty of them before. I can handle this."

"Yes, but the rules have been spelled out." Helena looked up from the letter she was writing home. "We've been warned time and time again not to break them, that if we socialize with instructors, we'll be washed out. And we are at war. This is no time to mess with instructors. We're here to train for a serious job."

"Oh my." Rita sighed. "We've all packed up, left home, and come together in the middle of this godforsaken desert plain while our men are out there killing men from other countries who are doing everything they can to kill our boys—our brothers and our sweethearts. Boys we might never see again. If this isn't a time to live, then when is a better time?"

"But we are living," Bea pointed out. She frowned at her notes.

"I don't know whether I'll survive the war." Rita lowered her voice. "Apart from that, I don't even know whether my little brother will live. Jake is eighteen, for mercy's sake. Every time he flies, my heart is in my mouth. He's gone and become a bomber pilot. Fudged his age and enlisted. He's gone to Florida."

"We have a friend who's training to be a bomber pilot," Nina said. "Eva and I worry about him every day."

Rita sat up on her bed. "Look, girls, if I was killed tomorrow, would I regret not seeing this man tonight? I felt something the moment Dan walked into the room." She gazed toward the open door as if to check that no one was within earshot outside. "Flying for my country comes with a risk, going out with Dan comes with a risk, but not doing either of those things just seems to me the dullest way to live. We could be killed any day up in those ratty old airplanes, and I for one never want to die with regrets."

A hot breeze ruffled the air outside, sending a brief shiver through the quiet bay.

"She's got a point. This whole thing is risky, and if we girls don't stick together now, what happens when we are out flying on military bases? What then?" Nina spoke softly.

"I'm with Nina," Nancy said. "We have to support each other. Judging each other is not the way to get through. We are going to have men coming into the equation during the course of the war. And in my opinion, the rules about dating them are too harsh." Nancy leaned on her elbow, her red hair falling down around her face.

"Well, all I can say is that I'm nervous for you right now, Rita." Helena stood up in her thin cotton dress. "The rules might not be fair, but Mrs. Cochran obviously feels they are necessary. Deedee won't listen to our opinions if you get caught."

"I won't get caught." Rita went to the showers.

Later, Rita stepped out of the bathroom, her beautiful face made up with a little powder and a touch of rouge. Her blond hair was pulled up into a French twist, and she tucked a gold lipstick into the pocket of the light belted trench coat that she'd put on over her dress.

"Girls." She glanced out at the quiet area between the barracks and the hangars outside. "A thought came to me while I was in the shower."

Eva lay on her bed, writing to Harry. She was certain she'd hear from him soon. At home on a Saturday night, she'd be going out to a dance hall. She'd be mooning over Harry. She put her pen down while Rita spoke. The girl had gumption, Eva would give her that.

"I think I need your help." Rita stood there, hands on her hips.

The girls looked up at her. The only sound was the hot breeze whistling outside the door.

"Thing is . . ." Rita hovered for a moment. "Well, thing is, Dan said there was a small gathering at one of the instructors' houses tonight. Would one of you girls be game enough to come out with me?"

Eva stared at the letter. What was she doing? Harry would be writing to Lucille.

"If I go on my own, you see, it would raise suspicions. No WASP is going to wander around Sweetwater by herself on a Saturday night. They could catch on to the fact that I'm meeting someone. We don't know whose eyes are watching us when we go out."

"I'll come with you," Eva said all of a sudden, before she could second-guess the crazy instinct to take such a risk.

"Evie?" Nina's brow creased into a frown. "Why?"

"'Cause, like you said, if we don't support each other, what's the point of this stupid war, anyway?" *And it's Saturday night, and I can't stand lying here. I may as well do something useful to help out a friend.*

Nina stared at her, but after what seemed an eternity, she reached out her hand across the cots.

"Give me ten minutes, Rita." Eva stood up. She opened her wardrobe and pulled out her favorite soft-green dress. "I'll be ready real fast."

When she came out a few minutes later, Eva fought a stab of conscience. The girls looked so innocent lying about in their pajamas and dressing gowns, their faces washed and free of makeup. Rita looked utterly out of place in her lipstick and high-heeled shoes.

But she was standing by the door, waiting, and Eva had made her a promise. So.

"Rita, Eva," Helena said, "remember that the gates to Avenger Field are closed at midnight, and you'll be washed out if you miss curfew. You don't want to have to climb back in over those cyclone fences."

"We'll be fine," Rita said. "You girls go to sleep, and in the morning, you won't even know we were out."

Eva sent Nina one last hesitant smile. Nina blew her a kiss and smiled at her. Eva could tell that her dearest friend was trying to be brave.

They stepped out into the warm night air, Eva following Rita up the long driveway that led to Fifinella and the entrance to Avenger Field.

"Rita," she said finally, her voice filtering into the darkness.

"Uh-huh?"

"About your brother. The bomber pilot?" The need to talk about bomber pilots seemed overwhelming right now. It was as bad as the need to stop thinking about Harry, but that was impossible, no matter what she tried.

The boundary of the airfield loomed in front of them, the tall cyclone fence as formidable as a barrier around a prison.

Rita paused at the gateway. Even in the dark, Fifinella looked so young and cute and innocent that Eva had to turn away.

Rita went out the gate first. It wasn't until they were on the highway, moving toward the small cluster of white houses where the instructors lived, that Rita finally started to talk.

"I know why my little brother's off flying bombers, Evie. I know why he's up there doing the riskiest thing you can do in this war."

Eva sighed. She knew why Harry was doing it too. It was because he wanted action. It was because he wanted to do something real. "You do?" she said.

"Well, when it comes to my family, the story goes back to the Great War. My dad came back from the Somme a changed man, or so my mom always said."

Eva stayed quiet, the sound of their dressy shoes clipping against the road the only noise in the dark. She was glad Rita was opening up to her. She'd always seemed a bit of an enigma—glamorous, adventurous—but Eva had no idea about her family life.

"My dad drank. At night, he used to be visited by these terrors. He'd flip. I used to think there was a demon inside him."

Eva had heard stories of shell shock, but she'd never seen it playing out.

"Thank you for taking this risk with me," Rita said suddenly, veering off topic. "I appreciate it. You know, sometimes, there's a special closeness of the confessional when folks are in cahoots and putting themselves at risk."

Eva stopped on the edge of the dry, dead stretch of grass that passed for a lawn in front of the instructors' houses. "It's no problem at all, Rita. I try to be a good listener, especially when it comes to my friends."

Rita's fair hair was illuminated under a streetlight. "Please don't tell the other girls, not Helena or Bea, in particular, what I'm about to tell you. Not that I don't trust them, but I sense that you and Nina might be a little less judgmental than Helena, and maybe Bea. Nancy is okay, but she's thick as syrup with Bea."

Eva frowned at Rita. "Of course, Rita. You can talk openly with me, and I promise it won't go any further."

Rita lowered her voice. "Eva, my dad murdered my mom when I was thirteen years old."

"Rita!" Eva reached out and pulled her into a hug.

"It was eight years ago today." Rita's words were muffled into Eva's shoulder.

"Oh. Oh my." Eva held her friend close.

"The only way I could deal with it, you know, the only way I could cope, was to get out of this world. Off it."

"Yes, I understand that . . ." Eva wanted to close her eyes and have this earth swallow her up. But she took a step backward. "Rita, I don't know what to say."

Rita's mouth was working into a small smile. "You know, Eva, sometimes, I imagine when I'm flying up there, my mom is waving at me."

"I lost a sister," Eva murmured. "My twin. And I do exactly the same thing when I'm flying. I wonder what it's like where she is now, up there. You can't help looking at the sky and thinking about folks you've lost, Rita."

Rita knotted and unknotted her hands by her side. "I'm awful sorry about your sister."

Eva reached out and rested her hand on Rita's arm.

"Jake is flying to get to *fight* about our mom's death, while I do it to be closer to my ma."

"Oh, Rita."

Rita's mouth worked. She caught and held on to Eva's gaze. "I hope you can see why I want to live my life as if every day matters, to follow my heart when it calls me. For my ma. Because you never, ever know when the life of a person you love is going to be cut short."

"You've experienced the very worst of loss. You understand it. You know how important living is."

"Thank you, Eva. For understanding." Rita turned toward the group of houses. "This is it, just how Dan described it." Suddenly, she patted a hand over her hair. "How do I look?" Her eyes swept over Eva.

"Stunning. You're a real stunner," Eva said.

The sounds of music drifted out of the house in front of them, and lights shone from the windows.

Rita knocked.

"You worked out your whole date over the communication device while you were in that horrid little trainer?" Eva hovered under the porch light. She was of a mind to lighten the topic before they went into the party, and to alleviate her nerves. The sounds of jazz filtered out onto the lawn.

"You bet we did." Rita cracked a wide grin.

"Well, you achieved a whole lot more than I did in that thing."

"You'll crack it. Don't worry about it," Rita said.

The front door swung open, and Eva's own heart skipped a beat at the sight of Dan Parker, even though his eyes flew straight to Rita, lingering on her and hardly noticing Eva at all. He raised a tanned arm up to lean on the door frame.

"Can I help you?" he drawled. "Are you girls by any chance lost?"

"Why, we were just passing through town." Rita put on a Texan accent too, as if she'd grown up the daughter of a rancher herself. "And y'see, y'all, we heard there was a party going around these parts, so we thought we'd knock on this here door. We heard the music, and we couldn't pass on by without checking this here hootenanny out."

Dan scanned the dark grassy area behind Eva, his eyes turning serious for a moment, honey colored in the light.

Eva forced herself not to turn around and check the road out too.

"Well, I don't like to leave a couple beautiful girls like you two standing out on my front porch. It wouldn't be the right thing to do, now would it?"

"Nooo . . . ," Rita said. "It would be ungentlemanly. A sin, in fact."

Dan stepped aside, and Rita walked right into the house.

"Come on in, Eva," Dan said. He frowned for a moment. "You feeling better now?"

"Yes, sir," Eva said, then threw her eyes to the sky at the way she'd addressed him. What was she supposed to call an instructor when she was at his house for a party that was strictly against the rules?

"Wouldn't want strangers to think that Southern hospitality didn't extend to these here parts," he said, following Rita inside.

"No, we would not." Rita turned and grinned up at him.

"Would you like to dance, beautiful girl?" Dan asked. He pulled a cowboy hat off a table and put it on her head.

Rita circled her arms around his neck.

Eva hovered at the edge of the room. Cole Porter crooned out from a gramophone in the corner, and a few men sat about in easy chairs. A cigarette haze hung over the room.

Eva did a quick scan of them and sent up a prayer of thanks that her flight instructor Reg wasn't here—nor was her ground school instructor.

One of the men stood up. "Hello, I'm Hank." He reached out and shook her hand, his grip firm. He glanced over at Dan and Rita dancing in the middle of the room. Hank ran a hand over his close-cropped head and turned back to Eva. "Sorry about my friend Dan here's manners."

"I'm sorry too!" Dan called. "Sorry, Eva," he said, head tilted to one side.

"Oh, don't worry about it." Eva grinned back at him.

Rita pulled him back into her arms.

"I'm Eva." She held out her hand to Hank. Wasn't going to tell them her surname.

"This is Phillip," Hank said.

A lanky red-haired man whom Eva had not seen before stood up from where he was sitting on a sofa and came to shake her hand. "Pleased to meet you, Eva."

"Charmed," Eva said.

Phillip went back and slumped on the sofa again.

"And John."

Eva was quite happy at not recognizing the slight man who stood up and greeted her either.

Then a girl appeared through a doorway. Eva's eyes widened. Beyond her, a small kitchen looked to be in immaculate order. Silver tins sat lined up like soldiers on the white countertop.

"Hey, Eva." Frances, a quiet girl whom Eva hardly knew from training came and rested her head on Hank's shoulder. He took her hand and led her to a sofa, pulling her down onto his lap.

Eva fought a rush of panic. She only hoped that what she thought of as Frances's discretion and silence extended to who was here tonight.

John was still by Eva's side. "Relax, Eva. We'll make sure you don't get into trouble. It's okay. Plenty of WASP break the rules and come to instructors' houses. They don't get caught."

"Well, I'm sure wondering about the wisdom of it right now," Eva said. But her shoulders dropped a little. At least John seemed friendly. At least she wouldn't be standing here staring at the four walls all night.

"Can I get you a drink, Eva? Gin?" He moved toward the open kitchen door.

"Sure . . ."

He held up a bottle filled with clear liquid. "Bathtub. There's a house in Sweetwater we all know about. This shady woman doles it out. The last WASP class spent a truckload of their pay on it."

"Okay." No wonder half the previous class washed out, then . . .

"Two fingers or one?" John held up the bottle.

"One. Please."

His expression morphed into a little smile. "We don't have any lemon. I apologize." He poured out a finger and handed her the glass.

Eva took a tentative sip of the drink. Fire burned down her throat. She coughed.

"My experience with bathtub gin is severely limited. To nothing!" She laughed and met his dark eyes.

He leaned against the kitchen counter, his legs crossed in front of him. "Take it slowly," he said, his voice soft.

Eva stared at the drink.

"It's a party," he said. "You can relax tonight." He took a step closer to her.

Eva backed away. "I only came here to support my friend. I'm not—" She cut herself off, feeling the telltale warmth of a blush flushing her cheeks red.

He threw back his head and laughed. "Okay, Eva. I'm not going to jump on you. Don't worry. Let's talk. How does that sound?"

Eva lifted her chin. "Shall I guess where you're from?"

"Let's see you try."

Eva took another sip of the drink. "Brooklyn," she said. "And if it's not too rude of me, I'd also take a stab and say you are of Italian stock."

"Not bad, not bad at all, Eva. Move to Manhattan and you're going to be right on the spot."

"Little Italy?" Eva felt her spirits lifting now. She tipped back the drink. Coughing violently, she ended up in a fit of giggles. "This is the most awful stuff," she spluttered.

"I know, honey! But we love it. It's the best gin in Sweetwater." John's eyes caught hers, and he let out a laugh. "Have another one, lovely."

"Yes. And two yeses . . ." She held out her glass.

"Two?"

"Two fingers." Eva held his gaze. "I can do it."

John leaned forward and refilled Eva's glass. "I should have cooked some Italian food for you to go with the gin tonight. I make the meanest pasta in Avenger Field. You should try it sometime."

"Don't you have to eat that without a knife?"

John chuckled. "Eva, yes. You can't eat spaghetti with a knife, honey."

"Very elegant, then."

"It is. We twirl it around a spoon."

"Your turn," she said.

"My turn?"

"I mean mine."

"Oh, I see." He put on a mock serious expression. "Didn't realize that mere students got turns, honey."

Eva giggled again. "Well, this one does. Where'm I from?" She tilted her head to one side.

He looked deeply into her eyes. "San Francisco. Your dad is a very ritzy lawyer, and you're here to escape some terrible engagement that you've been forced into against your will. You left the ring at home in a fit of passion and ran away to Texas. Your parents don't know you're here."

"Genius." Eva held up her glass. "So far off you may as well have pitched me in Timbuktu."

"Oh, come on." He leaned a little closer to her. "Tell me, then."

"You figure it out for yourself."

"Uh-oh, someone's relaxing now. We'd better clear the base."

He clinked her glass.

"Eva, you have no idea how many girls come out here to escape. I don't know what your story is, but I'd hazard a guess that has something to do with it."

"Well, turns out I'm doing the opposite." Eva stared into the clear liquid in the glass.

"How?"

"Boy I like is dating a Hollywood princess."

"Uh-huh. LA."

"Right."

"Well, in that case, you've come to the right place."

"Why?"

"Because there are plenty of handsome instructors out here."

"Who will get me washed out in one second flat! It would hurt your reputation too."

John sighed. "Well, that's the thing. It doesn't hurt our reputations when it happens. It's the girls who suffer. Every time."

"That's not right."

"One rule for you, another for us, I'm afraid."

Eva bit her lip. "I should check the time." The sounds of Rita and Dan chuckling filtered into the kitchen.

John leaned forward. He took her arm for a moment. "You know, Eva, every single one of the girls who come here are in it for the flying. And that's why I love teaching here. I see possibility in every one of their faces."

Suddenly, someone turned up the gramophone, and the house filled with jazz.

"Care to dance, Eva?" John held out a hand.

"One dance wouldn't hurt." Eva glanced at the clock on the kitchen wall. It was eleven thirty already. Half an hour and they had to be back. But one dance? One dance with a handsome stranger, what harm could come from that?

"One dance won't hurt." He took her elbow and led her out to join the others.

Rita was still slow dancing with Dan.

John gathered Eva into his arms. But when she closed her eyes, she saw Harry. Somewhere deep inside her, that little spark of hope just would not die.

The time flew. Eva lifted her wristwatch and frowned.

"Rita," she said, tapping her on the shoulder. "Rita. Five minutes."

"Oh, give me ten, honey." Rita looked like she was going to spend the whole night slow dancing in Dan's arms.

John looked at his watch. "I agree, you should go. Don't want to be climbing the fence, Dan."

"Climbing the fence would be a gas." Rita waved John away.

Eva chewed on her lip. Frances was dancing with Hank and in a world of her own. Phillip had disappeared.

"Rita, Frances," she said. "We need to get out of here now."

With only minutes to curfew, they were all three of them at serious risk of washing out.

# CHAPTER THIRTEEN

THE COMMITTEE: But these moral safeguards given to the WASP were only put in place to protect you young women, Mrs. Forrest. Surely, you can see that.

EVA FORREST: If relationships happened and were deemed inappropriate by the housemother, it was the women who were reprimanded every time. We were not protected. If you dated an instructor, you were washed out. I heard that instructors even washed girls out for *not* dating them. Eventually, the review board had to change the rules so that if a trainee washed out with one instructor, at least they could train with another one before being sent home.

The moon must have slid behind a cloud, and there were none of Nancy's stars to guide them back to Avenger Field after the party at Dan's house. Eva shivered when she stepped out onto the dark, still front lawn outside the instructors' buildings.

"The fact that there's no moonlight is an advantage," Dan said. "We can hoist you over the cyclone fence, but you risk being seen in our company if anyone is out on patrol." He had his instructor's voice back on, and in the silence, the reality of getting back to base safely took over from any thoughts of fun.

"I think we should definitely help you girls over the fence," John said. "We kept you out, we get you back in safely."

Frances walked in silence.

"Okay, then." Rita's expression was impossible to read in the darkness. "I'm game for the guys to come with us if you are, girls."

"We have no choice." Frances's tone was blunt and to the point.

"Okay with us helping you over the fence, Eva?" Dan asked.

"I think we should work as a team."

Their footsteps rang out something terrible in the quiet. Eva sped up her pace. It seemed an age before the boundary fence to Avenger Field loomed in front of them. Beyond it, on the runway, banks of planes were lined up, ready for the morning's classes.

"Everything's quiet." Rita's voice was like a clear bell in the dark. "No one in sight. I say we climb over, and once we are inside, we make our way around the aircraft, using them as camouflage."

Eva looked at the high cyclone fence with doubt.

Dan made his way right up to it. After he'd hugged Rita goodbye, he knelt down on one knee like a man about to propose. Rita hopped up on his shoulders, and he held on to the backs of her legs, standing up. She reached for the gaps between the barbed wire that laced the top three rows of the cyclone fence.

"Ready, Eva?" John's voice caused Eva to jump. But he knelt, and she climbed, carefully, from his knee onto his shoulders, just as Rita had done with Dan. Silently, she thanked whoever had the idea of daily calisthenics. Her balance and strength were sound.

"You climb over first, Eva," Rita said next to her. She turned toward Eva from atop Dan's shoulders.

Eva placed one leg over the top of the fence. Her balance tipped, and John wobbled violently underneath her.

"Sorry, Eva." He swayed again. The gin surged up dangerously into her throat. The wire dug into her palms, but eager to get off John's shoulders, she swung herself over the fence and managed to make her way down the other side, her footholds more than precarious and her heart thumping right into her mouth. Rita and Frances slipped down next to her.

"Goodbye, Rita," Dan called quietly through the fence.

Rita ran her hand along it. She started blowing Dan kisses.

"Rita!" Frances sounded sharp.

"Bye, girls," John said. "I enjoyed meeting you, Eva."

Eva sent him a quick wave and turned toward the runways. She dashed from the protective cover of one airplane to the next, the looming half-circular shape of the hangars her only goal. The training planes lurked like strange birds.

Once they were past the airplanes, Rita came to stand by Eva's side. "We'll team up and run to the barracks. Take cover in the trees when you can," Rita said.

Eva ran, keeping low as she tore from tree to tree.

Out of the corner of her eye, she caught a glimpse of Frances's slight figure disappearing toward the bays.

"She's an odd girl, that one," Rita said.

Eva wasn't going to risk the noise that too much whispering would bring.

Finally, they stepped up to the entrance of their darkened bay. Someone had left the door slightly ajar for them, and once they were inside, heads rose. Girls sat up, shadowy figures in their cots.

"Eva!" Nina reached out her arms. "I was worrying up a storm."

"We're fine," Rita whispered. "Sorry to keep you girls awake. We lost track of time."

Eva gave Nina a hug and made a beeline for her bed. A shape loomed up from the mattress under her blanket. Slowly, she pulled the bedding back. And turned to Nina.

"It was Helena's idea," Nina said. "In case anyone came by to check. One of the girls in the bay next door told her that someone was doing rounds with a flashlight. One of us! She was checking out beds. Seeing that no one had broken curfew.

"She never came into our bay. All we saw was a flashlight shining into our room through the window. We managed to stuff three of the pillows in your bed, and three in Rita's. She would have seen six sleeping shapes."

Eva fought her guilt. "Thank you," she managed. "Just thank you. You've saved my skin."

"Well," Rita said. "I most certainly owe you girls my heartfelt thanks. You risked your place here for us, and most especially, for me. And for that, all I can do is say that I appreciate it with all my heart."

Rita started handing out pillows. Eva pulled Nina's and Helena's pillows out of her own bed and returned them. She lay back, knowing sleep wouldn't come for a little while.

Not two minutes later, the door burst open, and Geraldine Martin, from a bay farther up the barracks, stood framed in the opening. Eva sat up, startled. Geraldine looked like a girl of around twelve standing there in her pajamas, with her short blond curls sticking up all around her head.

"Y'all have to wake up," she said. "Girls, I need your help."

"What is it, Geraldine?" Helena asked.

"It's Frances. She has been washed out. Caught breaking curfew. Deedee said she had no choice but to dismiss her from Avenger Field."

Eva rested her head on her knees.

"That darned Jenny Carlisle was waiting for her with her flashlight," Geraldine said. She wrung her hands. "Oh, girls, you see, Frances has been out before, but not this late. We were all exhausted after the Link Trainer session, and we all fell asleep, assuming Frances would come back before curfew. We should have left pillows in her bed."

Eva curled her hands around her sheets. If Frances had been washed out, then she and Rita should have been washed out too.

"Oh, girls. I'm worried sumpin' awful about her." Geraldine raised her hand up to cover her mouth.

Nina swung her legs over the side of the bed. She pulled her dressing gown on. "I hear you. What do you want us to do? Complain?"

Her heart racing, Eva pulled on her dressing gown too.

Geraldine paled. "No. It's not that. Complaining won't git us anywhere. It's worse. Frances has climbed up on the roof and won't come down. Oh, see, I'm in a terrible mind that she might do something stupid. She's in a real state. And she's alone up there."

Eva fumbled with the buttons on her gown.

"She hasn't made real friends here," Geraldine went on. "You girls are lucky to have each other. She's quite the loner, and now, well, she says she has nothin' to live for anymore."

Nancy, Bea, and Helena were up, pulling on boots, their movements flickers in the dark room.

"I know where there's a ladder," Nancy said. "I've done a bit of stargazing up on that roof since I've been here."

Rita's whisper was hoarse. "Oh, girls, it's entirely my fault! I'm going to confess to Deedee."

"No." Nina stood between Rita and the door, her hands on her hips. "Frances made her own choices. Washing yourself out is not the answer to this. And, Evie, don't you go getting any stupid ideas either."

"Frances is an adult," Helena said. The other girls bustled about to get ready in the dark. "She knew what the risks were. We all know the rules."

Eva stood, poleaxed. She threw a gaze toward Rita. Rita threw her arms in the air.

Finally, the girls headed toward the door.

Nina tugged on Eva's arm. "You were supporting Rita. That was all. It's not your fault."

Eva felt the dark fronds of her own betrayal curling in her stomach. Ahead of her, Nina pushed the door open.

"This is not right," she said helplessly to Nina's back.

Outside, in the deep-black Texan summer night, Geraldine talked softly to the small figure on the edge of the roof, but Frances sat in silence with her knees tucked into her chest like a little girl while the other girls paced uselessly, waiting for Nancy. Nancy brought a wooden ladder, hauling it to the base of the building. Helena checked the ladder was firm on the ground.

"Who's going up first?" Bea said.

"Me." Rita placed her foot on the first rung.

Once they were all up on the roof, whispering and finding places to sit, Nina reached out toward the staring, silent girl, placing her hand on top of Frances's. Her hands looked so small and delicate in her lap.

"I love the night sky," Nancy said. "Looking at the stars is something I will never tire of, no matter what happens in this darned war."

"It's beautiful," Geraldine said, turning her gaze upward. The clouds had shifted, and above them, there was an array of stars. "The sky out here is something else."

Eva kept her eyes locked on Frances, but the girl stared into space and did not open her mouth.

"They might be able to take you away from Avenger Field because you crossed some line, but no one can take your love of flying," Nina said.

"Well, I say it's damned unfair." Rita's words rang out, strong in the dark.

"Rita . . . ," Helena warned.

"It *is* unfair." Geraldine's voice was small. "I'm sorry we didn't do enough to help in the bay."

"It's not that," Rita went on. "It's a bum rap. It wasn't only Frances out late tonight. Why should she lose everything?"

"Frances hasn't lost it all," Bea pointed out.

"Bunch of fatheads." Rita let out a loud sigh.

Frances stared and stared at nothing. Eva worried that no matter what they all said, Frances was not hearing them.

"I am so sorry for the part I played in this." Eva's voice was small.

"Not your fault." Nina and Rita spoke at the same time.

"Rosie the Riveter. That's the job I'll be going back to." Frances's words were muffled in the dark.

Eva drew in a breath. She stared out at the ground that spread below the roof and shuddered.

"See that, up there?" Nancy said, her voice bursting into the night. "See that planet that's emerging right now?"

Eva sighed. She looked up at the sky.

"It's Saturn, the sun rising over Saturn."

Frances leaned forward and traced a pattern with her fingers on the roof. "I cannot believe this," she said. "I don't know what I'm going to do."

"We'll sit up here with you until morning," Nina said, "if that's what it takes."

Eva lay back on the warm roof, guilt snaking through her insides. And yet she also had to ask herself, would Hank ever admit that he'd kept Frances out beyond curfew tonight?

# CHAPTER FOURTEEN

THE COMMITTEE: Wasn't the work you did just like the work thousands of other women did during the war—simply another way of stepping up during the war effort, but still as civilians?

EVA FORREST: I would argue that there were two levels to which women stepped up. For me, working as an aircraft riveter at Lockheed was one thing, but being a WASP was far more specialized and militarized. Being a WASP showed our complete divergence from the accepted attitude that women had to act a certain way. Not only did we prove we could train in military style, just as men did, but we stepped up to the plate when our country called for us. We risked everything. Now, all we are asking is that we not be forgotten.

Frances spent the next morning alone, isolated from her own group. She was taken to the train station in the cattle truck at noon, a quiet girl sitting alone in the back. At instrument flight class that evening, Rita sat quietly in the back row. Dan spoke in a low, steady voice. The girls sat in silence. Gossip had gotten around.

By the time he was done talking, the sun had set and darkness had fallen. It was time to take the planes out at night for the first time.

Eva followed the girls to the runway. Nerves fluttered through her body at the thought of going up without being able to see the horizon. Harry had always taught her to watch the horizon. Suddenly, a sharp pang of yearning for him hit her. If only she knew he'd remain safe. And she'd kill to receive a letter from him, something that told her he was okay.

"Well, in spite of all the drama with Frances, at least we still have the stars," Nancy said. "You know, as an only child with older parents, I learned to use my imagination because I didn't have a whole bunch of siblings to keep me entertained. I'd lie and stare at the sky for ages, wondering what was beyond infinity. What a funny kid I was."

"I'm glad one of us is looking forward to tonight, because if I take my eyes away from the instrument panel, I'll most likely end up either halfway across the United States or nose down on the ground," Eva said. She tucked her arm into Nancy's. She was starting to really like this girl.

"We will be stacking you up over the airport," Dan told them outside.

The girls wound their turbans around their heads, but no one chattered.

"The airport will be divided into four quadrants with three layers of planes in each quadrant. Each of you will be assigned to fly at either five, six, or seven thousand feet, and you'll be assigned a quadrant. You need to circle in your assigned quadrant until you are told to change or come in and make a landing, a touchdown and a takeoff, and then go back to your place and keep on circling. None of you are qualified for instrument flying yet, so this is the next stage of our class. You'll not leave the quadrants until you are all confident with this exercise."

"I'm worried that I won't trust what my instruments are telling me." Nina turned to Eva.

"I know. Me too."

"You'll be just fine," Nancy said. "Both of you."

But the look on Nina's face showed she was unconvinced.

"Your safety is our paramount concern," Dan said. "We lost a couple students during night training exercises early on in the program. It goes without saying that we don't want any more losses . . ." For a moment, his gaze flickered over Eva's group of friends, lingering on Rita.

"Eva, honey, and Nina," Helena said in the flight line. "One way of getting used to instrument flying is to get here early and watch the lights, the white and red that are airplanes circling above the field, before you go up."

"I'll be watching before I go up, Helena. I'll be watching all those lights," Eva said.

Eva had been around twice in her quadrant. She'd taken off and done her landings, and everything seemed just fine.

Bea took off in her little basic trainer, the second aircraft they were flying in, the BT-13 Vultee, and Eva was cleared to take off down the runway for her third flight of the night. She focused on working with the plane, aware that this trainer had a more powerful engine and was faster and heavier than their primary trainers were.

But just as Eva's wheels left the ground and she sighed with relief that her takeoff had gone without mishap after having been awake all night, Bea, in front of her, clipped the high-tension lines at the end of the runway. And all the lights went out on the field.

The radio went out. The control tower disappeared. Eva was ascending. And there was nothing below her except the dark.

She fought panic. Her hands shook. It was all she could do to keep the aircraft on a straight course. That was what she'd been told to do in a situation like this. Harry had told her, Dan had told her: keep straight. Nothing in sight but the instrument panel.

What on earth was she supposed to do now? She could see nothing below her, and there was no way to guide herself up. She was just floating.

There were so many other planes in the air. All Eva could see was a sky filled with navigation lights twinkling around her. Nancy's stars were there, all right, but Eva could not help thinking they weren't any use to her with all their beauty tonight. There was no means of communication with another human being stuck up here. And Eva fought not to panic about Bea and to concentrate on her own flight.

Eva kept her plane steady. She only hoped the tower would come back on before her fuel ran out. Eva banked. She started to circle in the middle layer as she'd been instructed to do, but everything was wrong. She circled for a few minutes and knew that without any reference by lighting, natural or otherwise, a pilot was at risk of not knowing which way was up.

When, after what seemed like an age, Dan's voice came over the radio, Eva gripped the control stick harder.

"All of you, keep flying your pattern and be careful of anyone else. Keep your height." Dan had come up and was flying with them. He'd turned on his radio and switched it to broadcast.

But still, there was no way to guide herself except by the other girls' lights. There was nothing to do except to float. Girls were above her and below her. Eva checked her altimeter. She was steady in the middle group at six thousand feet. But should anyone get spooked with the lack of visibility, well, she forced herself not to think along those lines. And all the while, she was menaced with fear for Bea.

Eva lost track of the number of circuits she made before, finally, smudge pots appeared on the runways.

At last, the tower came back on.

"Stay in a holding pattern." It was Reg instructing them now.

Eva's gas was getting fearfully low. A film of sweat formed on her forehead. The dense heat of the turban was like an entrapment. Her right temple pounded.

She had to keep her head. Her mind was in orbit, and she had no way of turning back.

One of them was going to end up in a spin. Eva fought the urge to just close her eyes and go into a spin. End it. Give in to the inevitable. Her hand was slick on the control stick now.

She made interminable circles. Urgently, she needed what the men had in their planes. Relief tubes. If she were a male pilot, the relief tube would be in the side pocket in the wing, but there was no such thing for girls.

How was she going to fly long-distance tomorrow if she could not manage circles above the training runway without getting into a state? She wondered how the other girls were doing.

Eva reached back and pulled off her helmet and her turban, letting her thick brown locks fall loose around her neck.

Maybe she should wash herself out. Was this some hellish way of the world getting back at her for not getting caught last night?

Finally, after what seemed like an age, Eva was instructed to land.

And she did. She just followed instructions and landed the plane. When she was on the ground, she leaned forward. She rested her head on the instrument panel. "Thank goodness," she said.

She climbed out of the cockpit onto the wing. The first thing she saw was Nina. Nina had found Eva's plane and was standing alongside it with the ground crew.

"I didn't know who was who. I didn't know which one was you. I didn't know if you were okay." Nina held her turban unrolled in her small hands.

Eva reached for Nina and hugged her friend, holding her close.

"You know what?" Eva asked, her voice muffled against Nina's shoulder. "I felt like, instead of being free, I was locked up in that plane. It was the complete opposite of what I normally experience when I'm flying. And I still feel something awful about Frances."

Nina's voice flickered like the weak lights on the runway. "Slow down, Evie. You can't take everything on."

The ground crew was working fast, checking planes that had been taxed way beyond what they should have experienced tonight.

"Eva?"

"Yes?" Eva's eyes caught Nina's, bright in the dark.

"This is war, Evie. I know you are cut up about Frances. But we are going to lose classmates. Only a little more than half of us will graduate. After Sweetwater, we are going to have even more responsibility. And right now, it is our responsibility to learn to fly. Whatever happens, during any of this, we have to deal with it. And we'll do it together. Always."

Nina's words were humbling.

"Evie, let Frances go." Nina held Eva at arm's length. "There's nothing you can do now. She took the risk, she washed out. It was not and never will be your fault. Don't let it infect you, because I know you, and I suspect you are doing that."

Eva looked at the ground.

"And whatever you do, don't let anyone, not *any* of the instructors, know how spooked you were tonight."

Eva reached out a hand to Nina's shoulder. "Nina, I have to check on something."

"Everything okay?" Nina asked.

"Come with me a moment."

Eva strode the short distance to the ready room. "Bea hit the tension wires in front of me. That's why the lights went out. I want to check she's okay."

Nina kept pace beside her. "No one's said anything!"

Inside the hangar, Dan sat at the table along with Reg. They were both smoking cigarettes. Neither of them was talking, and neither of them looked as if anything were wrong.

"Is Beatrice okay?" Eva rushed over to Dan, resting her hands on his table, forgetting, for one moment, the chain of command.

"Why wouldn't she be?" Dan blew out a steady plume of smoke. "I have no reason to believe anything's wrong with her."

Eva stood transfixed, Nina silent beside her.

"Were you up there?" he asked.

"Of course I was," Eva said.

He held her gaze, his eyes level.

"Bea hit the high-tension line. Is she okay?" Eva asked again.

"Nobody hit the high-tension line, Eva."

Eva folded her, arms. "Is she all right?" she repeated. "I was right behind her in the flight line. I saw it happen. Can you tell us if she landed safely, please?"

"Eva," Dan said. He leaned forward in his chair. "Nobody hit the high-tension lines. Is that clear?"

Eva went out of the room, with Nina close behind.

While she had plenty to learn about flying, she had seen a different side to Dan tonight. Clearly, Eva saw that she had more to learn about the complexities that lay behind loyalty in the military forces. The instructors had not washed Frances out; Deedee had, because Frances was a woman who had broken a women's rule.

But were Dan and Reg not going to do Bea in out of military loyalty? Or was Dan being patronizing to Eva and keeping her locked out of what was going on with her classmate?

# CHAPTER FIFTEEN

THE COMMITTEE: If you received full military training without military responsibilities, we struggle to see why you are here, Mrs. Forrest. As civilians, you had advantages. For one thing, you could quit when you wanted to.

EVA FORREST: We received no GI benefits, no insurance, no veterans' educational or financial advantages. We were paid one hundred fifty dollars a month to train, but we had to pay for our own food, transportation to and from training, for our own uniforms. We were flying military aircraft, so we could not get private insurance, but because we were not military, we could not get military insurance. However, we were treated as if we were military in every other sense, from undertaking boot-camp-like training to daily discipline and military rules.

Eva sat up cross-legged on her bed, watching the doorway in the bay and willing Bea to come back from their night-flying exercise. The other girls lay around her, reading, writing letters, or, in Nina's case, studying madly for an upcoming algebra test. Clearly none of them knew about

Bea's mishap, except she and Nina. And right now, Eva would give her right foot to see her friend walk into their bay. Heck, she'd give her right foot just to know for sure that Bea was safe.

"Jeepers." Rita lay back on her bed. "Flying in quadrants with all of you around me and no lights on the runway scared me. I almost spun out."

Eva remained silent.

"I'm with Rita. Instrument flying is hard." Nina frowned over her algebra notes.

"I'll try to stay awake for Bea. She must be talking to the instructors." Nancy yawned, stretching her arms up to the roof in her pajamas. "But it's almost taps. And I sure as anything got no sleep last night." She lay back, and after a few moments, she'd fallen fast asleep.

A few minutes later, Helena appeared from the bathroom. Slowly, she unwrapped her hair from its bath towel and let her wet locks cascade down her back. "Beatrice is out late. Did anyone see her after the flight?"

Eva chewed on her lip. There had been no reports of any accident. She glanced around the room at her bay mates. The girls all had deep, dark circles under their eyes. The last thing she wanted to do was frighten them. They all had to fly tomorrow. They all needed a good night's rest tonight.

"I'm going out for a moment." Eva pulled on a light cardigan. The night was unusually cool. "Going to check on Bea."

She heard Nina's intake of breath. "Evie, I'm coming too."

"So am I," Helena said. "Give me five seconds."

Eva waited while Helena pulled her hair back into a wet bun and put on a skirt and blouse.

"You don't think anything's wrong?" Rita asked.

Eva took in the bags under Rita's eyes. It was unlikely her friend had slept at all last night. "Don't worry," she said. "I'll go find her."

Once they were out on the dry lawn, making their way across to the hangars, Helena linked her arm through Eva's. "Do you think she's in trouble or something?"

Eva kept her eyes trained ahead. Lights shone out from the hangar's wide-open door. "She clipped a high-tension wire when she took off. That's what caused all the lights to fail."

"What?" Helena stopped, hands on her hips. "Dan told us that it was an electrical fault."

"Technically, that wasn't a lie." Nina motioned them to keep walking.

Helena picked up the pace again. "I don't like the sound of this, girls."

"Neither do I," said Eva.

"But why would they hide it from us?" Helena asked.

Eva shrugged. "I don't know, Helena. Loyalty, protection of a student? Maybe Dan was affected by Frances being washed out last night. Either way, we're about to find out."

Eva blinked when she stepped into the hangar. Fluorescent light flooded the space. Dan and Reg stood near a table in a corner. At the sound of their determined footsteps, Dan turned to face them, his handsome features drawn into a frown.

Bea was nowhere in sight.

"Eva, Helena, Nina." Dan strode toward them. "We've had a civilian call. A local rancher. He was making his way home along a quiet road about half an hour ago."

Eva held on to Nina's arm. Her mind kept replaying that flicker of dying light over and over when Bea hit the wires and they sparked.

"Is Bea all right?" Eva asked.

Dan shook his head. "The ranch owner told us that a plane had come down in a field near his house. He was rushing out to the scene but radioed us first. I don't know anything more at this stage."

Nina's hand came down and clutched on to Eva's.

Right then, Nancy rushed into the room, hair flying and her dressing gown flapping behind her. "Sorry. Sir." She half saluted, then turned beetroot red in front of Dan.

"It's no problem, Nancy."

"I drifted off to sleep, and when I woke up, Rita told me these three had come searching for Bea. I knew she'd been gone too long. I suddenly panicked. Is everything okay?"

Helena reached out and touched Nancy's arm. "Nancy, Bea clipped a high-tension wire during the exercise tonight. There's no easy way to say this, but her aircraft has possibly gone down in a field."

Nancy blanched. "But she's my friend from back home. I couldn't stand it if anything happened to her. And what about her folks?" Nancy turned huge eyes to the other girls.

"Here." Dan reached for a jug of water on his desk and handed her a glass. "Nancy, we are doing everything we can to get to her as quickly as possible." He looked out the window. "I *hate* this."

Eva watched him. He was an instructor, and he had to be professional, but his feelings were there for them all to see.

"I can't stand being useless." Helena's voice cut into the room.

Nina reached out and took Helena's hand as well as Eva's.

"A recovery team has headed out to the field. All we can do is wait, Helena," Dan said.

Why had Dan not acknowledged Eva's concern hours ago? Why had he said that Bea had not had a mishap when she had?

"I was behind her," Eva said. "I was behind her when it happened."

"Eva," he said, eyes trained on her. "Beatrice is an excellent pilot. I want to focus on that. Okay?"

Eva's eyes locked with his. So he did want to protect Bea. His protectiveness was toward all the WASP trainees, even though he had feelings for one special girl.

"We'll get you girls some chairs," Reg said, appearing at Dan's side, placing a hand on Dan's arm. "I'll get them." His voice was gruff.

Reg moved slowly toward the side of the hangar, and with great care, he collected a stack of plastic chairs and set them out. "You must know that we are doing everything we can," he murmured. "We should have news very soon."

Eva sat down in silence. A plane falling from the sky was something entirely different from what they'd dealt with last night. Nina sat with her head in her hands, and Helena fidgeted in her seat. Nancy gripped her glass of water and frowned into space.

Reg and Dan chatted quietly a bit farther away across the hangar.

After about fifteen minutes, a member of the emergency crew appeared. He spoke quietly into Dan's ear.

Eva shuddered. Next to her, Nina drew a heavy breath.

When the instructors finally made their way back to them, the plastic seat under Eva felt like a slippery slope.

"Eva, Nina, Helena, and Nancy, Beatrice lost her bearings during tonight's exercise and panicked. She went way off course, spun, and decided the only thing to do was to attempt a landing. She, like all of us, lost contact with the radio tower during tonight's quadrant training exercise." He paused. "She is fine."

Eva slumped back in her chair, and Nancy moaned out loud with relief.

"Beatrice did the right thing tonight. She followed instructions not to abandon her plane once she'd carried out her forced landing. She stayed with it. The plane is safe. She simply waited until she was found."

Dear Bea. This was so like her. Eva could just picture her waiting. Not abandoning her plane to the cows.

"You girls will be able to get a good night's sleep tonight. Y'all must be very, very tired." Reg looked directly at Eva, and if she was not mistaken, he raised a brow.

Eva searched his face. Did he know about last night? She stared at the ground for a moment. This was becoming complicated. She had a lot to learn about loyalties among these folks.

"Who would like a nightcap while we wait for her? Coffee?" The relief on Dan's face was palpable. He was sagging with it.

"Yes, please," Nina said.

"I could do with a bucket of coffee," Nancy said. "Thank goodness. Thank goodness my dear, dear friend is okay."

A half hour later, and two cups of coffee having cleared her head, Eva almost collapsed with relief when the sound of a truck echoed through the hangar. Bea appeared in the doorway, holding her turban, her tiny frame overwhelmed by her hopelessly too-big zoot suit. Nancy was over to her before the others could get out of their seats, enveloping Bea in a great hug.

Eva ran over to their friend.

The thought of losing one of the girls out here was becoming more threatening than any fears Eva had of losing her own life.

# CHAPTER SIXTEEN

THE COMMITTEE: You were not trained by military personnel. Your instructors were civilians. As far as this committee can determine, the program was not military, and neither were the WASP in any veritable sense.

EVA FORREST: Our training was imbued with so many elements that were authentically military. We were all military in everything but name. From the beginning, we were taught that our responsibility was not to stay alive but to keep the person next to us alive. This military-style attitude of loyalty was drilled into us. What was more, the WASP gave us a military-style camaraderie that I have never experienced since in any other area of my life. Many of us came from homes where we did not have this. Being a WASP sung to our hearts. We felt like we only had each other because we trained on a base in one of the most isolated parts of the country. To be honest, I would get to the end of a hard day and realize that I hadn't even gone to the mail depot or thought about anything other than our training and being a WASP.

Eva propped herself up on her towel. The shade of a big tree by the Sweetwater public swimming pool was welcome, even though the weather was flowing by into autumn and there were only several weeks left until graduation. Nina lounged alongside Rita while Bea and Nancy chatted about the dance they were looking forward to that night at the Blue Bonnet Hotel in town.

"I'm so tempted to go buy a new dress for tonight, you have no idea!" Nancy said. "I saw this great little green number in the window of the dress shop, and I dunno if I can resist it. Nor do I know if I can afford it," she added, dropping her voice into a delicious, low, Texan-affected drawl.

"Green would look wonderful on you, Nancy," Nina said.

"It would bring out your lovely eyes," Eva said.

"I'm in the mood for a bit of fun." Nancy stood up, gathering her towel and duffel bag. "I'm going into the changing rooms to get dressed, and before I change my mind, I'm going to buy that little thing!"

"Good for you." Bea stood up too. "I'll come and keep you company, but I'm not even going to bother to dress up tonight. Don't see the point, but understand other girls do."

"Oh, don't be a heel, Bea." Nancy grinned at her. "Rita and Eva are so good-looking they'll be dancing all night! You and I gotta dress ourselves up a bit just so's we can compete."

Bea placed her hands on her hips.

"That gotcha!" Nancy grinned.

Bea took a playful swipe at Nancy, who ducked and laughed out loud.

"Well." Bea stood up to her full five foot three. "You and I will compensate with our brains. Although your brain is something scattered. You and your stars. I don't know about you . . ."

"You're the head of every class, Bea." Nancy chuckled. They made their way off to the changing rooms. "Which is why I need to console myself with that green dress!"

Eva sat up and shook her head, her lips forming into a lazy smile. This was a rare day off, and while some of the class were sunning themselves on the lawn between the barracks back at Avenger Field, stretched out on towels in their bathing suits, their bay had all chosen to jump in the cattle truck and come to the pool for a swim.

She stretched her tight muscles and wandered down to the blue pool. Autumn leaves fluttered from the trees overhead. They'd decided to make the most of the last warm days before the weather turned cold, which could happen suddenly and dramatically, they'd been warned.

Eva dived into the water, enjoying the feel of her body moving like silk. She started swimming lazy laps up and down the pool, coming to rest in the shallow end. A mother with a little girl regarded her.

"You one of those women pilots?" the woman asked.

"I am, ma'am. My name's Eva Scott."

"Pleased to meet you. I'm Rosie Harris, and this here is my daughter, Vanessa."

"I'm charmed," Eva said, smiling at the little girl, who shot her a cute grin before burying her head in her mother's bathing suit.

"Well, we weren't sure what to think of y'all when you first landed here," Rosie said. "I mean, folks around here weren't sure about women flying airplanes and all. It didn't seem right, somehow. Or proper. I dunno." She blushed a little.

"Oh?"

"In fact, there were bets around these parts as to how long you'd last. Because we had men stationed at Avenger Field before y'all came, you know."

"I know." The base was not new. But the WASP had taken it over for now.

"So there were bets that you'd not even be able to land your planes here, back when you started training here earlier in the year. My menfolk were predictin' that women would just crash their planes on the ground. But I tell you, the sight of all them airplanes landing ready for trainin', all flown by women and comin' in one by one, it was a sight I'll never forget, and I think it's grand. Y'all are serious pilots. I feel proud when I hear your planes up in the sky, Miss Eva. I'll tell you that."

"Well, I'm glad to hear it, ma'am. We appreciate being made to feel welcome, and I know that some of the townsfolk have been having trainees from the field in for Sunday lunches, so your kind hospitality is not going to waste on us."

"No, indeed. Your Mrs. Cochran got that organized so we could get used to having the young women around."

Vanessa started kicking and splashing in the pool.

"Well, guess I'd best git going!" Rosie said.

"Nice talking to you, ma'am," Eva said. And she smiled and took a few more laps up and down the pool.


On the way back to Avenger Field in the cattle truck, Eva rattled along with the rest of the girls, her damp head catching the breeze from the road.

Nancy showed off a glimpse of her green dress inside her brown paper bag. "Not gettin' it out while we're in the back of this rattly truck. But I'm excited."

"It looks just grand on," Bea said, her voice loud above the noise. "And it has sparkles. Sparkles that look like the stars Nancy loves." Bea rested her arms against the rails and raised her face to the sun.

Nancy bit her lip. "You know I wouldn't mind finding one handsome boy to dance with tonight. What do you think my chances are?"

"Huh. Don't hold your breath. Stop filling your head with such stuff and nonsense." But Bea's face broke into a wide smile.

They rolled up in the cattle truck, climbing out and jumping down onto the baked ground.

Deedee was waiting for them, arms folded.

"Now, you girls. Remember curfew. Not a stroke after midnight. The cattle truck will be there to pick you up at half past eleven outside the Blue Bonnet. And no stragglers. You're all getting closer to graduation with every day that's left now. Don't let me down, will you, ladies."

The girls hopped out of the cattle truck and made their way to their bays.

"You bet we won't," Nancy said.

Eva walked alongside Rita, her head down.

Once she was in the bay, Eva ran across to her bed. Propped up on the pillow, just like her mom used to do for her, was a letter with unmistakable handwriting across it. She'd know it anywhere in the entire world.

"Harry!" she said, throwing herself onto her bed. She tore at the envelope.

"Clear the decks," Nina warned. "Evie won't be on this planet tonight. I see he hasn't written to me yet!"

"Hmm," Rita said. "You've been very coy about whoever he is, Eva."

"I haven't heard about him either," Helena said. "You have to tell me. I should know! I want full disclosure. Haven't I earned that right?" She affected a whiny voice and then lapsed into laughter.

"You sure have, girl," Nina said.

But Eva was lost in the piece of paper in front of her. She read and read and had no idea what she was looking for, but her heart was thumping and pounding, and she let it do so while she drank in his words.

*Darling Evie,*

*How are you? I'm fascinated just thinking about your life ~~out there~~. It's difficult and easy at the same time to imagine it! I hope you and Nina are loving all the ~~"work"~~ and having a gas. I'll bet you're doing brilliantly. I'm doing fine. The food is good, and the other men are excellent company, and we are all getting along just grand. ~~It's hot here,~~ as you can imagine, but we love what we're doing, so it's fine.*

*I'm not sure how much those ~~censors~~ will take out of this, but they'll ~~black out anything that I can't share. I don't know if they'll be interested in any general details~~ that you and I always talk about, even if I keep ~~locations and weather out and be deliberately vague.~~*

*We are all getting pretty familiar with the situation here. Everyone is becoming proficient at the basics, and we are quickly moving on to more challenging stuff, ~~angles have to be precise,~~ I can tell you, and you need a good team with you up there. I'm dashing this off to you now ~~because tomorrow, we move from where we are.~~ The landscape around here is something amazing, and you know how I get to see it, just the same way you do. ~~I can't give you any more details, but~~ I can't wait to talk about it all with you.*

*Take care, dearest Evie, send my love to Nina, and let me know more about life where you are.*

*Much love, kiddo. I miss you something terrible.*

*Keep the far ~~horizon~~ firmly in your sights,*

*Harry*

While the other girls lined up for the showers, Eva read what she could of the letter over again. The censors had stripped it, but he sounded well. He sounded fine. She closed her eyes and thumped back on her bed.

Two hours later, they were lined up to get on the cattle truck, the sun setting over the airfield. Deedee stood by, counting the heads of her girls as they climbed aboard for the dance. The driver turned on the engine, and the girls gave a cheer as the truck rattled off to the Blue Bonnet Hotel.

Eva looked out over the plains studded with mesquite trees, Harry's letter burning a hole in her handbag. She wasn't letting go of it for anything tonight.

They stepped out onto the main street of Sweetwater, quiet except for the hotel with its fancy facade.

"Cheer up, Evie." Nina stood next to her, waiting to take their turn in the elevator to the seventh floor. The marble lobby gleamed around them, and in it, a few older men in cowboy hats lounged.

"There's nothing wrong." Eva smiled at her friends.

"Oh, I know. You've just got a big case of the Harry blues."

"I'm concentrating on keeping you away from all the cowboys." Eva nudged her friend.

Nina took a glance around the lobby at the forty- and fifty-something men who were still watching them from under their cowboy hats. "Don't git too excited, y'all," she said, putting on her best accent. "They all look 'bout your dad's age."

Nancy stepped into the elevator, her face shining, her pretty green dress twirling around her calves. "I, for one, am going to have a few dances and make the most of it. I'm in the mood to dance, and I don't care if my partner's eighty-three."

Eva felt a giggle well up inside her. "Oh, I do adore you, Nancy."

Nina pressed the button for the seventh floor. "My, being in an elevator seems so sophisticated. I could just ride up and down in this thing all night."

Once the elevator opened and let them into the ballroom, the girls stood on the threshold of the room and took stock. A clutch of aging cowboys sat at the bar, and a few older men in suits who were clearly traveling on business to the oil wells looked the trainees up and down, straightened up, and, as a group, adjusted their lapels.

"Well, this looks like a gas." Rita sighed.

But when the band struck up "Oklahoma," Nancy turned to the girls. "Hey there, you girls take off your high hats right now! I'm up for a whoopee of a time, and I'm gonna have one. Y'all can stand there mopin' if you please." She sashayed off to the dance floor.

Nina grabbed Eva by the hand. "There's no rule to say we can't dance with each other! C'mon, Evie!"

Two minutes into the dancing, a few cowboys adjusted their hats and came to dance with them.

Nina gripped Eva's back as she twirled her around and around. "Don't make eye contact with them." She giggled.

"I'm of a mind to think that Jacqueline Cochran would expect us to dance with them, but at the same time, we must—"

"Act with pure decorum." Nina laughed.

Rita appeared next to them in a flash. "My dears, let me join you." She pulled Bea over, and they started dancing in a group, swinging and jiving, Rita showing off all the latest moves, her long legs skipping.

Helena and Nancy were chatting with the cowboys, and one of them started twirling Nancy around.

"Good," Nina said. "She didn't get all spiffy for nothing.'"

Right before pickup time in the cattle truck, Nancy threw herself on a chair alongside the others, her face flushed and her legs stretched straight out in front of her. "Well, that was the most fun I've had in ages! It didn't matter a fig that there weren't any boys our age. You know, you girls sure know how to enjoy yourselves."

Rita handed Eva her glass. "Have a sip," she said. "In fact, finish it, honey. It's one heck of a bathtub gin. One of those businessmen bought me a drink, but I'll share."

Eva took the glass and finished it. "Here's to you, Harry," she whispered, her chest still heaving from all the dancing and twirling she'd done to make the most of the night despite the fact that he wasn't there.

At 11:25, the yawning girls made their way to the elevator.

"You know, if there wasn't a war on, dancing and boys would be the most exciting things in our lives," Helena said.

"Oh my," Rita said. "I think, Helena, you might be exactly right."

They all stood silent in the elevator while it took them back down.

# CHAPTER SEVENTEEN

THE COMMITTEE: Several of the committee members served in the armed forces during the war and recognize the closeness of camaraderie during service, but wasn't what you experienced in WASP not much different from sororities and clubs? It seems that all of this gained importance in your mind. If all you really want is a club reunion, then maybe you are wasting the committee's time.

EVA FORREST: No, sir. That is not the case. I am here because we are not recognized in the history of this country. Our contribution to the Allied victory in World War II is not recorded by historians writing official history books. Consequently, many Americans do not know the WASP existed.

The late-autumn sun was setting low over the airfield when Dan instructed the class about their major long-distance instrument flights. Over the last few days, the wind had turned colder, and the occasional flurry of sideways rain was a reminder that the Texan winter was not far away.

Eva's muscles still tingled from the brisk calisthenics exercise routines they'd done that afternoon. She'd followed the complex routines mindlessly, familiar now with everything the fitness instructor asked them to do. It was the only time during the day that she could get away without full concentration. Ground school was rigorous, and she'd become used to the constant study and assessment routine, but she'd worked hard and done well. And as for flight classes, she was more than aware that tonight's instrument flight in the dark was going to require utter focus. They were being graded on it, and one slipup could mean washing out.

"I *still* hate losing my horizon, Evie," Nina confessed in a whisper. "I'm in a panic, and I only hope I pass."

Dan paused for a moment to sketch diagrams on the blackboard.

"Me too," Eva said. "But at least the weather is cooler than it was when we first started night training exercises. I swear, those turbans—"

"I'm going to burn mine when we are done. I'm planning the bonfire," Rita said.

"Save me a spot, girls. I'll throw mine in with yours." Nancy chuckled and went back to her notes.

"Well, girls, we'll have to rely on the burning oil wells on the way to Midland. Nancy, your stars are scant tonight," Bea said.

"They are," Nancy murmured. "I'll try and call them up for you, Bea."

"You all set your courses for tonight's flights today during ground school." Dan turned back to face them. "And you've had plenty of practice with forced landings. If you do need to carry out a forced landing during this, your first long-distance night flight, then you are to proceed. We'd rather have you do what Beatrice did during the quadrant exercises than have you push yourselves to stay up there, resulting in disaster."

Eva saw the way Rita smiled at Dan and the way his eyes warmed in acknowledgment of her in return. She was glad for them. They had managed to keep their burgeoning relationship private as far as the wider class group went, but the glow on Rita's face was there for all of them to see.

An hour later, Eva sat in the cockpit of the advanced trainer with Reg behind her. She'd done a thorough preflight check and settled into the cockpit, feeling content for now, despite the task at hand. The advanced trainer was a honey of a little plane to fly. She got the all clear by the control tower, checked the wind sock for strength and direction, swung the aircraft around, and lined up on the center.

Lowering the flaps, she stood on the brakes for a moment and increased the power on the throttle, watching the needle on the tachometer climb. She applied maximum power quickly in order to get off the ground. Releasing the brakes, she hurtled down the runway, wincing at the thought that if any flying gravel flew up to chip the paintwork, Reg would make notes detailing every scratch in her report. But the wind had picked up, and there was nothing she or anyone could do about the chilled flurries throwing gravel up around the sides of the plane. The end of the runway approached, and she pulled back on the control column.

The plane eased off the ground perfectly, but Eva didn't allow herself any reprieve. She remained focused, watching the lights on the instrument panel that would be her only guide apart from burning oil wells and the odd lights that small towns and ranches threw up in the windy, dark night.

She'd become used to the Texan winds in the last few weeks. The weather was volatile now. For a moment, Eva allowed herself a wistful pang at the thought that she'd be home again in just fourteen days. Home for Christmas, hopefully with her silver graduation wings pinned to her chest and an assignment to an air force base. Anticipation about assignments was starting to dominate the conversation among the girls in the class.

Eva lowered the nose slightly, allowing the plane to pick up speed and rise into a steady climb.

"Your takeoff was well executed." Reg's voice came through the communication device. "Now look out for the fires on the oil wells. They will set your course to Midland."

"Roger."

She settled into a pattern of direction from Reg and provided a response, action, and report. The first of the oil wells burned in the blackness below. Eva focused on maintaining control of the plane. It was increasingly difficult the farther west they traveled. The winds strengthened as the flight wore on.

At last, they reached the twinkling lights of Midland, and Reg instructed her to turn the plane back toward Sweetwater. She was glad of his calm nature. With a pang, she thought of Harry, of the way he, too, was never temperamental or difficult in a plane.

Another plane twinkled past them in the distance; otherwise, she and Reg were alone in the cloudy sky. Eva resisted the urge to wave at whichever other instructor and one of her classmates were sharing the night with them.

She touched down at Avenger Field with a bit of a thump, but she taxied at perfect speed to the gate.

"Well done," Reg said once she'd taxied into the landing spot. "You're doing well. You were calm and well prepared tonight. You've been a solid student, Eva."

"Thank you." She held every finger crossed with the hope that all her classmates would have an equally straightforward flight.


Two hours later, the mess hall buzzed with the chatter of returning trainees. Only one girl had failed. She'd taxied faster than was safe on landing, jammed on the brakes, and skidded in the dust, only just missing hitting the gate. She sat surrounded by her bay mates. Eva only hoped she would not be washed out.

Helena finally swaggered in, wearing her zoot suit—still the only girl tall enough to come close to carrying off the thing with any dash.

"That was better than expected. But my, am I glad it's over." Helena sat down.

Eva cradled her hot coffee. "The wind's picking up for the others still out there."

The wind rattled the roof of the hangar now. The tin roof groaned in turn. Eva knew she'd been fortunate to be one of the first in the class to go up. Nina was still out, along with Bea, Nancy, and Rita.

Eva chatted with Helena about assignments, but she kept her eyes trained on the doorway, relief seeping through her whenever one of her bay mates came back.

Reg tapped her shoulder late in the evening. Eva turned to him. Something dark stirred in her stomach at the sight of his face. It was the color of white cotton blowing in the fields.

The wind outside swelled, its low wails and eerie whistles sounding like a pack of wolves baying on the lonely plains.

"Eva, Helena, Nina, Beatrice, and Rita. Please come with me." Reg's face contorted into a grimace.

Eva stood up with a jerk. Her chair flew backward, hitting the floor with a thud.

They'd been laughing and singing "Zoot Suits and Parachutes" to keep their spirits up. But now, Bea put her cup of tea down on the table and stood up next to Eva.

Reg stood almost as if to attention. The hangar seemed enormous, vacant. The sounds of their classmates' chatter swelled in and out as if from far away.

Something was wrong.

Nina, Helena, and Rita quieted. They stood up with Eva and Bea, following Reg to the instructors' offices. When they were all in his office with him, he closed the door.

"Girls, I want you all to sit down." Reg turned his back to them for a moment and rested a hand on the large wooden desk that was precisely organized with all his files and notes. He faced them. "Prepare yourselves."

Eva slid down into the last chair in front of his desk. Her heartbeats were as hard as gunshots against a steel door.

"Dan and Nancy were forced to make a crash landing during their training exercise tonight."

Rita reached out, her hand fumbling for Eva's. Eva took it, holding it in her own shaking fingers.

"Dan sent a radio call to the tower. They were facing multiple problems with their trainer. He said that the airplane was shutting down and their altitude was dropping dramatically. They came down nose first." Reg spoke low and evenly. "I'm sorry. There was nothing anyone could do."

Before Eva could catch her, Rita fell off her chair in a heap onto the floor.

The other girls tore to her side. Eva cradled Rita's head in her arms. Nancy, gone? Dan? She hurled her gaze back up at Reg. Is that what he'd said? Desperate for him to say they'd survived, she scanned his face.

But his jaw only tightened, and the way he looked at Rita . . . Eva thought, *He knows.*

He knew about Rita and Dan.

And yet, he had not washed her out.

"We have informed Jacqueline Cochran of WASP trainee Nancy Ward's death. Mrs. Cochran will provide the funds to get Nancy back to her folks and will organize to transport the body home. There is nothing else to be done. I'm so very sorry."

Rita lay, still unconscious, in Eva's arms.

"And Helena, Eva, Nina, Beatrice . . . Rita?" Reg cleared his throat. "We will be sending you all back out flying. Tonight. We've checked the weather, and the worst of the wind has passed us now. It will be smooth flying, but it's important you all get straight up again."

The girls stared at him in silence.

After a few horrible seconds, Bea nodded, and her voice shook when she spoke. "Of course, Instructor. We don't want any of us to get spooked up there. The best thing is to get right back up in the air."

"We have no choice but to push on during the theater of war. Take your time, and when you're ready, please report to the flight line." Reg left them alone with their grief.

That night, the bay was eerie and quiet. There were no usual soft sounds of the girls' breathing to send Eva off to sleep. Only the odd muffled sob punctuated the darkness. Outside, the night was still and uncanny. Eva hugged her gray blanket around her body and stared into the dark.

The worst in the room was Rita. She lay atop her cot, still wearing her zoot suit, her body curled into a ball. They'd only been made to take a quick circle over Avenger Field. Eva had forced herself to focus, after being sick in the bathroom before going up.

Bea's crying filtered into the bay, next to Nancy's empty bed. Eva slid off her cot and shuffled across the room in her socks. She stopped for a moment at Rita's bed, but her friend did not move when she reached out and stroked a tendril of blond hair that had fallen across her cheek.

As quietly as she could, she moved across to Bea. Bea leaned up on an elbow, staring at the bed Nancy had made up that morning with the rest of them, tucking in corners, lining up sheets. Even in the cover of darkness, Eva could see the tears shimmering down Bea's cheeks. Silently, Bea stared up at Eva and then moved over a little in her small cot. Eva slid in next to her, and in the stillness, she leaned her head against the other girl's while silently they both wept.

The next morning, Eva woke still next to Bea. She opened an eye to see Helena, Nina, and Rita huddled on Rita's bed. Rita was half propped up between Nina and Helena, sobbing now. Helena held Rita, whose whole body shook.

Outside, rain lashed the window. Bea went to pull up the blind. White sleet pelted at the glass. Eva hovered on Bea's empty bed.

"Come here, Eva, Bea." Helena patted Rita's bed.

Like a shot, they dived to Rita's bed, all of them huddled in their nightgowns, children who had been sent out to face something they could not begin to understand.

"She loved flying." Nina tucked her head into Eva's shoulder. "She died night flying. The stars were out."

"I'm sorry, girls." Rita let out a huge sob. "He was going to take me home after graduation in November."

"You'll come with us." Nina sounded resolute. "With me and Evie. Come to Burbank. We'll look after you."

Eva reached out and laid her hand on Nina's arm. The ruthless devastation of war had not come so close to her before. If this was the reality of it, Eva could only dream of a time and place in which it would never, ever come back again.


Nancy's and Dan's deaths were a distinct, somber rite of passage. After the girls crossed the turning point of grief, uncertainty about being separated after graduation increased throughout the class. The tension of where they'd all end up almost overrode their excitement over getting their silver wings and meeting Jacqueline Cochran and Henry Arnold. Graduation would be the end of an era, and who knew where they'd all be assigned.

Rita carried out the last of the training exercises as if she were an automaton. She forced herself to cope by shutting herself off in some place where no one else could get through. Outwardly, she was present, and she flew with an amazing determination and focus. Eva was only glad that Nina had invited their friend back to Burbank after graduation.

Eva found herself murmuring prayers for Nancy's memory and also, as she glanced at Rita's exhausted face, for Harry. Because if he were to fall out of the sky, she had no idea how she would cope.

Now, with a snowstorm brewing outside and flight class cancelled for the afternoon, Eva leaned forward over the long table in the mess hall and read through Harry's latest letter to her.

> *Dearest Eva,*
> *I expect you are ~~becoming an expert at the thing~~ we both love to do. I can't wait to hear all about it during vacation! I have some great news for you. After the last letter and the last round of work we had to do, ~~I've finished my training and have been assigned to a squadron. I can't tell you where I'll be stationed, but I can say that my squadron is one of the more experienced units in the US Navy.~~*
> *I'm still having a grand time, and getting to see a lot of the countryside from ~~you know where~~! That's the thing that's keeping me going, that and ~~knowing I'll see everyone real soon.~~*
> *Thank you for your letters. You know they say that news from home and friends is what keeps our men going out on the front. Even ~~snippets that pass by the censors~~ can mean a great deal to us, so thank you for writing so faithfully.*
> *Take care, kiddo. Must dash,*
> *Harry*

Eva laid the letter down. Nina was next to her, reading over her shoulder, her freckled face frowning in concentration, a mug of hot chocolate cupped between her cold, red hands.

"Oh dear goodness, I'm sure from what I'm reading that he's been assigned, Evie."

Eva couldn't find the words. Ever since Nancy's death, it was as if any naivete she'd felt beforehand about what they were all doing had been washed away.

"You okay?" Nina asked.

"I'm doing fine."

Nina touched her shoulder.

Eva sighed. "Thing is, I'm dreadful concerned about the ongoing reports in the newspapers here about the bugs in the bombers he'll be flying. I'm deathly worried. I just don't know if I can bear it . . ." She looked down. "The odds of him surviving seem so slim."

"He's a wonderful pilot," Nina said.

"Problem with being an aircraft mechanic," Eva said, "is that we know too much about those planes. Now I understand how my dad feels."

"That's true."

"Four Curtiss bombers were lost in midair collisions just recently, one lost into the water on launch, another straight in during bombing practice."

"He was one of the best aircraft mechanics Lockheed had, Evie. If anyone understands defects in an airplane—"

"Harry does," Eva said. "But I've read more stories of tailwheels falling off on landing and seven aircraft lost by one squadron alone. Why are they still pushing ahead with the Curtiss rather than reverting to the Douglas SBD?"

"It's not for us, nor for Harry, to decide, Evie."

Eva shook her head. "I know he only views me as a little sister, but I don't think Lucille knows or realizes one jot about the risk he'll take."

"When he sees you returned home, you'll be a graduated WASP." Nina's tone was soothing.

After Dan's and Nancy's deaths and all the brooding and sleepless nights, Eva knew that what she felt for Harry was not just a crush; it was a deep understanding. But most of all, it was turning into a slow-burning love.

# CHAPTER EIGHTEEN

THE COMMITTEE: The committee acknowledges that there were bonds forged between you, but this was in the style of flying Girl Scouts. It was not in any way military in the proper sense. If you are granted full military benefits, we will have every organization coming forward, including the Girl Scout volunteers who were on the ground. Do any of these other so-called friends you made in the WASP really view the experience as military, looking back? And if so, what possible justification do they have?

EVA FORREST: I lost contact with them all. I have written to them, but I haven't heard back. I had no choice but to move on.

THE COMMITTEE: So is this a personal revisiting for you, Mrs. Forrest? Are you simply here to try to reconnect with your long-lost friends? How could you truly have been sisters-in-arms, then, in the true military style, if your time there was so easily forgotten by your fellow WASP?

EVA FORREST: I do not believe that my fellow WASP could have forgotten our time together at Sweetwater. I believe that they felt the same bond during wartime as I did. But I was involved in an accident in the winter of '44 that killed one of my close friends, Helena Cartwright, a fellow WASP. I worry that I did something wrong in that accident. I have been unable to recall the details of what happened, and I have tried to reach out to my WASP friends. But I have never heard back. What if I broke our military-style code of putting my WASP sisters before myself? I worry that they washed *me* out.

Winter mist curled over the empty plains as the cold weather unfurled over Texas. Inside, the hangars were freezing. Trainees and teachers started coming down sick. But the girls flew the final hours they needed to graduate, bundled up in their leather flying jackets, woolen collars turned up to protect their necks. Their cheeks were flushed red with the cold, where four months earlier, they'd burned from the relentless sun.

Dan's replacement did not do anything to help morale. Their new flight instructor was an entirely different type of man.

Bob Sutton first addressed Eva's flight group on an exposed outlying airfield, his light-brown hair immaculate in spite of the icy breeze. His blue eyes were cold. "I know you women are nearly graduating. You must be clever girls to get this far. However, the fact is you're going to have trouble when you graduate. You'll either be target towing while our men shoot up at you from the ground, delivering new planes from factories to bases, or testing planes that have been repaired. It's all very well for you to have flown the three training planes here, but many of you won't be strong enough to fly the bigger planes that we need you to fly."

Eva sensed Bea tensing up.

"Women simply don't have the strength."

Bea cleared her throat. "I disagree, sir."

Swift as a cat, Bob rounded on her, frost curling from his mouth. "You have a problem?"

Their class had enjoyed a good run with instructors so far—Reg, Dan, and Hank had taught the women on the base with an attitude of respect, but gossip abounded about the way WASP were treated on some of the military bases across the country, and those bases were where they all were about to be sent. With only thirty percent of their class washed out so far, class 43-W-8 was working extra hard to remain focused and get through the last tests.

Eva had heard tales of past instructors who had washed girls out for very little reason, sometimes almost nothing at all. And that was the last thing they needed when they were so close to the end of their training. She admired Bea for standing up to Bob, but at the same time, she didn't want a touchy instructor's ire to ruin her opportunity to contribute to the war.

"I presume you are talking about bombers, sir?" Bea went on. Her tone was measured, calm. "Are you saying that we will not be strong enough to test or deliver them?"

"You'll struggle to fly them. It will be impossible for women of your height, in particular."

Bea rose up to her full height of five foot three. "We can prop ourselves up on parachutes and employ blocks under our feet to reach the pedals."

"This is the air force." Bob Sutton made no effort to hide his smirk. "Not some circus outfit."

"And we are professionally trained pilots."

"You are trainees. The multiple-engine aircraft are far heavier than what you've been training in here."

Nina piped up next to Eva. "Sir, our strength training and ground school have prepared us to handle a multitude of planes. We will be ready to fly every type of plane in the military. Unlike male pilots, we are ready to fly every type of aircraft there is."

He let out a snort. "You women have no idea what you're in for, frankly. You can't just strap on your high heels to reach the pedals. When it comes to planes like the B-17, men struggle to fly them. They land covered in sweat. You need to be aware that what you are facing will be impossible."

Helena raised a hand. "I don't think there's any reason a woman couldn't fly a four-engine bomber, sir. In fact, I understand that it's already happening on some of the bases. If the men do not want to test-fly repaired planes, then surely it should be a source of relief that women are prepared to take on that job."

Bob Sutton pressed his hands to his forehead.

Eva felt her mouth twitch.

"Class, today I want you to do check rides—stalls, lazy eights, turns, chandelles, and forced landings in the advanced trainer. You can come up with me first." He pointed at Bea.

When Bea followed Bob up to the advanced trainer, she turned around to the four of them in their group and sent them a shrug.

"What a big cheese," Nina said once he was out of earshot.

Rita stood silent and stiff on Eva's other side, her face pale in the cold. Eva glanced at the dark shadows that tarnished the delicate skin under her eyes.

Eva huddled in the open field with the others. In the warmer weather, they'd study in the outlying fields or use the time to write a letter home. But today, the windchill factor was below freezing, and they kept each other close.

"Bea got a ninety-seven on her math test again, and one hundred percent on navigation," Helena said. "I can tell you, if I'm sent to the same base as she is after graduation, I won't be complaining. She's one smart girl, and she won't take anything lying down."

"As was Nancy," Nina said.

"I so miss that girl's wonder at the world," Rita murmured.

Eva turned to her, glad to hear her voicing her feelings and thoughts openly with them. "I take comfort in the fact that she must be watching over us," Eva said. "And every time I go up there, I feel closer to my sister too."

Rita smiled, but the expression did not reach her eyes.

Bea brought the plane down in a perfect landing.

Amid the rattle of the prop engine, Rita reached out a hand and held tight on to Eva's own. "It's friendship that's gotten me through this terrible time. Thank you," she said when the advanced trainer's engine turned quiet. "Every day I miss him. I want to scream and shout at him being taken away. But I'm getting through."

Eva squeezed Rita's hand back, but across the windswept, freezing field, she could see Bob Sutton singling her out as his next victim. He was appraising her. Eva only hoped he knew she'd been getting top grades in her flight tests so far.

He marched over, stopping right in front of them with a click of his boots.

"Eva *Scott*." He murmured her surname like he was toying with a dying mouse.

"Yes, sir."

"Let's see you fly."

Eva tried to kid herself that she had nothing to worry about. They had only a handful of night-flying exercises to carry out and pass, along with meteorology finals in ground school. In total, Eva had only another ten hours of flying time left before graduation.

The problem was, since he'd replaced Dan, Bob Sutton had given out more unsatisfactory marks—U's—for check rides than all the other instructors put together. He'd washed out eight girls so far.

"What are you waiting for, woman?"

Eva stood up, collected her helmet and goggles, and moved toward the plane.

"Good luck flying in this wind," the mechanic on duty said.

The wind had worsened since Bea went up, and for one fleeting moment, Eva wished she were home. Sunny California seemed like a long-gone dream right now.

Eva carried out her preflight inspection and climbed up onto the wing. She slipped into the front cockpit with Bob Sutton behind her and pulled the hood down. She stared at the instrument panel. She would not be nervous. She would not let this instructor spook her in any way. Eva frowned at her hands, turned on the engine, and willed herself to complete her flight without a hitch.

The takeoff was smooth even though Eva's hands shook. She'd do this for Nancy's and Dan's sakes.

She carried out the required exercises, keeping her concentration fierce, shutting off one of the engines as they'd been instructed, and correcting the plane in a second as she'd been taught.

Finally, she landed and turned to face Bob Sutton in the rear cockpit.

His eyes were still narrowed, but there was a new glint of admiration in his look. "Fine form, Eva. Well done."

Eva turned away from him, raised her brow, and lifted the canopy over the cockpit. She went back to the waiting girls.

Nina came toward her. "Rebecca Marsh failed this morning. He washed her out. With only a couple weeks left. Someone's spreading the story."

Eva caught the fear in Nina's eyes, knowing that it was fear for Rita that worried her. Rita was flying as if she were against something every time she went up.

"Rita." Bob Sutton looked up from the clipboard that he kept attached to him like a vise. "Proceed to your flight."

Eva ran a hand over Rita's thin shoulder. The tall girl went to the plane. And from the time Rita took off, she executed every one of her maneuvers in the most glorious way Eva had seen.

# CHAPTER NINETEEN

THE COMMITTEE: Mrs. Forrest, how is your accident relevant to our decision to make WASP part of the military? We refute that you are here for anything other than personal reasons.

EVA FORREST: The WASP records have been locked away since 1944. No one can access them, because they are not military. Those records would contain the answers that I need about the accident. They would tell me whether or not I did the right thing by my fellow WASP and my sister pilot, Helena. And opening the records would make such information available not only for me, but for others as well. It would ensure that the WASP were part of history if historians could access our records and learn our story.

"Telling Ma to bring my woolen two-piece outfit, black pumps, and my silver studs for graduation." Nina sat upright on her bed, frowning at the letter she was writing home.

"Sounds fearful smart," Bea said.

"I'm gonna be terribly smart." Nina grinned right back at Bea.

"That's if we graduate, with Bob Sutton on the prowl." Helena stopped folding her clothes for a moment. "He's on the warpath, and none of us are safe."

"Nonsense, I'm graduating. I don't care how hard-boiled Bob Sutton gets," Nina said. "Evie, our moms will only need tweeds or something to wear when they come, right? My ma wants to know."

"Tweeds sound perfect. I'll tell Mom the same thing." Eva hated to think what her mom would make of Sweetwater.

"My ma says she and your mom have rooms on the same floor of the Blue Bonnet Hotel," Nina went on.

Eva glanced across the bay to Rita. All this talk of moms was not sensitive toward her. Chances were, Rita was not going to have anyone come watch her graduate next week.

Helena changed the topic. "Did you hear? They don't announce where we'll be sent until after we graduate."

"Dang it, that's frustrating," Nina said. "Evie, if we're separated, it's going to be mighty strange for us. I can't imagine it, to tell the truth."

"I'd love to be with you girls too." Helena put the last of her clothes away in her wardrobe and smiled, almost shyly, at Eva. "If the three of us were posted together, that would be grand."

"We could do with some organizing from you, girl," Nina said, still glaring at her own handwriting.

A shadow passed across Helena's face.

"We'd value your friendship." Eva kept her tone reassuring. "You know we would, Helena."

Helena's smile was full of relief.

"Don't know if we can request anything, but if we can, I'd like to fly cross country, either in California, Arizona, or Florida," Bea said.

"Sounds like a dream, flying cross country, better than doing short ferrying trips. And all the time in the world alone," Rita said.

"Imagine the lack of relief tubes." Nina closed up her envelope and placed it on her bedside chest.

"As long as I'm not sent to Camp Davis as a starting point, I don't mind where I go," Bea said. "Forty thousand men and fifty WASP? Not for me."

Eva stood up, suddenly feeling confined in the room. Outside, it was a clear Texan winter day, but freezing. She drew her cardigan around herself and stood for a moment on the front step of the barracks, raising her face up to the blue sky and the winter sun that shone down on Avenger Field. It was hard to imagine what going home would be like. Her mom's letters had been practical, perfunctory, and brief. Her dad wasn't a keen writer. He'd tacked on notes to her mom's letters, telling her he was hoping she was okay and that he missed her. She was looking forward to seeing them both, but she hoped her mom would cope with the news of her next assignment.

"Okay?" Nina stepped out the door to stand next to her.

"Just a little uncertain."

"Going back home throwing you off?"

Eva let out a soft chuckle. "You know, I'm a strange mix of wanting to go home and thinking I'm going to miss Sweetwater. I've become so very used to being out here."

"I'll miss Avenger Field." Nina folded her arms and sat down on the step. "I think it's the uncertainty, the not knowing where we'll all end up that's throwing me. And going home will be grand but strange. I feel like a different girl after the last few months. The reality of what we're doing has hit me. We're about to go off and do what we've been trained to do. I never thought I'd be a flygirl for the war."

Eva sat down cross-legged next to her. "Talking of flygirls and fly-boys, I had a new letter from Harry. He tells me Lucille is throwing a party in the ballroom at some swanky Hollywood hotel while we are home. It's gonna be on the night we arrive, and he sounded like it was gonna be a big deal."

"Evie? You don't think . . ." Nina turned to Eva. "Surely not." She sounded more decisive now. "This is Harry. Smart, sensible Harry. He wouldn't do anything rash."

"It's wartime," Eva said, staring out at the bleak barracks. "Folks are making decisions much faster than in peacetime. It's understandable. Just hard, thinking about it, you know."

"Lucille's wrong for Harry. What's she doing toward the war, anyway?"

"I have no idea. Sometimes, I want to just tell him I'm here, you know? But it seems a stupid plan when he's smitten with Lucille."

"I understand. But I think he's being a fool." Nina let out a snort and stared at the brown grass. November rains hadn't been enough to turn anything green out here. "Well, here's another suggestion. What if you meet someone swell on an air force base?" Nina nudged Eva with her elbow. "Hmm?"

"All I want to do on an air force base is fly planes. Problem is, I haven't met any man who comes close to Harry. I don't want to compromise, but the situation with Harry is impossible. I'll have to learn to live with it."

A plane buzzed, lonely in the clear sky.

"Well." Nina stretched out her legs. "I for one am going to look out for some handsome guy for you, someone to make our Harry jealous. Much as I love him too, he needs to see what he's missing."

Eva chuckled. "Oh, Nina. With men and women being so separated during wartime, I think we are extra susceptible to turning people into dreams because they're not there. But I do feel something deeper for Harry. And that's all there is to it."

"I could always thump him over the head and tell him to look at the beautiful Evie properly, not just see you like some kid sister around the block."

"I'd die if you did that."

"I know you would . . . makes you wonder whether Rita's philosophy was right, though, doesn't it?"

Eva sat in silence for a moment. "I've been thinking that."

A breeze stirred up the trees around the bay. "I'm awful glad you offered to bring Rita home," Eva said.

"Oh, it'll be a gas. Hollywood's full of military boys. Flyboys, marines. We might all meet beaux. But you are the most beautiful of the three of us, so I still think it's likely to be you who does."

Eva threw out a laugh. "Stuff and nonsense. If anyone deserves a beau, it's you."

Nina let out an infectious giggle like the schoolgirl Eva had known for years. "Oh, I'm holding out for the real thing, just as much as you are. I swear I'm never settling for some idiot. Jeepers, I'd rather spend the rest of my life nailing rivets than running around doing housework after some drip!"

Eva clutched Nina's arm, and Nina burst into a gale of giggles.


Deedee stood up on a podium in the hangar. Her blond hair was pulled back neatly, and she wore her dressy navy suit.

"Class Forty-Three-W-Eight, you have conducted yourself with excellence. Overall, you have one of the lowest washout rates of any group. We want to keep it that way now that graduation is so close."

"So do we," Bea muttered. "So do we."

"I know there has been a lot of speculation among you about where you're all going to end up. I cannot tell you which bases you'll be sent to, but I can tell you that the majority of you will be utility pilots."

"Polite way of saying we'll be test pilots for repaired airplanes." Bea's mutterings were just loud enough for their bay mates to hear, not loud enough to disturb Deedee's talk. "Darn it. But if that's what we have to do, then I'm not going to complain."

As for airplanes, many of the girls were keen to fly huge bombers and get started on the big four-engine airplanes, but Eva still much preferred the nifty single engines. She had no desire to lumber around in a bomber all day long.

"Many of you will be hop-flying planes when they're fixed and ready to go back into combat," Deedee said. She scanned the class. "Only a very select few will be sent to carry out target towing and searchlight practice. As for ferrying, again, there will only be a small group of you doing that. You'll all receive your postings when you are on leave after graduation."

Eva tightened her grasp on her flight gloves in her lap.

Bea let out a groan next to her. "Oh great. Well, I'll either be flying around in circles or hopping up in the sky and testin', then going straight back down to the ground again. At least she's told us."


At lunch after Deedee's talk, the girls filled their tin plates at the cafeteria in the familiar great long line that snaked around the mess hall. Rain pelted in sheets on the roof. Once they were at a table, their plates filled with corned beef and white sauce, Helena pulled her books out of her backpack. No matter that this was the last week before graduation, none of them were going to take any unnecessary chances.

"You're doing well, girls." Reg stood at the head of the room.

They all put down their forks.

"I'm impressed with your attitude, performance, and diligence. All of you are doing solidly. You've not had an easy run." His eyes searched the room and lingered on their table.

Bob Sutton came up behind Reg, his sharp eyes flicking around.

"One of our most promising graduating classes," Reg said, his tone mild but laced with something firm.

Bob sent Reg a quick, pointed look. "Is it? Really?"

"Indeed, Bob." Reg kept his voice measured.

"Well then," Bob said. "I guess it's not over yet."

Eva stared at her food, her appetite suddenly dulled.


A week later, the winter sun shone in a cerulean sky. Jacqueline Cochran stood on a raised platform in the freezing air. Henry H. Arnold, the chief of the air force, was by her side. She spoke for several minutes, and the girls stood and saluted them both, military style.

Eva had no idea how she had made it through; her final check was a heck of a nightmare—she'd messed up her landing, then taxied into the strip with her flaps down. She was certain she'd fail, but somehow, she'd passed, even though Bob Sutton had come through with his machete and washed out another two girls.

Now she felt a surge of pride when her name was called out, and she marched up to the platform to receive her very own pair of silver wings. Out of the corner of her eye, Eva saw her mom next to Nina's ma. Nina's ma clapped and clapped as if Eva had been awarded the Congressional Medal of Honor itself.

When Nina went up, her mom let out a whoop.

"Home to LA for two weeks!" Nina's face shone afterward at the dinner in the mess hall, which had been decorated with streamers for their class.

"You'd hardly know there was a war on with the spread of food you girls are getting out here." Eva's mom shook her head at all the food.

"We have to keep our military flying on full stomachs, Mrs. Scott," Nina said.

"Will you end up together, girls, do you think?" Helena's mother asked. The tall, elegant woman in her red outfit with a string of pearls around her slender neck ate delicately. Her class and beautiful manners had Eva intrigued.

"We can only hope that some of us will go to the same bases, Mother," Helena said. "I admit, I don't want to be separated from these girls."

"It's driving us all barkin' crazy not knowing," Nina said. "I'm half panicking with anxiety about being separated from Evie. I don't know what I'd do without my other half."

"We do know that most of us will be test-flying airplanes that have been repaired," Bea said.

Eva sensed her mom bristling at Bea's words.

"The task sounds extremely dangerous and risky," her mom said.

Eva bit her lip and willed her mom to keep her opinions quiet.

"Every time a plane goes in for repairs, Mrs. Scott, it has to be tested before it goes into military combat. The smallest flaw in a plane can be devastatingly serious if you're flying at four hundred miles per hour in combat." Bea looked at Eva's mom with genuine concern in her brown eyes.

Eva's mother sniffed. "Eva is trained as a mechanic. I've always said she would be better served going back to her job at Lockheed if all these planes need fixing for combat. She could do that there, if that is the need."

Eva held back her gasp. Honestly? Even after she'd just graduated?

"Are you saying that as test pilots, you will be taking up planes that no military pilot in their right mind would be flying?" Her mom was on a roll. "Surely, they do not expect a group of young girls to test planes that the military won't touch?"

"I am certain Jacqueline Cochran will ensure that our daughters are not put at any untoward risk." Helena's mother's tone was calm and rational.

Eva wanted the ground to swallow her whole at her own mother's lack of tact.

"The air force has to find out whether or not seemingly minor damage is reason to ground a plane," Helena said.

"To put it simply, they don't want to risk their highly skilled military pilots, because they are being used overseas taking abominable risks every day for our country. We girls might be taking up a risky role here, but the job has to be done, and trained pilots have to do it." Bea was at her most matter of fact.

"Maintenance test flights are routine procedure. They have been since airplanes started flying in the sky." Eva tried to smile at her mom.

"Yes, although . . ." Bea was frowning now. "The idea that the country's girls are expendable, and that male pilots are too valuable to fly planes that might be unsafe, is a good point. Especially when we are all trained."

"That was not my point at all," Eva's mom said. "My point was that you girls are not experienced enough to be sent up to test planes that men should and will be flying in combat. The country has gone insane sending our young girls up to do that."

"Maybe it has, Ruth." Nina's ma had been unusually quiet. Perhaps it was because she'd spent three days in a train with Eva's mom. "But given the choice between test-flying airplanes for the United States and fixing rivets on the factory floor, I know which my little girl would prefer to do. And I don't see why she can't fly any plane as well as a man. And, Ruth, didn't we raise our girls to have strong judgment? They're going to keep using that every day, no matter what their job."

Helena looked at Nina's mom, Jean, with new respect. "We are all, boys and girls, just doing whatever we can to further the effort for peace and for our country to win the war."

Finally, Eva's mom opened her mouth and closed it, and then to Eva's astonishment, she tucked in to her food.

# CHAPTER TWENTY

THE COMMITTEE: If you needed access to the records in order to understand the full nature of your accident, why did you not apply to see the records back in 1944?

EVA FORREST: I did not want to be seen as complaining by requesting the records, because the WASP were already under enough pressure in 1944. The publicity surrounding us became extremely unfavorable as the year wore on. Mrs. Cochran fought for WASP militarization, but public opinion; the Veterans Administration; the American Legion; and civilian pilots, who feared for their jobs, were all strong in their opinions against us. By June 1944, when the House of Representatives was to vote on WASP militarization, Drew Pearson for the *Washington Times-Herald* wrote insulting and patronizing articles about Jacqueline Cochran. He said that we were just glamour girls, costing the government too much money. It was reported in *Time* that the WASP program had been expensive and that men pilots could have been trained more quickly and cheaply than women. We were a small group and a unique organization. I did not want to draw any further disapproval toward us.

None of us wanted to make any waves, so we accepted the dangerous assignments, flew the old planes that men would not fly, and did not complain. By October 1944, the WASP were finally told they were going to be completely disbanded after Jacqueline Cochran wrote a long, last-ditch report, wanting the program to be militarized or scrapped. Because of the work of the WASP, the pilot shortage was not critical anymore, and Henry Arnold took up Jacqueline Cochran's ultimatum. The WASP were told they were going to be disbanded on December 20, 1944. The last class of WASP who trained were sent home without having flown one military plane. Jacqueline Cochran had fought for us and lost. If she could not win, how could a woman like me hope to get heard among all the hullabaloo?

Everything looked strange and different in the bedroom Eva had known all her life. It was as if the room had shrunk. Everything in it, from her student desk to her single bed to the busy pattern on her floral carpet, swirled in time with the throbbing tiredness in her head after the journey home to California that had taken her halfway across the United States.

And an envelope was propped on the pillow on her bed. Heart in her mouth, she went straight toward it, took it to her small desk under the window, and slit the envelope open. She scanned the letter twice. The winter sun beamed into the room, but Eva stood quite still.

Camp Davis, North Carolina. The assignment nobody wanted, on the base that all the girls dreaded. At the tough, bleak-sounding training ground for pilots to learn to use antiaircraft guns, Eva would be towing targets around in circles over the base while male trainees shot at her plane using live ammunition. So. She was one of Jacqueline Cochran's "select few." It was hard to know whether that was a compliment or not.

Eva moved around the room, bustling about to get her cardigan. She would have to keep stories of Camp Davis to herself when it came to her mom. She tried to push aside the rumors she'd heard that the base was surrounded by swamplands; huge tracts of unnavigable, thick marsh filled with quicksand; impenetrable waterways framed by thick forests; and lagoons. From what she'd heard, it was desolate, lonely, a landscape inhabited by strange marsh folk.

But what was worse, everyone said that for women at Camp Davis, unwanted attention of a more dubious kind from human pests was even more of a problem than the insects that swarmed up from the vast swamplands.

Eva walked out of her small bedroom, the envelope clutched in her hand. Her mother was resting in her room after the long journey home, having a nap before she had to cook dinner for the family.

Eva moved slowly down the narrow hallway. Once she was out in the blinding sunshine, the letter trailing behind her like a child's kite, Eva ran down the street toward Nina's house.

The small factory-issued houses with their faint smell of cabbages and wartime cooking floating out into the street seemed to fly by her as she ran past, trying to block out the pictures in her head of Camp Davis. She would have to keep her imagination in check.

The young vivid-green trees back here closed in on her after the vast brownness of the Texan plains. Everything seemed small and safe here, her house, her room, the streets.

Eva trudged up the short driveway to Nina's house. The gate swung on its rusted hinges, squeaking in the breeze. Eva hurried around back. Nina's mom came to the kitchen door, lugging a basket of washing on her hip. Eva ducked under the clothesline and leaned forward to kiss Jean on her cheek.

"Nina and Rita have just gone into her room, Evie. Surely they've missed you these past three minutes, honey!"

"Thank you." Eva's heart was half full of anticipation and half full of dread. Fact was, she had to prepare herself for the next jolt.

What if she'd been sent to North Carolina alone?

"Evie, that you?" Nina called from her room.

Eva's shoes clacked against the same patterned linoleum that lined the hallway of Eva's house. Nina appeared at her doorway, her cardigan wrapped tight around her small frame. Her eyes traveled down to the envelope in Eva's hand.

Rita was spread out on Nina's bed, facedown. She groaned a hello to Eva and lifted a hand in the air. "I'm beat, you girls!"

"Camp Davis," Nina said, her eyes darting to Rita. "Please, tell me I'm not going out there without you."

"You're not." Eva almost slumped with relief. "I was going to be strong if I was going alone, but thank goodness." She pulled Nina into a hug.

"Well, that's a good thing, now isn't it, Evie? We'll be together. That's something to be thankful for. I'm sure, together, we'll do just fine out there. Maybe the girls' rumors were too harsh about the place, eh?"

Eva let out a sigh. "Let's bank on that thought, Nina. We'll do just fine, I'm sure. And Rita?" she asked.

Rita lifted her head. "B-25 school. I had my assignment posted here to Nina's house. Flying the big bombers with the men at Mather Field, Sacramento. Apparently the school there is doing some experimenting with the bombers. I'll miss you gals, but the job don't bother me. I like having a lot of metal around me, and I suspect it's because of my height and my experience with instrument flying that I got chosen to fly the big planes. I like a lot of gauges and dials in an aircraft." Rita buried her head in the pillow again.

"She was told they're only sending twenty WASP to B-25 school. So Rita's also been chosen for a special assignment," Nina said. The sounds of Rita's soft groans of tiredness washed through the bedroom. "Apparently, they're sending two squadrons of white men, one of black men, and one squadron of girls."

"Well, that will be a gas, honey." Eva looked down at Rita. The sounds of her breathing steadied. She'd gone and fallen fast asleep.

"And Helena and Bea?" Eva asked.

"Helena was on the phone the moment we walked in the door. She's coming with us to Camp Davis. She nearly shrieked with relief to find out I was going too. And Bea's got what she hoped for: ferry command in Long Beach, California. She's in the best spot there is. So close to all the factories, she'll have access to every sort of airplane."

"Bea can fly anything if she puts her mind to it. I'm not surprised she was chosen to do that. I've heard of girls reading instruction manuals on their laps while they fly new planes. I can just imagine Bea doing that. Staying calm."

Nina glanced at the sleeping Rita. "Bea will be grand. She's just the girl to deal with that. Meanwhile, our challenges will be different. We're going to be eating mosquitoes, but you know what Jacqueline Cochran says. Don't say no to any job, and never complain, because if we do, military men will think it was only because we're women." Nina held up her chin, her blue eyes wide.

"Well, I'm not going to tell my mom about Camp Davis's reputation," Eva said. "I hope she doesn't hear anything from other sources."

Nina sighed. "Well, we'd best start getting ready for this party of Harry's now. Let's make the most of this vacation."

"Hollywood!" Rita murmured, half-asleep. "I've dreamed of that place since I was a little girl. Wake me so I have enough time to doll up!"

"I say we try and make the most of it, Evie." Nina held her eye.

"North Carolina, or Lucille's ritzy party tonight?"

Nina didn't miss a beat. "Both."

Back in her own bedroom, after a heavenly shower in the family bathroom, Eva slipped into a butter-yellow dress with a velvet belt and a tight-fitted bodice. She twirled in front of the old chipped mirror in her bedroom, her body taut under the chiffon. Months of daily calisthenics and handling heavy airplanes had her in tip-top condition. She applied a little powder and rouge, pulling her hair half up.

From time to time, she wondered whether Harry might decide Lucille was not right for him after all, with her glamorous ways. Right now, she still wished he might be of a mind to think about falling in love with a girl who cared about the things he cared about, who could pull her weight and had her own convictions.

Nina and Rita appeared at her bedroom door just as Eva was slipping on her patent-leather dancing shoes.

"Wow-wee, you look swell, Evie!" Nina whistled. "Harry won't be able to take his eyes off of you."

Nina's red dress clung equally well to her toned frame. Her blue eyes shone and were enhanced with a little mascara while her usually straight hair hung in loose waves that she'd conjured up.

Rita was just as stunning in pale pink, her blond hair swept up on her head. Her face was still a little pale with grief, but it was a good thing to see her dressed up and ready to go out.

"Harry?" Rita asked. She closed Eva's door behind her. And made a great show of lowering her voice. "Spill, honey. So he's the one you got that letter from. The boy you had your eye on back home. You sure didn't join in with any of the conversations about the instructors at Sweetwater, and you showed no interest in any of them local cowboys like some of 'em girls did."

Eva picked up her handbag. "Nothing to talk about. Honest, Rita. He's just a friend. More to the point, I'm his friend. End of story."

Rita folded her arms. "Nope. Spill. Goodness knows I need somethin' cheery to distract me, and a little happiness for one of my best girlfriends, why, what could be better than that?"

Nina sat down on the edge of Eva's bed, perching there in her red dress instead of throwing herself back on the pillows like she usually did. "Harry," she said, "is the local dish. Eva is the local beauty. You can go figure the rest."

"I am not the local beauty."

"You *are*," Nina said. "No one has such thick, lustrous hair and big brown eyes as you. And Harry, he's a green-eyed blond and a handsome flyboy! You'd be perfect for one another, except, our Harry's gone soft for this Hollywood girl, you see, Rita. Silly Harry."

"He was studying aeronautical engineering and working at Lockheed to fund himself through college," Eva told Rita. "But he's a fully trained bomber pilot. He's between assignments right now."

Rita whistled. "Brains and hardworking! He sounds worthy of our lovely Eva, then."

"Precisely," Nina said. "He is. But he just can't see beyond the glamour of Hollywood right now. We're stuck."

Eva folded her arms. "It isn't gonna happen."

"Anything I can do?" Rita asked. "Distract the Hollywood princess? Convince Harry he's an idiot for not noticing you?"

"I've offered so many times." Nina rolled her eyes.

"We have to get going." Eva picked up her bag. And right then, it struck her that she sounded exactly like her mom. She turned to Rita. "Thank you. But no. It's a hopeless case."

Nina moved to Eva's dark wooden dressing table and inspected her own pretty face in the mirror. "Listen to me, you girls, Harry or no Harry, we are going to a grand old famous hotel in Hollywood. There's a war on. We've just spent five months in the desert. I say we have fun."

"Here's to that, chickies," Rita said.

Eva heaved a sigh and followed them out the door.


"I've heard the Hollywood Roosevelt hotel is somethin' famous for movie-star sightings." Rita's face was all lit up. She stared out the bus window, entranced with her first sight of Hollywood Boulevard on a Saturday night. Women in silks and pearls strolled with fellas in tuxedos. There was certain to be a premiere happening somewhere in town.

"Oh my." Rita pressed her hands against the window ledge. "I couldn't feel more country girl if I tried! I'd trade all the movie stars in the world if Dan were here to enjoy this with us tonight."

"Dan was so handsome he could have been a movie star himself," Eva said. "He was a lovely man. Dan believed in you, and you'll always have that memory of him."

"I was privileged to know him, Eva."

"We all were," Nina said. She leaned her elbows on Eva and Rita's seat from where she sat behind them.

The bus rolled past the Broadway Hollywood Building. "Wealthy women go in there to have coffee while models come out and show the fashion collections. It's where they buy silk stockings and beautiful dresses."

"Ohh . . ." Rita's eyes were bigger than two round saucers. She squeezed Eva's arm and turned back to the window. "My mom and I used to dream of silk stockings."

"Oh, dreaming of silk stockings, I could write a song about that." Nina leaned her head back on the seat.

"A girl has to have a bit of imagination if she is going to get through sometimes." Rita's tone was a little more serious now.

"And at Stromberg Jewelers, the owner has lists of all the film stars' favorite jewels. So if you come in to buy something precious, he can tell you what they like."

"Sounds swell." Rita sighed.

Eva was pleased to see how Rita's cheeks shone for the first time in ages.

The bus pulled up outside the Hollywood Roosevelt hotel. Elegant people strolled through the front entrance. The hotel still spoke of glamour and hinted at the magic of the movies, war or no war.

Eva wandered in behind Rita and Nina. She tried not to stare like a half-crazed person at the vast lobby, dotted with palm trees and discreet chesterfield sofas. This was about as far from their usual social life as anyone could get. Eva clipped in her high heels across the Spanish-mission-style terra-cotta floors. She felt a sprig of nerves at the sight of old-fashioned waiters hovering with silver trays of champagne and canapés. Avenger Field may as well have been on the moon.

Even Rita was silent.

"Eva, Nina!"

Eva startled at the sight of the girl who she'd dreamed might have decided she wasn't in love with Harry after all. But here was Lucille, definitely present and oh so beautiful. Lucille leaned in to give Eva and Nina kisses scented with perfume that no girl from Burbank could hope to afford.

"Well, who is this?" Lucille's gaze swept over Rita. "What an elegant girl you are!" Lucille placed her hands on her hips, accentuated by her cinch-waisted cherry-red silk dress. Then she ran her soft white fingers over her charming curled blond hair. She smiled a slow smile, her dark-red lips curving upward to show off a set of delicate white teeth. Eva fought the urge to hide her own calloused, unmanicured hands behind her back. There was no way Lucille would be seen dead out in Texas, flying airplanes in a size-forty-four zoot suit.

"Lucille, this is Rita." Eva introduced the two girls.

Lucille reached out a hand and took Rita's with the softest of touches.

"My, you have beautiful hands," Rita said. "You'll have to excuse us roughed-up flygirls. Not sure that you've been doing much hard work with those fingers of late."

"Well, my, you are correct," Lucille said. "We have *people* for doing work around here."

Rita's eyes narrowed into slits. "Well then, you are a very fortunate girl."

"You're interested in airplanes, like Eva and Nina here?" Lucille kept hold of Rita's hand.

"I've just graduated as a WASP," Rita said, sounding proud of her achievements.

Eva took a glance at Lucille under her eyelashes. Lucille looked to be of a mind to sum Rita up.

Nina took advantage of the momentary lull in the conversation, a conversation that could erupt. "We'll go in and let you greet your guests, Lucille."

"Straight through to the door on the left of the lobby." Lucille almost sang the words. "The party's in the ballroom."

Eva swallowed and felt herself redden. "Is . . ." A bolt of panic flared through her. Why couldn't she just play it cool?

"Harry here yet?" Nina finished.

"Why, of course!" Lucille said, sweet as a key lime pie. "He's talking to Daddy," she said. "They're like a pair of perfectly cut gloves these days."

"Thank you." Eva swore she sounded like she was muttering to a schoolteacher.

"It's so *good* to see you, Eva and Nina," Lucille said. "Now, if you'll excuse me . . ." She turned to greet some new guests.

Eva heaved out a sigh. They made their way toward the ballroom. Gentlemen sat at the bar smoking cigars, handsome in their black-and-white suits and bow ties.

"Shoot," Rita mumbled. "She's a piece of work."

"And a determined one," Nina said.

They entered through the gracious double doors to the party. A plaque said that this grand room had been the venue for the first-ever Oscars ceremony in 1929. Round tables were scattered like lily pads on a pond for Lucille's party. Men in dinner suits lounged at tables decorated with ivy and red berries, and women in sparkling dresses, jewels glittering at their throats, floated under the mistletoe-bedecked chandeliers. A waiter appeared as if by magic and offered the girls champagne.

Eva scanned the room, a searchlight looking for its favorite target, until that old, familiar thwack in her chest hit her with a mighty thump. Even at the few feet that separated her from him, she could see that Harry's cheeks were tanned a deep brown. He was talking to a handsome, blond middle-aged man in a suit so well cut that it looked to have been fresh from a tailor on Rodeo Drive.

She half made a step toward Harry, only to feel Rita clutching at her fingers, pulling her back. Three young men had appeared out of the ether and were trying to engage Nina and Rita in chitchat. Eva turned to them.

"Well," one of them said. He was tall with white-blond hair and bright-blue eyes in a tanned face, which held a slightly surprised expression, like he'd just eaten a way-too-hot chili dog. "Where have you girls sprung from?"

He reached out to take Rita's hand, the glint of his cuff link flickering under the lights. He raised Rita's hand to his lips and dropped a gentle kiss on her fingers.

"Go say hello to Harry," Nina said. "We can deal with these boys."

The blond man leaned forward and murmured something in Rita's ear, and Rita threw back her head and laughed.

"Not yet," Eva murmured. "He's all tied up with some guy over there, who I'm guessing is Lucille's rich dad."

"Well, aren't you guys quite the dishes?" Rita placed her empty champagne glass back on a passing waiter's silver tray.

The blond young man—Rita's blond young man, Eva couldn't help thinking—took a freshly filled glass, and Rita accepted it, taking a sip with another tinkling laugh.

Eva sipped at her own untouched champagne, but the bubbles caught in the back of her throat.

"I'm Felix, and this is Jack." Rita's friend indicated toward the taller of the other two men.

The man he called Jack was mighty handsome. He had striking dark eyes and lashes . . . if only her heart were not as heavy as an unexploded bomb over seeing Lucille being so smug about Harry and her dad, she'd chat with him quite happily.

Perhaps, she should just do that . . .

"And this is Richard," Felix went on.

The other man, Richard, nodded. He was short and stocky, and his expression was astute.

"We are charmed to meet you," Rita said. "I'm Rita, and these are my friends Eva and Nina."

Nina held out a hand to Richard, as if she were some society hostess, not a girl who'd just got off a four-million-hour-long train ride from the middle of the Texan plains. "Pleased to meet you, boys. Are you back from the war?"

There was a silence. Awkwardness flared among the men, and Felix coughed, pulling his hand up to cover his throat.

"Well, perhaps you're all actors, then. I'm determined to meet an actor before I leave here tonight." Rita smiled around at them.

"Well saved," Richard murmured next to Eva.

"I'm an actor," the dark and handsome one, Jack, said. He took a sip of champagne, but Eva noticed a flicker of annoyance cross his chiseled features, like a ripple on a perfect wave.

Out of the corner of her eye, she spotted Lucille floating across the room to stand with Harry. Eva's stomach tumbled at the sight of him running his hand across Lucille's bare back and lingering on the curve of her waist.

Frowning, Eva switched back to Jack. He really was quite the dish. As good-looking as poor Dan had been. And his gaze was on her now.

She smiled, gave him a little encouragement. After all, they'd talked about Rita's philosophies.

"Eva wasn't it?" Jack's voice was smooth and deep. "Beautiful," he added.

Eva's eyes widened, and she turned to look up at him, sharp. "Oh, I see," she said, knowing she sounded coy. "Well, aren't you the charmer?"

"Where you from, Eva?" He smiled down at her, those chocolate eyes crinkling with warmth.

"Oh, Los Angeles." She waved her hand in the general direction of the ballroom doors. "You know."

"Telling me you live downtown?"

Eva took a sip of her champagne and giggled. "Maybe I am. What if I do, Jack?"

He raised a brow. "Hmm."

She squared up a bit, lifting her chin. "I live in the valley. I'm from Burbank."

"How intriguing."

"Intriguing?"

"Refreshing."

"Why?"

He leaned a little closer. "Eva, I get to meet a lot of girls through my line of work. Let's say I don't take them seriously and they don't take life seriously."

"Why do you think I would be any different?"

"There's something sweet in your expression. You look unsophisticated. You have no idea how rare that is to a guy like me."

"Oh, so you see me as some unsophisticated girl from the country?" Eva drew out the last syllables with the best Southern accent she could.

He laughed. "Never. Tell me, how does a girl like you know Lucille?"

"I don't."

He raised a brow. "Oh, so you've just walked right in tonight."

"Well, I do know her. But I'm friends with her boyfriend, Harry, you see."

"Ah." He shot a glance toward Harry, who was intent, still with Lucille's dad.

"So where do you come from, Jack?" She enunciated his name with crystal-clear clarity, as if she'd had elocution lessons all her life.

"Hancock Park."

Of course he did. It was old-money LA. But not an actors' suburb. "And you act as a career?"

"Trying to." He rubbed his hand across his perfect chin. "Are you interested in acting, Eva?" The expression on his face changed, as if he were willing her to answer in one way.

"Heck no." She went with the truth.

"Thank goodness for that." He stepped a little closer, leaned into her ear. The band had struck up a tune, and they had to shout a little louder to be heard. "What do you do, Eva? You look wonderful in that dress, by the way . . ."

"I just graduated as a female pilot—I'm a Women Airforce Service Pilot."

Jack's features sharpened. "You've trained, have you?"

"I have."

"I'm impressed."

Eva felt a smile play around her lips. "Thank you."

"I can't serve for medical reasons. I was rejected. All I'm useful for is acting." He raised his glass and shrugged. But the grin he gave her was heaven sent. He sure was good-looking. Eva thought it didn't take much imagination to see him as a matinee idol.

"Well then, now, more than ever, we need pictures to cheer us up, Jack." She smiled right back at him.

"I'm glad you see it that way. And I'm glad that you are contributing. At least one of us is."

Eva's smile changed swiftly to a frown.

"Eva," he said. "I hope this isn't too forward, but . . ."

Across the room, Harry dropped a kiss on Lucille's cheek. She beamed up at him, reaching to pat something imaginary from the stiff white collar of his shirt. The intimate gesture caused Eva to start.

"You're distracted." Jack's voice startled her even more.

She turned back to him, feeling a rush to her cheeks. She shouldn't have come here tonight. It was madness. Why would she want to hurt herself over again? "No, I—"

"Are you only on leave for a little while, Eva?"

"I am."

"Well then. This might seem mighty forward of me, and I don't want to monopolize you tonight, although, believe me, I am tempted . . ."

Harry led Lucille to the dance floor.

Eva swayed with sudden fatigue.

Lucille wrapped her arms around Harry's neck, and he led her in a slow dance.

"Would you consider letting me take you out for dinner tomorrow night? To Musso and Frank? It's a local place, and one my family's frequented for years. It's just a little way up along Hollywood Boulevard. If you're on leave, you might like a treat. It's a special restaurant."

"Dinner?"

Lucille pulled away from Harry. He was off at the side of the room again, talking with another man.

Before Eva could respond to Jack, Lucille was right next to her, breathless, her red dress a whirl. Lucille kissed Jack, Richard, and Felix in turn.

"Oh, I see you girls have met my favorite boys. I've known them forever. We went to school together, you see. Jack here was the high school dish. And I do *love* his family." Lucille laughed, turning to Eva and patting her on her bare arm. "I'm like Siamese twins with his mom. But Jack would never look at me for one minute. I was devastated by his rejection when I was twelve. Never got over it."

"No way." Jack put on a grin that would set the whole of Hollywood on fire. "Harry is perfect for you: he has looks, intelligence, and he's hardworking. Can't say I'm any of those things. You should stick with him."

Lucille trilled like a peacock. She even did a little twirl. Her red dress spun out around her body, showing off her toned legs to perfection. "Harry is a darling. But don't be ridiculous, Jack. You are quite the catch. Any girl would be lucky to have you on her arm. Including me."

Jack chuckled softly.

Lucille twirled off again to another group of guests.

Harry still hadn't seen Eva. She chewed on her lip. This was ridiculous. She'd have to go over and talk to him soon.

"Yes, then? Come out to dinner with me tomorrow night?" Jack's voice bit into her thoughts.

Eva couldn't tear her eyes away from Harry.

Jack took her hand and touched her fingers with a featherlight kiss. "Eight o'clock? How does that sound?"

Harry patted the man he was talking to on the back. The man looked like a wealthy, pompous man.

"Why not?" she said to Jack. "Sure, yes, why not."

"I can't wait." His hand was on her back. "I'll get your address before we leave tonight."

Finally, she managed to catch Harry's eye across the room. He startled. Harry excused himself from his conversation. He made his way to her. "Eva!" She saw him mouth her name.

"And Nina, forgive me," he said, appearing in a swish of expensive aftershave and an equally sophisticated dinner suit. His eyes ran over Jack standing next to Eva. He frowned and leaned down to kiss Nina first.

"Hello there," he said, holding out his hand to shake Jack's. Harry pumped Jack's hand a little harder than might be polite. "Harry Butler."

"Jack Forrest."

Harry turned to Eva, his eyes running over her face. "Dance with me, Evie," he said, his voice dropping. "I'm sorry, I wasn't certain if you'd be here tonight. Lucille wasn't sure whether you'd come after all your traveling. I wasn't looking out for you, and we need to catch up."

Suddenly, all the irritation she'd felt toward Lucille evaporated. Here was Harry. It was the war. He'd survived his first few weeks so far. "I'd love to dance with you, Harry," she said. "Excuse me a moment." She smiled up at Jack.

The thing about war was that you couldn't take any of your friends' lives for granted. Just seeing him here, all her irritation evaporated.

Jack nodded in a formal way. "Of course."

Harry took Eva's hand and led her toward the dance floor. The band played Glenn Miller's "That Old Black Magic," and Harry drew her into his arms. He placed a hand around her waist. "Tell me what's on your mind, kiddo. I can see something's getting to you. And it's wonderful to see you, by the way."

Eva rested her chin on his shoulder. "My head's been full to bursting these past months," she said. "You know, about training."

"I do. And I'm certain you'll make a brilliant pilot. I would fly with you any day."

"Thank you." Eva's insides couldn't help but dance too.

"Any news about where you'll be stationed?"

"Camp Davis."

Harry held her at arm's length. "Evie. I've heard stories about that base—"

"Honey?" Lucille was at their side in a flurry of red dress and expensive perfume. "I'm right here and I want to dance."

A warm expression passed across Harry's face, tender and indulgent and kind. "Of course."

He let go of Eva, and she stood there while Lucille laced her fingers through his own. "Kiddo?"

*Kiddo.* Eva stayed still.

"I want to talk. I have a few things I want to say to you about Camp Davis."

"I guess we could do that." Eva managed to smile.

He drifted off, and Eva searched the room for Nina. Suddenly, she wanted to go home.

Anywhere was better than here.

# CHAPTER
# TWENTY-ONE

THE COMMITTEE: But if you really needed to access the WASP records, Mrs. Forrest, why didn't you make any attempt to contact the government after the war was over in order to access them?

EVA FORREST: With all due respect, sir, after the war, we were all having babies. We didn't talk about the war and were encouraged to move on. To forget. We didn't talk about it. Eventually, we almost did forget. When the government said we were done, my husband said the same thing.

"Going out for dinner with a gentleman from Hancock Park?" Eva's mom eyed her over her cup of chicory coffee the next morning in the kitchen. "Who did you say this man was?"

"I didn't." Eva pushed her mussed-up curls back from around her face. She'd slept twelve hours after the party, and her mom was already on her midmorning pick-me-up, not breakfast. Warmth flushed Eva's cheeks, and with all the unaccustomed sleep in her own bed, she felt like she'd been hit over the head with a baseball bat. "Jack Forrest went to school with Harry's girlfriend, Lucille. Jack is an actor in Hollywood."

"Tell me more." Her mom smiled, almost in a conspiratorial manner.

"He's just a boy." Eva pulled a piece of bread out of the bread bin. She opened the toaster and placed the slice inside it, staying right next to the counter to keep a close eye on it. The toaster was temperamental, bread was precious, and if she burned her toast, her mother would not allow her to take another slice.

"He's a gentleman, by the sounds of it, dear."

"Maybe he is."

"It's not every day that your daughter gets asked out by a gentleman from Hancock Park. We need to show him that you appreciate his gesture." A whimsical look came into her mom's eyes.

Eva opened the toaster door and turned the bread. "Well, he's nice and all, but it's hardly anything to get excited about."

"You see, a man like that could help us. All of us. Dear, your father will never make enough for us to retire with ease."

The bread was crisp on one side and soft and white on the other. Eva turned to her mom. "What, Mom? You and Dad are in financial trouble?"

Her mom lit the gas stove and filled the kettle from the kitchen tap, the sound of the water trickling through the kitchen. "Oh, you know how it is, dear. Your father has never earned much at the factory."

"I'm hoping you're exaggerating? I thought we talked about this. Dad said Lockheed was still flat out with war orders and that he was fine."

"Oh, come on. All I'm saying is that if you married well, it would take the worry out of it. I'd always know you would help us, should we need you to do so, dear."

"Mom! Please—"

Her mom held up a hand. "Eva, I would also love to see you with a house full of kids. You know, if I'd had more than just you and Meg, my heart wouldn't be so broken at the thought of you leaving us again."

Eva's toast was cooked on both sides. She started to butter it. Ever since Meg's death, things seemed so much harder. Every conversation with her mom seemed loaded with regret. And her mom had put everything into her daughters. She and Meg used to sigh together about what it would be like for their mom, coping with an empty nest . . .

Her mother reached for one of the high cupboards in her kitchen, the one where she kept her best china set. She pulled out a rose-patterned teacup and saucer and a teapot, adding a scoop of tea leaves to the hot water from the stove.

"Now, Evie. If you are going to start dating, that gives me something to get excited about. It's a focus, dear. I would suggest that if you like this boy, then there would be nothing wrong with seeing what the possibilities might be with him back here." Her mother let the tea brew only for a few seconds, just like Eva liked it, and she handed Eva the steaming tea in the cup she reserved only for company.

Eva pulled a chair out and sat down with a thump. Cautiously, she eyed the elegant cup. Had her mother already pigeonholed her as a married woman in Hancock Park?

"Possibilities? I don't think there are any, at this stage."

"How about we go shopping this afternoon and buy you a dress? Rose and Semple. How does that sound?"

"Honestly?" She took a reviving bite of her toast.

"You bet your buttons."

"Mom! You are unstoppable."

"You need to show this Jack Forrest that you are worthy of his people. You're a lovely girl, Eva."

"I can buy my own dress. You forget. I've saved up my income from WASP training, even though it's not much. But I can't afford Rose and

Semple. I'll get something down on Main Street. That'll do just fine. And then, we'll see."

But her mom eyed her like a cat. "I gave in and let you go to WASP training . . ."

Eva put down her toast. "Seriously?"

"You allow me to buy you a dress for this dinner date."

Eva stood in front of the mirror. Her hair was curled and clipped up with a tortoiseshell-and-diamanté clasp that her mother had loaned her. The deep-navy-blue dress her mom had insisted on buying for her dinner date with Jack Forrest was ruched in the bodice, showing off her slim waist, and swirled around her tight calves.

"Oh, hi-de-ho." Harry's voice swung and simmered behind her. But then he stood dead still in the reflection of Eva's mirror and let out a whistle.

Faint traces of his aftershave filtered through the air, and she stared at him standing there, his hair looking damp as if he'd just got out of a shower, with his white shirt and camel-colored trousers neatly pressed, covering his tanned and toned frame.

She raised a hand to one of her cheeks that had suddenly taken on a mind to burn.

"Kiddo, you are gorgeous."

Eva did a Lucille-worthy twirl.

A flicker of amusement caught in his eyes.

"Seriously? I'm still 'kiddo' in this dress?" Her voice came out cracked.

He came into her bedroom and leaned on the dressing table, his expression shifting. "Oh, sorry. *Eva.*" He tilted his head to one side. "Where are you off to?"

He was looking at her in a way he'd never looked at her in his life.

Eva stood opposite him, suddenly shy.

200

"On a date."

"Is he worthy of you?" His tone was more serious than she'd ever heard.

"You know him."

"Do I?" He held her gaze. Something in the room shifted.

"Jack Forrest." The words burned and scratched in her throat. It was as if he held her reflection in his eyes. One word from him, and she swore she'd be in his arms.

"Oh, Evie. But I cherish what we have. What will happen to that?" His words were quiet and still, and they hung between them as if balancing on a swing bridge over an impassable ravine.

"Eva!" her mom called. "Jack's here."

"Go," Harry said. "Go to him."

Eva's chest rose and fell, and if she moved one step, she'd fall over her shiny high heels onto the floor.

"Go out with Jack." His voice was barely audible in the dim, quiet room.

One word, and she'd give her sincere apologies to Jack this minute.

"Evie!" Her mom moved up the hallway to the front door. "Honestly, I don't know what you're up to. I'll have to let Jack in myself." She tutted loudly.

"I'll go out the back way," Harry said, still holding her eye.

He started to retreat.

Eva fought the urge to reach out to him, to grab him and to bury her head in his shoulder and to ask him to slow dance with her, just like she'd seen him do with Lucille.

But before she could open her mouth, Harry was gone.

Eva leaned over, pressing her hand into her familiar dressing table. She heard her mom's voice drifting from the front entrance.

"Mr. Forrest. I'm Eva's mother. I'd invite you in, but I'm sure Eva is keen and ready to go out. *Evie*, dearest?"

Eva closed her eyes. Harry's presence lingered in the air.

"Mr. Forrest is here to pick you up! And he's got a bunch of roses the size of a Christmas tree in his arms. Can hardly see the man for them. Eva?"

Eva gathered her handbag, lifted her chin, plastered a smile on her face, and went to the front door, which was obscured by a huge bunch of red roses, with Jack's handsome face peeking out from behind.

Eva stepped into Musso and Frank as Jack held the door open for her. Elegant tables set with gleaming silver and crystal were dotted around the room, which was lined with leather banquettes and rich wood paneling.

The maître d' appeared. "We have your usual table, Mr. Forrest."

Eva raised a brow.

"How are your parents?" The waiter led them to a secluded booth overlooking Hollywood Boulevard.

"My parents are well. Thank you, Roberto." Jack waited for Eva to slide into the booth before gliding in next to her himself. He ordered champagne for them both and then leaned forward, reaching for Eva's hand, bringing it up to his lips, and brushing her fingertips.

"In the back room of this place, Hemingway used to mix his own mint julep."

Eva was glad for the distraction of Jack's conversation after the heady interlude with Harry. She'd alternated between frustration and longing all the way here in Jack's father's glamorous car. Jack had told her how his dad had managed to keep the car during wartime because he was a busy doctor.

"I love Hemingway." She smiled at him. It wasn't his fault, her feelings for Harry. She let her hand rest under Jack's on the deeply polished wood.

"Olivia de Havilland and Joan Fontaine come here for birthdays. It's a very important place when it comes to the world of Hollywood."

"Do they?" Eva leaned her chin on her hand.

"Why, indeed, they do. Are you interested in the movies, Eva?"

"Hollywood seems about as far away from Burbank as Avenger Field from New York. But I used to like to go to the pictures with my friends on a Saturday afternoon, before we signed up for the war, that is."

He looked down at the table for a moment and stayed quiet.

"My friend Harry used to watch the newsreels that come on before the movies. So I'd go with him sometimes." Eva felt herself redden.

Something dark passed across Jack's handsome brow, but he stayed quiet.

"The glamour of acting is enchanting." Eva flurried about for words.

"Is it?" he asked.

The waiter brought their bottle of champagne, pouring it with a flourish for them.

"Oh my, look at that!"

"It's not easy sometimes. Being stuck here. Being useless."

"I'm so sorry, Jack."

"But at the moment, I'm filming down at Santa Monica. During wartime, there aren't as many actors left here, so, lucky me, I get parts all the time."

"Well, that's something," she said, her voice soft.

"You have beautiful eyes," he said. "I know it's a cliché, but you do."

"Oh, well, thank you. It's nice to be appreciated." Eva sat up. "You know, would you please excuse me one moment?"

"Of course." Jack slid out, standing with stiff formality while Eva walked across the restaurant to the powder room.

Once she was in there, leaning against the beautiful marble basin, framed in the mirror beside a bunch of roses as big as the ones Jack had brought her, Eva stared at herself and splashed a little water on her forehead.

She pressed her lips together, opened her handbag, and applied a little more lipstick, as if that would help.

The fact was that Harry was in love with Lucille. She could tell by the way Jack looked at Eva that he was keen. And she sensed a vulnerability in him that was endearing somehow. Perhaps, Jack needed someone to tell him that not being in the war was okay.

Eva went back out to the restaurant, threading lightly through the tables with their few glamorous wartime guests. The blackout curtains were closed, and Jack stood up the moment she came back toward their table.

"Thank you for coming out with me tonight, Eva," he said.

Eva slid back into her seat. She leaned forward, her hand touching his on the table. "Jack," she said. "It's a pleasure. Thank you for inviting me. Now tell me more about Hollywood."

She smiled at him while he talked about his work.

Eva's mom burst into Eva's bedroom the following morning. Eva sat up in bed, rubbing her tired eyes. Her mother stood with her arms folded, her head wrapped in the turban she wore while she swept the house.

"Eva?"

"What is it?"

"Harry." Her mom sounded irritated with her, more irritated than usual, if you could put it on a scale. "Harry is here again."

*"Harry?"* Eva was awake in one second flat.

"Were you expecting him?"

"Not at this very time, no." Eva grabbed her dressing gown and threw it on. She stood up by her bed and pulled the blackout blind open. Bright midmorning sunlight flooded the room. "Oh goodness. I am of a mind to sleep for another hundred and twenty-six hours."

Eva's mom tutted and shook her head.

Eva took a step toward the door, but her mom blocked her.

"No lady entertains a gentleman dressed in her sleepwear."

"Mom, just because I've been on a swanky date with Jack doesn't mean I can't go see Harry in my pajamas." Although, her mom had a point. Lucille would look like she'd just stepped out of a fancy Hollywood hairdresser, even if it was six in the morning.

Eva raised a doubtful hand to her head.

Her mother rolled her eyes to the ceiling. "Go take a shower and clean up."

"Don't let him go away." Good thing she had all that practice with sub-three-minute showers back in Texas.

Her mom stayed in the doorway. "Eva. What is going on?"

"I don't know what Harry wants." Eva darted a look to her bedroom door. "Where is he, Mom?"

"Chatting with your father. He's going to help him mend a hole in the fence."

"Oh for goodness' sake, stop them. Dad'll take him over." Eva threw her hands in the air. "Distract him, Mom. Tell him I'm right on my way."

"All right, then." Her mom hovered for a moment. "But, Eva?"

Eva stood still.

"Be careful. Harry's clearly involved with Lucille. I don't know for the life of me why he's coming around here to see you. I'm not sure that you children know what's in your own heads. And you had a lovely dinner with Jack. Remember that, won't you. Mark my words, don't shoot yourself in the foot."

Eva frowned. "Thank you, but honestly, I can make up my own mind."

"I try, Eva. I try." Her mom threw her arms in the air and marched out the door. "Gerald?" she called. "Bring that boy back inside, and we'll give him coffee."

Eva scooted to her wardrobe, choosing and discarding outfits like a girl in a terrible rush. Fifteen minutes later, she was showered and ready in a pair of cutoff blue jeans and a red T-shirt, her curls piled up on her head like she used to wear them when she was twelve.

Harry and her dad sat at the kitchen table. Eva's mom had placed a whole round of her homemade biscuits in front of them, and they were in the middle of talking about Lockheed's planes, poring over diagrams, with brochures spread out in front of them.

"Here she is! Sleeping Beauty." Her dad smiled up at her, looking mildly proud, Eva thought, although she could not imagine why right then.

"Morning, Daddy, Harry."

Harry was leaning heavily on the table. He looked up at her. "Eva, can we go talk somewhere?"

Eva had her hand halfway into the bread bin.

"Let me buy you breakfast." Harry was already standing up. "Mrs. Scott, Mr. Scott, please excuse me for rushing off like this. It was lovely to see you both."

"You always have such charming manners, Harry. It was fine to see you too." Eva's mom smiled at him.

Eva turned to follow Harry out the back door, and her mom caught her eye, mouthing something at her and gesticulating wildly behind Harry's back.

Eva shrugged, and Harry held the door open for her.

The whole walk to the local diner, Eva was flooded with confusion. Dread at what he wanted to talk about mixed with anticipation that would not leave her be.

# CHAPTER
# TWENTY-TWO

THE COMMITTEE: If you honestly are here to support your fellow WASP, why not continue trying to reach out to them in order to resolve your personal matters rather than take up the committee's time?

EVA FORREST: I have tried and tried to reach out to my old WASP friends, but for thirty years, I have not heard back. This felt like some sort of punishment I did not deserve. And for women like me, who were affected detrimentally by accidents, having access to health care and records is vital so that we can thoroughly understand what happened and be given help to move on. Without access to the official WASP records, I cannot have the answers I need. I also believe there must be other, fellow ex-WASP who need health care and may not be able to afford it.

Harry held open the glass door to the local diner. The sight of the old black-and-white-tiled floor and the waitresses flitting around in pink dresses with caps brought back memories of their high school days. How often had she sat here with Dylan, Nina, and Harry before war had complicated all their lives?

Eva went to a booth in the window overlooking the high school they'd all gone to. A waitress poured them coffee from a glass pot.

The girl blushed when Harry flashed her a smile.

He turned to Eva once the waitress was out of earshot. "Evie. There is something I have to tell you. I hope that you will . . . understand."

Eva stared at him, feeling her eyes widening into two huge pools. "What is it?" She was going to have to sit through whatever this was.

"The navy is planning a strike."

"I see. Harry, I know you're the best pilot there is, but please, be careful."

Harry stared at her hand. Something crossed his face for a moment, and after a second, he reached out all of a sudden, covering her hand with his own.

"Recently, a small task force struck the Japanese naval base at Rabaul and damaged several warships. A far larger strike is being planned, with four other carriers involved."

Eva looked up at him, meeting his eyes.

"Rabaul is the major enemy base in the South Pacific."

"When do you leave?" She pushed her cup of coffee away.

He lowered his voice. "First thing in the morning, Evie. I'll be gone before you wake up."

"Harry—"

"Would you folks like something more than coffee? Doughnuts, a biscuit?" The waitress was back, making eyes at Harry.

"I can't eat," Eva said.

"I'll have a doughnut," Harry said. "And I'll get some toast and a milkshake for my friend here. You still like chocolate malt, right? Texas didn't change that? I told your mom I'd buy you breakfast, sweetheart, and a promise is something I always stick to." He dropped his voice, and Eva's heart froze. He still held her hand. "Evie, our skipper is a veteran dive-bomber who flew at Midway and Santa Cruz."

"What's your squadron's record like?"

He frowned for a moment. "Don't tell Lucille what I'm about to say. But you're a pilot, you understand."

She turned back to him, incredulous. "Not when it comes to you." She punched the words out. "Not when it comes to you."

"Here we are!" The waitress placed their order down on the table. "Doughnuts were made fresh this morning."

"Thank you," Harry said. His eyes held on to Eva's and did not move. "Evie," he went on when the waitress had gone. "Don't."

"I'm not just a pilot," she said, her words threading like a silk ribbon between them, flying so close, yet not touching them.

"I know that. But you understand."

And then she nodded. In a different way from Jack, Harry needed her to be strong. He needed her to be what Lucille could not be, and he needed her to understand.

"Tell me what you want to say."

"The SB2Cs had major structural problems. In one incident, the whole tail section separated from the plane."

Eva stared at her toast.

"I'm telling you this because I don't want you to worry. I want you to know that while we are flying them, we've taken steps. We have a new maintenance officer to serve with our crew. He has intimate knowledge of the planes." He looked at her, searching her face, as if trying to seek her reassurance.

She sensed his own thread of fear. "I have faith in you, Harry," she said. She wanted to say what he wanted to hear. "You know how to check a plane. And you are the best pilot I know."

"The fact is, I'm much more worried about you," he said.

"No," she breathed. "Don't be ridiculous."

He leaned forward. "We need to talk about Camp Davis. Your mechanics there will have to deal with multiple aircraft, and the shortages of properly trained mechanics are rife on the bases, with so many men at war."

"We're all dealing with the circumstances of war."

"No. Insist on checking the planes yourself before you fly. Please. Both of you. You and Nina."

"Harry, the fact is, I'm going to be towing targets around while men shoot at me. That's a little different from what you're doing—"

"There's something else I want to talk to you about. Something I need to say."

She knew she'd be ill if she ate a bite of food.

He frowned. "I decided to make a commitment to Lucille. I've asked her to marry me, and she's said yes. I . . ." His voice drifted off.

Eva was silent. The implications of what he'd just said took slow shape in her mind like a Texan storm brewing in a thunderous sky.

"I couldn't go away after this break and leave her not knowing where she stood. And her father—"

"You sound like you're justifying it. You don't need to explain your reasons to me. Honestly, this is your decision."

"I'm not doing that. Evie, I . . ."

Eva wanted to walk out of there and scream in the street. She wanted Harry to ask her to marry him; she wanted Harry to tell her she was the one; she wanted Harry to share his deepest fears and his dreams with her, for every night of whatever was left of their lives. And she wanted to wipe out this entire conversation with one of her mom's feather dusters as if it had never, ever happened after all.

"Well then," she said. "Congratulations." Annoyingly, heartbreakingly, tears wanted to pool in her eyes. She turned away from him, swiping at her cheeks.

"We'll announce it officially when I return. I didn't want you to hear it from . . ."

Lucille? Neither of them uttered her name.

"I know how girls can be."

Eva did not look at him. "I should get going. I'm sorry, I'm unable to eat right now. I'll pay for my own breakfast."

He stood up.

She stood up too, and handed him a dollar.

His mouth worked. "No, Evie." He shook his head at the money.

Until suddenly, he grabbed her into an awkward, lopsided embrace. Closing her eyes, scrunching them tight so that the tears that threatened to wreck her composure did not tumble out, she leaned against his shoulder, breathing in the smell of him. Then she pulled away as fast as she'd fallen into him.

She looked down. She was still clutching his hand.

Silently, Eva pulled his fist to her heart. Then let go of it, letting it fall down between them.

Somehow, this goodbye felt like the last note in what had been a beautiful song.

"Be safe. Take care of yourself."

His eyes searched her face.

"Just survive this darned war," she said. "Because I can't deal with—"

"Please, sweetheart—"

She turned, raising a hand behind her.

"Evie?" That upward lilt in her name rent her heart in two, but she could not turn right back around and tell him everything she felt, knew, dreamed.

He loved Lucille. Enough to marry her.

Head down, she hurtled out the door.

Eva spent that night staring at her ceiling. She may have blinked, but she did not doze. When dawn broke, cracks of yellow light slipping around her blackout curtains, she pulled them open and allowed the sunlight to stream through the glass.

Harry would have gone to the Pacific by now.

Eva got up and showered and dressed.

Nina was taking Rita to the beaches, to Santa Monica, to show her around. Eva finally wound up at her dressing table. She ran a brush through her hair.

"Eva?" her mom called. "Jack is at the door."

Eva stilled her brush.

Jack.

She gathered herself and made her slow journey down the hallway.

Her mom came to meet her halfway. Eva's dad was out on the porch, chatting with Jack.

Eva's mom stopped her, reaching out to hold her by the arm. "Eva, Jack Forrest is fond of you. And he's rich."

Eva closed her eyes. "Not now, Mom. Harry's gone to war."

Her mom's sigh was audible. "I know, dear. I understand."

Eva's hands shook by her sides.

"But, dearest, you could do far worse than marry a man from Hancock Park. Don't let your feelings for Harry cloud your common sense."

"Mom." Eva's voice was dangerous and low. "Believe me, marriage is the last thing I want to talk about today." She went past her mom to the front door.

"Hello there." Jack was leaning against the veranda post in blue jeans and a white shirt.

"Hey." Eva hovered at the doorway, suddenly self-conscious when her dad turned around and smiled at her. He looked as excited as her mom was to see Jack.

Her heart plummeted to the red sandals she wore.

"Feel like a drive?" he said. "I'm not filming today."

The sound of an airplane buzzed overhead.

Jack rattled his car keys, his face breaking into a wide smile. "How does that sound? Unless you got different plans. I was a bit presumptuous coming over here without calling, but I couldn't resist the temptation, and it's a beautiful, sunny day."

"I'll let you two make plans." Eva's dad moved toward the front door. On his way past Eva, he patted her on the head as if she were a little girl.

Eva stood on the threshold, her arms wrapped around her body.

"I thought you might like a spin in my car?"

After a few moments, she shrugged. "Sure, Jack. I'm happy to come for a drive with you."

"Well then, what're we waiting for?" he said.

A few locals turned and stared at Eva and Jack cruising through Burbank in his dad's cream Chevrolet. Was his family experiencing the war at all?

Jack's hand rested on the steering wheel. "It's delightful, Eva, that you are happy and willing to jump in my car when I call, but I'm bursting to tell you where we're going."

Eva kept her gaze focused on the road. What would happen when Harry got to Rabaul? Perhaps the ship's chaplain would say a prayer for them all. And he'd stand there with his squadron, straight and tall, before they all roared off into the sky. "Where did you want to go, Jack?"

He tapped the steering wheel with his fingers. "Honey," he said. "I hope you don't mind me calling you that?"

Eva turned to look out the window. "I guess that's okay. In a friendly sense."

"I'd like to take you out to my set. I'm the villain in this particular picture." He sounded a little shy. "I'd rather be the handsome hero, of course, but a credit's a credit."

"I suppose it is better being the villain than nothing . . ." When Harry took off, would he wind his way through thunderclouds or a clear blue sky? What height would they have to go to before the dog-fight started? Twelve thousand feet? That would be about right. Below, Japanese aircraft carriers would hover in the misty sea. And there'd be enemy planes. Dogfights.

"I'm not needed on set today. Otherwise, I would have picked you up at five a.m. I thought that would be too presumptuous." He laughed.

Eva had been awake at five.

Jack's smooth Chevrolet made its steady way toward the beaches. They pulled up near the pier, and Eva threw open the car door. She ran ahead of him, across the lawn, toward the shore. The sea lay in front of her, blue and steady and beautiful.

Soon Jack was right next to her. He reached out and stroked her cheek. "Eva, you are the most beautiful woman I've ever seen. You know that?"

"Don't be crazy," she said in the sunshine, focusing on the azure sea. "You're surrounded by movie stars."

"Movie stars are not the girls I want to date."

Eva kept her gaze on the water. Destroyers, cruisers, warships would all be below Harry. He'd dive down to, say, eight hundred feet, then open the bomb bays, throttle back, and nose over. The sounds of the exploding bombs would ricochet through the air, renting the quiet, rocking and concussing Harry's plane. Then fire in the ocean and the sky full of Japanese Mitsubishis and Zekes, all come to protect their own.

How many Helldivers would be lost? Under attack by the Japanese Zekes. All she could do was pray that his fellow pilots would come by if he needed them. She knew that in her dreams at night, she'd be willing him to get out of there at max speed.

Eva stilled her thoughts. She knew too much.

The sea sat so still in front of her eyes.

Swiftly, Jack wrapped his arms around her waist from behind her. She startled a little.

"You are nothing like the others, Eva," he said.

Eva pictured Lucille and her sophisticated Hancock Park allure. "But what about the girls you meet through your family in Hancock Park?"

At that, he threw his handsome head backward. "You have no idea what those girls are like. I, you see, am a catch to them. If they are not plotting to marry me, their mothers are."

"I'm sure they are. You would hate that."

His eyes twinkled, and he took both her hands in his. "There is not one ounce of the mercenary in you."

She sighed at the thought of her mom.

"The fact that you are off flying in the war. Well," he said, "that salves my conscience. I'd like to be with someone who can do something, unlike me." He pulled her closer, into his arms.

"Oh, I'm only doing what little I can."

"I'm proud of you, Eva. Immensely so. And a little in awe." He took her hand again, leading her toward the beach. "I don't feel like our dates are like another audition to you. I'd love a girlfriend who is there for me, not one who wants to act and is self-absorbed."

"Oh." Eva screwed up her nose at this strange compliment.

The movie set was near the pier. A makeshift fence had been set up all around. Black tarpaulin was wrapped around it, and a security guard stood at the gate. Warner Brothers vans sat like black beetles in the parking lot.

They made their way down toward the set, and Eva was silent, Jack pointing things out. When a young woman emerged from the gate, she came straight toward Jack and waved.

"Jack, honey," she said. "We might need you after all. Director wants to do another take of yesterday's scene."

"Oh, honestly?" Jack said. "Celeste, meet Eva. Eva, Celeste Varini."

The red-haired girl held out an immaculate hand. "I'm charmed, Eva. Jack, where did you meet such a lovely girl?"

"The Hollywood Roosevelt. At some ball. I was the lucky one to discover her."

Celeste's eyes lit up. "You're new in the industry?"

Eva shook her head. "Not at all, although I think my mom would like it if I was."

"Really, honey?" Jack put on a drawl. "You're tellin' me she's not proud of her girl flying airplanes in the war?"

"You fly airplanes?" Celeste's smile was accessorized with a dimple.

"I do. I'm about to go to an air force camp in North Carolina and tow targets for our aviation trainees."

Celeste let out a high-pitched whistle. "Well, Jack. That'll be full of flyboys. You'd best watch your back, with a girl as pretty as this."

"Oh, I know. Don't worry, Celeste. I'm staking my claim right now."

Eva looked down at the sand.

"Say, Eva, would you like to come have a look at the set?" Celeste asked. She held out an arm to Eva.

"Why not?" Eva said. Everything seemed unreal, as if things were moving and she were standing still.

"Celeste knows her way around," Jack said. "I'll go and check the production schedules and meet you afterward, Eva. I want to get you safely home."

Celeste wound her arm through Eva's. "Come on. Let me show you how Jack's world works."

Eva bit her lip, and she wrenched her thoughts and her gaze away from places and dreams that were beyond the horizon, to what was right here in front of her eyes.

# CHAPTER
# TWENTY-THREE

THE COMMITTEE: Mrs. Forrest, are you here in the hope of attaining some sort of reparation for women who suffered during the war?

EVA FORREST: That is not my intent. I am recalling the facts as they happened. But I do believe that I have shared with you all the ways in which I think we suffered what we would now see as discrimination, although we did not have that label back then. We just accepted our second-class status in society, and we did all the things men did without the benefits that men doing the same jobs were given. After the war, we accepted the way we were treated and went back to our traditional roles—many of us did, anyway. Now, with the air force announcing they are training women as pilots for the first time, we are here to show you that we flew too.

Eva stood on the platform in the train station, her kit bag at her feet. Jack swept through the early-morning fog wearing a navy greatcoat, heading straight for her. Rita pretended to swoon. Jack bent down and kissed Eva, and a woman passing by stopped in her tracks and gaped.

"I'll think about you in the wilds of North Carolina," he murmured.

"And you can think of me while I'm flying in circles over Dismal Swamp." Eva stepped back.

Jack held her at arm's length, and then he reached forward to tuck a tendril of Eva's hair behind her ear. "You go fly for the both of us, Eva."

"We're all doing our part as best we can," she said.

Rita and Nina were stealing glances at them. The grin on Rita's face was as easy to read as an instrument panel on a baby PT-19A.

"Goodbye, Jack," Eva said. "It's been a gas meeting you."

"Write to me?" he said, his hand lingering in hers.

"Sure," she said. "I will."

The train let out a great whistle. Her mother and father stepped forward from where they stood with Nina's mom.

"You stay safe in those airplanes." Eva found herself buried in her mom's favorite rose-scented perfume. "And remember, if ever you want out, you can come right back home," her mom said.

"Goodbye, Mom."

Jack pressed something into Eva's hand.

"Go on, honey," he said. "Open this on the train."

She threw a confused glance up at him. Because what she held in her hand was a small velvet box. She stared at the little thing.

But he swept off into the Los Angeles mist—his coat swinging behind.

"Evie?" Her dad stepped out from beside her mom, an endearing expression on his gentle face. "We'll miss you something terrible, dearest."

Eva threw her arms around his neck. "Bye, Dad."

"Promise me you won't take any risks." His words were muffled yet crystal clear.

"Of course I won't. I promise." Eva clung to him for an instant. "Dad, you know Meg would want me to go."

And for one moment, her dad held her gaze. And then he nodded. "She would."

The train whistled again. Eva turned to the tall blond girl standing slightly apart from the rest of them.

"Goodbye, Rita." Eva held her hands out to her friend. "You take care. And write us. Write as often as you like."

"And you listen to me, Miss Evie. Promise me you'll enjoy that handsome beau of yours. He sure is something else." Rita held her at arm's length. "And as for your Harry, well, I only hope he wakes up one day."

Eva felt the little box in her pocket and bit her lip. "Not sure Jack's my beau, and Harry is definitely not mine, but thank you for your thoughts. Rita, stay safe in those bombers, and whatever experiments they are doing, I know you'll shine."

"Oh, come here, you two." Rita grabbed Nina as well and pulled her and Eva into a three-girl hug.

Eva tucked her arm into Nina's and blew her parents a final good-bye kiss. She felt a tug of sadness while Rita headed off to her platform, her knapsack swinging by her side.


The corridor was crowded with troops, and the stench of cigarette smoke was laced with sweat. Eva followed Nina, but every carriage they looked into was full.

"We should have boarded earlier." Nina's voice was worn and thin. "You're going to have to watch you don't get too distracted with that man. He's moving awful fast, Evie."

Eva stopped for a moment. She opened her mouth to reply, but people were shuffling and pushing behind her. She had to keep moving.

Ahead of her, Nina ducked her head into every compartment before continuing on.

"Here's one with space." Nina looked up at Eva, her face pale. "Two flyboys in here, that okay?"

"Sure." She frowned at Nina's washed-out countenance. "You okay?"

Nina wiped a hand across her brow. "It's just the packing, and you know . . . saying goodbye to my mom."

They hauled their kit bags up onto the overhead nets, and Nina sank down in her seat.

"You got water, Nina?"

Nina held up a canteen. She sat back in her seat and closed her eyes.

The platform was crowded with families—women and children reaching up to the train windows for a final touch of their loved ones' hands. Eva glanced out the window and saw her dad in the crowd, standing tall above most folks. She pulled the window half-open.

"Dad! Bye!" She waved at him, frantic, suddenly wanting him to see.

He caught her eye, and his face split into a grin. He blew her a little kiss. Before long, the train kicked into motion, and they were off along the tracks. Eva sat down in her seat with a thump, the unfamiliar clatter of wheels on rails was something they were going to have to get used to again. Eva felt the stirrings of excitement, that soon she'd be in a plane, feeling no weight underneath her, only air.

Nina settled deeper into the seat. "I'm going to have a nap. You know, you're right, Evie. I'm something awful beat."

"Well, there'll be plenty of time for napping on this journey." Eva sat back, grateful for their seat. Groups of personnel still lined the corridors, eyeing their compartment and moving along.

Before five minutes were up, Nina was fast asleep.

Nina's breathing was steady, and the men in the compartment talked quietly about aircraft carriers. Eva pulled out the little box that

221

Jack had given her from the pocket of her cardigan and gasped at the sight of the exquisite bracelet of diamonds and silver that lay nestled inside.

"Someone's got a rich beau." The red-headed boy about Eva's age sitting opposite her leaned forward and let out a low whistle.

Eva raised her head with a start.

"It's gorgeous," he said, his eyes crinkling into a smile. "For a gorgeous woman, if you don't mind me saying."

"If we have to share this carriage, I think we should keep the conversation proper." But Eva did smile back at him.

"Sorry if I've caused offense," he said, his eyes still bold.

"I'm not offended." Eva held his gaze.

The second man in the compartment reached out a hand. "I'm Walter, and this clown here is my friend Samuel. We're headed for Camp Davis. Where are you girls going?"

Eva sighed. "I'm Eva, and this here is my friend Nina. And we're going all the way to North Carolina as well."

"Your friend here looks out for the count." Samuel folded his arms. "I, for one, can never sleep on a train."

"Oh, well, I hope you like reading and card games, 'cause you have an awful long time to stay awake," Eva said.

"You girls WASP?" Walter eyed Eva.

"We are. Going to tow targets for you, I presume, while you shoot at us from the ground."

"Well, it's nice to know who we'll be shooting." Samuel sent her a mischievous grin. "Tell me, I'm intrigued to know why a beautiful girl like you would want to don a flight suit and fly our ugly airplanes?"

"Sam," Walter warned. "Leave her alone."

Eva placed the jewelry box inside her handbag and clipped it tight. "Same reasons you do, I suppose."

Sam chuckled. He held out a packet of cigarettes. "Cigarette, Eva?"

"No, thanks," Eva said.

The men lit up, their cigarette smoke filling the air with a haze. The train swept past the suburbs of LA. Every now and then, Nina's eyes flickered. A line of sweat trickled across her forehead.

Eva reached across and touched her on the arm. "Nina? You like some water?"

But Nina didn't stir.

After they'd wound their way out of LA, the train snaking through the desert, Sam pulled out the table between them and laid down a pack of cards. Eva played a few games of gin rummy with him.

The train rolled along into Arizona, daylight giving way to an endless pool of dark, no lights showing the way, with the blackout on in full force. Eva struggled to find a comfortable resting place for her head. So far, Nina had woken only once, padded to the restroom, and returned. Refusing food, she'd fallen fast asleep again.

Fingers of pink light stretched across the horizon the next morning, the train still moving across arid plains. Eva opened her eyes, only to be hit with shock. Nina's breathing was labored, and the dark circles around her eyes had swelled into purple blooms. Eva reached out to touch her friend's hand. It was hotter than one of her mom's saucepans on the boil.

Eva pulled back in alarm.

"Nina!"

No response.

Eva stood up, her body stiff. She cast about wildly in the cabin for water. Nina's canteen sat next to her, hardly touched. Eva panicked that her friend had slept through the journey, and Eva had failed to make sure Nina had been given a drink.

Gently, she propped Nina's lolling head up against the back of the seat.

"Eva, is there anything I can do to help you there?" Walter's voice was soft in the otherwise quiet train.

"She's feverish."

Eva turned to look up at the slim, neat-looking man. In spite of the fact that they'd been traveling for twenty-four hours, he looked and smelled as clean as he had when they'd boarded the train.

For the next day and a half, Walter held Nina in his arms. He made a makeshift bed for her, pulling the armrests down so that she could lie flat with her head in his lap, and while Samuel and Eva took turns alternating between lying and sitting up on the seats opposite, Walter insisted on sitting up and cradling Nina himself.

"It's what I'd expect anyone in my circumstances to do for my own sister," he said.

Nina's fever worsened as the journey wore on. Sweat poured down her face. She was unable to maintain coherent conversation. Eva bathed Nina's forehead and held her hand, talking to her, although she couldn't hear a thing. She found a group of officers in a carriage and asked for a doctor, but there was not one on the train.

They heaved their way into New Orleans, and Walter eased Nina up to a seated position. They had an hour stop. No time to find a doctor. The train was not going to wait for Nina. The thing was to keep her fluids up until they arrived in North Carolina.

"All I want is an infirmary and to get there," Eva said, the sound of the train against the tracks starting up again.

"I'll get her to the infirmary for you," Walter said.

"I'll be right alongside you, Walter." She was only thankful for this quiet, calm man.

The Deep South gave way to the jungle and swamplands of North Carolina, and Eva was rocked with exhaustion and increasing panic. Nina slipped in and out of consciousness. When she was sleeping, she muttered incoherent words.

Two of the officers checked on her regularly but decided that since she was not worsening, her condition largely remaining the same, the best thing was to get her to the base and to urgent medical care. Eva started counting the hours until they'd transfer to the bus that would take them to Camp Davis. The very least she hoped for was a warm welcome, a hospital bed for Nina, and a hug in Helena's capable arms.

. The cold at Camp Davis was as still and icy as the greeting in Sweetwater had been warm. Eva almost fell off the bus from Jacksonville onto the bleak-looking base. Rows of dank wooden huts sat in the sand. A narrow runway ran alongside.

No one greeted them; no one said hello. Eva pushed aside memories of Helena and Nancy meeting them at Sweetwater. She walked straight past airmen who only looked her up and down.

Walter carried the desperately ill Nina in his arms, and Eva trudged along next to them, carting both her kit bag and Nina's while Samuel took Walter's and his own luggage to their bay.

"Excuse me." Eva stopped a trainee outside one of the long lines of makeshift barracks. "We need directions, if you please, to the infirmary."

"Straight in the direction you're goin'." The boy looked down at Nina, made a face, pulled his cap down, and moved on.

Eva marched on next to Walter.

"I see it," he said. He stepped up his pace. "Thank goodness."

Eva walked on, her head held high. They passed groups of airmen lounging on the front porches of their bays. Eva swore she heard a couple of sneers at the sight of Nina.

The worrisome stories Eva had heard about this place seemed startlingly real right now. She'd heard of women here being derided as powder-puff pilots and how the WASP at Camp Davis had been restricted to flying tiny planes—the two-seater single-engine Piper Cubs. But Jacqueline Cochran would not want them to be intimidated by that. They had not trained for five months to be put off by a place with a bad attitude. They were here to do their job.

Sand blew in isolated flurries around them on the dusty pathway between the barracks. Through the gaps between buildings, Eva caught glimpses of airplanes lined up on the runway, all painted the same color—army green for aircraft that were out of action, planes that were only to be used for gunnery practice.

Eva held open the door to the infirmary. A middle-aged nurse took one look at Nina and asked Eva and Walter to leave Nina and her kitbag in the infirmary until further notice.

"I'll come back tonight to check on her," Walter said. Even through the filter of exhaustion, his brown eyes were sincere.

"Thank you," Eva managed. She was swaying on the spot. Despite the bleakness of this place, surrounded by jungle and blown by the sea winds, she was grateful to be off the train and, through her fatigue, only felt immense relief that Nina would finally get the care she needed.

Walter laid a hand on her shoulder, then turned to go away.

Eva huddled her leather WASP jacket around her. Marching on, she swore she'd find the women's barracks alone after two airmen whistled at her when she was about to approach them for directions.

"Prettiest clay pigeon an ack-ack ever saw," one of them jeered.

Eva held her head high and decided to continue straight ahead.

"Hey, why don't you stop and talk to us? You stuck up like the rest of the women out here?"

Eva marched so that Jacqueline would be proud of her, and in her head, she hummed an old WASP song, "Goin' Back to Where I Come From," while working her way logically around the huge base, with its rows and rows of identical structures, until she found the administration building.

Reaching up to open the wooden door, she went inside. A small office was furnished with two desks and a typewriter. A man in his sixties sat at one desk, and a woman who looked to be in her forties stood up to greet Eva.

"Yes?"

"Eva Scott, reporting for duty, ma'am. I'm a WASP."

"I would assume as much." The woman turned her back to Eva, leaving her standing there.

After ruffling around in a filing cabinet, she pulled out a form, attached it to a clipboard, and handed it to Eva. "Check these details are correct, miss."

Eva scanned the form, forcing herself not to take any of this personally, forcing herself to view this as exactly what it was—a base.

Eva handed the form back. "It's all correct," she said.

The woman looked down at it. "Report for dinner in the mess hall at seventeen thirty. Breakfast at six fifteen. After that, you'll see your flight assignments for the day posted in the women's anteroom. You've been assigned to bay one hundred thirty-one. It's empty."

"Yes, ma'am."

The woman took a step closer to her and sent a glance to the older man. "I would suggest you watch yourself. Pretty girl like you. Stick to your fellow WASP, and check all your planes, every time you go up. There's an awful lot of different types here, if you know what I mean."

"Different characters, you mean?" Surely the woman was not referring to color or background.

Something flinty passed across her face. "Well. You can take my warning as you see fit. I was only trying to help."

"Thank you, ma'am," Eva said.

"That will be all, miss."

Eva heaved her kit bag back up onto her shoulder and went off outside again.

The wind whipped up her hair. Standing still as if she were lost seemed like the worst of a bunch of bad ideas. Eva moved with purpose, glancing at the bay numbers. She'd walk all over base if she had to, until she found her sleeping quarters.

After twenty minutes, she'd passed scores of tents and buildings and located the mess hall and the WASP anteroom. Both were clearly marked. Finally, she stopped outside a forlorn-looking bay marked 131 on the far row of the camp. Beyond her building, a barbed-wire fence ran the length of a thick forest. That must be the edge of Dismal Swamp.

Eva pushed back memories of that night when she'd scaled the fence with poor Dan, Rita, John, and Frances. There sure weren't going to be any parties or late-night forays with all the quicksand out here.

Her heart heavy, Eva pushed open the door to the windswept bay.

A hush hung over the empty, silent room. Even in the late afternoon, it was dark. Dust motes floated in the hazy air. Four beds lined the walls, and the wooden floorboards were bare and dirty. Eva threw her bag on a bed. She needed to find the showers. And once she'd washed up, she'd unpack and prepare for what she'd come here to do. She'd simply get on with the job.

# CHAPTER
# TWENTY-FOUR

THE COMMITTEE: Mrs. Forrest, while you give some stirring reasons for militarization, you are missing the point. The WASP were never intended to be military. They were regarded as an experiment.

EVA FORREST: The families of the thirty-eight women who died for our country may have a different view of that.

On her first morning at base, Eva wrapped her leather flying jacket tight against the freezing wind, trusting her instincts and memory to get her to the infirmary. She had a half hour to visit Nina before breakfast, and she was not leaving her friend unseen before she went up flying on her first day. Her boots trudged up the dirt road, sinking into the soft pools of mud leftover from recent rains. This was nothing compared to what lay beyond the barbed-wire fence, out in the swamps. Finally, she came to the base hospital, pushing the door open and entering the small reception area.

Another middle-aged nurse was on duty, her head bent over a form.

"Good morning." Eva wasn't going to wait like she did in the administration building. She was going to spend whatever precious minutes she could with Nina.

The nurse's head popped up as if in surprise at Eva's audacity to speak first. "Yes?"

"Excuse me, ma'am, but I was wondering if there was any news on my friend Nina Rogers."

The woman pulled out a file from a stack on her desk and glanced through its contents. Eva scanned every expression on the nurse's face. Eva dragged her hand up to wipe her tired forehead. She'd not slept much in the cold bay, huddled up with her one gray blanket, worrying about Nina and Harry. She desperately wanted news of his mission.

"You are a friend of hers?" The nurse didn't raise her head.

"Yes. I'm her . . . best friend." Eva bit her lip after pronouncing the childish words. But she was. And she needed to show these people that Nina had family out here, that she wasn't alone. "I've known her since I was five years old. Please. If you can give me any news of her, I'd be more than appreciative."

The nurse looked up then, scanning Eva's face from under her white cap. "Miss Rogers has a fever. A bad one, mind you. At this stage, we think it is influenza, and we hope she will recover from the fever in a few days' time. I don't think there's anything to worry about."

Eva felt her shoulders collapse with relief. "Thank you. I am extremely grateful to hear those words."

The woman had her back to her. "You may go on in," she said without turning around. "Please sign the visitor log on the desk, and you can stay fifteen minutes."

Eva moved past the reception area into the first long room, lined with cast-iron beds. A couple of men lay sleeping, and another trainee lay with his leg raised in a white plaster cast.

She spotted Nina's familiar shape in the farthest bed, her brown hair splayed around her on the white pillow. Eva came closer and saw her pale face against the white pillowcase, her eyelids flickering slightly as she slept. She sat down and held Nina's hand awhile.

"Evie!"

Eva turned to see a familiar figure coming her way.

"Oh, thank goodness. Helena." Eva reached forward, holding the tall girl in her arms.

"They told me at the administration building that Nina was in the infirmary, and I thought you'd be fast asleep and exhausted, so I came here." Helena frowned down at the little shape in the bed. She took off her gloves and hat, laying them on her kit bag and standing there in her unbuttoned camel-colored coat. "What on this earth went wrong?"

"A fever caused by influenza." Eva had hardly uttered the words when a silhouette appeared at the door. "Oh!"

Walter marched down toward the bed. "Nurse told me I'm visiting the most popular patient in the ward." He spoke in a whisper and held out a hand to introduce himself to Helena.

"Walter Rivers. I'm pleased to meet you. I take it you're Helena?"

Helena gave him her most gorgeous smile. She turned to Eva, eyebrows raised.

"It was a long four-day journey," Eva said. "Walter helped look after Nina the whole way here."

"Oh . . ."

Eva suddenly realized she had a lot to tell Helena. She smiled at her as Walter leaned down over Nina, running his hand over her forehead.

"There now, she's looking calmer than she was on the train. I do think she is cooler too. What do you think, Eva?"

Eva laid a hand on Nina's forehead. "She's not as hot as she was during the journey. But still, I so want to sit with her today. I can't bear going up flying and leaving her alone here."

"Ah, she wouldn't want you to be not doin' your duty, Eva," Walter said. He stood up straight, adjusting his training uniform. "Let's hope she makes a super quick recovery. Once she does, we'll all do something together. Go out."

Eva glanced out the window. Gray dawn was unfolding on the base. The facades of the wooden buildings stared back at them in the bleak landscape. "I hope we can find something fun to do out here."

"Oh, don't you worry about that," Walter said. "When we get some time off, we'll make sure to enjoy it. Now. Since my friend Nina here is sleeping again, I'm going off to breakfast. I've never known a girl to sleep so much!" He winked at Eva and Helena and went out.

"Oh my, who is he?" Helena whispered.

"I'll tell you at breakfast. We need to be in the mess hall by six fifteen."

"Well, in that case, they'll have to put up with my kit bag as well as me," Helena said. "After my journey, I'm not missing breakfast, and if they're putting me up in an airplane this morning, I'm not going unless I've had a good cup of coffee, imitation or otherwise."

Eva linked her arm through Helena's.

"And how was your leave?" Helena said.

They made their way to the front entrance. "So much to tell you," Eva said.


At breakfast, Eva scanned the newspapers for any news of Harry's squadron. There was nothing in any of the papers yet, and she only wished she could go off base into one of the local towns to sit in a theater and watch the three newsreels a day that informed folks of what was going on in the war. She'd written to Harry early this morning, using the V-mail system, knowing that her letters would be read in Washington and then sent on a microfiche reel to the front. All she needed was one word from him to say he was fine, but could she expect such a thing after their last encounter, and would he keep writing to her now that he was formally engaged to Lucille?

After Helena had changed into flight gear and put her things in their bay, Eva took her friend to the WASP anteroom. Now that she'd eaten and Helena was here, the base seemed a little less bleak.

"Here goes," Helena said. She climbed up the steps to the anteroom, laughing at the comical sign on the front door: **WASP NEST! DRONES KEEP OUT OR SUFFER THE WRATH OF THE QUEEN!** "We might be on a base with one hundred thousand boys, but we girls are going to make sure we have our space."

"Oh, we certainly are," Eva said.

She pushed open the door. A girl she hadn't met in the mess hall yet was examining the flight schedule that was pinned up on the wall above the tables dotted around for the WASP to wait.

"Wendy Turnbull." The girl held out a hand and shook Eva's and Helena's when they introduced themselves. "Welcome to Dismal Swamp."

"Oh, I already have a thing about that swamp," Helena said, shrugging off her jacket and putting it on the back of a chair. "Any plane would sink into it and never be seen again."

"Happened to the last two girls in your bay," Wendy said.

Eva stopped in alarm. The atmosphere in their bay had been icy when she first got there, but the WASP before them had gone down in the swamp?

"Rumor has it that someone had messed with their engines, and that caused them to go down," Wendy went on. She glanced at the other girls sitting around at tables and waiting for their turns to go up. "We're not allowed to complain, though, although Jackie knows, and I think she will do something. I hope."

"You are kidding me." Eva sighed.

Helena remained silent by her side.

"You need to carry out your own inspections out here, girls. It's nothing like as friendly as Sweetwater," Wendy said.

"I've gathered," Eva said.

"The mechanics are hopelessly understocked with parts. We girls just have to be aware of it, and we have to look out for each other." Wendy patted Helena on the back. "But we all don't want to let Jacqueline down. We don't complain ourselves, or we'll likely prove our commanding officers right and be sent off base."

"Great," Helena said. "Thank you for bringing us up to date, Wendy."

A group of five other WASP came bursting in from the cold, cheeks pink, chatting animatedly. Eva and Helena introduced themselves.

Helena looked up at the schedule. "At least there is plenty of flying here, Evie, even if it is in circles."

"As long as we're in the air," Eva said. "And as for any foul play when it comes to our aircraft, I know my way around a plane, and so does Nina. Helena, if you ever want either of us to check your aircraft with you, then just call on us."

One of the girls, a short, dark-haired girl who reminded Eva of Bea, went to the door. "Time for us to go out," she said.

"Come on Helena and Eva," Wendy said. She held the door open for the group. "Looking forward to introducing you to our commanding officer." She snickered.

Eva picked up her helmet and goggles and followed the other girls out the door.

A short man with iron-gray hair under his military cap was out on the tarmac, head up, shoulders back, and wearing only a short-sleeved shirt in spite of the wintry morning. Behind him, the forest glistened green. A burst of sunlight threw a streak of light through the clouds.

Eva took in the sorry roundup of drab demilitarized planes that they'd be flying. The commanding officer glared at the small group of WASP who stood up straight on the edge of the airfield. The girls formed a line in front of him. Eva wanted to huddle in her leather flying jacket. She'd gotten too used to her beloved Californian sun again.

"I understand we have two new pilots." The officer scanned the group. "Identify yourselves on the double."

Eva stepped forward. "Eva Scott, sir," she said.

"Helena Cartwright, sir."

"Back in line."

Eva kept her eyes ahead.

"I'll keep this brief. For those of you who've heard this before, it won't do you any harm to hear it again." The tone of his voice was harsh.

"I'm your commanding officer. My name is Officer Grant. Now, here are some things that I tell every woman who's come to work at this military base. You are no different."

Eva heard Wendy's sigh.

"The men's squadrons don't need any help."

Eva felt her lips tighten.

"They appreciate being released for better jobs elsewhere. The only positive thing about having you here is that some of the WASP end up with beaux, and our men need a bit of comfort. Any women in that position will find themselves with consistent flying partners. I suppose you women have your uses, even in war."

On her other side, Eva sensed Helena tensing up like a tight coil.

"No time for messing around with hair curlers or lipsticks. I emphasize that particularly when it comes to you two new girls, given your obvious . . . attractions."

Eva forced herself to focus on the slight movements in the distant trees.

"Your flight suits are ridiculous," he said. "You look like a pack of clowns."

Eva resisted the urge to show him exactly how she'd tried to adapt her suit with safety pins and stitches, to show him just how ridiculous it was being forced to do her job day after day in such a thing.

"Today, you'll be testing artillery level tracking. You'll be flying back and forth and round and round for several hours at a time over the camp. You'll be in the little L-5s. Just remember, these planes are dispensable, and you are dispensable."

A couple of male ground crew came to stand with Officer Grant.

"You'll be towing sleeves behind your plane while our trainees shoot live ammunition at you. Occasionally, you'll see smoke and explosions on the sides of your aircraft. That will be the men hitting ahead of target. Some of you will come down with bullet holes in your planes. The men are playing for real. It's a dirty assignment, and we need you to keep your wits up there. Your ground crew are here. Off you go."

The women stepped out of line. Eva walked alongside Helena to the ground crew. Her friend let out a long sigh.

"Heaven help us," Wendy said. "Welcome to Camp Davis, girls."

The following night, Eva lay alone in the cold bay. After two days of flying for six hours straight while the trainees tracked them with artillery, followed by ground school and further training, training that would go on for another six weeks, the strain of the long journey and the new routine was finally catching up with her. She had a half hour before dinner, and she lay back in the bare room, her eyes falling closed.

A few minutes later, the sound of Helena coming in woke her. "I've been into Wilmington. Evie, I've been to the stores."

Eva sat up, rubbing her tired eyes.

"I've bought some real nice decorations for Nina, for when she gets well."

Helena pulled out a couple of lace doilies.

Eva felt herself soften. "That's kind of you," she said. "I know how much Nina will appreciate those little touches. If we can make her feel at all at home here, that will only help her recovery."

Helena busied about, placing a small decorative piece of lace on Nina's chest of drawers. She lifted a photograph of Nina's mom, Jean, in her backyard at Burbank that Eva had placed there for her and put it gently atop the doily.

Next, she pulled a colorful throw rug out of her bag and lay it next to Nina's standard GI cot.

"That is gorgeous. Look at all the colors in it. Someone's put a lot of effort into that."

"It looks a whole bunch better to me, Evie." Helena straightened her pile of textbooks on weather, flying, and artillery and placed a couple of her own modern novels next to Nina's bed. "At least we're allowed a few more decorative touches out here than we were at Sweetwater."

"Thank you, Helena." Eva caught the girl's eye. "You know, I'm real glad you're here. I'm glad there's three of us out here at Camp Davis."

The next morning, Eva went to the infirmary extra early. Last night, she'd hardly slept. The nurse told her that Nina was stabilizing, and Eva found herself wakeful and wanting to see Nina sitting up for herself. During the night, she'd been plagued with memories of Meg's illness and the up-and-down reports they'd received from medical staff. In the end, she'd gotten out of bed, sneaked into the bathroom, and written a letter home to her mom and dad, telling them news of Camp Davis, reassuring them that everything was fine with her. Then, her writing paper pressed to the wall and the door shut so as not to wake Helena, she'd written to Harry's parents, asking them if they could relay any news of his safety, knowing they could not mention locations or battles, troop movements, or direct locations in the mail. She just needed to hear he was alive.

So far, in the constant scramble for news of loved ones, brothers, beaux, and cousins at war, she'd only found a few scant details of his squadron's battle at Rabaul in the newspapers on base, that on takeoff, one bomber pilot had gone into the water, and that there had been a prolonged dogfight in the air, but that ultimately, a Japanese destroyer had been hit and burned while two other warships were also hit. Eva had to force herself not to let her imagination or her worries run wild. The government had started releasing more graphic details of the war, and images that had been strictly censored of boys being hurt were now more readily released. Eva had no idea what she would do if she actually saw anything on a screen or in a paper, an image of someone she knew or loved.

Now she pushed the infirmary door open. She bustled into the nurses' reception area, and from the ward, the sounds of Nina's giggles sent Eva's spirits soaring into the air.

"Good morning, Eva." The nurse looked up from her station. She'd become accustomed to Eva, Helena, and Walter these past few days. "Our patient is well on the way to a full recovery."

Eva wanted to punch the air with her fist. "Thank you, ma'am, you have no idea how relieved that makes me feel. I was so hoping to hear that things had improved even more this morning."

"Go on in so you're not late for breakfast." The nurse gave her a genuine smile.

Eva stepped into the now-familiar long room.

"Well, hello there." Walter was right by Nina's side. He turned to face Eva, his brown eyes lighting up into a smile. "We're on the mend. Much better."

"Evie!" Nina held out both her arms, and Eva leaned in to give her friend a gentle hug. Her freckled face was still pale, but her eyes had lost that awful dull edge.

"I've managed a whole egg this morning. Powdered, but at this point, who cares about that?" Nina patted the bed next to her. "Come on, sit with me here. I can't wait to get up in the sky again. I'm bursting to get back in the cockpit. You showing the flyboys here how things are done?"

Eva slid up on the bed next to Nina. "The commanding officer is something brutal, and the boys are too busy shooting at us to see our skills in the air, so all we can do is fly in circles, or in straight lines up and down the beach. There's no chance to show off. The noise from the gunfire is something else, but we girls are staying focused. The good thing is there is plenty of flying. Soon, you will be up there too."

"Well, sounds like you need a break. I hear you and Helena haven't been out for an evening yet. So Walter here and I have been makin' some plans." Nina's gaiety was infectious.

"That didn't take you long. I like your attitude, Walter!" Eva threw Walter a glance.

The smile on his face was a little bashful. "Well, you see, I'd like to take you three girls to the officers' club. Maybe tomorrow evening. The nurse thinks Nina could do well with a little cheering up. Thought we'd come pick her up in a jeep and drive her there. It's only a ten-minute walk from here around the camp, but I'm not riskin' getting her out in that cold."

"Sounds fun." Eva couldn't help nudging Nina with her elbow. "Doesn't it, Nina?"

"The nurse tells me Walter here's been visiting me daily." Nina shot a glance at him under her eyelashes.

"He held you all the way from Arizona to North Carolina," Eva said. She was better. Eva couldn't contain the smile that wanted to burst out.

There was a silence.

Walter coughed and looked down at his boots.

Eva fought the urge to giggle.

"Well, I'd best be getting to breakfast." Eva eased herself off the bed. As she did so, she squeezed Nina's hand. And her friend squeezed her hand right back.

Two hours later, Officer Grant addressed the WASP on the freezing tarmac. "Today, you'll be taking out A-24s, our two-seater dive-bombers, to ten thousand feet. That's as high as you can go without oxygen. A conk out, a loss of speed, or a sudden up- or downdraft and you'll be in the soup. Our gunners are testing radar tracking. You girls need to keep your wits about you. You hear me?"

"Yes, sir," the girls answered.

"I don't want to lose any of you." He turned around for a moment, standing with his legs wide apart. When he turned back, his expression was more thoughtful. "It's a dangerous mission."

He indicated for them to go to their aircraft.

"You know the rumors?" Helena kept pace next to Eva. "Exposure to radar can make you sterile."

Eva kept her pace steady next to Helena. "I don't fancy complaining to Officer Grant about that." She stopped at her assigned A-24. Her plane's tires had been replaced with standard truck tires. She sighed and made her way around the plane.

"Helena, you call on me if you have any concerns at all about your aircraft."

"Oh, perfect. Thanks, Evie. I'll holler if I need you." Helena glanced at Eva's sorry aircraft and marched on to her plane.

Eva began carrying out a thorough preflight inspection, Harry's words of warning echoing in her mind. She'd be spending four hours in this dark-green-painted baby, so she checked everything three times before climbing up on the wing, slipping into the cockpit, and sliding the canopy closed.

Once she was in the air with the other WASP, Eva flew back and forth up the coast, enjoying the peace without artillery being shot at her and trying not to think of what her mother would say at her being exposed to radar, which could stop her having children of her own.

Below her, the Atlantic stretched gorgeous and blue. White caps dotted the sea where two years ago, U-boats had wreaked havoc, causing the locals in North Carolina to wake up to the sounds of regular explosions. Cargo ships traveling up the coast were attacked mercilessly. The navy had managed to put a stop to it, and now the battle against U-boats was concentrated up the northern part of the coast.

When her time was up, Eva took a smooth landing, but after four hours up there, the seat had become hard and her back ached. She stretched, arching her back once she was on the ground. After lunch, they'd report straight to ground school.

Once her flying for the day was done, Eva stood in front of her mirror, ready to go to the officers' club, her blue party dress looking ridiculous in these conditions, in this climate, not to mention the mud. But it was the only decent outfit she'd packed in her kit bag. She wasn't going to go to the officers' club in a flight suit or her Santiago blues.

"You look gorgeous." Helena applied a little lipstick next to her. "I for one am looking forward to a night out." She pulled her woolen coat over her dark-green evening dress.

Eva shrugged on her own coat. The sound of a jeep pulling up outside their bay ricocheted into the cold night. She followed Helena out to the porch. Nina waved at them from the front cabin of a rough old jeep, wrapped up in her red coat, a beret sitting atop her long hair. Walter hopped out, his uniform immaculate, brass buttons gleaming in the dark.

"You girls want a ride?" he said.

"I didn't realize you were an officer, Walter," Helena said.

"Fully trained at Randolph Field, Texas, before the war." Walter stood upright as if to attention. "I've always been interested in taking on extra antiaircraft training, so I put my hand up to come here."

"Well, we are most grateful that you did." Helena stepped into the back seat of the jeep. Walter held the door open for Eva too.

He closed the door with a snap, and Nina turned around to them, her face more animated than it had been for weeks. If Eva were honest, she'd say that a pink flush shone from her cheeks.

"Well, hello there, Miss Nina," Helena said.

"Hey, honey," Eva said.

"Hey there, Evie, Helena." She winked at them.

Walter walked around the side of the jeep.

"Someone's got a gorgeous beau." Helena dropped her voice.

"Isn't he somethin' else?" Nina said.

Walter was back in the jeep, and in two seconds, he had the engine fired up. "Couldn't let you ladies trudge through the mud in your party shoes."

They rattled along the dirt road up to the officers' mess, passing groups of flyboys who whistled at the sight of the dressed-up girls through the windows of the jeep.

"And that's another reason why I didn't want you walking." Walter eased the jeep around a corner to another, identical row of wooden buildings.

"I just say hello right back to them and don't let them intimidate me." Eva had become used to the attentions of the men.

"Oh, I'd be furious," Nina said. "Tell them to go stick it and stare at something else."

Walter threw back his head and laughed.

Eva grinned and held on to the rattling doors of the jeep. Her little friend was back.

Walter pulled up outside a large building. The sounds of classical music drifted out through the blackout curtains. A couple of potted plants sat at either side of the entrance, and the sign on the door warned anyone who wasn't an officer to keep out.

"Welcome to the officers' club, girls." He was out again, holding the doors open and helping Nina.

Eva gave Nina a hand on her other side up the short steps that led to the building's porch, shocked now at the slight figure of the usually healthy girl she'd grown up with. Nina's coat hung from her frame, and she halted at the top of the steps, her breathing fast.

"Well done, Nina," Eva said.

"Never thought I'd be so grateful for the ability to climb a flight of stairs." Nina's face broke into a faint replica of that grin that Eva loved.

Inside, twenty or thirty people stood about on a floral carpet in a smoke-filled, hazy room. A long mahogany table was set out with glasses of wine and platters of food. Eva stood for a moment, adjusting to the pretense of more opulent surroundings than she'd become used to since arriving here. Officers chatted with a few other WASP and women who might have been locals from Wilmington and the towns surrounding the base, but mostly, the room was filled with the conversation of men.

"Let's get a drink, girls." Walter led them to the table, offering them all glasses of wine.

"Nina, what would you like?" he asked, his tone attentive.

Eva found herself watching how he interacted with Nina. Nina looked up at him, her face reddening into a slight blush. "Orange juice, please. I'm not ready to delve into alcohol yet."

Walter handed her a juice and led them all to join a group of other young officers.

"Well, well." An officer who looked to be in his late twenties brightened at the sight of Eva, Helena, and Nina. "What do we have here?"

"Three WASP," Walter said. "Who have been up at ten thousand feet today."

The officer whistled. "I heard they were sending you girls up testing altitudes," he said. "Tell me, how are you finding life out here at Camp Davis?"

"Oh, we're just fine," Helena said. "Getting used to the mud and all!"

"Indeed. Bryce Collins." The man reached out a hand to Helena. She shook it, and he leaned forward to chat with her.

Walter was leaning in close to Nina in turn, whispering and making her laugh. She threw back her head and chortled when he clearly told her some anecdote about one of the other officers, an older, serious-looking man who walked past.

Jack's diamond bracelet glimmered on Eva's wrist under the lights.

"Evie!" Helena was right next to her again. "What in the name of heaven is that?" She picked up the bracelet and peered at it.

"Oh, it was a gift." She turned it over doubtfully.

Helena's officer friend Bryce leaned forward to look at Eva's wrist. "Well, that's a gift from a man who's serious. You got yourself a boyfriend, I'd say, miss."

Helena tucked her arm into Eva's and took a few steps away. "Excuse me one moment, Officer," she said to Bryce.

He ducked his head in acknowledgment. "Secret ladies' business. I know when to keep well out of things."

Helena drew Eva to a quiet corner spot. "Evie. You are keeping something from me?" She picked up Eva's wrist.

Suddenly, Nina was right by them. "Say! Whoa! What's that? I've never laid eyes on so many diamonds on one girl's arm in my life." She narrowed her eyes. "Evie . . ."

Eva chewed on her lip. Nina held Eva's arm up to the light.

"Oh, hadn't you seen that before?" Walter was by Nina's side.

Nina rounded on him. "What? You've seen this before me, Walter?"

"And me!" Helena said.

"And Helena. We three girls are tight," Nina said. She turned to Eva. "There are two boys who could have given you that, Evie, and one of them's engaged and not into grand gestures, so . . ." Her face fell into a scowl. "I guess it's that *other* boy."

Eva's gaze traveled slowly over Nina's face. What was her problem with Jack?

Right then, a few officers started to dance with some of the women. The music changed, and the room exploded with Glenn Miller's "In the

Mood." They'd cleared a space on one side, and people started putting drinks down and working toward the makeshift dance floor.

"Oh, this makes me miss New York," Walter said. "Nina, would you like to dance? Promise I won't exhaust you."

"A little jitterbug never did anyone no harm." Nina grinned up at him, looking as mischievous as she used to when she was twelve.

"Sounds grand, Nina." Walter took her arm and led her to the floor. Helena watched on, her expression wistful.

"Girls? Helena, Eva, would you like to dance?" Bryce said.

"Sure. Come on, Evie." Helena grabbed Eva by the arm. "Let's let off some steam with these swell guys."

Eva dropped her arm with the fancy bracelet by her side. For now, she'd forget her mixed feelings about Jack. She followed her friends instead, forcing herself to push painful memories of her last meeting with Harry aside as they threatened to intrude, weaving her way through the noisy, chatting crowd. In a few moments, they were all jitterbugging together, and that was all that seemed to matter.

Two hours later, Nina was flushed but sitting up on a chair at the edge of the room, her head resting on Walter's shoulder. Eva and Helena chatted with a fine group of officers, whom they'd danced with ever since they hit the floor.

"Eva? Helena?" Walter appeared at Eva's side. "I'm taking Nina back to the infirmary. You girls all want a lift back to the bay?"

"Yes, please, Walter." Eva didn't fancy walking all the way back in the mud. Rain had started pelting the roof, and today, they'd had a fall of sleet.

Once they were snuggled back in the jeep, Helena's head resting on the window in the back seat, she started singing a slow rendition of "Zoot Suits and Parachutes," her voice lilting in the dark. They made their way through the night back to the infirmary, and Nina took up the tune. Soon Eva was singing along with them, a sense of nostalgia for their days training at Avenger Field running between them, even though they seemed so far away.

Walter pulled up outside the infirmary. He sat for a moment, looking straight ahead in the front seat.

Helena let out a yawn. "Gee, I'll be an interesting girl to wake up at six a.m."

"Nina," Walter said, something special and soft in his tone.

Helena flashed Eva a glance.

Eva found her heart beating hard for her dear friend. Walter was a lovely man. Was he about to ask Nina out?

"Nina," Walter went on, sounding almost shy, "I hope you don't mind me askin' you this in front of your friends and all, but thing is, I was wondering if you'd like to go out to the pictures with me. In Wilmington? I've got Wednesday night off."

Helena gave Eva a nudge.

"Walter, I'd love that."

Eva felt a smile spread across her face.

Outside, the rain had softened into a slow-falling mist.

"Well, I'm happy to hear it." Walter climbed out.

"You sleep well, Nina," Eva said.

Nina turned to the girls. "Had to be a silver lining to getting sick." She sent them a wink.

Walter opened the door to help her out of the jeep.

"They're letting me out in two days, Evie," Nina said.

"I can't wait to have you back, honey!"


The last couple of days without Nina seemed to drag, and yet Eva knew that every mission she flew was taking her one step closer to having her friend back with her in the air. She sat in the anteroom, a cup of coffee clasped in her hands after a morning of routine antiaircraft tracking.

The sounds of the guns ricocheting around her plane was something she was becoming used to as a constant ringing in her head.

"Mail drop." Wendy pushed the door open, still wearing her helmet. "Eva, Helena. Letters for you."

Wendy passed five envelopes to Eva. Eva's eyes flew over the handwriting. She sifted them. Her mom, Bea, Rita. Jack. Nothing from Dylan—although she'd heard that he'd taken up a teaching post in Upstate New York, somewhere quiet and as far away from his memories as he could get. From Harry, not a thing. But the fifth letter in her hand was from his mom.

"At last," Helena said. "Mail seems to take an age to get out here."

Wendy pulled out a seat. She held a few letters in her own hands.

The room went quiet, and Eva frowned at the letters. She couldn't help it. She had to read Harry's mom's letter first. She slipped her nail under the seal.

> Dearest Eva,
> First, let me say how delightful it was to hear from you. We are so very proud of you and Nina. I know how much boys like Harry appreciate you.
> When it comes to Harry, I can tell you that he is fine. I know how much, of all people, you and Nina are aware that loose lips sink ships, so you will understand that I will keep my information far briefer than I'd like.
> Harry's written to tell us not to worry, he's fine and he's enjoying steak breakfasts! He said ~~the other boys in his squadron~~ are cheerful company but that they had ~~lost one man recently~~. He couldn't tell us about anything else, not even the weather from overseas, as that would give away too much. That's all he's said.
> I write to him daily in the hope that my letters from home give him comfort. I know Lucille writes to him real

*regular too. Life is mighty quiet here with all of our young folk off at war, but we are doing our bit. We are going on* ~~with our ration cards.~~

    *God bless you, dear,*
    *Louise Butler*

Next, Eva opened Rita's letter.

*Dear Evie, Helena, and Nina,*

    *I'm mighty missing you girls, and you know me, I'm gonna pack as much into this precious letter as I can.* ~~I bet it gets censored~~*, but I'm following the idea of* ~~no weather, no locations, no details that are risky. I hope it gets through those censor people~~*! You know me!*

    *I hope you girls are having a ball and are swinging! I'm thinking it's a gas that I'm seen as more of the Mercedes-Benz or the Cadillac type of girl, rather than the sports-car sort.* ~~A lot of the men are drafted out here. They don't have the love of the flying we girls have, you see. So it's different. Mighty different when it comes to morale than it was when we were together. But the WASP here are great girls. We're holding our own and determined to outfly the boys. You'll see!~~

    ~~Oh darn it, this information won't help any enemy alien. Some of the boys seem a ton more scared than we girls when it comes to flying the bombers. I was flying with a man as my copilot, and he had it in his head that our automatic pilot wasn't working. I told him it was, because I'd checked it, but he wanted to go back to the line. I told him we had to take off, and finally we did. That boy was darned scared, he was.~~

*~~And the other day, a plane exploded right in front~~*
*~~of me before we took off. Again, my copilot wanted to~~*
*~~turn around and stay on the ground. But I insisted we~~*
*~~fly, and the captain of operations ordered us to take off.~~*
*~~I had to deal with the boy moaning and turning green~~*
*~~the whole flight.~~*
*Other than that, not much to report. But it's fun,*
*~~competing with the boys. We're doing Jacqueline Cochran~~*
*~~proud.~~*
*Missing you,*
*Much love,*
*Your friend Rita*

Eva shook her head, smiled, and opened Bea's letter. Would Rita ever get the hang of wartime censorship?

She handed Rita's letter to Helena and read Bea's steady writing.

*Dear Evie, Nina, and Helena,*
*Well, I hope you three are doing fine out there. I'm well.*
*Enjoying my job and getting to see a lot of the ~~countryside~~.*
*Overall, it's good work, and I have no complaints. I've*
*been told to keep my letters positive to avoid ~~the censor~~*
*~~scissors~~, so here goes. ~~I'm gonna do my best to be vague.~~*
*Last week, I went ~~the whole distance across the coun-~~*
*~~try~~. I tell you, I don't miss that weather where we were,*
*because I hit a ~~storm~~. It was so big I couldn't see anything*
*else, and it came on so sudden. ~~I tried to fly over it, but~~*
*~~I couldn't. I tried to fly under it, but I couldn't do that~~*
*~~either. I looked for someplace to land, saw an airfield,~~*
*~~and landed. Five minutes after, another plane came in,~~*
*~~and it was another girl right behind me.~~ I reckon we were*
*scattered all over that night.*

*How are you girls doing?* ~~Is it as bad as they say?~~
~~One thing I am going to warn you about and hope~~
~~this gets through to you, I'll try. We all have to be careful~~
~~with our inspections, doubly so, because one girl found a~~
~~vial of acid chewing holes in her parachute. One girl had~~
~~to come in for an emergency landing because her coolant~~
~~and fuel lines were both in the red, and she found they'd~~
~~been crossed. The engine had seized up, and she landed~~
~~without hydraulics. So we're being extra careful. I hope~~
~~you three do too, because there are some mighty bad things~~
~~happening. Some men still cannot handle women flying~~
~~airplanes. The other girls warned me the moment I got~~
~~here. Of course, some folks are also traitors to the United~~
~~States. So please be careful.~~

*But apart from that, I have this rewarding job to
do, and these great people to work with. I'm living well
and eating well.*

*Well, girls, that's my news. I can't wait to hear from
you all.*

*My love,*

*Bea*

Eva took back Rita's letter from Helena and held up both Rita's
and Bea's letters to the light. They were both heavily cut out by censors,
and she knew they understood the rules. So what was so important that
they'd wanted to write her about?

Jack's letter was written in a sloping hand with expensive fine blue
ink on embossed thick cream paper. He was acting, working on his film,
but his dad was encouraging him to give it up and take on a sensible
job, especially once the war was done. In fact, Jack said, his dad was of
a mind to have him married.

Eva placed Jack's letter down on the table and pushed it away when she read that. Marriage seemed as alien and irrelevant out here as the moon. And yet Harry was engaged, and here was Jack suddenly throwing the word around as if it belonged to the everyday. Finally, she opened the letter from her mom. To her surprise, she felt herself smiling at the mention of mundane things at home.

She stood up, going to the flight schedule that was put up for the rest of the day. She was going up in half an hour, flying in circles over the swamp.

"Sounds like Rita and Bea are doing grand," Helena said.

"It does from what was not cut out," Eva said. She felt a sudden compulsion to get up in the air, even if it was flying around and around with no destination in sight.

# CHAPTER TWENTY-FIVE

THE COMMITTEE: Jacqueline Cochran knew that the WASP program was an experiment, Mrs. Forrest. Which is why she did not push for military recognition.

EVA FORREST: Jacqueline Cochran did put her foot down in the end, after waiting for Congress to militarize us while we all got on with the job. But by the time she did so, the war was winding down. There was not such a great need for pilots. In fact, the army was starting to draft out our trained male military pilots as ground crew because that was the need. But these trained men wanted to fly, so they said that they could be better used doing the ferrying, target towing, and testing jobs that the WASP were doing. After a battle with Jacqueline, some strong support for the male pilots, and derision for Jacqueline Cochran from our newspapers, the loudest voice being Drew Pearson of the *Washington Times-Herald*, Congress deactivated the WASP. And Jacqueline Cochran lost her opportunity to fight for military recognition again. That is why we are here now.

THE COMMITTEE: And so ended the issue of women flying for the military.

EVA FORREST: Only temporarily.

On her first day back flying, Nina tucked into her lunch like a girl who'd not eaten for months. Outside, light rain fell. Eva's zoot suit was wet, her hair was damp, and the air in the hall was humid and close.

"I can't tell you how much I want to get up there and really fly." Nina sipped at her mug of steaming tea. "Take a plane for a spin. Floating around, stuck in that darned drone this morning was worse than being held captive in the Link Trainer. I swear I was sweating ships. Eva, I was hoping you'd make a real mistake so that I could at least get to operate the controls. You have no idea what it was like to have someone else fly your plane while you just sit there like a dummy."

It was clear from the outset that Nina had not appreciated her first assignment, being chosen as a small girl to "fly" one of the air force's bright-red drones while it was controlled by a twin-engine mother ship, a C-78. A trainee beep pilot had flown the C-78 while Nina had sat in the experimental drone. She was allowed to operate the tiny craft only if the trainee pilot messed up her controls in the aircraft, making a mistake or getting into trouble. Officer Grant had been watching Nina's every move.

Eva blinked as they left the mess hall and stepped into the sudden sunlight that saturated the base now that the rain had stopped. The trees in the surrounding jungle swamp glistened.

"Nina?" Eva stopped at the edge of the tarmac. "I wasn't going to suggest this, because I wasn't sure if you were well enough and all, but Officer Grant's allowing us a free flight this afternoon. He wants us to practice our cross-country skills. I'm up for it, but I didn't want to push you. What do you think?"

Helena stretched next to them. "I'm going back to write letters home." She patted Nina on the arm and moved off.

A Curtiss A-25 dive-bomber sat at the ready on the tarmac, ground crew milling around.

Eva stared at the great airplane. The A-25 was a Helldiver. It was fitted with a large bomber bay. Suddenly, she was filled with a yearning for Harry. She hated to think of how they'd parted ways, and he'd not written to her since he left home. There'd been nothing other than the letter from his mom.

It seemed impossible to know what to write to him now.

"Evie, you have no idea how much I'd like to take that airplane up for a long spin. You can't imagine how dull it's been, stuck in that infirmary and not being able to fly."

"Let's go." Eva grabbed Nina's arm, and they made their way to the great aircraft. The ground crew moved around with them, carrying out inspections on the same plane that she was so worried about Harry flying out in the Pacific.

Once they were done, Nina gripped Eva on the arm. "Evie, I've got an idea."

"Love your ideas, always have, always will."

"Why don't we hug the coast, travel north? The Atlantic will be glistening today. Why don't we go all the way up to Kitty Hawk? There's a carrier based up there."

"Kitty Hawk? Near where the Wright brothers made their first flight?"

"The very place. I feel like a bit of adventure given it's my first day up in the air again. It's a celebration, us flying back to one of the places aviation began." Nina's eyes shone. "I feel like it would be grand to go visit the boys on the carrier."

"You want to land this thing on the *carrier*, Nina?"

Nina pulled on her helmet. "I need to do something that makes me feel alive again. I need to celebrate being well."

"You sure you're well enough for that, though?"

"I'm bright eyed and bushy tailed."

Eva went to the wing. "Well, I'll do it with you, then. Not letting you do this on your own."

In unspoken agreement, Nina hopped into the front cockpit. "Gonna sit on the parachute so's I can reach the pedals, Evie."

Eva strapped herself into the back cockpit. "I'm so relieved you're better, honey."

Nina called out the window to the ground crew to request they remove the chocks. Next, she leaned out and called for them to clear the prop. Nina asked for permission to taxi, and Eva could have bottled the thrill in her best friend's voice. Nina taxied the huge airplane out to the holding point, increased the throttle, and asked for permission to take off.

They flew up the coast, over the inlets and the ocean, toward Kitty Hawk, and the whole way there, Nina sang at the top of her voice "Zoot Suits and Parachutes," "Buckle Down, Fifinella," and "I'm a Flying Wreck." Eva joined in, and the world spread below them, the rain giving way to sunshine.

"This is Delta Thirty-Five. Permission to land on the carrier."

Eva saw the telltale way her friend's shoulders shook with laughter.

"From Camp Davis," Nina said, keeping her tone mighty sound.

"Permission granted," the male voice crackled through the radio.

"No other aircraft in sight," she confirmed. She continued downwind, her little hands gripping the control stick on the huge plane.

Nina slowed, lowering the flaps. Eva's eyes scanned the narrow landing opportunity below. But Nina brought the bomber in perfectly. She turned off the engines. Eva slid back the canopy, unbuckled, and climbed out.

The linesmen coming to check them in stopped dead in their tracks.

*"Girls?"* one of them shouted. He turned to his companion, his hands in the air.

"What can we do for you, ladies?" The other one moved toward them, eyes brimming with mirth.

"What a pleasant change from Camp Davis." Nina spoke almost under her breath.

"You bet." Eva adjusted her zoot suit.

The men took in the size of Nina and then stared at the huge bomber.

"Well." The taller of the two boys reached out to shake their hands. "I'll be darned. Welcome to Kitty Hawk!"

"We'd like some fuel, please," Nina said, grinning up at the two boys. "So this is where the navy pilots practice carrier landings."

"For sure." The shorter boy led them to the office.

Nina and Eva signed in, and the officer in charge looked at the girls and then out at the plane and shook his head. "Well, I'll be," he said. "How come you're flying the navy A-24?"

"They are air force versions." Nina stood to her full height and spoke proudly. "Without the folding wings the navy needs."

The officer insisted on taking them on a tour of the base. Afterward, the linesmen took them back to their great lumbering bear of a plane and shouted to Nina and Eva, "Come back again!"

Nina gave them one of her most winning smiles, her flight goggles and helmet over her two swinging braids. "One day, we'll see you again, boys!"

# CHAPTER
# TWENTY-SIX

THE COMMITTEE: Mrs. Forrest, while the committee acknowledges your personal reasons for coming to Washington, and while you give a stirring argument for Mrs. Cochran's hopes that this group of civil women aviators might one day be militarized in 1944, the fact is we do not have any proof that the WASP were a de facto military organization. The fact remains that you were simply civilians called in to help. There was nothing military about it.

EVA FORREST: But what about the fact that I was given a full military discharge by my commanding officer at Camp Davis when I left in '44? Is that not proof that, even then, we were seen as part of the military by our superiors, even if the government did not see us that way?

THE COMMITTEE: You were given a full military discharge? Why would that be, Mrs. Forrest?

EVA FORREST: Because I believe that the officer concerned recognized my contribution and the circumstances under which I left to be equal to that of any man on the base.

The following afternoon, deep-gray clouds bruised with purple framed Officer Grant through the window in the WASP anteroom. Eva drew her leather flying jacket around her. It was going to be freezing flying out there as the afternoon gave way to darkness. The entire WASP cohort sat listening to him. Eva had become hardened to his cast-iron tone.

"You'll be undertaking searchlight missions this evening. The exercise is scheduled to run for four hours from nineteen hundred hours until twenty-three hundred hours. Understood?"

Nina was pale and exhausted next to Eva, and Helena sat forward, frowning in concentration at his words. Eva worried that they'd pushed things too hard flying up to Kitty Hawk the preceding afternoon, and now, Nina had to fly again tonight.

"You'll be flying a racetrack pattern up there. You'll fly at different altitudes while the artillery men follow you with their searchlights. It's essentially instrument flying. If you look outside, with all the searchlights trained on you, you'll lose your vision and won't even be able to read the instruments. Is that clear?"

"Yes, sir." The women spoke in unison.

"Very good. Report back here after dinner."

Nina collapsed on her bed back in the barracks, not even bothering to take off her flying suit. From the shower, the sound of Helena singing a lilting version of "As Time Goes By" rang through the otherwise quiet bay. The wind rattled at the flimsy doors and shook the windowpanes.

A crack of thunder sounded somewhere out at sea. Eva lay down on her bed and closed her eyes.

Helena gently woke her, dressed in her zoot suit, with her goggles and flying helmet tucked under one arm.

"Time to go to the mess hall," she said. "Nina was starving. She's already left."

Eva rubbed her eyes. "I'll follow you."

Helena opened the door, and a shot of freezing air burst into the room. Sand blew in horizontal patterns in the light cast by the hurricane lamp outside the bay.

Eva picked up her goggles and leather jacket and went out into the gathering storm.

# CHAPTER
# TWENTY-SEVEN

THE COMMITTEE: Are you telling the committee that you honestly believe your contribution to the war effort was equal to any man's in the war and so you were worthy of a full military release?

EVA FORREST: We women were not allowed to enter into full combat duties. If we could have, we would have done so. I believe that I stepped up to serve my country just as any man did. I completed full military-style training; I lived in military-style conditions on a military base; I risked my life for my country day after day and lost two sister pilots. Clearly, we were more than civilians, and at least one officer recognized this and gave me a full military release after the accident.

Jagged cracks slashed the cream paint on the ceiling above Eva's head. She lay staring at it, flickers of recognition filtering into place only to dance out again. Her eyes opened and closed, and she did not seem to have any control over them. Not anymore. It was the smell in here that reminded her of something, or someone. Nina. Nina had spent days in here too. And now, Eva was here instead.

Eva tried to raise herself up, but her head pounded, the sweep of searchlights flashed into her vision, and the rattle of an engine was obliterated by the roar of thunder somewhere. She tried to turn, but her side burned and her head pulsed hot and thick. Her cheeks stung, and pain raced up her arm to her neck.

A hazy face loomed in and out of focus. A white coat.

A cool hand rested on her temple.

"Nurse!" A man's voice.

Everything swooned.

"Miss Scott?"

She fought to stay awake but felt her eyes drooping. Blackness engulfed her again.

Bright light this time. An elderly man in an ill-fitting tweed suit with a shock of white hair stood by the bed. A deep crease indented the skin between his rheumy eyes. A nurse hovered beside him. A watch was pinned to her breast.

"Ah," the man said. "I see we are awake, Miss Scott."

Eva tried to open her mouth, but her eyes fell closed again. Heavy. She managed to flicker them open, but only with huge effort.

"There we are," the nurse said. "Are you thirsty?"

The back of Eva's throat was parched. With every ounce of her strength, she tried to nod her head.

"Meperidine, Nurse. Can you swallow something, Miss Scott?"

Eva tried to raise one wrist, but pain soared gloriously up her arm. She shook her head, her eyes a pair of wide pools.

Eva felt the leaden pull of darkness again.

# CHAPTER
# TWENTY-EIGHT

THE COMMITTEE: Mrs. Forrest, do you know of any other WASP who were given military discharge other than yourself?

EVA FORREST: I don't know if any other WASP were given a military discharge, but mine was recognition from the military that the WASP had contributed in a way that did the air force proud.

The gray blanket wrapped around her knees was thick and scratchy. She'd been placed in a wheelchair by a window. The light that came in from outside obliterated the blackness for sporadic, spectacular seconds before she dived back down into her own endless night.

A plane swooped to land outside. A bomber. They'd placed her so she could look out at the runway. Her arm was bandaged up, and her side still burned with pain. The infirmary shook as the huge plane swept by.

"How are we today?" The doctor crouched down next to her, the collar of his blue shirt peeping above his white coat.

She looked up at him, entreating him for news of Helena. "Please, tell me, where are my friends? Where is Helena? Helena Cartwright. We flew together on a searchlight mission, but all I can remember is leaving the bay. Has my friend Nina Rogers been to visit?"

"Miss Scott, why do you think you are here?" His voice seemed to come from nowhere.

Eva winced.

The roar of another plane shot into the room. "No!" She reached out and gripped the doctor's arm, her five fingers wrapping around his feeble old joints. "Stop!"

"Nurse." His voice hardened.

Eva felt the sting of an injection, and her breathing started to come in shallow puffs.


Eva tried to focus on the face in front of her, but the features were blurred and strange. With heroic effort, she forced herself to pry her eyes open. And felt a jolt of shock in her chest. Had she lost her mind?

"I'm going to take you home as soon as I can," he said.

*Jack.*

"Where is Helena? We were going flying together. I want to speak to her, to Nina. Please, for goodness' sake. Will someone tell me what's going on?"

"Shh now," he said. "We'll get you home safely and soon."

The nurse came, her footsteps soft and now familiar in this hellfire of a place, and Eva felt sleep drift over her again.


The sympathy card from her parents sat by her bed, and when she woke up, she stared at her mother's loopy handwriting, her dad's neat script.

Jack sat next to her in a plastic chair; every now and then, he offered to get her a glass of water or fix her some juice. Eva eased herself up a little, pressing her hands into the rough cotton sheets.

"Jack? Please tell me what's going on."

He reached out a hand, looking up at her over the page he was reading. A script, Eva supposed. She'd seen him sitting there next to her before. Usually, she drifted back off to sleep before she could talk to him.

"What is it, honey?"

She searched his face. "How long have you been here?"

He pulled off his black-framed glasses and ran a hand over his chin. Tiny lines spread from the edges of his eyes, which were rimmed red with tiredness. "A couple weeks. I don't know." He turned to her. "How are you feeling today?"

"Helena, Jack. And where is Nina? Is she still here, are they not allowed to visit?"

Jack's eyes darted to the nurses' station. He rolled up his wad of paper and tapped it on the side of the bed.

"Jack?"

"Eva . . ."

"Is Helena okay? I'm having trouble remembering details, Jack. Something is wrong with my memory."

"You need to rest."

She lay back. And then, the nurse.

"Must not be worried, Mr. Forrest. She'll get agitated." The nurse's words seemed familiar somehow.

Sleep was familiar too. She felt her eyes closing, dull.


A few days later, or maybe it was the same afternoon, Jack placed a jar of daffodils on the small table beside her bed, the yellow blooms too bright for her eyes. Outside, the sound of planes droned in the sky.

"Jack, I need to know about Helena. Is she okay? Please."

Jack clasped his hands between his knees and stared down at the floor, his dark brow furrowed.

Eva moved slightly, adjusting her sore side carefully on the pillows.

"And I want to see Nina. If there's some restriction on who is allowed in here, then please tell them Nina is an exception."

Slowly, he raised his head. His eyes collided with hers, and in one split moment, his expression adjusted to blank, to that you-are-in-a-hospital-and-need-to-be-treated-with-the-finest-kid-gloves look that every doctor and every nurse had worn since the moment she started to wake up.

"You came all the way here for me?" she asked. "That is way beyond what I would expect of you."

"It's nothing. There's nowhere I'd rather be than by your side. And, Eva, everything is fine."

Eva hauled herself up in her bed, wincing at the sharp pain that shot up her side at the sudden, unfamiliar move. Jack leaned forward, helping her to get into a more comfortable position. She closed her eyes, focusing, trying to draw the words out.

"Please don't just tell me everything's fine. It worries me. Can you give me more information? Is she out flying with Nina? Was she hurt? Please, Jack. I have to know."

"Nurse?" Jack's voice resonated through the room.

Eva tried to reach for his arm, but he remained focused on the nurse coming straight toward them now.

"Everything all right here, Mr. Forrest?"

Eva stared at the nurse's uncompromising white pressed uniform, at the neat-as-a-pin badge that was stuck to her chest.

"Please." She ground the words out. "Will someone tell me about my friend Helena."

Jack looked up at the nurse, their eyes meeting as if in complicity.

"You need to tell me the truth. Please."

Silence.

Jack sighed and stared back down at his hands, which were clasped between his knees again.

The nurse reached out and leaned her hand against the top of Eva's bed. "Eva, you're having trouble remembering details of your accident. It's important we don't agitate you or upset you further so that your memory starts to restore itself naturally. Until then, we want you to relax. Not worry about things. Just let the memories come back, and try not to think about it. Would you like to read a book?"

"Helena is one of my closest friends. I can't read a book and not know that she is okay."

Jack looked up at her, his expression clouded. "Evie—"

"Not many people call me that, Jack." Harry does. *Oh, Harry.* Eva groaned and leaned back into her pillows. "Sorry," she managed to breathe. "But is she okay?"

"Are we all right here?" The elderly doctor was by her bed. Eva stared at him, useless from where she lay. He was wearing a suit. His cool hand came down, touching her forehead. "Your temperature is good. You're doing well, Eva."

He pulled his hand up, but Eva clasped it, grabbing it before he could move away. "Please. Doctor. I need to know about my friend. My copilot?"

"Eva. Miss Scott." Slowly, he sat down on the side of her bed. Jack went to stare out the window. "How much do you remember of your accident?" the doctor asked.

She shook her head. Outside, the sky stretched, gray and cold and endless. "I don't remember anything after waking up in the bay. We were going out on a searchlight mission. Me and Helena were preparing to fly together. I was tired, and I took a nap before dinner. Then, nothing. It's awful strange and scary for me, Doctor. But my concern is not for me. I want to know what happened to Helena. Is she okay?"

The doctor sighed. "Eva. We've been trying not to upset you, trying to keep you calm in order to assist your memory."

"What?" She tried to ease herself upright.

The doctor's grip on her hand was firm. "But if you think it will help you to know a little more, then, well. I think it would be all right to tell you a little more. But I want you to promise not to dwell on it. That won't help restore your memory, Miss Scott."

The nurse's gaze flickered toward the doctor. "Doctor, I wanted to ask—"

But he held up a hand. "Thank you, Nurse. I'll make the decisions here. Miss Scott, I'm sorry. There was nothing we could do to save your copilot. I don't want you dwelling on it. I want you to try and accept that these things happen. You know, if you were well enough, we would have had you right back up in the sky before now."

Tears formed, pooling behind Eva's eyelids and falling unbidden down her cheeks. She pulled her hand out of the doctor's clasp, bringing it up to her heart. Dear Helena. Her wonderful, beautiful friend. Gone? In a flicker of time?

"I'm sorry. There was no hope, Miss Scott." There was nothing to be done. "I'll leave you here with Mr. Forrest."

Eva heard his whisper to Jack. "Don't talk about it. Distract her. Brooding will make her condition much worse."

"Of course, Doctor." Jack's voice was soft, reassuring.

Did they have no idea what it was like to lose a close and wonderful friend? Suddenly, images of Helena swam into Eva's mind. The way she'd tried so hard to organize them all, the way she'd slowly become closer to Eva and Nina than anyone had ever been since Meg. Now she realized that they'd come to value Helena as a new and vital part of their little trio. It was unthinkable that they would not see her again.

And what she had suffered, Eva had no idea.

"Sir?" she asked, straining to try and reach out to the doctor.

"Miss Scott," he said. "I want you to rest."

"How much did she suffer?" Eva asked, agony tearing at her voice.

"Mr. Forrest. You know what to do." The doctor rested his hand on Jack's shoulder for a moment before looking at Eva. "Miss Scott, I have to go now. You should think about something else, I want you to do that for me, do you understand me? Let your copilot go. The most important thing is to forget, not remember. Otherwise, we will all go mad after the bloodshed is over. Is that clear?"

"But—"

The doctor held up a hand. "I have to go. Just relax, like I am. Read a book, play a game of cards, and talk about something else. This is a war. We are all enduring our own personal trials, Miss Scott. It doesn't do to dwell." He walked away.

"Jack?" She turned huge eyes to him. "I can't believe this. Please. Someone needs to tell me what happened. Did I do anything wrong? What went bad in the flight? Helena and I are . . . were . . . good pilots. We were able pilots, Jack." She choked on the word *were* and brought her hand up to her mouth.

He was next to her, cradling her against his chest. She leaned into him, not caring that her side burned. All she saw were pictures of Helena, of that girl who had held their bay together and looked after them all, putting pillows in beds when she and Rita were out late, protecting them, helping them make up their beds on the very first morning, gradually winning their hearts.

"Where's Nina?" Uncontrollable sobs racked her body. Dry, shaking sobs.

"Honey . . ."

"Where is she? Can you get her here now?"

He whispered into her hair, holding her and stroking the back of her head like her dad used to do when she was small and she'd fallen off the swing or taken a tumble from her bike.

Jack took in a deep, heaving breath. "She's gone, gone to another base for an advanced program testing altitudes with your friend Wendy. It's classified."

"What?" Eva asked.

"I'm taking you home. They told me a few days ago we could get you out of here once you were more lucid. And I think it's best we go very soon. You need to get out of this place. You need to get home."

Eva rested her head back against his shoulder.

Silent, rough weeping shook her, and Jack held her tight.

"I'll look after you," he said. "I want to take care of you, Eva. I'm here."

Three days later, Jack eased her out of the infirmary bed and into her wheelchair. Her side still burned, and her arm was wrapped in a sling. Her head ached and thumped something awful, and the cold, gray base seemed all but dead to her without Helena and Nina here. Jack pushed her toward the infirmary door. The wind howled and whistled against the windowpanes.

"Goodbye, Helena," she whispered.

"Goodbye." The nurse handed Jack a slew of pills. "These will help make the journey home more comfortable and a little easier for you too, Mr. Forrest." The nurse leaned down and spoke in a loud voice. "Mr. Forrest knows exactly what levels of medication to give you. Please listen to him. We have briefed him, and he will take care of your recuperation from now on."

Jack started to wheel her toward the door.

"Thank you, Nurse," he said.

Eva stared straight ahead.

Jack wheeled her out to the small dark-green bus that would take them to the station. She'd signed the discharge papers that had arrived at the infirmary from administration, with Jack sitting next to her and passing her the pen.

She had no choice. She had to leave. Helena had been taken out in a coffin; she was being rolled out in a wheelchair. Jack carried her up the bus steps. The driver stowed the wheelchair at the front of the bus. A few boys on leave watched while Jack settled next to her, handing her a couple of pills and her canteen filled with water. The bus ground into action, and Eva turned to see Camp Davis disappear in a swirl of sand.

It seemed every time she woke up during the train journey, Jack gave her pills that knocked her out again. She took them only because they dulled the terrible pain that hit her every time she woke and realized Helena was gone. The train journey was a blur. At last, they pulled into the station in LA, and through the window, she saw her parents standing on the platform waiting for the train. She stared at them through the window. Her mother clasped her handbag with both hands, and her father stood rigid, tall.

Jack wheeled her out onto the platform.

"Oh, thank *goodness*." Her mother leaned down, grasping Eva's hand, before reaching up to kiss Jack on both cheeks. "Jack, we owe you everything."

"Evie." Her father crouched next to her, holding her. "Welcome home." His voice broke, and he turned away, his hand swiping at his cheeks.

They made their slow way down the platform.

"Jack's been a marvel." Her mother sounded anxious.

Jack pushed her through the station they'd left from with all those hopes and dreams intact.

"I don't know what we would have done without him. I was so grateful that he stepped in." It was as if her mom wanted her to acknowledge Jack.

"He's been wonderful," she said, knowing she sounded half-dead.

Military personnel crowded the platform. As if in a dream, Eva scanned the faces. What about Walter? Images flooded her hazy mind. He would be missing Nina something terrible now that she'd left the base.

Eva tried to open her mouth, but words would not form right now. Instead, the sound of Rita's and Nina's voices flew down the platform in her imagination, just as they had only weeks ago.

"You are so very lucky to have him. What a blessing. He dropped everything and went out to bring you home. It's been a nightmare of worry at this end." Eva's mom sounded insistent. "He has been very good to you, Eva."

But her heart was back in North Carolina; her heart and her thoughts were with Helena. She didn't know when they would ever stop.

Back in Burbank, things seemed to move even faster. The sun beat down on Eva's parents' yellow house, and it was as if the dark, cold winter in North Carolina didn't even exist now that she was back here. Camp Davis may as well have been on another planet. As soon as they were done with the rigmarole of getting Eva out of the car, her mother bustled to the kitchen to put coffee on for them all. Eva stood in the hallway, leaning heavily on Jack. Nothing had changed back at home, but everything had changed for her.

"I made your favorite coconut cake, Jack!" Eva's mom's voice trilled down the hallway.

Eva turned to him. "My mom knows your favorite cake?" Her voice was still weak, but she was able to feel the sense of surprise that her mom's statement brought.

He dropped a kiss on top of her head. "Your mom and I got to know each other while you were away. I was missing you." He leaned forward, absently, stroking a tendril of hair away from her forehead. "Your mom and I have become good friends."

Eva felt something ill stir in her stomach.

"Jack?" her mother called. "Coffee?"

"You go rest." Jack led her to her room, helping her down onto her bed. The sounds of his footsteps were loud and unfamiliar in the hallway, a six-foot man striding through their tiny house.

Out of place. He didn't fit in here with her family.

Her father came into her room, holding her kit bag against his chest. "Dear," he said. "Where would you like me to put this?"

The sounds of Jack and her mother's laughter rang through the house.

Eva's and her dad's eyes caught. "Please put it on the floor," she said. "Dad—"

"Best let them deal with things until you get better. They just get on well, is all." Her dad's voice was quiet. His eyes searched her face. "Evie?"

"Yes, Dad?"

"Dearest, I'm so sorry. I'm sorry for the terrible loss."

Eva leaned back on her pillows. Remembering the time she and Nina had sat here, poring over the *Life* magazine. "I want to see Nina," she said. "I so want to see her."

"I know, dear," her father said. He hovered, seeming awkward. "I'd best let you get some rest."

"It's good to see you, Dad."

"It is a relief to see you back home. I just don't know what we would have done." He turned, leaning with his hand on her desk for a moment, lingering there before shaking his head and leaving her room.

# CHAPTER
# TWENTY-NINE

THE COMMITTEE: You would need to prove that you received a military discharge and were in some way recognized during the war. We presume you do not have the discharge in your possession thirty years later, and even if you did, the document would have to be verified.

EVA FORREST: I brought all my personal WASP records with me. My letter of discharge is in the hotel here in Washington.

THE COMMITTEE: You still have a full military discharge from Camp Davis in your possession?

EVA FORREST: But of course, sir, I do. I would never have thrown it away. Not even in the state I was in on my return home, sir.

Eva sat out on the back lawn of her mom and dad's house a few weeks after she'd arrived home, in one of a pair of striped deck chairs that Jack had bought. Her dad was clipping the hedge, and the sun shone on a perfect, mild early-spring day. Blossoms drifted from the neighbor's tree that overhung the fence.

Her mother came out the back door. "Popping over to the neighbor's house for a moment." She bustled out the side gate.

Her father stopped working briefly and came to crouch down by Eva's side.

"How are you feeling today, my love?"

She turned to him, things still seemed to swim a little. "I put all my WASP things in a little box," she said. "My silver graduation wings, my discharge certificate, my letters of acceptance, and my graduation certificate. I'm not going back to fly for them, Dad, ever, am I?"

Her dad sighed for a moment. "No, dear. No. You're not. In time, your memory should heal, but you need to rest for now."

Eva forced herself to focus on the garden. The doctor had told her to look at what was around and not think too much. "I wish Harry was here. I wish I had one old friend around. You know I love being with you and Mom, it's not that, it's just that things feel so different without Nina and Harry."

Her dad brought a hand up and rested it on her arm. "Harry will take good care of himself, Evie."

Eva drew the knitted patchwork blanket that covered her knees closer.

Her dad was quiet for a moment.

"You honestly okay?" he asked.

"I wonder if I did the wrong thing. Going off like that, thinking I could do something toward the war."

"Evie, don't—"

"But I thought I could do anything. I thought I was strong and invincible, and look what happened. I feel as useless as Dylan now. I miss him too. I guess war makes either fools or heroes of us all."

"Eva, I want you to listen to me. And I want you to stop that talk." He glanced around and lowered his voice. "Tragedy is the price of war. The irony of fighting for our own country is that it makes us all human, it shows us how powerless and vulnerable we can be, no matter what side we are on. Believe me, I lived through the last one. This one is yours. No family will come out of it unaffected. But please, Evie, I have something I want to say."

"Yes, Dad?" She leaned in.

"Whatever they tell you, you did the right thing going to fly for the war. Don't ever forget that. Promise me."

"They?" She tried to sit up, only to be wrenched back down by her sore side. She sighed and slumped into the deck seat.

"Eva, you were and still are a wonderful pilot. And a brave person. You should be proud of what you achieved. Never let anyone tell you anything else."

"But I'm washed out."

"Folks have been discharged for lesser injuries. You were doing the job that the air force wanted you to do, and an awful accident occurred. That is it."

She traced patterns on the blanket with her fingers. "I don't know anything about the accident."

"Eva, best to move on from that. I have something else I want to say."

She looked up at him. His face was framed by the blossoming tree, and the sun beamed through the pink flowers all around him.

"I'd hate to see you lose that spark that we all love. That *Harry* in particular loves." The last word lingered between them, spoken.

"Harry's marrying Lucille, Dad." A breeze picked up in the yard.

"I don't think that will ever change what you share with him. You know about things that run deeper than most, Eva. Just remember, some folks don't realize what's important in this life. Harry does, and you see that in each other. Just wait. It's the most important thing that can run between two people. If it's meant to be, it will happen."

Eva brought her good hand up to rest on the bandage that still encased her arm. "Maybe," she said. "I don't know anymore."

"War can do that too, Evie. Take your faith and make a mockery of it." He reached forward and held her hands. His voice was a whisper. "I believe in you. I believe you are strong and will be able to cope on your own again soon. Your mother and Jack, they mean well, it's not that they don't mean well . . ."

She looked up at him. Words started to form on her lips, but she couldn't make sense of them.

"Eva!" Her mother bustled back through the gate onto the lawn. "It's time for your bath, dear. And Jack is coming to take you out for dinner. He'll be here soon. Oh, come on, you two. Chatting away like a pair of birds. How would we ever get anything done with you two running things? Hmm?"

Her father reached down and dropped a kiss on Eva's forehead. "Remember what I said. Evie, I know you are tired now, but please . . ."

Her mother removed the blanket and helped her out of Jack's low-slung deck chair.

# CHAPTER THIRTY

THE COMMITTEE: Mrs. Forrest, in the light of what you have told us, and in particular now that you will be providing us with evidence of recognition by the air force in the way of a military discharge, we will adjourn now to discuss the matter of WASP militarization. We will make our decision available to you once we have reached a conclusion. Thank you, Mrs. Forrest, for your time.

EVA FORREST: Thank you, sir.

"You poor dear." Eva stood with Jack on the threshold of his parents' home. Jack's mother opened the front door wide, and Eva stood in front of her in kitten heels, her side still aching, but at least her arm was free of any slings. "How charming to meet you, Eva."

"Hello, Mrs. Forrest," she said.

"What a time you've had. Broken bones too numerous to imagine, and your poor head." Mrs. Forrest stepped aside, allowing them to enter her fine home in Hancock Park.

Jack leaned down and kissed his mom on the cheek.

"She is beautiful. You are right, Jack." The elegant middle-aged woman eyed Eva with a knowing look.

Eva hovered in the unaccustomed baby-pink dress that Jack and her mother had bought for her to wear. Lined with rows of tulle under the full skirt, it was gathered on the décolletage with a silver clasp. Around her neck, Eva wore her mother's fake pearls. She had no idea how Jack and her mom had managed to procure a dress with so much fabric in wartime.

"Come in, Eva." Jack helped her down the hallway. "Mother," he said when his mother tried to take Eva's arm. "We're doing fine here."

His mother stepped aside. A slight frown creased her otherwise smooth forehead, her short, wavy dark hair looking as if it had been freshly set at the hairdresser, bright-red lipstick on her rosebud mouth. "I don't know what to do, dear, how to help."

Jack steered Eva into an expansive living room. A baby grand piano sat at the window, and yellow silk sofas were dotted around on a carpet that was like a soft green sea.

A man turned from the window to pace across the room. "Welcome," he said, shaking Eva's hand. "Lovely to meet you." He seemed to scrutinize her, his strong eyebrows knitting together above his dark eyes.

"Thank you," Eva murmured. "Sir."

She allowed Jack to help her onto one of the sofas. Thankful, she slipped down into it and rested back a little.

And her mother's warning came into her head. *"Dear, these people are from Hancock Park. Quality folk. You are a lucky girl for Jack to take an interest in you. Make sure you don't go upsetting any of them. Particularly his mother."* After that, her mom had squeezed her hands. *"This will be a wonderful opportunity for us all. I've been working hard to get this happening with Jack, Evie. Don't blow it. There's a good girl. You have a wonderful future ahead of you if you play your cards right. Trust me, we'll make this happen for you."* Eva had stared at her mother. *"And remember, you are not well right now, but later on, you will thank me for this. And Jack. You should be forever grateful to him. And you should make the most of his feelings for you. There is no reason you shouldn't be very happy with him."*

Jack sat down next to her. He rested his hand in hers. "Mother, Father, I'm so pleased that Eva is well enough to meet you now. She's had a mighty rough run." He spoke in clipped tones, differently from how he spoke with her own mother.

His father brought over a small glass of lemonade and handed it to Eva.

"Thank you."

"Thanks, Father," Jack said. "Don't want to be giving her anything stronger just now."

"No, I'm sure not." Jack's father sat down opposite them, leaning forward, cupping a tumbler of amber liquid in his hands.

"Did you hear anything about the role, Jack?" his mother asked.

"Not yet," Jack said. "Filming starts in three weeks in Malibu. It's one of those beach gigs they're doing like hotcakes now."

His mother shifted a little in her seat. "I caught up with Lucille's mother today."

Eva's ears pricked up.

Jack's mom sipped from her small glass of sherry. She crossed her slim legs at the ankles. "They're all about this engagement. This Harry sounds like a nice boy, and a hard worker, which makes up for his background. He will be good for lovely Lucille. Even though he does not come from—"

"Mother. Please."

"The point is . . ." Jack's father took up the thread. "Lucille's old man told me he's got a place for this young Harry at the Royal Academy of Engineering in London after the war. Harry and Lucille will get married, and they'll go straight to London. Should give the boy a leg up. He's lucky to have met someone like Lucille, and she's utterly smitten, so Noel says he's doing everything he can to help and to make it work for the young couple."

"Harry is a friend of yours, Eva, isn't he?" Jack's mother asked.

"Yes. He is a friend." She was struggling to keep up with the conversation here. Harry was going to London? If only she could let up on the pills from Camp Davis. They were still knocking her around something awful.

"Lucille's mother mentioned that some of the other girls from around here will be at the party tonight . . . have you seen Lila or Jane lately, Jack? I saw the lovely young Jane out in the street the other day. She's delightful. And she asked after you, Jack. I know none of those girls interest you. Although, I do admit, I can see why." Her last words were a hasty sprinkling of sugar dusting a perfectly baked pie.

Jack sat up. "I'm sure she did, and I'm sure you were very friendly toward Jane, Mom."

"Well, of course I was." She sounded bristly now.

Eva patted down the soft fluffy fabric over her knees.

"So what if you don't get this role, son?" Jack's father asked, sounding harder now.

Eva felt the flicker of something in Jack next to her. The pressure on her hand increased just enough . . .

"Then I audition for another one, Father," he said, his voice quiet. "It's how the industry works."

His father cleared his throat. "And you must know that Brian Manning will give you a job anytime, son. You have backup. I'd suggest taking it. You can't seriously go on with this acting idea."

Jack scowled at the floor.

Eva felt Jack's hand tighten around hers and cling on.

His mother brought her hand up to gather the pearl necklace around her neck. No doubt hers was real.

"A job selling insurance." Jack's dad's voice boomed. "There could be worse things. And there will be opportunities galore in *that* arena, mark my words, son. After the war . . ."

Jack stood up to leave. "Father, I only wanted to bring Eva here tonight to meet you both. We must be going. The party starts at eight."

His mother stood up too, anxiety sweeping across her face. She glanced at Eva. "I'm sorry we have not had the time to talk with you properly yet, dear. You must think us terribly rude."

But her husband was right behind her. "That's enough, Elizabeth."

Eva bit her lip.

Jack bent down to kiss his mother.

"She's lovely," she heard Jack's mother say. "Beautiful, but not sophisticated. We can work to make things a little less rough around the edges."

"Sure, Mom," Jack said. "I understand where you are coming from."

Eva gulped. What did she just hear? She could hardly trust her own ears these days. Her head swirled, and she reached blindly for something to hold.

Jack's father held Eva's hand and shook it hard. "Wonderful to meet you, Eva."

With Jack's arm around her, they made their way through the green front garden to his car that was parked on the quiet street. Eva waited while Jack held the car door open for her.

He drove toward Hollywood Boulevard. The party tonight was in the very hotel where they'd met. She was starting to associate the Hollywood Roosevelt hotel not only with movie stars, but with Jack and his glamorous friends.

Eva looked at him. "Harry will go to London after the war?" Her voice seemed disembodied. Everything did.

"It would be a great opportunity for a boy like him, Eva. He will be doing what he loves, designing airplanes, and will have a beautiful wife. All I need to do is get this acting going, and we'll be sitting pretty too. You wait . . ."

He pulled into the driveway behind the Hollywood Roosevelt hotel, and an attendant came around to park the car. Eva caught a glimpse of a familiar figure sweeping in the back entrance, her arm hooked in that of a well-dressed man. Lucille. Eva felt a swell of panic.

Eva allowed Jack to help her out of the car, but her eyes strained after the girl who was disappearing fast into the hotel, her party dress swinging.

# CHAPTER THIRTY-ONE

THE COMMITTEE: We are pleased to announce that in light of all the testimonials from the WASP whom we have interviewed over the duration of this hearing, we have come to a decision. We have voted that the WASP be given full military recognition, and this bill will be passed in Congress in the very near future. Due to the fact that we have been provided with evidence that they were regarded by the military as a de facto military organization and due to the fact that they trained and lived in full military fashion while flying air force aircraft in service for their country when we needed them, with thirty-eight women pilots making the ultimate sacrifice for the United States during the war, Congress acknowledges that these women have earned a place in our military and they were not simply civil aviators during a crucial time in our history. We congratulate them. They will not be forgotten, and they should be proud of the service they all gave to our country.

"Jack!" Lucille leaned into Jack, resting her head on his shoulder. Eva gazed around the ballroom in the Hollywood Roosevelt hotel. Crowds of sophisticated girls chatted with men in uniform. Suddenly, Eva was haunted with memories of the last time she set foot in this grand room, when Harry was dancing so intimately with Lucille. She shuddered, drawing her gaze away from the space where they'd danced, and she tucked her arm into Jack's.

"Lucille, you remember Eva Scott?" Jack asked.

Lucille looked down at her. Eva could have sworn that she shot Jack a complicit glance.

"Hello there, Eva." Lucille's voice softened to Eva's surprise.

"Hello, Lucille."

A swarm of young men came to surround Lucille. They carried her off to the dance floor. All but a couple of boys who remained standing with Eva and Jack.

"You haven't introduced us," one of them said, giving Eva a grin.

"Well, this is Eva," Jack said. "Eva, this is Clyde and Edwin."

Eva held out a hand, and each boy shook it. They were in uniform. Eva started at the sight of boys in military dress so close to her. Suddenly, she felt the need for some fresh air. The sound of flyboys marching across the airfield toward planes in Camp Davis beat in her head. She closed her eyes for a moment before forcing herself to come back to where she was.

Jack started a conversation with Edwin.

"And where did you meet Jack?" the one called Clyde asked.

Eva focused on the young man's face. She swallowed, but her throat closed over and stuck.

The room seemed too bright, too noisy.

"Here," she said. "In this hotel, in this room."

"So you're the one looking after the man who can't go into service."

"Oh, I'd hardly say that," Eva said.

"You been doin' anything during the war, Eva?"

"I've been flying airplanes," she said. And the moment she did so, she heard the sound of an airplane rattling away in her head. She made a face. It must have been his uniform or something about this guy that was sending her mind back. Triggering something. She frowned at him.

Clyde let out a chuckle, and then another one. He winked at her. "Ah, that was a good one. For a moment, I thought you were serious!" He laughed again, throwing his head back.

"But I was." She looked at him sharply now.

"A girl flying airplanes! What a joke that is. Hey?" He leaned a little closer to her.

"Why? What's wrong with that idea?"

Clyde stood so close to her that she could see the individual specks of fair stubble on his chin.

"Tell me, did you fly bombers, Eva? That your game? That what you did?"

"Yes. Sometimes we flew bombers. We WASP fly every aircraft the air force has. I flew, let's see, about a dozen different sorts of planes."

Clyde let out a snort this time. "A dozen different sorts of planes? You are priceless. Were they paper airplanes, gorgeous?"

"I'm sorry, but that is insulting."

"Next, you'll tell me you got in and flew a B-29!"

Eva opened her mouth. But Clyde was sauntering away into the crowd, his shoulders shaking with laughter.

"Okay there, Eva?" Jack asked.

She felt Edwin's gaze on her too.

"That boy wouldn't believe me when I said I flew planes just now." She looked up at Jack. "Why, I never."

Jack patted her on the arm. "Evie," he said. "That's over now. Sure, some folks won't believe what you did. But you know that I'm only proud of you, and supportive."

"You are?"

"Of course I am," he said. He leaned closer to her. "But here's a little word of advice. Whatever you do, don't tell people you flew during this war. No one's going to believe that women are capable of such a thing. You just tell them you volunteered, my sweet. Don't muddy the waters. You know what I'm saying?" He dropped a kiss on her forehead. "Are we clear now?"

Across the room, Eva caught the glint of the diamond on Lucille's ring finger, sparkling and shining under the crystal chandeliers.

After the party, Eva slipped in the front door of her parents' house, using the key her mother had given her now that she was officially dating Jack and was coming home a little later than she'd ever done back before she left for Sweetwater.

"That you, Eva?" Her mom's voice rang out from her parents' bedroom, stopping Eva dead in the hallway.

"Yes, Mom."

"It's awful late. Get some sleep."

Eva leaned against the wall, catching her breath, her chest heaving. She'd been fighting for air the whole way home. Jack had taken a detour up the hills so they could look at the view over the San Fernando Valley, but all Eva wanted to do was get back and be alone. What she'd started to hear and see back in that ballroom had scared her. Was her memory returning, or was there something seriously wrong? She narrowed her eyes for a moment. What if it was the medicine that had caused her to hear the sounds from Camp Davis? Should she stop taking the pills her mom dished out to her each day?

Eva almost fell down the hallway to her bedroom. The sounds of her father's snoring drifted out into the house.

In the dark, she sat down at her old school desk; hand shaking, she pulled open a drawer. Eva pulled out a lined pad of note paper and began to write.

In half an hour flat, she'd filled pages and pages for Nina and Harry. Tomorrow, she would give them to her mother to mail. In the midst of all of this—Jack, her mom, her mind playing tricks, her injuries—she knew one thing. She needed her old friends.

Unless this was some nightmare, she was certain they'd both write straight back.

Three weeks later, she'd not heard a thing. Nothing from Harry was fair enough. He was hardly going to have time for letter writing from where he was stationed in the Pacific, and he couldn't tell her anything anyway, but still, Eva battled nightly fears that he was not safe. And every day, Eva waited to hear from Nina, and nothing came.

A month passed. Her mom checked the mailbox daily. Not a letter, not a word.

"I want to go visit Nina's mom," she told her mother one afternoon while her mom sat sewing in the living room. Eva put down the book she was pretending to read and waited while her mom frowned over the pattern she was trying to copy. "I can't walk all the way there, though. I'll ask Jack to drive me to see her. I've asked him to a couple times, but it's always too late in the evening by the time he gets here after filming."

Her mom put down her sewing. "Nina's mom has gone away. She's visiting her sister down in San Diego. I told you that."

"Is she? I don't recall you telling me that, Mom."

"Dear, please don't worry yourself. Everything is fine. Hold this fabric for me while I get my measuring tape."

Eva held the bolt of fabric while her mom turned to her sewing box.

"I really should have taught you to sew. Flying airplanes was the least useful thing you could have learned."

Eva sat back in her chair. "Well, I guess I won't be needing to sew if I end up marrying Jack, now will I, Mother? I'm of a mind to think I won't be needing to do anything at all."

Ruth Scott smiled down at the pattern she was cutting out. "And that, my dear girl, is like a beautiful tune to my ears. You can have a house full of kids and in Hancock Park to boot. Dreamy, Eva. All this has turned out so well. In the end."

That night, Jack pulled up outside the house after dinner. Eva stood at the front door, holding on to the frame, and he made his way up the lawn to help her. Once he'd kissed her on the cheek, she was unable to hold in what was on her mind.

"Jack, I cannot understand why Nina would not write to me." She leaned on his arm. They walked slowly down toward his sparkling car.

"I don't want you worrying about that or anything else. Remember there's a war on. Give things time." He squeezed her hand.

"Well, I suppose so," she said. Was she being too impatient? Mail didn't always come in regularly at Camp Davis. And letters did get lost . . .

"I've got something I want to show you today. It's a surprise." He opened the car door for her and helped her inside.

Jack drove in silence toward Santa Monica.

Eva stared out at the landscape of LA.

He pulled up just beyond the pier. "Come walk with me. I'll help you along the beach."

Eva went to open her car door, but he'd leaped out his side and was ready to help her out. "Thank you. I'm able to walk a little farther by myself now, and I can get out of a car, you know, Jack."

He jolted back a little, but then his face broke into a kind smile. "Eva, I'm here to help you. Just let me, okay? I adore you. All right?"

The evening was mild, and a few couples strolled along the beach. Jack leaned down and took off his espadrilles.

"You can't be sad tonight." He stopped, moving to stand in front of her, grinning at her, and blocking her way a little bit. He reached out, tucking his hand under her chin.

"I'm not sad," she protested. "I admit I'm confused, though. You see . . ." She was tempted to open up to him about the troublesome experience she'd had at the Hollywood Roosevelt hotel. But he reached out to her, taking hold of her waist. And she decided to wait. This was something she'd rather confess to Nina or Harry. They'd known her longer and would not think she was going insane.

"Marry me?" he whispered, nestling his head close to her own. "Marry me and come live in Hancock Park? I own a house there, did I tell you? My parents gave it to me for my twenty-first birthday. I don't want to live there all alone. And I'm in love with you. I adore you. Eva, please, let's make this official. I can't wait any longer. You're the perfect girl for me."

Eva's mouth dropped open.

"You'll make the best wife. And you know what?"

"I . . . can't think."

"You're going to make a beautiful mother as well."

Her side throbbed, and suddenly, a picture unfolded in her mind. Lucille in a wedding dress, Harry waiting at the front of the church. She brought a hand up to her mouth. Harry had not written back to her. He'd be writing to Lucille. She was being naive thinking he felt the same way about her as she did about him. The last time she saw him, had he been trying to let her go? And yet, here she was, clinging to him, clinging to something that she swore was between them. Something that the harsh light of reality was showing her did not exist.

Helena was gone and Nancy was gone.

Bea and Rita were far away.

Nina was busy, understandably, doing high-level military work. Eva should not be surprised her letters back were taking a while.

Eva was the one who'd washed out. She was the one who'd failed.

And that left Jack. Jack was here, and he was taking care of her. Harry might be her fantasy, but Jack was her reality. He'd come all the way to North Carolina for her. Was she seeing and feeling everything all wrong? After all, her mind was playing tricks on her. Who and what could she trust?

Marrying Jack, she'd make everyone happy. Her mom, finally. This way, she could put everything right, make up for all the tragedy and the loss that had happened while she was away from home. It was as if the pattern were being set for her. All she had to do was say yes.

Imagine the fallout if she said no . . .

"I'll marry you, Jack."

He leaned down to kiss her, and Eva wondered whether she'd just grown up.

On a sunny afternoon in spring, Eva stood at the entrance to a grand church in Hancock Park. All she could see down the aisle were flowers decorating every surface and wreaths of roses adorning the end of every pew. Jack's mom had gotten all her friends to raid their gardens. War or no war, she'd insisted that it was just once that her only son would be getting married. Eva wore Jack's mom's diamond tiara on her head, and the matching diamond necklace he'd given her glistened. On her wrist, she wore his bracelet, and glowing on the ring finger of her left hand was Jack's engagement ring. Slowly, Eva had become used to wearing his ring, to the way it felt and the way it glinted at a new, different life.

Her dad took her arm to give her away. The organ swelled into the bridal march, and at the front of the church, Jack stood handsome and tall in his black suit.

Eva hesitated for a moment, unable to squash pangs of sadness that Nina was not here with her as her bridesmaid. She'd still not heard anything from Bea, Rita, or Harry either, but her mom had reassured her that she wouldn't be the only bride without attendants. It was one of the prices of getting married in wartime.

Nevertheless, every day, she'd listened for the postman. Every day, she'd gone out to the mailbox when he came. And every time her mom came back from the stores and had checked the family's post office mailbox, Eva had trailed her like a child, begging her to tell her that a letter had come.

The first person Eva laid eyes on when she stepped into the church was Lucille, her cheeks blooming and her lips painted a pearly pink. Eva held her head up, returned Lucille's smile, and walked down the aisle toward Jack.

At the reception, in the back garden under a white tent outside Jack's house, Eva thanked his mother and father for being good to her, while the whole time, she still felt sick at the thought of Harry and Nina not being there. She'd not heard back from Nina's mom, even though she'd sent letters to her address in Burbank in the hope that her mail would be forwarded on to San Diego.

Jack drove them away from the reception toward a hotel on the beach for their wedding night.

"You can't imagine how guilty I feel, Jack." On their left, the Pacific Ocean glimmered in the late-afternoon sunshine.

"Guilty, my love? That's not a word I want to hear on our wedding day."

"It's been months, Jack. I'm worried that I must have done something wrong during that flight. Otherwise, why would they all cut me off?"

"Eva," he said. "Don't worry. Your happily-ever-after is here."

The next morning, she sat cocooned in Jack's arms overlooking the beach on the balcony of their hotel. The sea sparkled in front of them, and the sand was a glorious golden yellow. Fresh fruits sat on a platter, along with pastries that Eva had never seen the likes of, not even before the war.

"You should try this," he said, holding up a precious strawberry to her lips.

She leaned back into his chest. Silently, she took the strawberry. Helena couldn't do this. Helena would never get married. Helena was gone for good.

She'd sat awake most of her wedding night, curled in an armchair by the open window while Jack slept. Outside, in the murky darkness, the sea called of Harry, and the sky only served to remind her of her girlfriends. Were they somewhere out there flying tonight? What if her suspicions were founded and she had done something wrong in that plane, and what if that was the reason none of her friends were writing back . . .

# CHAPTER
# THIRTY-TWO

*Washington, DC, November 1977*

The gavel came down on the WASP bill, and the House of Representatives moved straight on to the next matter in two seconds flat. After weeks of debates, Eva sat in the gallery in a state of disbelief with the small handful of dedicated women pilots who had helped fight for this cause. The WASP were military, with full recognition as part of the armed forces. Finally, it had happened, but the way Congress handled it, it seemed as if the momentous decision were of no consequence.

Gradually, as if coming to life in slow motion, the small group of women who had worked so hard for the last few weeks stood up in the public gallery and encircled each other in their arms. They filed out of the Capitol Building into the bright Washington sunshine, blinking for a moment on the steps before turning to each other in astonishment.

"So what now?" Eva asked. "Did anyone else feel like Congress was acting as if that was just part of a normal workday routine?"

One of the middle-aged women who'd fought alongside them all wiped a tear from her eyes. "This is a big deal. It's of massive consequence for us. And you know what? I just don't want to go back home and behave as if this has not changed anything in our lives. I say that we should all ensure this recognition has an impact on us, whether it makes us prouder of ourselves or gives us more self-belief or even if it just stops us from telling people we simply 'volunteered' in the war. Because I for one am sick of doing that."

Eva stared at the woman standing opposite her. She was from another WASP class, her experiences were different from Eva's, but in the end, they were all fighting for a common ideal.

"I agree with you," Eva said, standing a little taller. "Going home and taking up our old lives without reflecting on what this means to us would be a real shame. We need to keep today with us. Always. We need to remember the women who died flying for the WASP. We must not pretend our time as WASP never happened."

A couple of men started climbing up the steps toward them. Two of the ex-WASP went down to hug their husbands. Eva said her goodbyes to the other women for now.

Traffic wound its way up and down the wide boulevard below. And just as the women were about to go their separate ways, a familiar figure made his way up to them.

"Bruce." Eva walked down to Henry H. Arnold's son. This man, a lobbyist, had allowed the WASP to make their headquarters in the Army and Navy Club, to use his secretary, his office, and his phone. He'd provided unmitigated support for them, partly because he believed in the cause his father, Henry, had believed in along with Jacqueline Cochran, and partly because he appreciated what the WASP had done for the country. He'd sat by during their campaign and helped them deal with Congress. And now they'd won.

Bruce stood in front of Eva for a moment.

"We've done it, Bruce."

"If my father were here, he'd salute you." Henry's gray-haired son looked at Eva with pride.

"And I would salute him right back." Eva smiled at him.

And for the first time in years, as she stood there outside the Capitol Building, she felt the stirrings of the old fire that used to burn within her before the war that changed all their lives. She felt her old hope and optimism coming back to life. It was a good feeling, and it was one she never wanted to lose again as long as she lived.

The next morning, Eva woke late. The celebrations for the WASP victory had gone well into the early hours, and she'd enjoyed every second. And now, she sat up. She was not going to let a little champagne headache stop her from finishing what she'd come here to do. She'd fielded a barrage of questions from the committee about her personal life, but she'd deflected them and pushed on, never giving up. She was proud that she'd managed the battle for the WASP with dignity, but there were still answers she needed. Bruce Arnold had promised her he'd call as soon as he'd accessed the WASP records. At ten o'clock sharp, the phone next to Eva's bed rang.

"Eva?" Bruce Arnold sounded as if he were in the next room.

"Good morning, Bruce."

"How are you?" He sounded as whip-smart as any of Eva's old WASP instructors.

"I'm ready for the next steps, Bruce. I'm prepared for whatever your searches might bring." Eva rested her hand on the brown quilted coverlet, the diamond engagement ring she'd worn since her wedding day back in 1944 sparkling on the bed.

"Can you meet me soon?"

"Why, yes, I can." She raised her wristwatch and looked at it. "Where are you, Bruce?"

"I'm in my car. I'm calling from my car phone, and I'm driving to your hotel."

"Oh, I see. A car phone." Of course he'd have a car phone. She'd seen a few of them recently.

"Can you come down to the lobby and meet me in the next few minutes?"

"Is everything all right, Bruce?"

But he had hung up.

Eva stood and went into the small en suite bathroom, brushed her teeth, and applied lipstick before picking up her handbag. On her way to the door, she glanced once more at the phone. She should call Jack to touch base, but their conversations had been strained while she was here in Washington. Hesitating for a moment, and unable to face a confrontation, she walked down to the lobby.

Bruce walked through the swinging glass doors just as she stepped across the marble floor.

"Eva."

Eva accepted the kiss he gave her on the cheek.

He scanned the lobby, his sharp eyes scouring the room, taking in the people dotted about.

"Let's go for a walk. It's not very private here."

Eva took in a shaking breath, and they stepped out into the freezing air. Bruce walked a couple of blocks, staying quiet apart from the odd chitchat. Soon, he turned off the main road so they were on a quieter, residential street. Wooden houses with steps leading to front doors and Christmas decorations twinkling in windows lined the road. A light blanket of snow lingered on the lawns. Eva drew her overcoat around her. She'd never taken to these cold East Coast winters.

Finally, he started to talk. "You told us that Helena Cartwright flew with you out on a routine searchlight training mission back in January 1944, and that you cannot remember anything about the flight. You said that she was killed in the accident that caused you to have to withdraw from service."

Eva kept pace with him. She told him about trying to reach out to Nina and never hearing back. "I hate to think what the records might turn up. I've had flashbacks about the accident, and I worry about Helena's death to no end. But I have to know." She stopped for a moment.

Bruce stayed quiet.

"You see, Bruce, I saw something I have never seen before during a recent flashback. I saw myself crawling across the tarmac to rescue Helena. Not knowing whether I did the right thing or not has been a nightmare that I've lived with for thirty years. It's almost as if I haven't known who I am since that night. After the accident, not being able to fly, I lost my purpose. I realize now that I let people run my life for me because I lost confidence in my own abilities. And I was worried about my own state of health because the flashbacks were starting, even then. When my old WASP friends would not respond to my letters, well, you can imagine the impact not knowing and being cut off from them has had."

Bruce was quiet beside her. "I was able to access the official records this morning. First thing. I insisted. As you know, I have military clearance, and I was there at o-eight-hundred hours. I understand how this has affected you, Eva. I saw the pressure you were under during the committee hearings."

Eva's freezing breath escaped in white puffs from her lips.

"I suggest you prepare yourself," he said.

Eva closed her eyes. The last time she'd heard those words, it had been when Instructor Reg Tilley told them that Dan and Nancy had been killed.

"I didn't deserve the luck to survive," she said. "Not when Helena and Nancy died. I think I struggled with guilt over that afterward.

You know what it's like to be part of the military, to want to put your friends first . . ."

Bruce Arnold reached out and laid a hand on her arm.

"Helena Cartwright was not the name listed on the flight records of that accident. I double- and triple-checked."

Eva heard the rise and fall of Bruce's quiet breathing beside her. "What, Bruce? But what happened to her, then?"

"Nina Rogers was the name of your copilot in the accident, Eva."

The sound of a little warbler singing a sweet, sad song came from one of the street's skeletal trees.

*Nina?* Eva reached for something, anything. She was about to fall. All that she could grab on to was Bruce Arnold's steady arm.

He grabbed her, holding her gloved hand in his own.

"Nina? But then that means . . . my little friend died?" The sidewalk swam, and a car swished up the road, spurting snow from its back wheels. Heat, cold, fire, all these things seemed to sweep through her faster than she could keep up, and all the while, a voice inside her screamed—*No!*

And deep down, had she known all along? Had she lied, not to another person, but to herself?

The street spun.

She was spiraling too. Down, down toward the ground.

Bruce heaved her upright.

"I think we should go sit down." His voice came from some strange place.

He held her elbow and led her down the street, pushing the door open into a warm coffee shop. Eva stared at the room, the occupants, the people. Nina had not lived to see adulthood. She'd never had children, a husband. What about Walter? He'd been lovely. They might have been happy together.

A great sob racked her body. She doubled over, right there in the coffee shop. Nina, with her plaits and wide-eyed optimism and determination and her complete love of flying.

Of course. Nina had never abandoned her.

She would never have not written. Why had Eva believed it could be so?

And one answer came to her. She felt the inevitable, sinister thump of dread in her stomach. *Jack.* Jack had never told her Nina was dead. He'd let her believe Helena had died instead. And so had her mother.

Bruce eased her into a booth. A waitress came and hovered.

"Is everything all right here, sir?"

Suddenly, Eva felt the burn of the waitress's gaze. Her face flushed. The tragedy, the loss, the waste of Nina dying. And the waste of thirty years thinking something else.

"Two strong coffees, please. And a shot of brandy in each, if you can." Bruce spoke quietly to the waitress.

He leaned forward. "Eva, listen to me. I know what it's like to lose someone in the military, and I'm truly sorry this is so unexpected. I'm truly sorry that you haven't known about this for years."

When the waitress came back with their drinks, Eva moved her hand as if it were not part of her, lifting the small china cup to her lips. She tried to swallow, but a lump formed in her throat. Nina had not been able to see the sunshine. She had not felt the touch of rain. And Nina had died a terrible death out there.

"I wrote to Nina. My husband told me he'd mailed the letters."

Bruce shook his head. "I'm sorry, Eva. What about your other friends in the WASP?"

"Oh, I wrote them too. Never heard back. Rita, Bea." She punched out the names. "Jack posted those letters for me too. And yet, I never heard from them, not once." She shot her head up for a moment. "Bruce? I did not do anything wrong? Tell me I did not leave her to die, because if I did, I cannot—" She cut off her own words. Stared at him. "Was it all my fault?"

He reached out a hand and placed it over her own.

"The investigation after your accident found that the interior catch on the door in the front cockpit was faulty. The inspection sheet that was cleared before the flight showed the all clear, so we think that something went wrong during the flight. The fire in the engine, perhaps, could have caused the door and the front canopy in the A-24 to expand."

Eva brought her hand to her mouth. "So she was trapped on landing, in the front cockpit?" She felt her mouth working. "What was I doing?"

"Eva, the cockpit split in two on impact. Nina's half of the plane was separated from yours when the plane skidded to the tarmac. Witnesses reported that they could hear her screams while the cockpit burned. It was a shocking accident, and it's understandable that you became confused afterward. It's understandable that your memory blocked it out. Your section of the cockpit, the back part, was halfway up the runway. Hers had hurtled forward away from you. It was some distance away."

"But what should I have done?"

"You managed to get out of the rear cockpit and crawl away from the plane."

The tarmac; the flashback she'd had in the market. Sickness spread through her at the thought of what Nina had gone through, how she hadn't known.

"Then for some time, you were in a coma. You slipped in and out after a while. You had no memory of the flight, or the accident afterward."

"Dear goodness."

Bruce Arnold kept his hand on Eva's. "There was nothing anyone could do."

# CHAPTER
# THIRTY-THREE

Somehow, Eva managed the flight home to LA. She acknowledged airport staff, talked a little to her fellow passengers, but her heart was back in Camp Davis. One day, she'd go back there, back to that marshy, wild landscape so that she could at least say her farewells to Nina.

At LAX, Jack's car was parked in the short-stay parking lot. It was the first thing Eva saw through the sliding doors leading out of the airport. He climbed out from the driver's seat, and she walked over to him. He reached out to take her luggage from her and store it in the back of the car.

"No, that's fine, I can do it myself," Eva said, prizing it away from him and heaving it into the trunk.

"It's too heavy for you," he muttered, flicking a glance to the driver behind them, who was waiting to take his spot.

"I've been hauling it myself all the time I was away."

She turned from him, staring out the window once she was in the car.

"You okay?" he asked, climbing into the driver's seat. "Don't tell me you've come back in a mood."

"Is Alex home?" Eva's voice seemed disembodied.

The airport passed by them in a swish, and they were out on the freeway.

"He's staying with some friend. I forget who."

Eva frowned. "Really?"

"Haven't spoken to him for a while."

Eva tapped her hand on the door of the car.

"He was being difficult."

"*He* was being difficult?" Eva could not help the way her head shook in disbelief. "Come on, Jack."

"Takes after his mother."

"What did you just say?"

He pulled out onto the freeway. The silence between them was a frozen layer of ice above a stream, a stream that was running cold, or had it stopped dead long ago?

"Forget it," Jack said. "Oh, all the drivers are here. They're all out today." He pulled into another lane, swerving across the traffic, the wheels whistling against the road. "It's been a nightmare with Alex since you left. He has no darned idea, that kid. You've spoiled him. You know that?"

Eva felt her fists clenching and unclenching by her sides. Her throat burned with unspoken words, and she knew, right then, that what was in had to come out. "Jack, can you please stop the car?"

"What?" he said, eyes on the freeway, head lowered. "Eva? Jeez, what's wrong with you now? I can't stop the car. We're on a freeway. Calm down."

"I'm asking you to stop. Please." She spread her hands out to either side of her on the warm vinyl seat. Took in some deep breaths.

Jack swooped the car off the freeway, then onto a quiet street. "What is it?" Irritation and boredom and what-are-you-doing-now laced his three words, hung in the air, a toxic, fuming mess.

He turned off the engine.

They sat in silence.

"We accessed the crash records." Her voice was dull and low.

He leaned his head back against the driver's seat. "Oh great. I see."

"Jack."

He did not move.

"You never told me."

His voice was quiet. "What was I supposed to do? Beat you over the head with the truth?" He brought his hand up to his chin, running his fingers over the slight stubble that she used to think was sexy. Once. "You weren't coping. You needed to be taken care of. I did that."

"I should have been told the truth. You, Mom—"

"What good would it have done to upset you further? Leave it alone, Eva."

Eva stared straight ahead. "You knew I thought Helena was in that plane." She spoke through gritted teeth. "You knew that I wrote to Nina, over and over again. What happened to my letters? What did you do with them, Jack?"

"Letters weren't going to go anywhere. It was not in your best interest to send them off."

Eva reached for the car door.

"There was no point in your writing to Nina." He let out a sardonic laugh. "Come on, Eva! We just thought you'd realize, in time. I assumed you had. We never talk about the war. Who does? Nobody does!"

"Oh, I know that now!" She flicked the door open.

But he reached across, holding her arm.

She turned to him, and she whispered, but her words may as well have come out as a wretched scream. "My letters to Bea, to Rita? What about those?"

He shifted in his seat.

"Jack? Did they ever write to me? Any of them?"

He dropped her arm. "Their letters are at home. I never did anything with them. I simply never gave them to you."

"I want to read them. And I'm getting out of this car now. I'll make my own way home. Get a taxi. Or a bus. I need to calm down right now, Jack."

"Read them, but don't blame me if they upset you. You're clearly having a crisis. Where are you going?"

Eva climbed out of the car. She leaned in the window. "You know what, I have no idea."

Jack stared at her. After a few moments, he just shook his head and laughed. "For pity's sake, Eva. I've had enough." He turned on the engine and roared off.

He did not look back, and Eva stood alone under the endless blue she once loved. She was on a slight ridge, under the Californian sky. It was the same blue sky that she'd flown through with Harry. The far horizons shimmered all around her. She'd not noticed them in a very long time.

# CHAPTER
# THIRTY-FOUR

*Four months later*

One fine spring day in March, Eva drove to her first flying lesson, with Alex right by her side in the car. She stopped outside the Hollywood Burbank Airport. The strings of alfalfa that had hung in the air during the war might have disappeared, and the aircraft were a little more modern and streamlined these days, but the excitement that laced its way through Eva's belly at the sight of those little planes lined up through the wire fence was as thrilling and raw as it had been when she saw the same sight out at Sweetwater, when Helena had been there to welcome her and Nina after that long, tiresome journey through Texas in the train.

"Mom, this is awesome." Alex squeezed her hand from the passenger seat next to her. "I never thought I'd get to learn to fly alongside you. Not that you are learning." He laughed, in that adorable nineteen-year-old way.

"Oh yes, I am." Eva caught the warmth in his eyes with her own enthusiasm, with her own decision to live her life, for Nina, for both of them from now on. "I'm learning to do everything again, sweetheart."

A little primary trainer swooped down the runway, lifting into the air in a smooth arc. Eva squeezed Alex's hand right back at the sound of it. After months of therapy at the military hospital, the sound of plane engines no longer set off one of her bad turns. She drove on into the parking lot that surrounded the terminal, finding a parking spot while the airplane engines whirred and buzzed around them like a happy tune.

She turned off the car engine and waited while Alex got their gear from the back seat. There was no turning back. These last few months had been filled with times when she could have changed her mind about leaving Jack; about moving to an apartment in Los Feliz, right near the one that she'd admired during her WASP interview; about returning Bea's, Rita's, and Helena's letters. And she could have changed her mind about taking up flying lessons again, but now, being here, she knew that the decisions she'd made in the past few months were right for her, at last.

Eva held open the glass door that led into the terminal for Alex and made her way toward the front desk. The young woman behind it smiled when Eva gave her name.

"I understand you learned to fly in Burbank during the war, ma'am?"

"I did." Eva smiled.

"Welcome home."

"Thank you, miss." And it did feel like being home again, being surrounded by planes and folk who loved to fly.

Their instructor came to meet them at the reception desk. She was tall and blond, and she reminded Eva of Rita, or of the girl Rita had been before she started her own helicopter flight training business, something that Eva had been delighted to learn about in the letter that her old friend had written straight to her after finally, finally hearing from Eva after thirty years.

The young woman held out her hand and spoke with all the confidence of Helena, who had recently told Eva how she had married a Boston teacher and ended up working in scientific research.

And when their new instructor sat her and Alex down and started talking about the logistics of the little Piper Cherokee that would be their primary trainer, the young woman showed all the practicality of Bea, who wrote with enthusiasm that she had raised five children, worked as a librarian, and taken great delight in being president of her kids' school's PTA.

All her friends had been unanimous in two things: Eva should definitely train to be a flight instructor, and they would come to a reunion to see her whenever she said the word.

Eva brought her hand down to her coat pocket. Inside it, Bea's, Rita's, and Helena's recent letters sat like talismans. She wanted them with her when she went up today, even though the doctor had given her the all clear to fly. And around her neck, she wore her dear silver necklace for Meg. And next to it, she'd placed a little silver locket in honor of Nina, with a photo of her in braids.

Her friend Nina. The girl who had shared all her youthful dreams. That companion of her younger days, whose own days had been cut tragically short. But she would always be with Eva. No matter what. She'd hold Nina close until the day she died. And she would never let their girlish dreams down, ever again. She'd fly for the both of them now, in every aspect of her life.

The young woman stopped for a moment before leading Eva into the ground school classroom.

"I'm delighted to meet you," she said, flashing an almost hesitant smile that reminded Eva of herself at nineteen. "I heard from our bookings team that you flew planes in the war. That you were one of our newly famous WASP?"

Eva smiled. "Why, yes, I did, but that was long ago. I'm in sure need of a little refreshing when it comes to my flying skills."

The instructor led Eva to a spacious classroom filled with three rows of desks and shiny white plastic chairs. "Sit down where you like. We are honored to have you here."

Eva slid down behind a desk on a chair next to Alex. She pulled her favorite pen out of her shoulder bag. And opened her old book full of notes from ground school. She'd kept it, and she'd found it. And now, it was time for it to be put to good use again.

The instructor still looked at Eva with something like intrigue. "And you learned to fly right here in this airport?"

Eva smiled at the punch in her belly brought by that memory. "Yes, I did."

"I hope I can teach you as well as your last instructor did."

Eva felt a blush spread over her cheeks.

In her left pocket, she curled her fingers over letter number four.


After their ground school lesson, Eva drove with Alex toward her parents' old house with the window wound down all the way. She let in the afternoon breeze, savoring the spring after the winter and the accompanying drama with Jack.

The little original Lockheed factory houses still lined the streets where she'd grown up, but the paint on their yellow house was chipped and faded now. Eva's parents' driveway was dotted with tall weeds. It seemed nobody was taking care of her past here. Eva had not been back to Burbank since her parents had moved to a small apartment near the farmers' market not far from the house where she and Jack lived, until both parents had died in their seventies.

The sting of what she had thought was Nina's rejection had kept her away from her old neighborhood, spurred on and encouraged by Jack.

She moved on past her parents' old house, driving along slowly in companionable quiet with Alex, until she came to Nina's old house, stopping outside it for a moment in the still afternoon. Alex sat silently beside her, letting her remember. Letting her reflect.

Eva could swear that the sounds of Nina's mom's singing filtered out into the street.

Eva sat, a middle-aged woman looking at ghosts that had long gone, until after a while, she allowed the memories of her times with Nina to wind their way into the past again and turned on her car engine to drive away down the familiar old streets.

She stopped outside the cemetery.

"You okay to do this?" Alex asked.

"I am."

She gathered the sheaf of roses she'd brought with her.

"Mom?"

She hesitated, one hand on the car door.

"Would you prefer to do this on your own?"

She held his gaze. "Thank you, Alex."

"I'll be right here waiting for you. Always," he said. "I'm here if you need me."

She hugged him, then climbed out of the car and walked slowly toward the white-painted gates that led to the little gravestones beyond.

Above her, a lone airplane drew lazy eights in the azure Los Angeles sky.

Eva stopped for a moment, shielding her eyes and watching it do its maneuvers, before making her way down the driveway that led into the graveyard, flanked by rows of the dead.

Somehow, for the first time in over thirty years, she did not feel as if she had no sisters left.

Nina's small gravestone was white. It sat silent in the sunshine, resting among a whole row of other folks who'd been killed in the war. Eva stood at the foot of Nina's grave awhile before she bent down to place her beautiful bouquet of yellow roses on the place where her little friend had been laid to sleep.

She startled a little at the sound of footsteps, a voice. Finally, she brought her gaze up from Nina's resting place, her lips drawing into a smile.

"Kiddo."

He stood there, opposite her on the other side of Nina's grave. Looking the same, looking like Harry. She felt a warm smile spread across her face.

"It's been a long time." He held her gaze, the man whom she'd loved like her North Star. "It was good to hear from you."

The sun glimmered on Nina's gravestone. Harry bent down, running his hand over the warm stone before looking up at her, the sun catching his eyes now, his still-handsome face.

"I'll never forget her."

"I know, Harry."

"I'm so sorry about everything that's happened."

"I'm sorry that I never got your letters. Not one."

"Not your fault, no apologies . . . Evie, how are you?" Something crossed his face, and he took a step toward her.

She fought the urge to pull him into her arms. "Learning to fly again."

"Turns out neither of us was very good at flying with our wings clipped." He took a tentative step closer.

Nothing had stopped her loving him, not a war, not being married to the wrong person, and not even tragic loss and the loss of the girl she'd once been.

Her dad had been right after all.

"You too?"

"Evie, we both got into marriages that everyone assumed were right for us. I think our rich spouses wanted to do everything they could to keep their playthings." His eyes were still locked with hers. "But now, I want to undo the worst mistake of my life."

"Lucille?"

"Lucille upgraded back in London a long time ago. She fell for an earl." His lips twitched.

"Oh." Eva brought her hand up to her mouth, trying to hide her giggle. "I'm sorry."

"You're not taking me seriously, kiddo."

"Oh, but I am."

He reached out, pulling her into a hug.

"I let her go because I always loved you more," he whispered into her hair.

She closed her eyes at the sound of the words she'd wanted to hear since they flew together, she and Harry.

"I never stopped loving you." She rested her head on his shoulder.

"It's time for me to fly back home, for a new start with you."

Harry pulled her close, and it was as if they were doing some old slow dance, decades too late. Or maybe, just maybe, it was exactly the right time.

# AFTERWORD

This story began with a personal family history, then spread to a fascination with the true stories behind the WASP, before finally evolving into this story, with Eva, Nina, Harry, Rita, Bea, Nancy, and Helena taking up the thread in their own ways. I have long been intrigued by airplanes and the air force. My parents were both members of the air force during the Second World War. My father flew for the Royal Air Force in Europe, dropping parachutists over occupied France. I remember him standing in our back garden at home, watching modern air force planes flying overhead for demonstrations in the eighties, and I could sense the World War II flying veteran in him, but he didn't talk about his time in the war much at all, and I knew only a little more about my mother's experiences. She joined the Women's Australian Auxiliary Air Force in 1941 as a teenager fresh from school. She was stationed at a pilot's training base in remote South Australia for six years (which is flat and hot like Texas), and she told me how formative this was for her in terms of the wonderful friendships she made and in the sense that these women all pulled together, living in tin sheds and running the base while male pilots came to train. Women in Australia were not allowed to fly during the war, and when the war was over, my mother had to forgo the place she'd earned at university because she got married, as so many women did.

I was intrigued and wanted to know and understand more about women in the air force now that she's gone. I traveled all the way from Australia to Sweetwater, Texas, where I visited the WASP museum and Avenger Field, journeyed through the state by road, and spent time learning about the WASP from the wonderful then president and CEO of the WASP museum, Ann Hobing. Many of the anecdotes in this book are inspired by true stories from the real WASP but adapted by me into fiction—Bea hitting high-tension wires, Frances sitting on the roof and all the girls spending the night up there supporting her, Rita fainting after her vaccinations, the trials of the Link Trainer, and the girls sneaking out to have bathtub gin with the instructors while their bay mates put pillows in each other's beds to stop them from getting caught. The conditions at Camp Davis and Avenger Field were all researched in depth, and there were similar crashes to those in the novel. Eva and Helena may have had to do a little more training out at Camp Davis before they were authorized to fly, but I allowed a little poetic license for the purpose of moving the story along. As for Eva's military release, this is inspired by the true story of a WASP who provided her formal release document as evidence that the WASP were regarded as military, and this turned the corner in the fight for military recognition that the WASP carried out in 1977.

As well as traveling to Sweetwater, Texas, and reading WASP diaries and letters home, I went to California and stayed in the Hollywood Roosevelt hotel and discovered old Hollywood with the help of the lovely April Clemmer.

You may be interested in some of the books that I read as part of my research for this novel:

- *WASPs: Women Airforce Service Pilots of World War II* by Vera S. Williams

- *Seized by the Sun: The Life and Disappearance of World War II Pilot Gertrude Tompkins* by James W. Ure

- *Nancy Love and the WASP Ferry Pilots of World War II* by Sarah Byrn Rickman

- *Slacks and Calluses: Our Summer in a Bomber Factory* by Constance Bowman Reid

- *Flying for Her Country: The American and Soviet Women Military Pilots of World War II* by Amy Goodpaster Strebe

- *Helldiver Units of World War 2* by Barrett Tillman

- *Fly Girls: The Daring American Women Pilots Who Helped Win WWII* by P. O'Connell Pearson

- *A WASP Among Eagles: A Woman Military Test Pilot in World War II* by Ann B. Carl

- *To Live and Die a WASP: 38 Women Pilots Who Died in WWII* by William M. Miller

- *Wings over Sweetwater: The History of Avenger Field, Texas* by Major Bennet B. Monde

- *US Air Force in World War II* by Thomas A. Siefring

- *United States Aircraft* by Bill Gunston

- *The Story of Hollywood: An Illustrated History* by Gregory Paul Williams

After a drawn-out fight, the WASP were given military recognition by President Carter in 1977. The WASP had been forgotten for thirty years. Finally, President Barack Obama awarded the WASP the Congressional Gold Medal in 2009 "in recognition of their pioneering military service and exemplary record, which forged revolutionary reform in the Armed Forces of the United States of America."

# ACKNOWLEDGMENTS

I would like to thank my wonderful editor, Jodi Warshaw, for her highly valued guidance and expertise throughout the whole process of writing and editing this book. I am incredibly fortunate to work with Jodi. Thanks to the entire team at Lake Union Publishing, including Danielle Marshall for her support; my adored developmental editor, Tegan Tigani, who worked tirelessly on this story with me; my meticulous copyeditors, Laura Petrella and Erin Cusick; the careful proofreader, Valerie Paquin; cover designer Shasti O'Leary Soudant for her beautiful cover design that I adore; my author relations manager, Gabriella Dumpit, for always being there; and my project manager, Nicole Pomeroy, for overseeing the production of the book. Thank you to my amazing agent, Steven Salpeter, for his much-appreciated guidance and support; to Ann Hobing at the WASP museum, Sweetwater, Texas, for the wonderful conversations we had about the WASP; and to her staff for talking so generously with me. To Tracy Balsz for her help scouting for locations in Burbank, and to pilot Dorothy Shorne for her generous assistance with planning the flight scenes. My heartfelt thanks

to the late pilot Tom Lawson, for reading the flight scenes and for helping me further refine them. I will never forget his kindness, and I will
always remember him. To Margie Lawson, who inspires me to work
hard at my craft. My dearest thanks to Geoff for his constant support.
Thanks and love, always, to my children, Ben and Sophie.

# ABOUT THE AUTHOR

*Photo © 2014 Alexandra Grimshaw*

Ella Carey is the international bestselling author of *The Things We Don't Say*, *Secret Shores*, *From a Paris Balcony*, *The House by the Lake*, and *Paris Time Capsule*. A Francophile who has long been fascinated by secret histories set in Europe's entrancing past, Ella has degrees in music, nineteenth-century women's fiction, and modern European history. She lives in Australia with her two children and two Italian greyhounds.